MISTAKEN IDENTITY

A PRIDE & PREJUDICE VARIATION

J. DAWN KING

D1601321

Quiet Mountain Press

Published by Quiet Mountain Press LLC

Follow J Dawn King on Twitter: @jdawnking

Like her on Facebook: www.facebook.com/JDawnKing

Or connect by email: jdawnking@gmail.com

Please join my mailing list at http://jdawnking.com for news about latest releases.

ACKNOWLEDGEMENT

To write a novel with a mystery element, the research is quite different than for my typical Regency novels. Therefore, I need to thank Rob and Skyler from Umpqua Survival in Roseburg, Oregon for their knowledge of ballistics, weaponry, and how to load and fire an early 19th century black powder pistol on horseback. You, sirs, are high caliber ROCKSTARS!

Allen Van Dolah shared his knowledge of horses with me. I am very appreciative since this helped me to not have the poor animals doing things a horse simply would not do. For example, did you know that an experienced rider would not be able to approach a strange horse without a bridle or halter, jump on its back, and ride like the wind? Being a town girl who is allergic to animals, my information came from old Westerns on TV where cowboys did it all the time. Of course, I had to delete the whole scene. But can you imagine Darcy and Elizabeth running for their lives where he leaps onto a horse, pulls her up behind him, then races away from their enemy? How romantic! How exciting! How fictional!!!

Nicole Clarkston is relentless in encouraging (pushing) me to get words on paper. In retrospect, I thank you. (Insert smiley face emoji) My daughter Jennifer shared the elements of mystery writing with me. I hope I remembered all of them (smiles sheepishly).

I would like to thank Serena Agusto Cox. You always make the finished product sparkle. I'm grateful.

Happy reading, my friends.

CHAPTER 1

*F*itzwilliam Darcy heard the gun's repercussion a second before his perfectly formed beaver hat flew off his head. Dismounting, he hurried to retrieve it. Less than an inch from the top was a hole on one side where the bullet entered and another opposite where it exited. Brushing the dirt from the brim, he glanced around. He saw no one. Dismissing the gunshot as being from a hunter who aimed wide of his intended target, Darcy remounted and hurried away before the person who fired the shot could reload.

That was the day prior in Kent.

The next afternoon, in the middle of the business district of London, a bullet pierced the side window and back panel of his carriage. Shards of shattered glass littered the floor. The leather squab where he normally sat now possessed a gaping hole in it, exactly where his chest should have been. Had he not positioned himself in the back-facing seat to lay the pile of papers he gathered from his man of business on the bench, Darcy's life's blood would be pouring from him.

His heart pounded from the sound and the implications. To be fired upon two days in a row was not an accident. Someone wanted him dead.

Yelling at his driver to hurry away, Darcy's eyes scanned the passersby through the void where the window glass should have been. At first glance, those who stood their ground appeared harmless. One man looked to be at least eighty years of age. Likely, he was hard of hearing so was entirely unaware of what transpired. Another appeared to be not yet old enough to shave. Both of his arms were wrapped around a younger lad and a little girl with the same sandy blonde hair. It seemed he was no more than an older brother whose first instinct was to protect his family. There was no place he could have quickly hidden a firearm with his arms engaged as they were.

It was the third and final person who caught and held Darcy's attention. The lady was his sister's height, or a little taller. She was dressed in a fashionable dark green traveling garment with a matching bonnet. Her headwear concealed the color of her hair. The brim shaded her face. Yet, as Darcy looked at her, she boldly tipped her chin to stare back at him—her large dark eyes as angry as he had ever seen on a person. Those eyes—he would not soon forget them.

Surely, it could not have been a female who wanted to do him harm. Perhaps, she was merely startled from the sound.

As the coach turned the corner leading to Darcy

House, the young lady stepped away from the walkway into the street. Lifting her hand, she gave him a saucy salute, her fingers formed into the shape of a pistol before she slipped into an alley to be lost amongst the crowds.

Good Lord! It was her!

* * *

"Tell me everything," Colonel Richard Fitzwilliam, Darcy's older cousin and best friend, demanded. "From the moment you left Darcy House until you returned, I want to know where you went, who you saw, what they were wearing, and what they were doing. Who wants you dead?"

Darcy's heart pounded fiercely until he feared Richard could hear it.

"Blast it all!" Darcy borrowed his cousin's favorite curse with no guilt or regret.

When he turned toward the tray holding a cut crystal carafe full of France's finest brandy, Richard stopped him before a drop touched the Baccarat stemware.

"No, Darce. You need a clear head for this. The sooner you start speaking of your experience, the more accurate your details will be. Delay will do neither of us any good."

This was the reason why the first thing he did upon returning to Darcy House was request the immediate presence of his cousin. When they were both upset, Richard's mind was clearer. His talents were wasted on the battlefield. Should the War Office have used him to plot strategy, the conflict with France would have been long over.

"Fine!" Darcy ran his hands through his hair. Dropping into a chair opposite his cousin, he began. "Yesterday, I was called on a fool's errand to Kent by Aunt Catherine. She has taken it into her head to choose a wife for her parson, who happens to be an idiot."

"I cannot imagine Aunt Catherine choosing well," Richard mused.

"She would not. Nor would her imbecilic clergyman." Darcy inhaled slowly, his mind going back to the day prior.

"I decided to ride. The weather was fine, and I knew I would need to clear my head after spending as little time as possible with the dreaded duo." His already sensitized body shuddered at having been in the same room with Lady Catherine and Mr. Collins. They were two peas in a very overripe pod.

"But I digress." Waving his hand in the air to dismiss the thought, he continued, "On my return to London, I made my usual stop at the inn in Bromley to rest my mount and sample their beef stew. After my repast, I left Bromley behind. I was two or three miles west of the inn when I registered a gun firing immediately before my hat hit the ground. The sound was close. It startled my horse and myself."

"Go on," Richard insisted.

"It actually took a few seconds before I concluded I was in danger," Darcy admitted. "Once I realized it was likely a hunter with bad aim, I retrieved my hat, remounted my horse, and rode home a bit quicker than my normal pace."

"Did you see anyone?"

"I did not." Darcy closed his eyes to picture the scene. "The road was lined with trees on both sides. There were no houses or cottages visible. I scanned the area before I left."

"Did you see any game? Where there was a gap in the trees, who or what was behind them? Were you two or three miles, Darcy?"

His eyes shot open. "It was two miles and I saw nothing. No deer. No rabbits. No birds. No humans." Despite knowing why Richard was demanding answers, it did nothing to ease Darcy's frustration.

"Close your eyes again, Darce." Richard's voice calmed. "Go back to the inn at Bromley. Were there coaches in the yard? How many animals were in the corral? Who was in the tap room? Did anyone attempt to make conversation with you?"

Relaxing as best as he was able, pictures began flashing inside his mind.

"There was a well-worn black carriage with paint chipped from the edges. Inside was a lady with three young children—all girls. They were hanging outside the window trying to garner the attention of the man. The gentleman was attempting to get help with one of the horses, I believe. His clothing was plain and clean. I... I remember hearing his wife ask if there was enough to stay the night and have a meal. The man shook his head no."

"Very good." Richard's praise was rare. "Did they leave before you? Which direction did they travel?"

"They were still at the inn when I left. By then, the one horse was unhitched. Before you ask, it was a rather tall Welsh Cob as old as the two of us. The blacksmith was tending the animal. It limped, favoring its foreleg. Even though the family were headed toward London, there was no possibility they could have caught up to me within those two miles."

"I see. Anything else?"

Another image popped into his head.

"A lady was seated inside the building. Her back was to the door. I did not see her face."

"Yes? Good! Tell me everything about her." Richard sat forward in his chair.

"Although she was mature in form, her wavy hair hung down her back like a schoolgirl's. It was a dark shade of brown, reaching about six inches from her waist."

Richard cleared his throat. "What was she wearing?"

"Her traveling coat was...*Oh my WORD!!!*" He suddenly lost the ability to swallow. "The woman who shot at me today was wearing the same garment. It was so dark a green it almost looked black. Her hat was the same color. There was one ostrich feather on the side. It was fastened with a black rose made from ribbons. The lace on her collar and sleeves was black. When she turned to see who entered the room, her eyes..." he gulped. "Her eyes were as dark as the midnight sky with bolts of lightning streaking from them. I assumed at the time that she resented her meal being disturbed."

"Well, cousin, I am positively delighted a finely-dressed woman finally caught your attention, even if she is trying to kill you." Richard smirked.

"Not funny, Richard!" He knew what his cousin was about. Richard often used humor to dispel tension. This time it failed.

6

"Do you know her?"

"I do not keep company with females who carry and know how to use pistols—especially in London."

"Yes, well, this can be the subject of debate for another time." Richard sat back in his chair. "I know how little you share your business. The likelihood of anyone other than your staff or Lady Catherine knowing your destination yesterday would be almost slim to none. Am I correct?"

"You are."

"Then let us go back to Kent. Was there anything out of the ordinary with Aunt Catherine or Mr. Collins? Did nothing stand out?"

Darcy ran his hand over his chin. While in their presence, he tried to ignore everything spewing from the mouth of his aunt and her parson. However, bits and pieces must have pierced his cerebrum.

"Mr. Collins appeared to be having something of a difficulty. Whatever it was, concerned Lady Catherine. I assumed there was a disturbance in the parish. This was not agreeable to our aunt—although why it is her business to decide how he should act is difficult to fathom. She did heap glowing praise upon her parson for providing spiritual guidance and comfort to Anne who is, according to our aunt, 'distressed at not yet becoming the mistress of Pemberley.'"

"Bah!" Richard scoffed. "When have we not heard the same from Aunt Catherine? If she had her way, you would have wed Anne once the both of you could toddle your way to a chapel." He shook his head. "What else do you recall?"

"Aunt Catherine spoke at length of an entail on a small

estate Mr. Collins would inherit when the current resident dies. The family has several daughters. Asserting her
authority, Aunt Catherine insisted he depart for the shire
to marry one of the young ladies. She has allowed a fortnight for him to complete the task and return to Rosings
with his bride, despite it not being long enough to have
the banns read. All I can say is 'the poor girl' to whichever
one catches his eye."

Richard chortled. "I daily thank the heavens that I am
not the focus of Aunt Catherine's matchmaking attempts.
Having you, with your hefty purse, grand estate, and
charming, good looks in her boresight is entertainment
enough."

Even without his aunt's constant haranguing him to
marry her fractious daughter, Darcy would never have
turned to her for marital advice as the parson had done.
Lady Catherine's marriage to his uncle had been volatile
and miserable. What did she know of a happy relationship
between a man and a woman? She loved to argue and
always insisted on having her way. Since Anne was very
much like her mother, Darcy would never offer for a lady
whose personality guaranteed that any peace at
Pemberley prior to her arrival would vanish as soon as
she stepped through the door.

Richard cleared his throat then continued, "If these
gunshots are related, then someone knew you traveled to
Kent. They also knew your destination today. I suggest
you speak with your grooms to see if there were any
innocent-looking ladies who asked after your schedule."

Darcy's confidence in his household staff was absolute.
Nevertheless, several of the grooms were young and

impressionable. If the lady caught and held his attention despite not seeing her face up close, he could only imagine her power should she turn those magnificent eyes upon a lad embroiled in those adolescent years where they first noticed how females were built differently than themselves.

"I will ask."

"Good." Richard stood to take his turn pacing the floor. "Another option we need to explore is that the lady, or someone she has in her employ, has been watching Darcy House, following you when you leave. Have you noticed anyone out of the ordinary lurking about?"

"I have not." Darcy's confidence in the security he had set up to protect himself and his sister was shaken. To have someone who meant him harm get close enough to his home or to those who worked for him for the purpose of doing away with him, was unthinkable. It was his sole responsibility to protect his sister and his staff. Should something happen to him, Georgiana, who three months earlier proved her vulnerability by agreeing to elope with the worst scoundrel of Darcy's acquaintance, would be left as easy prey for others who would use her to gain the pearl of the Darcy fortune, Pemberley.

"Hmm..." His cousin came to a standstill, tapping his lips with his bent knuckle for the longest time. Darcy knew to not interrupt. Richard was mulling the details over and over. Silence was the best help Darcy could give him. Finally, his cousin slapped his hand on the mantel. "From the angle where the bullet entered, she would have been able to see clearly through the window. She would have known you were not in your usual seat before she fired the shot. She did not aim to kill, did she? It was your attention she wanted."

"She achieved her goal." Darcy thought back to the damage to his carriage. In response, his breathing quickened, his heart rate increased, and the small hairs on his forearms stood tall.

"Who is this woman?" Richard growled. "You have not kept a mistress whom you tossed out into the street. You do not flirt or increase expectations with young ladies, which irritates the women and their mothers but should not inspire violence. Darcy, according to my mother, who has given your marital prospects a fair amount of consideration, you are not a man of deep romantic passion. In fact, Mama despairs of you ever becoming emotionally attached to anything other than your sister or your estate."

Darcy nodded. Every word his cousin spoke was the truth. His honor would not allow him to raise a lady's hopes and dreams of becoming mistress of Pemberley when he would never have any of them as his wife. His aunt, Lady Matlock, dangled a bevy of the latest debutants in front of him every year at the beginning of each season since he inherited Pemberley—to no avail.

Dropping back into the chair, Richard tapped his fingers on the arm. "Darce, we need to get you out of London. Either go to Pemberley where any stranger would stand out or...better yet, go no farther than St. Albans, Brighton, or Oxford, which would leave little opportunity for an ambush on the road. They are, any of them, close enough. Contact with you would be swift. According to the rumors floating on the wind, very soon I will be leaving for the continent to pursue a network of spies. I could, however, supply someone from my regiment to pose as a local recruiting officer for the Regulars. My commanding officer would be well pleased to have more bodies to order about."

Darcy immediately saw the wisdom of Richard's suggestion. Considering his options, the best was a recent invitation from his close friend, Charles Bingley. The younger man was hosting a small party at his newly leased estate not far from St. Albans. His request to Darcy was twofold. Initially, it was in repayment for the many times Darcy welcomed Bingley and his family at Pemberley. Only later was it revealed that the invitation was also for the purpose of reassuring Bingley, who feared he made a colossal mistake in putting out so much money to lease and refurbish Netherfield Park. This was the first time Bingley was responsible for overseeing all of the details, large and small. He felt he needed Darcy's assistance.

If Darcy left immediately, he could be at Netherfield Park within four hours.

His mind listed all he needed to take care of before he could leave. His priority was the protection of his sister. "Will you see Georgiana settled at Matlock House?"

Both men shared guardianship of Georgiana Darcy. She would be safe with Richard's parents.

Richard nodded. "I will. Her studies with her masters could continue and Mother would have someone who actually paid attention to her to fuss over."

Darcy nodded. His sister continued to suffer from her near elopement with the son of Pemberley's former steward, George Wickham. She was terrified of making another mistake. Being under the tutelage of Lady Matlock would give her confidence—he hoped.

Before the October moon began lighting the night sky, Georgiana was escorted to Matlock House by none other than Richard himself and Darcy was in his largest undamaged town coach heading north.

CHAPTER 2

*L*ongbourn bustled with activity as five young ladies prepared for the grandest social event of the autumn season in their part of Hertfordshire, the Meryton assembly. Typically, everyone in attendance was known to everyone else. When the news reached the Bennet household that the premier estate in Hertfordshire was let at last by a single man possessed of a fortune and it was reported he brought friends, the excitement level erupted like Mt. Vesuvius, spilling anticipation into every room.

Elizabeth Bennet was as eager as the rest of her sisters to meet the mysterious family residing at the neighboring estate of Netherfield Park. Rarely did anyone new attend the assembly. Thus, the possibility of standing up with a stranger was thrilling.

Their mother, despite knowing nothing of the current occupant, had already selected Mr. Bingley, with his rumored five thousand a year, as the future husband for Elizabeth's eldest sister, Jane. According to Mrs. Bennet, the pair would be wed before the winter holidays, which gave them slightly under two short months to meet, decide they were perfect for each other, post the banns, and be joined together in holy matrimony.

Elizabeth was eternally grateful that she was not her mother's favorite. To be paraded in front of a stranger like a butcher choosing a cow was offensive. Jane, too, found their mother's attitude to be a challenge. Yet, her innate kindness and goodness allowed her to see the motive behind her mother's distress. If none of the Bennet daughters married well, they would be left impoverished and homeless upon the eventual loss of their father. Even though their estate had a Bennet as master for almost two centuries, Longbourn was entailed to the heir's male. Since there were no sons born to the current Bennets, the estate would go to a distant cousin, Mr. William Collins, parson to Lady Catherine de Bourgh in Kent.

Their mother cared not if Mr. Bingley was young or old, kind or cruel, handsome or pig-faced. In her opinion, what mattered was that he had the funds to lease Netherfield Park. His wealth, her sole criteria, was enough to consider him attached to one of her girls. Well, that and a promise to care for the rest of the new Mrs. Bingley's family, in particular his mother-in-law, when the inevitable happened to Mr. Bennet.

Elizabeth dug through her ribbon box for hair pins. She needed two more to finish her sister's coiffeur. Setting aside a scrap of fabric that would match her own dark green dress, she found the needed pins.

"I do hope Mama is not too forward with her attention to Mr. Bingley," Jane mused. "The assembly tonight shall be crowded, and the music loud. I pray she will restrain her tone at the very least. It would not do if she could be heard over the dancing."

Elizabeth teased, "If Mama had her way, she would tuck iron shackles and a chain in her reticule in case she gets close enough to capture Mr. Bingley before Lady Lucas, Mrs. Long, or Mrs. Goulding can reach him."

"I suspect you mean to be funny, Lizzy, but I cannot laugh." Jane sighed. "I do wish to meet someone who is kind and gentle, loyal and true. Perhaps Mr. Bingley, or one of his guests, will turn out to be the man of my dreams."

Jane Bennet was the loveliest of all Elizabeth's sisters. As Elizabeth twisted the last strand of Jane's flaxen locks into a curl, pinning it snuggly into place, she replied, "I hope he does not have a wart at the end of his nose, that his breath does not smell of Papa's stockings, and that he is not shorter than you."

Jane spun toward her sister. "Oh, Lizzy. Mama cannot keep herself from wishing. Nevertheless, I will not marry a man I cannot admire and respect. Should Mr. Bingley be less than a gentleman should be, I will distance myself from him no matter what Mama says or wants."

"Well said, Jane!" Elizabeth tapped her sister's shoulder, turning her back to the mirror. Pushing the final pin into place, Elizabeth leaned down until both faces were looking back at them. Where Jane was fair with twinkling blue eyes, Elizabeth's hair was a nondescript brown and her eyes were almost raven black.

The disparity of Elizabeth's appearance was often commented upon when the five Bennet girls were together. Jane, Mary, Kitty, and Lydia had the same petite stature and fair coloring as their mother. Elizabeth was taller. Her darker hair and eyes came from the Bennet side of the family.

Kissing her sister's cheek, Elizabeth gazed unseeingly out the only window in their chambers. Marriage was serious business. Being attached to an unscrupulous or belligerent man would cause no end of misery that would last a lifetime.

"Charlotte said there were only three men in the party. One of them already has a wife," Jane said.

"Did she comment upon their character or their appearance?" Elizabeth asked.

"Charlotte did not see them, Lizzy. She was repeating what her father told them after visiting Netherfield Park to welcome Mr. Bingley and his guests to the neighborhood."

"I see," Elizabeth grinned. "Mama is sure to be disappointed because her last report was four plain-looking, poorly-dressed females and eight handsome single men."

The uncertainty as to the exact size of the group had caused no end of drama in the Bennet household. Rumors circulating the parlors of Meryton reported anywhere from seven men and two ladies to twelve men and six females. Since those primarily occupied with the speculation were mothers with unattached daughters, the number of gentlemen in their imaginations always outnumbered the ladies. Thus, Mrs. Bennet was unsure if it would be only one daughter who would be marrying or if there would be enough males present to dispose of all five of her girls at once.

"Beware, Lizzy," Jane smiled. "With two unmarried gentlemen in the Netherfield party you, too, are in danger of becoming the target of Mama's matchmaking schemes."

Elizabeth snorted. In imitation of her mother's high-pitched whine, she said, "Mr. Bingley, how lovely to make your acquaintance. Allow me to introduce you to your future bride, my loveliest daughter, Jane." Elizabeth curtsied. "To the other mystery male, she shall offer me like a cooked goose on a platter." Elizabeth hissed like the oldest gander at Longbourn. "My Dear Mr. Plumbottom, pray welcome your future wife by offering to stand up with her as no one else will, I am sure. She is far too quick with her opinions, so I pray your advanced years have rendered you hard of hearing in addition to...oh, Mr. Plumbottom, you are short on teeth. My Lizzy does have a penchant for soft foods. Look! You already have so much in common. Go now! Dance!"

"Plumbottom? I cannot imagine that is his name." Jane giggled. "You are too hard on yourself, sister dear. One of these days you will meet a man who will only have eyes for you, then you will need to bite your tongue."

Elizabeth smirked. "Then let us pray that Mr. Bingley and his guests are impervious to Mama's schemes, blinded to our flaws, and uncaring that our dowries are small."

Gathering their gloves and shawls, they headed downstairs to join the rest of the females in their family. As was usual, their father had elected to remain home to enjoy the quiet.

* * *

CAROLINE BINGLEY TURNED in front of her mirror to make certain that she was well turned out from every angle. Her gown, a dark blue paisley with a front panel of silver, swirled around her legs with each turn. The silver ribbons and lace twinkled in the candlelight. The delicate sapphire necklace sparkled against her skin; the largest stone nestled between her ample bust, which was elegantly displayed by the perfect fit of her gown.

Her sister burst into her chambers. "Caroline, are you not yet ready? The others are already downstairs. Charles is pacing, mumbling to himself, and Mr. Darcy stands at the fireplace, his disdain at being kept waiting is a fearsome sight to behold. Gilbert is on his second glass of port. If you do not hurry, I fear the men will leave without us or they will talk themselves out of attending. Then all of this trouble to get dressed up will be for naught."

"Louisa, if I am to procure a marriage proposal from Mr. Darcy, I need to be seen at my best." Caroline made another turn in front of the mirror, stopping midway. "Come here and fix this," she commanded the maid standing in the corner. "One of the loops in the ribbon is larger than the other. I cannot be seen like this," she sneered.

As the servant rushed to fix the bow, Louisa approached to see how badly tied the ribbons were. "Good heavens, Caroline, the one loop is barely a quarter inch wider than the other. If you do not quit fussing, Mr. Darcy will not have a chance to see you. The small fortune you paid for that gown and those jewels will be wasted. Charles will be upset. The cost of leasing this property, plus the furnishings you chose, have him nervous about how little funds he has left. You had better be successful with Mr. Darcy or we could be facing the poor house, all of us."

Running her hands along the silver ribbon under her bodice, Caroline pushed up, lifting her breasts until little was left to the imagination. "He will be mine. Pemberley will be mine. You wait and see."

* * *

AS JANE HAD SPECULATED, the rest of the attendees at the assembly were packed into the room from one wall to the other. Charlotte Lucas was standing close to the door waiting for Elizabeth.

"Have they arrived?" Elizabeth asked as her outer things were whisked away by waiting staff. The musicians were beginning to tune their instruments. Before long, dancing would begin in earnest.

"Not yet." Charlotte grabbed Elizabeth's hand and pulled her close. "Lizzy, I am in need of some assistance."

"What is wrong?" Rarely had she seen Charlotte ruffled.

"Mr. Bingley requested the first dance with me. My father was overjoyed to the point that he failed to consider what he was agreeing to when he accepted."

Under normal circumstances, Charlotte, who adored horses, could ride like the wind. However, the new gelding her father had foolishly purchased from an itinerant vendor had at first presented a docile persona. As soon as Charlotte mounted the beast, he lowered his head, raised his hindquarters into the air, and kicked out with his hind legs. Caught off guard, Charlotte had landed with the full force of her weight on her right knee. The bruise and swelling had yet to go down. Even the thought of twisting and turning during a dance had to be painful.

"Oh Charlotte. I am sorry. Surely, it should be your father who should make this right?"

Charlotte shrugged. "Yes, it should. However, he is far too busy being the master of ceremonies to consider what he has done to me."

Without hesitation, Elizabeth stated, "Then allow me to speak with Mr. Bingley."

Jane reminded her, "You have not yet been introduced, Lizzy."

Observing the obvious distress lining Charlotte's face, Elizabeth said, "Pray do not worry, either of you. I will find a way."

Taking Charlotte's arm, she helped her to a chair at the side of the room. "Can I get you anything for your comfort, my friend?"

"If you can keep me from the embarrassment of having my situation spoken of publicly, I will be forever grateful." Charlotte's face turned a pasty white from pain. "I should not have come. Father insisted."

The demands of a stubborn parent were as familiar to Elizabeth as breathing. Nodding, she noted, "Should the Bingley party be fashionably late, the first set will be over. You will not need to dance, and I will not need to speak to the gentleman."

"We can hope." Charlotte smoothed the fabric of her gown over her injured limb.

Charlotte Lucas, at twenty-seven, was considered by

the gossips of Meryton to be an object of pity for there was nothing more undesirable to any of them than to be an unattached female with no prospects. Elizabeth knew better. For the past several years, her friend was anonymously writing articles about life in a country town for the widely distributed circulating paper, *The Times.* Although the pay was minimal, Charlotte was frugal, saving every farthing she earned to live independently should the need arise. Elizabeth would do anything to help her reach her goal.

Charlotte whispered, "At least from here I will be able to gather material for my writing. Perhaps our newest neighbors will add much needed drama so I will not need to be as creative as usual."

Elizabeth chuckled, "You are a wicked woman, Charlotte Lucas." She wandered back to the entrance in hopes of subtly being able to catch Mr. Bingley's attention before he entered the fray.

Within moments, three men and two well-dressed ladies stepped through the doorway where servants helped them with their outer garments. Elizabeth ignored the ladies while in search of Mr. Bingley. Was he the short, heavy-set man with the thinning hair? No, for one of the ladies was attached to his side. By the way they were blatantly ignoring each other, they must be the married couple. Was it the tall, handsome man who stood at the back of the party next to the youngest of the females? She clung to him like a burr on wool stockings. Would a sister do that to a brother? If she was shy like Jane, then she would.

Elizabeth shrugged. The only other new arrival was a

handsome young man with a large smile on his face. Since he had entered the room without waiting on either female, Elizabeth suspected he was Mr. Bingley's guest. Therefore, she concluded the tall man was Mr. Bingley himself.

Winding through those waiting to dance and the staff, Elizabeth made her way to his side. Before she could speak, the shorter man returned to his host. He was dressed colorfully in dark green and gold with his hair perfectly coiffed in Beau Brummel's Brutus style, giving the appearance that he was taller than he was.

"What lovely partners we will have for the evening. Why, I do believe the music is as good as in town. You must dance with someone other than Caroline or Louisa."

The taller man scoffed, making a terrible first impression on Elizabeth.

She could hear the disdain in his voice as he said, "I certainly shall not. You know how I detest it unless I am particularly acquainted with my partner. At such an assembly as this, it would be insupportable. It would be a punishment to stand up with any female already inside this room."

Goodness! Why would a man of the world attend an assembly if he had no intentions of dancing or mixing with the neighborhood? Was he weak of character? Was he easily led? Or was it his purpose to impress others with his status and rank?

"I would not be so fastidious as you are for a kingdom!" cried the younger man, "Upon my word, I have never seen so many pleasant girls in my life. There are several of them who are uncommonly pretty."

Elizabeth followed his gaze to where Jane stood next to Charlotte. Both were lovely, indeed.

"Which do you mean?" the tall man asked as his eyes swept in Elizabeth's direction. "Her?"

Elizabeth dropped her gaze to the floor, counting from one to ten to keep from calling him all the names a lady never used in public.

DARCY WAS TAKING a risk being at an event surrounded by people. Yet, by being pressed into Bingley's carriage with four others and being surrounded by a multitude of the local populace, he was as protected as he could be.

What had moved him to take a chance on being exposed to someone who meant him harm was Caroline Bingley's brash statement that if he remained at Netherfield Park, she would stay behind to keep him company. Calculating the odds, he decided that having a bullet fly towards him was less detrimental than being permanently attached to Miss Bingley.

He abhorred public assemblies, especially where he was the stranger. Within seconds he would hear speculation about his estate, his income, and his marital status. As soon as he could safely leave where Miss Bingley was engaged to dance with someone else, Darcy would request the carriage and return to Netherfield Park, alone.

"Yes, her. She is as lovely as the others," Mr. Bingley's kind-hearted guest responded.

Elizabeth peeked at him from under her lashes. Everything about him from his outstretched hand and furrowed brow, indicated he was uncertain how to react to his host's cruel comments. That he tried was meaningful, something she would certainly share with Jane and Charlotte.

The lout continued, "She is tolerable, but certainly not handsome enough to tempt me. I am in no humor at present to give consequence to young ladies who are so bold as to actively seek an introduction by approaching me in a doorway. You are wasting your time with me."

Of all the arrogant oafs on the planet, she was faced with the worst. The man's fate was sealed. Elizabeth would do anything to keep horrible Mr. Bingley from attempting to stand up with Charlotte or to marry Jane as Mama dreamed. His manners were atrocious.

Inhaling slowly, Elizabeth wondered how Sir William had deigned to offer his daughter to the ogre for a dance. Mr. Bingley's attitude would have wounded Charlotte far more than her injury had she been in anticipation of standing up with him for the first set. It was considered an honor to open the dance with revered guests. Additionally, his insult covered every other female in the room, not just herself. *Brute!*

She was livid. Clearing her throat to gain his attention, she looked him directly in the eyes. Scathingly, she asserted, "Mr. Bingley, you are no gentleman!"

"You!" the rude man stepped back from her, holding

his hand out as if to fend her off. "Who are you and how did you know I would be here?"

"I have no possible idea of what you are speaking." Elizabeth crossed her arms over her chest. She was so angry that she was shaking. *How dare her mother attempt to tie sweet Jane to such a man! How dare Sir William attempt to subject his daughter to dancing with the dolt! Thirty minutes would have been a punishment!*

Ignoring her, the beast called to the friendly man who was headed toward the ballroom.

"Bingley, I am leaving now." A man of his word, the monster spun on his heels and departed.

In the confusion of the younger fellow trying to get the dunce's attention by calling out, "Mr. Darcy," Elizabeth became aware that she had inadvertently addressed the wrong man. Mr. Bingley was the amiable one. Mr. Darcy was the bullish ox with a foul temper and an abominable character.

The rest of the party followed. As the newly revealed Mr. Bingley passed by, he addressed Elizabeth. "Say, I apologize for my friend. He is not himself today. May I inquire as to your name, Miss?"

Dipping into a curtsey, Elizabeth spoke quickly, "I will not hold his conduct against you, sir. I am Miss Elizabeth Bennet."

"Do extend my apologies to Miss Lucas. I anticipated our dance."

"Consider it done, sir."

"I thank you, Miss Bennet." With a smile of regret, the man gathered his greatcoat, gloves, and hat then departed the building behind the rest of his party.

CHAPTER 3

*I*gnoring the other four occupants in the carriage, Darcy's mind raced. He was angry with himself. *Why had he walked away?* For his own personal safety, of course.

Wishing he could go back to the assembly and demand the woman identify herself and her purpose in wanting him dead, he knew that was out of the question. He was right to leave the building immediately. Still, he could not conceive of how the same woman who attempted twice to kill him could have known he would be in Hertfordshire, in Meryton, at a public assembly, no less. Who was her informant? Who was treacherously providing private information to her to keep him at risk?

Darcy could not begin to guess. Richard's interview of his stable hands had turned up nothing. A discreet inquiry of his household staff had resulted in the same.

The lady was as bold as brass, showing herself in public where an arrest could have been made. She was brimming with guile, making herself up to fit in as a country maiden so she did not stand out. Had Darcy not seen her eyes, he would have looked right past her. Whatever her purpose, with Darcy's connections, she would be swinging from a rope before the next quarterly assizes were held.

Blast!

He would have known her anywhere. Her dress of dark green fabric was strikingly like the traveling cloak of the marksman. Her hair was darkish brown. Yet, it was her eyes that gave her away as being the attempted murderer. They were as filled with anger as they were in London.

His mind kept repeating, who was she and why did she want him dead?

He would need to contact Richard immediately.

"Mr. Darcy," Caroline Bingley clutched his arm, finally wrenching his attention away from his plans.

Inhaling to calm himself, Darcy realized that the other occupants of the carriage all had their eyes trained on him. Darcy's hand covered his mouth, keeping the words he wanted to spew to himself. The others could not know of his inner distress.

His skin crawled with the idea that someone intruded on his privacy, discovered his plans, then secretly followed his every move.

Blast it all! Had he not been fending off the unwanted attentions of Caroline Bingley when they stepped into the assembly hall, he might have noticed the woman earlier. He could have discretely asked if she was known in the community. He doubted it since she was standing alone at the entrance. If only he could have discovered her name, it would have placed him one huge step towards knowing her purpose.

"Mr. Darcy, I feel exactly the same as you." In her quest to become the mistress of Pemberley, Caroline Bingley would have agreed with him even if he proclaimed the moon would be purple on one side and bright green on the other. Her attempts to gain his attention were ridiculous. "There was not one ounce of fashion to be seen. It would have been insupportable for you to offer to dance with any of the daughters of those ruffians."

"Caroline! I saw several ladies there of uncommon beauty." Bingley rarely spoke up to correct his sister's poor attitude. However, his kind nature would be outraged at any slight to a young lady, known or unknown. He tugged at the hem of his favorite waistcoat, dark green and gold with shiny brass buttons. "I did not see any ruffians at all."

"Pshaw!" Miss Bingley would have none of the attention focused on anyone other than herself. "No, Charles. You may have judged some of them as comely, however, Mr. Darcy has a more discerning eye."

Darcy was unimpressed with her temerity. There was no basis for Miss Bingley to claim that she was privy to his private opinions. He had not once taken her into his confidence. Nor had he said anything to her insipid sister Louisa Hurst or her brother-in-law Gilbert.

However, the conversation had served to slow his breathing and settle his thoughts. He needed to do everything within his power to gain information about the lady. He needed to carefully consider how to proceed so he did not place himself in even greater danger.

"Say, Darcy, I made an acquaintance of one of the ladies this evening. She was a pleasant girl with lovely eyes. Her surname is Bennet. There is an estate not three miles from Netherfield Park that is the home of the Bennet family. They have five daughters. If all of them are as lovely and kind as Miss Elizabeth Bennet, then our time in Hertfordshire will be made more enjoyable."

"Charles, we were hardly there for more than a few minutes. How on earth did you come to meet her?" His younger sister inquired.

"Why, she approached the area while we were handing over our outer clothing. I was able to ask her to send my regrets to Miss Lucas with whom I was promised for the first set."

"Her? You call her a beauty?" Miss Bingley sneered. "Why, with her mousy-brown hair, dark eyes, and her quaint country dress that was at least a year out of fashion, she would never be considered a favorite by the *ton*. I do believe I gave my maid a dress made from that particular shade of dark green cloth several years ago."

Darcy sat up. "The lady with dark eyes and a green dress? You spoke with her?"

"I did, indeed."

"Her name? What did you say her name was?" Darcy demanded, his heart pounding in his chest.

"Miss Elizabeth Bennet." Bingley paused. "If I recall correctly when her father came to welcome me to the neighborhood, their estate is Longbourn."

"Bennets of Longbourn," he repeated under his breath.

Miss Elizabeth Bennet! He would write to Richard as soon as he could excuse himself from company.

"Say, Darcy. I wanted to ask. Were you not feeling well this evening? You said nothing earlier, but you turned pale in the entrance of the Hall, then quickly departed. May I call the apothecary for you?" Bingley asked.

"No, I am well," Darcy replied without thought. "I merely saw someone I never expected to see in Hertfordshire."

It was too much. He should not have uttered a word. Charles Bingley would have accepted any excuse as a reason for rudely turning away from a public assembly. His sisters, on the other hand, looked between themselves, their noses lifted to the same angle in disapprobation of the neighborhood. That they considered him a confederate was abhorrent.

To set matters straight, Darcy added, "Rather, I thought I saw someone I recognized. Upon further reflection, I believe I was mistaken."

He could tell by the glances they gave one another that the sisters did not buy his claim. In truth, Darcy could care less. There were far more important matters to ponder.

* * *

Who was this Elizabeth Bennet to Mr. Darcy? Caroline fumed inside. Any female who caught and held the attention of the master of Pemberley would pay dearly for distracting him away from her. Caroline wanted him and what Caroline wanted, Caroline got.

No sooner had the carriage arrived at Netherfield Park than Mr. Darcy hurried to his chambers.

"Charles, I believe a conversation is in order." It was not a request. Obediently, her brother and the others followed behind her. Hurst shut the door of her private sitting room firmly then turned the key.

* * *

"WELL DAUGHTERS, am I to expect any young men to approach me in the morning with an offer for your hands?" Mr. Bennet teased.

"Papa!" The youngest three kissed the man before heading above stairs. The baby of the family, Lydia, chanted, "I am sure Mr. Bingley's friend will not be asking for Lizzy's hand. Eleanor Goulding was standing close enough that she heard him say that my sister is not pretty enough to tempt him to dance with her. Can you imagine? Why, I would perish with shame should some wealthy man say that about me."

"What!" Mr. Bennet growled.

The girls' mother entered the conversation. "Yes! Yes! Not five minutes had passed after the Bingley party arrived and departed that I had not heard the insult from at least three different people. Upon the fourth telling, it became tiresome," Mrs. Bennet sighed. "Lizzy does not lose much by not suiting *his* fancy; for he is a most disagreeable man, not at all worth pleasing. So high and so conceited that there would have been no enduring him! Not handsome enough to dance with! I wish you were there, my dear, to have given him one of your set downs. I quite detest the man." She sniffed into her handkerchief. "With him taking off with Mr. Bingley, all my hopes were dashed to pieces. Of course, so were the hopes of Lady Lucas, Mrs. Long, and Mrs. Goulding. Thus, it was not a total loss."

"I praise you for showing forbearance under such dire circumstances." Her husband tipped his head slightly as she, too, bussed his cheek before retiring to her rooms.

"Lizzy?" His dark eyes were softened by genuine concern. "Were you crushed by his comment?"

Jane, who would never interfere in a private conversation, quickly bade their father good night.

Elizabeth waited until they were alone. "Papa, his opinion matters little to me. He is a mean sort who would not know quality if it slapped him in the face."

Mr. Darcy was a puzzle to her. It seemed almost as if he was afraid of her, which was entirely odd since she had never before seen him or heard his name. Elizabeth had told none of her party nor anyone else what he had said. Despite the gossip not coming from her mouth, it had quickly circulated the assembly. Rather than cry, she laughed off the man's insults. He was the one in error. If his expressed opinion landed him judged as deficient company, it was his fault, not hers.

"That's my girl." Mr. Bennet wrapped his arm across her shoulders. "Do not allow him to rob you of your joy, Lizzy. The exchange would hardly be fair. You are a pearl. He is nothing more than a clod of dirt, is he not?"

She smiled. Yawning, Elizabeth decided that the best course was to find the blessing in the situation. Had he been willing to subject the ladies of the assembly to his presence, Elizabeth might have had to dance with him. *Heaven forbid!* Chuckling, she took herself off to bed.

BEFORE BREAKFAST, Darcy sent the letter to his cousin. He was astounded that he had found the woman so easily. A thought unsettled him, what if it was her intention that she was discovered? A cold chill shot down his spine. What did she want of him?

His peers generally disparaged the minds of females as being far inferior to their own. Nonetheless, Darcy knew from history and his own experience that some women were exceedingly intelligent. His mother was a clever woman. Richard's mother was also possessed of a sharp mind. Lady Matlock navigated the upper levels of society with the shrewdness of a master chess player, as did her close friend, Lady Barrington. Many times, both Lady Matlock and Lady Barrington were able to procure information that aided their husbands in making wise political moves. According to Richard, the person currently running the network of spies pilfering secrets from the British government was female. Additionally, Queen Elizabeth was quoted as saying, "Though the sex to which I belong is considered weak, you will nevertheless find me a rock that bends to no wind." The decisions she made during her lifetime had generally proven her words true. As well, Catherine the Great was ruthless enough to change a nation as well as her personal life. She knew what she wanted and how to achieve her goals.

Was Elizabeth Bennet equally as astute? She had

boldly drawn his attention as if she was wanting him to see that it was her who hunted him. She had stood by the door, waiting to pounce on him like a panther on her prey.

Did her daring camouflage ignorance? No, he could not imagine it would. If it was her in Kent, then she was as skilled with a firearm as he was. The shot that removed his hat was remarkable. Taking into consideration the breeze, the movement of his horse, and the angle, that he had not lost his life was a tribute to her artistry with a weapon. Firing through a crowded street and his carriage window was also a noteworthy feat. Had she not been aiming to cause harm; he could have admired her finesse. Was she a cold-blooded assassin who felt a sick sort of joy from taunting him before she ended his life with a bullet between his eyes?

He shuddered as a trickle of fear traveled up his spine. Well, he would be no easy target. Now that he was aware of her location, he would continue his life as before with the exception of not wandering about alone. There was protection in numbers. Not only would it be a distraction for her, but it would also provide him with eyewitnesses when he captured her. No one, male or female, played Fitzwilliam Darcy for a fool!

In the blink of an eye, he knew his course. Rather than remain on the defensive, which left him vulnerable, he would do as Richard would do and go on the offensive. His first task would be to learn everything he could about one Miss Elizabeth Bennet.

His goal that morning had been to encourage Bingley to remain inside the house, possibly reviewing the estate's accounts. Now, his course was set. Calling for Netherfield Park's steward, Mr. Morris, they would ride the fence line between Bingley's estate and Longbourn. If she was hiding behind a grove of trees in hopes of a clandestine attack on a single rider, she would be disappointed.

CHAPTER 4

*A*utumn was Elizabeth's favorite time of year. The remnants of summer blending with the hints of upcoming winter rendered the days glorious for a pleasant stroll through the newly harvested fields. The heat from the day before had vanished during the night. Glancing out the window to a sky bereft of clouds, she would need her pelisse and shawl to stave off the morning's chill.

Her choice of direction was familiar. Oakham Mount beckoned her.

Grabbing an apple from a low-hanging limb in the orchard, she rubbed it on her skirt. The first bite was always the best. Juice shot to the back of her throat as her tongue tasted the sweet tangy flavor. Raising her face to the sun, she placed the fruit in the pocket of her summer gown to remove her bonnet. No one would see her casually garbed.

Stepping back to the well-worn path, Elizabeth hummed a tune from the assembly. Long after the Bingley party left the building, there was a lull in the dancing permitting the musicians to rest. After Elizabeth's sister, Mary, performed her normal dirge on the pianoforte, Miss Mary King delighted the gathering with a rendition of Thomas Moore's *My Lodging is on the Cold Ground.*

Wishing her voice was equally as lovely, Elizabeth shrugged. While she sang in tune to the music, she was no skilled vocalist. Nevertheless, it did not stop her from breaking out into song as she strolled. There was no one to hear her, other than the birds. Their interest was in their own music and the worms poking their heads above the soil.

Believe me, if all those endearing young charms,
   Which I gaze on so fondly to-day,
Were to change by to-morrow, and fleet in my arms,
   Like fairy-gifts fading away,—
Thou wouldst still be ador'd as this moment thou art,
   Let thy loveliness fade as it will;
And, around the dear ruin each wish of my heart
   Would entwine itself verdantly still!
It is not while beauty and youth are thine own,
   And thy cheeks unprofan'd by a tear,
That the fervour and faith of a soul can be known,
   To which time will but make thee more dear!
Oh! the heart, that has truly lov'd, never forgets,
   But as truly loves on to the close;
As the sun-flower turns on her god, when he sets,
   The same look which she turn'd when he rose!

Hmm! Elizabeth could not help but wonder if the words were true. If her mother and father had ever been in love, it had not stood the test of time. They rarely agreed. Instead, they acted as if they were strangers with completely different interests occupying the same house. Yet, the affection between Charlotte's parents had endured changed circumstances, the ravages of age and illness, along with the birth of six children of which Charlotte was the eldest. Lasting love was possible.

An image of the mean-spirited man accompanying Mr. Bingley popped into her mind. To be joined forever in marriage to such a creature would be intolerable. Hah! That would never happen. Her father would not force her to wed someone she despised, no matter how much wealth *he* might bring to a marriage. Nor would that brute Mr. Darcy ever be interested in her. No, she could easily imagine him with a high-born lady of means who would fill their nursery with an heir and a spare before ignoring him to live the life she desired. They would be two miserable people in an equally miserable marriage.

Perhaps Miss Bingley was his intended victim. As close as she was standing to the man, she must have been agreeable to the match. *Foolish woman!*

The caw of a carrion crow alerted her to the presence of *Jeanne de Valois-Saint-Remy*, a thief of a bird named for the Frenchwoman who once stole a necklace intended for Queen Marie Antoinette. Several times, Elizabeth set a treat to her side when she was engrossed in a book only to find that Jeannie, as the bird was nicknamed, had pilfered the biscuit or scone. The crow was bold enough that she would perch with her treasure just out of Elizabeth's reach before flying off to wherever her nest was located.

Without looking up, Elizabeth made certain her apple

was tucked deep inside her skirt pocket. *"Va-t'en. Vous n'obtiendrez rien de moi aujourd'hui."* Elizabeth taunted as she continued towards her goal. The silly crow would gain nothing from her today except a phrase from one of her old French lessons.

Less than twenty steps later, she reached her destination. Oakham Mount was barely elevated over the lush Hertfordshire valley. It's wealth to the landowners was a small hole in the limestone where a steady stream of water emerged. Following the natural curvature of the rocks that created a narrow embankment dividing Longbourn's fields from their neighbors, the spring along with regular rainstorms added much needed moisture until both Netherfield Park and the Bennets had an abundance of water to keep their crops irrigated.

"Hello!" Someone called from across the brook.

Elizabeth looked up to see three horsemen. Mr. Bingley and Mr. Morris, Netherfield Park's steward, had dismounted. Mr. Darcy, who was flanked by the others, stared at her from his superior height. His horse had to be sixteen hands. Additionally, he was a tall man. His stance was one of arrogant superiority.

Well! Her courage rose with any attempt to intimidate her. She glared at him before offering a warm smile of welcome to the others as she replaced her bonnet, quickly tying the ribbons under her chin.

"Good morning, gentlemen. A fine day to survey the area, is it not?"

"Indeed, it is," Mr. Bingley grinned. "Do you walk here often?"

"I do, Mr. Bingley." She gestured to where the stream

began. "I enjoy contemplating small beginnings, then envisioning where the droplets travel. I find I am able to broaden my world without leaving Meryton."

"What a brilliant concept," Mr. Bingley nodded. "I shall have to find my own small beginnings to ponder."

What a kind man to give consideration to her ramblings. Jane will like him.

"Mr. Morris, is your family well?" The steward served at Netherfield Park for as long as Elizabeth could remember.

"They are. I thank you for asking."

As a matter of courtesy, she should next acknowledge Mr. Darcy. Looking at him closely, Elizabeth judged him as having the possibility of being handsome, had his coloring not been pasty white and his lips not been puckered like he had sucked on a sour lemon.

Without an introduction, Elizabeth could not address Mr. Darcy directly. Another glance at the disapproval on his face stirred her gratitude for the manners of the day.

"You spoke French. Who were you addressing?" he insisted, despite the fact that he should not have spoken to her.

Of all the rude people she had ever encountered, this man was the worst!

"Darcy!" Mr. Bingley's face registered shock.

"Sir, I do not believe it is any concern of yours." There was no power on the earth that would have had her admitting to the oaf that she was speaking to a crow. Turning back to Mr. Bingley, she said, "Do enjoy your ride. It is time for me to return to Longbourn. A pleasant day to you." She curtsied to the two friendly men. "Mr.

Morris, pray tell your wife that we would be delighted to share our pears and apples. Our larder is full."

"I thank you, Miss Lizzy. She will be pleased to hear it, and I will be pleased to eat her preserves."

Grinning at the man, Elizabeth added, "Will you be taking the gentlemen to see the caves on your ride this fine morning, so they know the places to avoid?"

The steward nodded, "Absolutely! I will let them know where it is safe to ride and where it is not."

Smiling, she walked from the area, ignoring Mr. Darcy. Needless to say, her poor opinion had not been improved upon by this second contact. No, Elizabeth could not conceive of them ever being able to pass a polite quarter hour in the same room with equanimity.

Miserable man!

* * *

TERRIFYING chills covered Darcy's whole body when he heard Elizabeth Bennet's French. "Go away. You will get nothing from me today," she had said. Who was she addressing? Did she have a partner in her crimes? *Blast it all!* Placing all the pieces of information together that he had gathered about her so far—she was skilled with weapons, she spoke French (albeit not well), she freely traveled unaccompanied, by her own words she was passing information to others, and she was sly—what if she was the French spy that Richard was chasing? The implications were too horrifying to consider. However, it explained everything.

He was not the target. It was Richard.

With his greatest threat casually strolling away from them, there was no risk for him to separate from his grouping. "Bingley, I need to send a message to my cousin. Pray continue your ride. I will speak with you later." Turning, he raced back to the stables. Before his horse came to a complete stop, he swung his leg over and dropped to the ground. Hurrying to his chambers, he grabbed paper and quill. Within mere minutes he was done.

Richard,

Not only is she here, but I now believe I am not her primary target. Your idea that she meant to gain my attention is correct. Through me, I believe that she might be attempting to get to you.

She introduced herself to Bingley as Elizabeth Bennet. Are you familiar with the name? There is a family of Bennets at Longbourn, not three miles from Bingley's estate. She could have assumed the identity. I would put nothing past her.

When you come, which I know you will, take care. This woman is as sly as any I have known. Danger lurks in Hertfordshire.

Darcy

The note was soon on its way with the express rider using Darcy's fastest mount. He was to wait for the colonel to reply before returning to Netherfield Park.

Darcy paced his chambers, gaining no peace in any of the ten steps from one end of the room to the other.

He remained isolated until early evening when the rider returned. Breaking the seal, he ripped the note open.

Darcy,

Headquarters has me on a wild goose chase. I am leaving for

Spain in the morning. I doubt I will return to England before spring. Your mission is reconnaissance. Discover all you can about her without danger to yourself. You are far more important to me alive then dead, dear cousin.

Major Robert Gerring will be arriving this evening. He will stay at the inn in Meryton. He will pose as an old friend of mine from Cambridge, which will explain to Bingley why you will be spending a great deal of time with him. He is an intelligent man who is trustworthy.

Be cautious, Darcy, and take care of Georgiana while I am gone. Wickham is not the only fortune-hunter on British soil.

RF

Running his hand over his face, Darcy reread the note, hoping he would find an indication in between the words of Richard's intentions to head north. Instead, the man who was his most trusted friend was sailing into enemy territory. He prayed God would protect his cousin.

Wishing the circumstances were different would change nothing. If Richard trusted Major Gerring, then he needed to do the same.

CHARLES BINGLEY WAS a humble man and a generous host. He never complained when Darcy had business to care for nor did he insist on being entertained by his guests. As well, he readily admitted that the ambitions of his sisters were outrageous.

"Darcy, unlike Caroline and Louisa, I will not complain about you being absent from my table." Bingley leaned forward in his chair. "What I will do is offer any help or resources I have available to assist you with whatever is consuming your time."

"I thank you, Charles."

Darcy met Bingley shortly after the death of his father. The younger man had recently inherited a large fortune when his own father died. The Bank of England, where the Darcy family kept the majority of their funds, had a few bankers who were less careful than others with the investment portfolios of their clients. When Darcy happened to see the young man headed in the direction of one of the risky financial managers, he intervened. Directing the young gentleman to his own man of business at the bank had protected Mr. Bingley's fortune and cemented a friendship that would stand the test of time, Darcy had no doubt. Bingley was one of the few men he could trust.

Bingley patted his stomach. With his legs stretched forward and crossed at the ankles, he was the picture of pleased satisfaction.

Darcy said, "You are enjoying being the master, are you not?"

Bingley grinned. "I am. Netherfield Park is a fine property. As Miss Elizabeth said earlier, it is my small beginning. In the future, with a little luck, I plan to have a far more extensive property to pass down to future generations of Bingleys. Oh, certainly not as grand as Pemberley. But one I can call my own."

"A worthy goal," Darcy said.

"Say, Sir William Lucas of Lucas Lodge has invited us to gather with a few families from the neighborhood tomorrow evening. Caroline and Louisa are loath to socialize with the local gentry. When I suggested they remain at Netherfield, they said they would wait to see whether you chose to attend before they decided."

Darcy moaned. "Bingley, this form of manipulation on the part of your sisters is repugnant to me. They will not dictate with whom I spend my time or where I will or will not go." Deciding to put his foot down once again, he continued, "Your sister's attempt to engage me as a husband will never work. Nothing she could do or say would induce me to offer her the position as mistress of Pemberley, despite how badly she wants to be Mrs. Darcy."

"I have told Caroline as much," Bingley admitted, then shrugged. "But what else can I do?"

From the corner of his eye, Darcy caught the movement of light pink lace-covered fabric pausing by the opened door before moving on. Miss Bingley. If she heard, which likely she had, Darcy would suffer no regrets. Her ambitions would not be satisfied by him.

If Charles Bingley had a weakness, it was his tendency to allow others, particularly his two sisters, to chart his course for him. Although he was not entirely weak-willed, for Darcy had seen him stand up to others when needed, the fact that he permitted Caroline and Louisa to interfere in his affairs without consequence was a failing of which Darcy hoped the younger man would eventually outgrow.

Bingley asked, "So what do you say? Shall you accompany us to Lucas Lodge?"

If Elizabeth Bennet would be in attendance, it would be a perfect opportunity for reconnaissance. Although he wished his cousin was present, Darcy would press ahead with his investigation. "You say that other families would be there?"

"Yes. Sir William mentioned that the Longs, the Gouldings, and the Bennets had already confirmed their attendance."

"I will gladly join you." Until Richard's reply, Darcy would have declined to attend. Now, nothing would keep him away. "By the by, one of the senior officers in Richard's regiment who is an old family friend, will be in the area recruiting for the Regulars. His name is Major Robert Gerring. If you do not mind my absence, I will occasionally accompany him as he surveys the area."

"Wonderful!" Bingley grinned. "The ladies do appreciate a man in uniform. Will he be lodging here at Netherfield? As an associate of yours and Richards, he is welcome."

"How kind of you, my friend. No, he will stay at the inn in Meryton since his schedule each day will vary based on who and where he visits."

"Will Colonel Fitzwilliam be joining us as well?" Bingley eagerly asked. "He certainly knows how to enliven the staidest gatherings. With him under my roof, we will empty every covey and fill my larders with game."

"No, I am sorry to say that Richard sails for the continent in a few hours."

Visibly disappointed, Bingley said, "Well, that is too bad for him and for us."

Darcy agreed. Without Richard, he would be the one to gather the needed information to prove Miss Elizabeth Bennet was a spy and discover why she was trying to kill him.

For his first action, he needed to locate Major Gerring.

* * *

DARCY'S MEETING the next morning with Major Gerring was productive. They had spent almost an hour in a private sitting room at the inn in Meryton before venturing into the tap room so they could be seen socializing together.

The major was about Bingley's height but that was where any similarity ended. Darcy's first impression was that the man had to be as strong as a bull. Even with his economy of movement, the muscles of the officer's arms and the width of his shoulders identified him as a force of nature.

"Mr. Darcy, my assignment is first and foremost to protect you. Therefore, I would appreciate it if you would inform me before you wander outside alone. I am at your service so will be able to join you within a short period of time. In addition, my goal is to learn if your Miss Bennet has any ties to the woman we are seeking."

Absent-mindedly, Darcy commented, "She is not *my* Miss Bennet."

Major Gerring shrugged. "Until we determine otherwise, she certainly is your Miss Bennet. As Colonel Fitzwilliam instructed you, your task is to seek her out to gain whatever information you can as long as the circumstances are safe. As well, any impressions, even something seemingly small, might be just what is needed to discover the person who is feeding her information. We care not who her contacts are in France. It is the traitor amongst us who is the greater danger."

"I will be attending a small party at the home of Sir William Lucas this evening where the Bennet family are scheduled to attend. Should I ask my friend to see if you can be included?"

"I thank you, Mr. Darcy, but no. It is best if I remain on the outskirts to catch anyone attempting to run or hide."

"Very well."

The major continued, "You should know that a militia will be arriving here on Tuesday next. We will need to pay particular attention to any interactions between the Bennet family and the officers. A link in our prey's chain of deceit could be quickly established if Miss Elizabeth Bennet were indeed our target, which would allow her to feed information to her sources. If you would watch the Bennets, I will follow whichever officers attach themselves to the family."

ELIZABETH WAS SEATED NEXT to Charlotte when the Bingley party arrived. In her heart, she hoped Mr. Darcy had left the area.

The Lucases were wonderful hosts. The evening promised to be pleasant. However, good fortune was not with her that night. Mr. Darcy had not been in the room a full minute before his haughty stare swept the room only to settle upon her.

Elizabeth's response was involuntary. Her chin lifted

as her left brow shot towards her hairline. Holding his gaze, she refused to be the first to blink.

"Hey, Lizzy," Charlotte's brother came bouncing up to her like a puppy. "I saw a gal who looks just like you as I was leaving London this morning. She had the same brown hair and dark eyes, was about the same height, but she wore her hair down like you used to. Do you have a cousin or someone in your family who is a twin to you?"

It took a moment before his words sank in.

"I beg your pardon, Johnny." She gave her full attention to the young man. John Lucas had recently reached his majority. His father had grand plans of his son being welcomed at St. James by the *haut ton*. At heart, John was a farmer. He loved nothing more than straight furrows dotted with a healthy yield. After only two days in the city, he had returned home. "I was not attending."

"I can see that you were not, Lizzy," he teased. "I was just saying that I saw your twin in London. She even had a dark green coat just like the one you wear. For as long as I have known you, I don't recall ever hearing you had a cousin who looked so much like you that I, who have known you since you were born, doubt that I would be able to tell you apart."

"Is that so? Tell me, how did you know it was not me?"

"When I yelled 'Hello Lizzy', she failed to respond." John replied, shrugging.

What a puzzling situation. There were very few cousins on her father's side. A smattering of distant relatives still lived close to Ramsgate in east Kent, if she recalled correctly. Nonetheless, she was personally unacquainted with any of them. "I shall have to ask Papa when we return to Longbourn. I am only sorry he was unable to attend, or we, the both of us, could find out if the lady and I might be related."

Her curiosity was roused. She was an anomaly in her household. It would be interesting to discover if she had a Bennet relative who resembled her closely. Elizabeth chuckled. "I can only wonder if she finds enjoyment in a good book, leisurely strolls, and finding humor where possible."

Charlotte rested the back of her hand on her brow in a move so dramatic the others laughed. "Do let us hope there are not two of you, Lizzy. The world simply could not contain more than one."

Looking up, Elizabeth happened to catch Mr. Darcy's eye. The look of surprised uncertainty on his face spoke of a multitude of questions for which he needed answers. At the most, he should have been unconcerned whether she had any family who looked like her. At the least, confusion was far more attractive on the man than anger. *Whatever was he about?*

John Lucas was not yet done. "Say, Mr. Bingley, will your party be attending our Guy Fawkes Night bonfire? I loaded up my cart with fireworks while I was in town. It should be a spectacular show.

Mr. Bingley's excitement was palpable. "I love bonfires and fireworks. Of course, we will attend."

Elizabeth smiled at the joy radiating from his face. What a fine match he would make for Jane, should they both be inclined.

CHAPTER 5

*D*arcy's mind was spinning. The implications of what young Lucas said were daunting. Who was this other woman? If Miss Elizabeth Bennet was not a French spy who had twice shot at him, then who was she?

Stepping away from the Bingley sisters, he moved towards her, hoping to overhear something to either absolve her or indicate her guilt for there was yet a possibility that the female Lucas saw in London was the innocent one.

He had no ability or desire to be stealthy in his approach. At the same time, he was a guest whose manners would reflect on how well the Bingleys would be established in the neighborhood. Darcy had almost reached her side when he recalled that they had not been introduced. *Blast!* Scanning the room, he located their host. Crossing to the man, Darcy knew what to expect. As soon as he made his request, Sir William would assume there was a romantic interest on his part. *Bah!* That would never happen!

Within moments, he was standing directly in front of his target. He was in control now. He was the hawk to her mouse...until she gazed up at him with those magnificent eyes.

One second, he was the master. The next, his throat dried up until he could barely swallow.

When she turned to help her friend stand, Darcy discerned two important facts—she was kind and Miss Lucas was injured.

Dash it all! How was he to proceed?

Mischief shot from her eyes as she spoke directly to him. *"Bonsoir Monsieur. Aurons-nous quelques instants de conversation polie, ou énoncerez-vous sans ambages votre intention comme cela semble être votre habitude?"*

Despite the nerves arising from the threat of danger, he wanted to laugh. Her French was not perfect, yet it was clear enough. *'Good evening, sir. Shall we have a few moments of polite conversation, or will you bluntly state your intent as seems to be your habit?'*

While there was a slight chance that she might not be a murderer or a spy, he now had undeniable proof of her impertinence.

"I beg your pardon, ladies." Darcy gestured to the chairs behind them. Needing to regain a semblance of control, he addressed Miss Elizabeth's friend. "Pray be seated, Miss Lucas. Although you cover it well, I can see it is painful to remain standing."

Sir William had arranged for a servant to slide a chair closer to Miss Elizabeth. Darcy grabbed the back and pulled it to the other side of Miss Lucas. He wanted no public display that could give rise to rumors of his interest in his possible assassin. Thus, he gave his full attention to the host's daughter. Perhaps he could discover what he needed to know by taking a circuitous route.

"Miss Lucas, I understand your brother recently returned from London. Do you often journey to town?"

"I do not, Mr. Darcy," was her quick reply. Slightly tipping her head to the side, she studied him closely. "I find I am content to enjoy the beauty of Hertfordshire as each season brings new colors and textures to the landscape. Is your home located close to London?"

"I have a house in London, but my home estate is in Derbyshire. Like your shire, Derby changes each season, although far more dramatically than here."

He loathed polite chatter. Next, he supposed they would speak of the roads or the weather. Before he could redirect the subject matter, Miss Lucas added to her thought.

"Sir, where my inclination is to remain at home, my friend eagerly anticipates a trip to that very shire although she is forced to wait until the summer months." Miss Lucas glanced at Miss Elizabeth before returning her attention to him. "She has never before been as far north as Derbyshire. Her desire to explore new places should be satisfied when she sees the rocks, mountains, and the lakes of your district, I believe. When Lizzy is not in London with her favorite aunt and uncle, they often take her along on their travels. She recently returned from Kent and has been there several times. It is a life she loves."

His breath quickened. She had recently been in Kent? He could not stop himself from asking, "How recently?"

If the reply was as he expected, Miss Elizabeth would be the lady he sought.

Miss Elizabeth cleared her throat. "Since you are speaking of me, I will answer for myself, if neither of you mind." She grinned at her friend before glaring at him. "Why do you ask, Mr. Darcy? Has there been something noteworthy I would have missed by my not being in London? Perhaps there is a new play at the theater you have seen where we might compare impressions had I also been in attendance? Or was it a change of exhibit at the museums that left enough of an impression that you wanted to share your opinions with someone who was also familiar with the items? Pray tell me, sir," she leaned towards him. "What is it you are anxious to share?"

"No! No! That is not it at all." He sat back in his chair, distancing himself from her words. Elizabeth Bennet was kind, impertinent, and shrewd—rare commodities in the young females of his acquaintance. Thinking of the possibilities, his mind finally settled on a line of reasoning that would work. "I merely wondered if you were in London recently whereupon you might have spied your counterpart as did young, Mr. Lucas."

"Spied, Mr. Darcy?" She tapped her chin with her finger. "What a curious choice of words considering your reaction to overhearing me at Oakham Mount. Is there a clandestine purpose for your being at Netherfield Park? Do we need to worry that Napoleon is set to invade London and beyond? Are you who and what you appear to be, sir?"

What! How had they gotten so far away from his purpose that he was now in a position where he had to defend himself?

Before he could utter a sound, a voice rang out from across the room begging Miss Elizabeth to play for the gathering so there could be dancing.

As Miss Elizabeth excused herself and walked away, his eyes could not be restrained from following her.

From his side, Miss Lucas reassured him. "Our Lizzy is full of mischief, and you are her current target. Do not fear, Mr. Darcy. Her wit, although rapier sharp, is not deadly."

He gulped. How much did Miss Lucas know? Target? Rapier sharp? Spies? This did not look good for him, not good at all.

CHARLOTTE LUCAS WAS as opposite in character to Elizabeth as was possible. She loved Elizabeth like a younger sister. However, that did not make her blind to her faults. Elizabeth Bennet would stubbornly cling to her opinions until proof could be dangled under her nose. Lizzy's middle name should have been 'Mischief' instead of Rose.

Charlotte believed in a female using whatever opportunity presented itself to push herself forward. That evening, a wealthy, handsome man had singled her friend out. Like her, the Bennets needed to use every advantage to settle their futures. Whatever his purpose, Charlotte would help things along.

* * *

OUT OF THE corner of her eye, Elizabeth watched the interaction between Charlotte and Mr. Darcy. There was only an occasional comment exchanged followed by long pauses where her friend tapped her fingers on her skirt to the time of the reel. Mr. Darcy appeared decidedly uncomfortable with everything about the evening. Perhaps he was displeased with her efforts on the pianoforte. Or maybe the pounding of the men's boots on the wooden floor where the carpets were rolled back was giving him a headache. Either way, he looked pained, like he would rather have been alone in a quiet room with a snifter of French brandy.

Mr. Bingley sought out Jane as soon as he entered the room. Mr. Hurst had comfortably settled himself next to the table with the food and drink. His wife and Miss Bingley stood by the door, undoubtedly hoping for a quick exit. Neither looked happy to be there. Both of the ladies watched Mr. Darcy's every move. Occasionally, Miss Bingley's eyes would shoot toward where Elizabeth sat at the pianoforte. Quickly, they darted back to the gentleman and Charlotte.

Elizabeth chuckled to herself. He was a puzzle, this Mr. Darcy. If she did not know better, she would have thought he considered her to be a French spy. How funny, in an odd sort of way.

Her mouth dropped open, whereupon she snapped it closed. *Oh, my goodness!* Did he *really* think she was involved in espionage? Was he an agent for the British Government looking for traitors to the crown? Had he received a report that someone from Meryton was threatening an overthrow of England by cooperating with Napoleon?

No! It simply was too outlandish to consider, was it not? Meryton was as quiet and settled as any small farming town in England. Rarely did anything or anyone disturb the peace unless one of Mr. Caudle's pigs got out of their pen.

As her fingers danced over the keys, she studied him surreptitiously. His clothing was top quality. Why, the jewel holding his perfectly tied cravat in place was stunning in its size and clarity. Sapphires had always been her favorites, far more than diamonds, which Jane preferred. His waistcoat was silver, white, and vibrant blue which looked remarkably fine against the black of his coat and trousers. His thick hair had a slight curl to it in the back where it hugged his neck. His face was clean-shaven, except for well-trimmed sideburns. He looked like money rather than an agent of the crown. As the muscles of his face relaxed while sharing conversation with Charlotte, Elizabeth had to admit that he was exceedingly handsome. In this, he certainly met her mother's criteria for a perfect match. For Elizabeth, he was far too prickly to want to be close to. No, she would avoid him completely.

As the song was ending, she gave attention to the music in front of her.

Did he actually believe she was a spy? *Goodness!* While the mere idea was absurd, she could not laugh off a threat to her good name. Any negative connotations to her character would settle her future as miserable. What was worse could be the damage to her sisters' prospects for good marriages if her name suffered from any accusations, be they false or not. No, she needed to take Mr. Darcy's presence in Hertfordshire seriously. She would no longer seek to find merriment at his expense. She would watch him so she would know how to act.

* * *

THE BRAYING laughter of the youngest Bennet girls hurt his ears. The two should have remained in the school room.

Unaware that his displeasure was displayed on his face, he was horrified to hear Miss Lucas's subtle reprimand.

"Sir, with little effort you will discover that the eldest Miss Bennets are as unalike their younger sisters as black is to white." Miss Lucas added, "We are often in company. Thus, it is easy for us to overlook Kitty and Lydia's small indignities because we allow our love for them to cover any errors. Those who are newly out have yet to receive the training needed to be in more mature company. With that said, they are most welcome here." She leaned slightly closer. "We are not in London, Mr. Darcy."

He stammered. Never had he been chastised by an unattached female. Ever! What could have been her motive?

Miss Lucas was not yet finished. "Mr. Darcy, Elizabeth Bennet is my dearest friend. She would do anything to protect her family, her country, and anyone she loves. We are a close-knit community. All of us would do the same."

A sickening feeling started in the pit of his stomach

then rose to almost choke him at the throat. Miss Eliza beth had deftly evaded his question about whether she was recently in London. She was clever, as was her friend. In fact, in reviewing the exchange, he was left with the knowledge that he knew nothing more than when he had sat down. As a reconnaissance man, he failed utterly. When he wrote his report to Richard that night, he would have nothing to tell him other than the possibility there might be a twin to the current object of his curiosity and concern.

Deciding he needed a different approach, he asked, "Would you tell me of Mr. Bennet? He has been conspicuously absent."

Miss Lucas smiled. "He is a good man and a wonderful neighbor. He rarely can be moved from his bookroom. Lizzy is his favorite since she shares his love of reading. Additionally, he is unequaled when it comes to strategy although Lizzy is a close second. When the chess board is brought out, they are worthy of watching for neither will give way to the other out of familial regard." She said, "He wakes early to peruse the dailies for news. He is strong of opinions, enjoys a lively debate, and loves nothing more than to test the mettle of those who enter his sanctuary. Very few will beard the lion in his den. Lizzy is one who can."

He nodded. "I see." Considering each expression of her description, he found that he was anticipating meeting the man. He, too, was an early riser. "I thank you, Miss Lucas. You have been a delightful companion." Receiving honest, intelligent advice was always welcome, even if it came from a new female acquaintance. Standing, he offered, "I would gladly bring you something to drink should you desire."

When she declined, he walked to where Bingley was engaged in conversation with the eldest Miss Bennet. Ignoring them, Darcy pondered what he needed to share with his cousin. Perhaps his best tactical move would be to wait until after he spoke with Mr. Bennet before penning his report. Of course, he knew not if Richard remained in England or if his ship had already sailed.

Since he could do nothing at the moment, he relaxed enough to be more aware of his surroundings. Hurst was imbibing rather freely of the punch. His wife and Caroline Bingley were avoiding any contact with the "ruffians", as they had labeled the residents of Meryton, and Bingley had found the loveliest unattached female in the room.

Bingley asked Miss Bennet if she preferred London to the country. Darcy could not fail to hear her reply.

"Why, no, Mr. Bingley. The quietude of the rural areas of England deeply appeal to me. It is Elizabeth who enjoys an occasional journey to experience the bustling activity of city life. In fact, if there was not a war with France, she would be off to Paris without hesitation."

"Paris?" Bingley asked. "Why would she want to go there? For the latest fashions? I hear from my sisters that they are already available with certain modiste's on Bond Street."

"I am afraid that fabric and lace hold little appeal to Lizzy. She is curious about new places and new people. Why, just yesterday in London, she..."

The conversation was interrupted by another Bennet

girl. "Jane, Kitty tore her hem. She needs you to make repairs right now."

Darcy, who had leaned towards them, was irritated. What had Miss Elizabeth been doing the day prior in London? He desperately needed to know. When Miss Bennet walked away, following her sister to where a third Bennet was examining her hem, Darcy stepped back into the shadows. He was in no mood to listen to Bingley's raptures over the eldest Bennet's beauty. He needed to consider the cold, hard facts.

Elizabeth Bennet was in London. She had recently spent time in Kent. She spoke French. She was a known strategist. She longed to go to Paris.

Upon my word! It was HER!

CHAPTER 6

*A*t exactly four o'clock the following afternoon, an unexpected visitor arrived at Longbourn. At least, Mr. William Collins' arrival was not anticipated by anyone other than Elizabeth's father who had received a letter stating his intent a fortnight prior. He was the dreaded cousin who would inherit Longbourn at the death of one Thomas Bennet, Esq.

The parson was a tall, heavy looking man. His air was grave and stately. His manners were formal. His attitude was...well, several times Elizabeth caught him tripping over his avarice to appear humble. He had not been inside Longbourn for a full quarter hour before he offered his admiration of Mrs. Bennet's daughters, the hall, the dining-room and all its furniture, the excellence of the paintings hanging on the wall, and a quilted piece of fabric separating a vase of flowers from a side table.

"One of my fair cousins must have fashioned this fine piece, I suppose," he said, his voice slightly nasal as he fingered the cloth. His elbow bumped the vessel overflowing with orange, pink, red, and purple gerbera daisies, splashing water onto the table and his sleeve, frowning at the flowers as if they were at fault, he added, "To display the efforts of a child in her youth could be considered a kindness from a loving mother, I suspect. Lady Catherine de Bourgh," he paused before continuing in hushed tones. "You have heard of her, of course. She is the exalted patroness of my humble home at Hunsford Parsonage in Kent. Her estate is second only to Pemberley in Derbyshire, held by her very nephew, of whom I am certain you have also heard. After all, Hertfordshire is not far from London where those of exalted rank are regarded as the scions of society."

"Mr. Collins, I have never heard of Lady Catherine or her nephew," Mrs. Bennet snorted. "Nor did one of my daughters craft that table runner. We are perfectly able to purchase products from the haberdashery in Meryton for use in our home."

Elizabeth observed in shock and awe as the man spent the next twenty minutes admonishing his hostess for her ignorance and groveling for being in error over who had stitched the piece under the flowers. By the time he paused long enough to take a breath and possibly gather his thoughts for another tirade, Elizabeth counted him as the most ridiculous man she had ever met. When added to Mr. Darcy's oddness, the marital prospects of the Bennet household had not improved with the gentlemen's addition to Meryton society.

She wanted to roll her eyes. Had the vase not been one of her mother's favorites, Elizabeth would have bashed

Mr. Collins over the head with it to get him to stop talking.

Oh, good grief! He was now rambling on and on about Lady Catherine's estate...and Lady Catherine's perfect daughter...and Lady Catherine...and Lady Catherine... Elizabeth finally started counting how many times in a single sentence Mr. Collins uttered the phrase, "my esteemed Patroness, Lady Catherine". His average was once. However, he uttered the accolade two times in a very long sentence. *Amazing!*

What a dolt!

Finally, to protect her own mental stability, she allowed her mind to wander, knowing that Mary, Kitty, and Lydia had each stopped paying attention to their guest shortly after he first opened his mouth. Jane, of course, was too kind to do anything other than give him the attention he desired. *Silly girl!*

Automatically, her mind stood the two men next to each other, Mr. Collins on the left, Mr. Darcy on the right. They were of equal height. Both had dark hair and eyes. Both had perfect posture. Mr. Darcy's clothing had a better cut and fit than the wool of Mr. Collins' garments. Both men were idiots.

She harrumphed. No, Mr. Collins was foolish in his opinions. Of Mr. Darcy, Elizabeth decided she could not yet put him in the same class as the parson. Mr. Darcy was impossibly rude...and... and... she sighed. He was kind to Charlotte. What did that mean? That he had conde-scended to give their host's eldest his full attention to the exclusion of others had elevated Charlotte in the eyes of those in attendance at Lucas Lodge. Later that evening, Charlotte whispered to Elizabeth that she found the man to be exceedingly handsome and somewhat agreeable. *What!* How was that even possible? While she could admit that his looks were fine, the man was so lofty in his own opinion that the minions in Meryton mattered not to him.

Yet, he acted the gentleman towards Charlotte.

Elizabeth desired nothing more than to discover that there was no good at all to be found in Mr. Darcy. He had offended her vanity and possibly viewed her as a danger to England. How on earth was it possible that he was nice? *Inconceivable!*

Of course! Why had she not guessed it before? Mr. Darcy was merely cozying up to Charlotte in an attempt to gain any snippet of information to be used against her. The beast!

Mentally bouncing back and forth between Mr. Collins and Mr. Darcy the realization came to her quite clearly. Both men were cut from the same cloth, thinking they were residing far above the Bennets. They were each of them moronic but only one of them was a danger to her.

"Charles, you must do something!" Caroline Bingley fumed as she paced the parlor. "Mr. Darcy ignored me through the whole of the evening. Instead, he acted the moon calf over pitiful-looking Eliza Bennet and her homely friend."

"What do you expect me to do?" her brother raised his hands into the air.

Caroline hissed, "I expect you to promote me as the perfect wife for Pemberley."

"You mean, as the perfect wife for Darcy?" Bingley corrected her, which increased her ire.

Growling, she approached her brother's chair. "You promised Papa that you would take care of me, seeing I get all I deserve from life. Well, I deserve Pemberley."

"I don't know," Bingley hemmed and hawed. "Darcy does not seem too keen. He told me point blank that he would not have you."

"Bah!" Caroline scoffed. "He has no clue what is good for him, or rather, *who* is good for him." She sneered, "If you do not act quickly, Brother dear, I will happily let Mr. Darcy know of the gaming losses you and Hurst have had at the tables. He will not be pleased to find out how much you owe, I imagine."

"But," Charles balked.

"No, Charles," Caroline stepped back to address the other three. "We need money to elevate ourselves to the position we deserve. Mr. Darcy is our chance, our only chance. Flirt with Miss Bennet if you want but do not get serious unless you discover her dowry is as large as Georgiana Darcy's. If not, you need to look elsewhere."

He nodded. "Yes, Caroline."

DARCY HAD A PLAN. One that did not include Major Gerring.

After sending an express updating Richard with his suspicions and breaking his fast with Bingley, he told his host he needed some time to gather his thoughts on an important matter of business. Bingley respected his privacy. Bingley's sisters did not.

Louisa Hurst and Caroline Bingley were ambitious. With the eldest Bingley female safely and securely wed to Gilbert Hurst, the two sisters had paired up to achieve their greatest desire, entering the first circles of society on the tailcoat of the Darcy name. To do this, a marriage between Caroline and himself was their immediate goal. As he had told Bingley, never would that happen! Darcy shuddered. Being joined in matrimony to Miss Bingley would be like having a ten-foot boa constrictor in his house, yearning to squeeze every farthing and ounce of respectability from his soul.

"Mr. Darcy, the morning is lovely and unseasonably warm. The autumn colors should be at their zenith. Mightn't you join us for a stroll in the garden?" Miss Bingley fluttered her eyelashes at him, her mouth in a perfect pout.

He wondered if she practiced the pose in front of her mirror. He had seen it a thousand times on the faces of the London debutantes seeking his attention. Darcy would not barter his fortune or his good name with a female who simpered and pandered to him in hopes of becoming the next mistress of Pemberley. No, he would marry a woman of character once he decided it was time to begin filling his nursery.

"I apologize, Miss Bingley. My business will take me

away from Netherfield Park for the morning." He bowed. "If you will pardon me?"

Not waiting for their reply, he left the breakfast room satisfied that he would have the privacy he needed for his plan. Within minutes, he was dressed for a leisurely jaunt in the countryside, a small pistol in his pocket and a sharp knife in his boot. Strolling unaffectedly away from the house, he hurried his pace once he was out of the direct view of the windows. Turning to the west, he plotted his course towards Oakham Mount.

HURRYING TO HER FAVORITE SPOT, Elizabeth remembered to grab an apple from the tree for Jeannie. Once she was seated atop the smooth stone to the right of the spring, she bit into the fruit, loosening the tasty morsel.

"Jeannie, where are you? Come for a treat and good conversation, I beg you, for I have had a tortuous hour spent with a man so impressed with his own opinions that he had no need to hear anyone else's." Tossing the piece of apple to a nearby patch of grass, Elizabeth again entreated for the crow to come. *"Viens petit oiseau. J'ai besoin d'oreilles qui ne me jugent pas pour ma mauvaise opinion d'un homme désagrêable."*

Yes, she would love to have an unbiased listener so she could pour out her heart about a disagreeable man. But which one?

The sound of flapping wings heralded the arrival of the crow. Ignoring her, the bird darted to the piece of apple. Cawing her pleasure, she devoured the fruit then looked to Elizabeth for more. Happy to comply, Elizabeth bit off another piece then tossed it to her.

"Ah, *Jeanne de Valois-Saint-Remy*, what am I to do? Papa told me before I left Longbourn that his cousin is here to select a bride from amongst my sisters. Mama has decided that Jane is meant for another which leaves me next in her quest to rid herself of daughters. Jeannie, he is a stupid man who would make a sensible wife miserable. He is full of conceit and his manners are ill-suited to me."

She bit off another fragment for the waiting crow.

"There you go," she paid no attention to where the apple landed. The crow would have no difficulty finding it. "In addition, I have become aware of a worrisome situation in London. There is a lady with similar looks who caught the notice of John Lucas. What could be her purpose? What sort of a female would she be who wears her hair down like a girl who had not yet left the school room? What is her intention in putting herself forward so that strangers notice her in a crowd? I cannot imagine! Nevertheless, if John thought it was me, mightn't others do so as well? I have many acquaintances in the city who are long-time friends of Aunt and Uncle Gardiner, Jeannie. If this lady...at least I hope she is a lady...if she acts inappropriately where one of these friends would notice, it would ruin me and with it the hopes of my sisters."

Elizabeth was made aware since her infancy that society's standards for females were that women were required to be modest and dutiful, even-tempered and without opinions, always keeping their reputation spotless in all matters. Therefore, when she was away from Longbourn, she was cautious with her expressions, holding her assessments and conclusions close until she determined if those who could hear were able to be trusted. She had the freedom of speaking openly at Long-bourn and in the neighborhood. Her friends knew her well enough to know that she was not malicious. However, it simply would not do to offend someone who would malign her teasing until her good name and those of her sisters were soiled.

"And then there is Mr. Darcy. What is he about? He acts like he is aware of some dark secret that could ruin me as well. Or perhaps he..." A thought occurred to her that shocked her to her core. "Jeannie, what if that lady has already done something vile? What if Mr. Darcy witnessed her evil intent, then thought it was me when he saw me at the assembly?"

Her heart was racing. Clasping her hand to her throat, she spoke her thoughts aloud. "Jeannie, what if he believes me guilty of something truly terrible? He has the connections and the wealth to have me arrested and tried." She flung her hands into the air, startling the bird. "This is in every way horrible! I was in London with my aunt the day prior to the Bingley party's arrival. He would have no way of knowing my purpose was to care for the twins because their nanny was needed at home or that I had a service to perform for Charlotte."

Standing to pace back and forth, Elizabeth clasped her hands around her middle. "Jeannie, this is dreadful. What am I to do?"

The bird cawed as if she understood the seriousness of the matter. Hopping to a rock a short distance from the grassy area, Jeannie flapped her wings violently before raising her voice with one shrill caw after another.

Something was upsetting the crow. Knowing it could not be the words she had uttered, Elizabeth set the apple aside then went to investigate.

CHAPTER 7

*T*hat blasted crow!

Darcy was reeling from all he had learned from eavesdropping on Miss Elizabeth. Nothing she said implicated her in attempted murder. At the same time, he had to consider the skill of an operative who could repeatedly escape Richard and his men. Her intellectual acuity would rival his Cambridge professors. Was this lady crafty enough to have discovered his presence without his knowing, then acting the part of an innocent who gleefully diverted his attention to a poor stranger who happened to look like her?

There was something very wrong about the situation. Where was her pistol? Where was the female who saluted him to let him know that he lived that day only because it was her desire? She wore the same gown and bonnet she had the day before. The pale pink fabric matched the color of her cheeks. No, it was not exactly pink. Rather, it was the blush of a fresh peach. Her pallor and the way she withdrew from him rather than stepping closer puzzled him. Why was Miss Elizabeth seeking escape instead of making the demands that would satisfy whoever had hired her?

Part of him felt ridiculous thinking her earlier conversation was with an individual from the network of spies passing information back to the French. The other part remained on cautious alert. As it was, he heard her footsteps rapidly approaching. Whether or not she knew he was there, the crow did.

Standing, he turned to face the one person on the planet who could be his executioner.

She startled, then immediately began backing away from him. "Mr. Darcy? Whatever are you doing here? Why were you hiding? What do you want?" Her voice shook. Her eyes darted to the side before quickly returning to him.

Instead of seeking protection for himself, he stepped towards her. Instantly, she jumped backwards, thrusting her palms in front of her as if those small hands could avert any danger.

"Miss Elizabeth, pray calm yourself. I mean you no harm." He stood his ground, his arms at his sides.

"What do you want?" she demanded, continuing to move away from him. "I carry no coins with me and shall scream bloody murder should you attempt any harm of my person."

"Harm? Never would I do anything to hurt a woman. Ever! Miss Elizabeth, I shall not harm you if you allow me the same kindness." Holding up his hands, he showed her they were empty of anything he could use against her. "I have questions for you as I am certain you have for me. Mightn't we discuss our futures amicably?"

"Futures, Mr. Darcy? My future has nothing to do with you."

In a moment, she spun on her heel, running quickly down the pathway. Moving around the rocks with a familiarity he did not have; she widened the distance between them.

There was nothing for him to do but give chase. He could not afford to lose this opportunity to gain needed information from the source of his troubles.

His long legs ate up the distance.

The crow that he had cursed only moments before, must have been counting on more of a treat from Miss Elizabeth since she swooped close to the top of the lady's bonnet. Momentarily distracted, Miss Elizabeth failed to place her foot safely in the middle of the path. The tumble she took rendered her motionless.

Blast!

Running to her, Darcy dropped to his knees beside where she lay. She was on her side facing away from him. Her skirt had ridden up, exposing trim calves and well-used walking boots. Her bonnet was askew. Her arms that she had thrust out to catch herself were dotted with mud.

"Miss Elizabeth, are you...?

Her only response was a moan.

"Miss Elizabeth, pray tell me that you landed upon your pride and that no other parts of you are injured." He suggested, hoping beyond hope that she was conscious. He closed his eyes as shame rushed over him. "I promised you that I would not hurt you, yet you are injured because of me."

There was nothing else for him to do but check for injuries. The instant he rested his hand on her shoulder, she sat up and slapped at his hand...except she missed.

The base of her palm hit him square on the right side of his nose. His vision blurred as tears trailed down his cheeks and blood began dripping from his nostril.

"What!" he sat back on his heels. Patting his chest for the linen handkerchief he carried in his pocket, he finally located the cloth, using it to mop up the worst of the damage. Pinching the bridge of his nose, he tipped his head back to stop the flow.

"Mr. Darcy! Sir, I apologize..." the lady sputtered. "I mean, I am not sorry that you are no longer chasing me, but I do feel slightly bad that I injured you."

His left eye opened to see if she appeared sincere. She had already covered her ankles and was employed in straightening her bonnet.

"Only slightly?" he chuckled to himself. "Are you injured?"

She groaned, closed her eyes, then admitted, "My ankle turned, causing my fall. Like Charlotte, this will keep me from dancing, I am afraid."

"I am sorry to hear it," he honestly admitted. "I apologize for following you after you insisted that I not. I owe you a debt for going back on my word. I meant you no harm."

"Mr. Darcy, pray let us get one thing straight," she insisted. "I am here on the ground because of a greedy crow, not because of you." Her smirk was followed by obvious concern. "What are your intentions toward me, Mr. Darcy? Before you reply, you should know that I have gathered a sharp stone in each hand that I will wield to protect myself should you mean physical harm."

He pulled his handkerchief away from his face, waving the bloody cloth like a flag. When she opened her fingers, a rock the size of her fist rested in each palm. He nodded.

"It is wise for a lady to protect herself. However, I truly meant you no harm. I do wonder though if you will extend to me the same courtesy."

She looked confused. Finally, after a lengthy pause, she replied, "I give you my word that should I need to take aim against you for any reason, I will leave your battered nose alone."

"Well, alright then. If that is the best you can offer, I will accept." He stood, looking to gauge the distance between the orchard and Longbourn. "As I see it, we have three options. I can offer you my protection by waiting until someone comes to rescue you. This would allow us to clear up any confusion between us."

"Confusion, sir? I cannot imagine what you are referring to since we are barely acquainted."

Was she sincere? Or was she a skilled actress like the heroines on the Drury stage who could night after night pull a viewer's heart out with their plaintive cries during a tragedy? He was uncertain.

"Our second option is for me to leave you here while I go for your father. I could explain my presence to him as we walk the path back to you."

"Mr. Darcy, I would appreciate it if you would explain your presence to me right now," she insisted.

He ignored her. "Our third option is for me to carry you to your home."

"No!" Her response was immediate. "Pray do not give number three any consideration. Should my mother see any contact between the two of us, the cry will go out around the neighborhood that I have been compromised by you. I will *not* have my name attached to yours, Mr. Darcy. Therefore, I beg that you go to my father, explain that you found me injured, you then offered me your help, which I refused, and tell him where to find me. Do not accompany him back. Do not offer any other explanation which my mother, my sisters, or our guest could hear, I beg you."

Her request was entirely reasonable. Nevertheless, it did not sit well with him that her rejection of him was so complete.

What was he thinking? Although she was not currently acting like a murderer and a spy, she might in actual fact still be one. *Had her blow knocked all the sense out of him?* Gazing down at her beautiful eyes, he began to wonder at himself. For almost eight and twenty years he was immune to feminine charms. For a certainty, there were ladies he had found attractive and appealing. Despite this, none had made him feel this confusion and doubt like this lady had. He longed to protect her.

Of all the imbecilic ideas! Protection? He should be protecting himself! And was that even the emotion coursing through his veins? He did not know. It was a strange feeling, a first for him.

"Mr. Darcy, will you get my father, please?"

From his height she appeared fragile and small, an injured soul seeking help.

Making his decision, he extended his arms, saying, "Let us move you out of the mud to the grassy area under the oak tree which should protect you from the damp and from a greedy carrion crow."

Helping her to stand, she tentatively put weight on her injured leg, only to hiss as she lifted the limb back off the ground.

Scooping her into his arms, he carried her to where the path straightened into a direct route to Longbourn. Something about their position felt remarkably right.

Was he insane? Having his foe wrap her arms around his neck should not have his heart thumping like the native drums he had read about where South Sea islanders welcomed treacherous strangers into their huts. This was Elizabeth Bennet, possible murderer. He should not be experiencing ideas that...well, they unsettled him with pictures of curling up together in front of a fire on a cozy rug after...

Get ahold of yourself, Darcy! He needed to be rid of her—now!

Choosing a level spot covered in tall grass, he gently lowered her legs until she was able to stand on her uninjured foot. Once she transferred her hold from around his neck to the tree trunk, he removed his coat to spread on the ground.

"Mr. Darcy, it would be better if you did not leave your garment behind," she suggested, her tone firm.

"My first duty is your comfort, Miss Elizabeth. I will express the need for caution to your father. Surely, he will bring along with us only those whom he can trust with your reputation...and mine."

She continued to protest. As he had done before, he listened to her concerns but said nothing as he spread his coat so she would not be sitting directly upon the ground. She could fold the edges over herself, warming her, should she choose.

"Mr. Darcy, if you are not nearly as stealthy as you imply you are, the damage to the both of us will not be easily undone."

"Then I will be my stealthiest."

She growled.

Once she was settled, he left for Longbourn. Looking back, he was shocked to see the lady with her head bowed, her hands clasped together beseeching their Heavenly Father in prayer. Did assassins pray, he pondered as he quickly moved down the pathway. Perhaps not all of them did, but when he saw her lips moving in silence, he knew that Miss Elizabeth was pleading for help...or forgiveness.

CHAPTER 8

*E*lizabeth could no more have kept from watching him walk away than she could reach up to catch a star from the sky. Mr. Darcy had proven himself to be equal parts rude, confusing, and... kind. *Who was this man?*

Resting her head against the tree trunk, she tried rubbing the throb from her ankle. The pain was beginning to ease, which meant it had not been a sprain.

Relief was not her most immediate concern. From infancy she was taught that a female's most valued commodity was her good name. How she was going to protect her reputation from harm from their newest neighbor was unknown. Although she was not as religiously inclined as Mary, she sought guidance from someone far smarter than anyone she knew.

After pouring out her heart in earnest supplication, Elizabeth felt she could list her greatest concerns with clarity. Primarily, she needed to avoid an attachment to either Mr. Collins or Mr. Darcy. After rushing away from the former and sending the latter off on his errand of mercy, was such a task humanly possible?

Secondly, why had Mr. Darcy been lurking at Oakham Mount? Was his eavesdropping planned? Had he returned to Oakham Mount in hopes of seeing her again? For what purpose? If he meant her harm, her injury would not have stopped him. Therefore, what were his intentions?

She wished she knew the answers because it would shed light on so many things that confused her. Was he attracted to her? Surely not! His insult at the assembly was clear and concise. Was he afraid of her? It seemed so, but why? She was as harmless as a fly, despite bloodying his nose.

Oh, she was a wretched girl, feeling an inner glee at having pained him. His words at the assembly had hurt. She imagined his nose hurt, too. Elizabeth grinned.

Moments later, Mr. Darcy spun on his heels returning to her side. *What did he mean by it?*

She gulped, holding the stones tighter in her fists. She would fight him until her last breath if he meant to harm her.

"I beg your pardon, Miss Elizabeth, but I simply cannot waste this opportunity to gather information that will save lives, especially my own."

She had not expected conversation. She squeezed the rocks in her palms, wishing for a more obvious weapon. "I do not follow, sir. Are you in danger? Am I?"

Stopping, he seated himself on the ground not six feet from her, his legs stretched out in front of him, his arms relaxed at his side, his empty palms face up.

Yearning to be further away from him, she pressed her

back into the tree, swinging her legs around so she could easily roll up onto her feet with a leap to run as fast as she could from the area, if needed. Her ankle would suffer for it, but it could not be helped.

Glancing around, she sought a fallen branch she could use to strike him, if necessary, preferably one with a jagged point on the end.

"Miss Elizabeth, a few days past, on my journey from Kent to London, my hat was shot from my head. At first, I concluded it was done by a hunter with bad aim. In retrospect, it could have been by a female who was strikingly similar to you in looks."

"What?" Elizabeth had not expected what she heard. "How do you know it was a woman who shot at you?"

Darcy nodded, "Good question. I had stopped at an inn where the lady in question appeared to be waiting for someone or for her horse to be rested to continue her travel. I left before she did. However, I was enjoying the warmth of the sun and the brisk air so was not hurrying my journey. There is a path parallel to the main road similar to the one we are on that my cousin and I often use to exercise our mounts without causing disturbance to other traffic. It has many straight stretches so a person could easily leave the inn and arrive ahead of me, especially if she was familiar with that portion of Kent. It is my belief that this was exactly what that lady did."

A woman fired a gun at him? On purpose? Good heavens! He must have been even more rude to that lady than he was to her!

Giving him her full attention, she stopped looking for something she could wield as a sword. Instead, her eyes shot to his, watching him so as not to miss a word. *Was this a trick, something to catch her off guard so he could pounce?*

"The following day, the same female fired upon my conveyance, this time aiming for my heart. It was a fluke for me to seat myself on the opposite side of the carriage that day, which ultimately saved my life. When I caught her eye afterwards, she saluted me as if it was solely up to her whether I lived to see another day."

What in the world? "Mr. Darcy! She wanted you dead? How horrible for you!" Elizabeth dropped the rock as her hand went to her chest. She scooped it back up. "What did you do to her?"

"Nothing! I did nothing. Until I caught sight of her at Bromley and in London, I can say with full honesty that I had never before seen her."

Considering the implications, she reached the only conclusion available. "You thought I was the lady with the pistol, did you not?"

"I did." He rubbed his jaw then removed his hat to run his hand through his hair. "When I saw you at the assembly, I assumed you had followed me with the intention of hitting your mark."

"Never!" she insisted. "Oh, I see," she muttered to herself as her mind raced. To him, she said, "I know that I am not the woman you seek. I have never fired a gun in my life, nor do I have evil intentions towards you, Mr. Darcy. Until you arrived at the assembly, I had never before heard your name." She paused in consideration. At his nod, she continued, "Is this why you eavesdropped upon my conversations with the crow? And why my speaking to the bird in French was of concern to you? Did you think me to be a spy as well as a murderer? Mr. Darcy!" Lowering her hands to her lap, she fisted them in the soft fabric. Her breathing was rapid, she could feel her pulse at her neck and down the inside of her arms. "I am a lady. I love my country and my fellow man. I have a plethora of witnesses who can vouch for my reasons for being in London, as well as my exact location at any given time since I never once left my uncle's home on Gracechurch Street."

"You were in Kent." Mr. Darcy challenged. "Miss Lucas said you had recently traveled with relatives to the area where I was first attacked."

"Sir, I returned from Kent twenty-one days ago. I did not leave Meryton again until my aunt summoned me to care for her children. I returned home the morning of the assembly." She inhaled to regain control. By then, she was shaking. "Are you familiar with Otford near Sevenoaks? At his nod, she continued, "There is a scholar with access to old legal records kept in the former bishop's residence who often provides information to my uncle and others who use contracts to buy and sell properties. This man understands how to clearly interpret boundary lines and prior ownership. It was to this area of Kent that we traveled."

"You are speaking of Mr. Archibald Sutton?" Mr. Darcy asked.

"You know him, then?"

"Any man who has an estate where the location of boundary markers is questioned knows Mr. Sutton." He pondered a moment before asking, "Tell me, what is unusual about the outside of his house?"

Elizabeth chuckled. He was testing her.

"Are you speaking of the single turret on the right rear corner, or the delightful shade of orange paint slathered over the surface?"

He stared directly at her, studying her as much as she was studying him. They were both wary. Finally, he nodded, apparently satisfied with her reply.

"Mr. Darcy, as I mentioned, witnesses who are not bound to me can be provided who would not be influenced by familial attachment in what they saw or did not see. I beg that you make it your next course of action to obtain proof of my innocence. I, Elizabeth Rose Bennet, have never had the intention of causing you or England harm."

As soon as his chin dipped in acknowledgement, she added, "Nevertheless, I cannot know what the lady John Lucas saw has in mind for you. I beg you to do everything within your power to discover her purpose since it means your life and my reputation."

Pulling his knees up, he rested his arm across the top.

"In truth, I had not given consideration to the repercussions against your character."

Selfish man!

"However, now that I am aware, I suggest we both speak with your father. He will want to protect the interest of every member of his family."

"In that you are correct, sir." Elizabeth watched each of his movements cautiously as he stood, brushed the grass from his trousers and pulled on the sleeves of his shirt.

"My father will be very concerned. Nonetheless, you should know that my father's cousin arrived earlier. He is a pompous man who is interested in everything about Longbourn since he will inherit when my father dies. Should he happen to overhear anything he feels would affect his future, I have no doubt that he will inform his 'esteemed Patroness, Lady Catherine de Bourgh." The last was said in an imperious tone.

"My aunt?" Mr. Darcy slapped his right hand to his chest. Horrified, he asked, "You cannot be speaking of her parson, Mr. William Collins, can you?"

Of course, the arrogant Mr. Darcy was related to the equally haughty Lady Catherine! Elizabeth grinned. "I can, Mr. Darcy."

A deep red flush covered Mr. Darcy's cheeks. "And *this* is the man your mother intends you to marry?"

"Mr. Darcy! How would you know of my mother's plans?"

Despite it seeming humanly impossible, his blush deepened. "You mentioned it to the crow." He paced back and forth in front of her. "This is in every way terrible, Miss Elizabeth. Your father's cousin is an imbecile who believes the sun rises and sets with my aunt. Lady Catherine is so blinded by her position in life that she has no care about reality nor any empathy for the feelings and beliefs of others. If this threat to my life, plus a hint of your resemblance, should get back to her..."

His steps lengthened, his chest rose and fell rapidly, and his breath could be heard from the one nostril she had not bloodied.

Mr. Darcy came to a stop in front of her. Without

pause, he blurted, "Once he knows that I am close by, he will not be able to restrain himself from intruding in every activity in which I involve myself. He would count my breaths and report it to Lady Catherine if he could. Good heavens! If he tells her that I am here, she will believe herself in the right to interfere. Her *modus operandi* is as subtle as inviting an elephant to a tea party believing that no one would notice." Removing his hat, he ran his hand through his hair. "Without a doubt, her meddling would end in everyone knowing your business and mine, which would destroy your good name and possibly my life."

"Lovely woman," Elizabeth whispered under her breath. "Then we must do all we can to avoid the possibility of them finding out."

"We?" he asked.

"Sir, I will do anything to protect my good name, which safeguards the future of my sisters. If this includes putting myself in physical danger, then so be it. They mean everything to me. So, yes, we as in you, my father, and I will use our brains and any resources within our power to protect your life and my reputation." Elizabeth pushed up with her hands, standing carefully on her uninjured leg. "If you would help me to find a walking stick, I will proceed home. I have no doubt that Mr. Collins has already invaded Papa's bookroom. Therefore, I will ask that Papa visit you at Netherfield Park where you might speak with him privately."

"No," he blurted. "I am sorry, but Mr. Bingley's sisters will attempt to learn why your father would seek me out. They have their own agendas in keeping track of me, which I abhor, mind you. If Bingley was not a good friend, I would never acknowledge either Miss Bingley or Mrs. Hurst."

Elizabeth was surprised at his bluntness.

"Pardon me, Miss Elizabeth. These are desperate times for each of us. I cannot believe that hiding information from each other will serve either of us well."

She agreed. "If Mr. Collins believed anything would affect Longbourn or one of my sisters, he would interfere."

"I concur."

"There might be a way, sir." Leaning down to pick up his coat, she shook it out. "Should you tell my father that it is Charlotte Lucas who needs assistance, he will quickly come with his cart. He knows of her injury and her propensity to walk out as I do. This will not be a surprise to him. I imagine that Mr. Collins would not want to assist someone wholly unrelated to him."

Mr. Darcy nodded. "She appeared to be a sensible young woman."

"You do not know the half, sir."

"Very well," he took his coat from her after assisting her back to the ground. "I am finding it is very hard for me to leave you here knowing you are in pain, Miss Elizabeth. If it were not both of our futures at stake, pray know I would never have been able to walk away."

"Just go, Mr. Darcy. The sooner you leave, the sooner my father will arrive so I can make it home after we discuss our situation. He is a smart man, my Papa. If anyone has any ideas that can help, it will be him."

"Very well." Donning his coat, he added, "I will return."

After he left, Elizabeth meditated on all that she had learned. He had thought she tried to kill him and that she was a traitor to the crown. She giggled. How ridiculous! Sobering, she considered the consequences if she could not adequately prove her innocence. Possibly life ending!

CHAPTER 9

*D*arcy was correct. Mr. Collins blathered on about the grand privilege of being in the same room as him. Ignoring the fool, Darcy attempted to explain the situation to Mr. Bennet. Unexpectedly, the parson had every intention of "helping" rescue poor Miss Lucas since Lady Catherine would insist it was his Christian duty. Mr. Bennet, apparently eager to be left alone, offered to remain behind, leaving the younger men to be heroes to their neighbor.

Thinking quickly, Darcy said. "Sir, the only reason I did not go directly to Lucas Lodge for aid was because Miss *Elizabeth* Lucas insisted that you would not only provide a cart and pony for her safe return, but she was also confident that having five daughters of your own, you would be in the better position to assist her without involving others."

Mr. Bennet's eyes snapped to his as soon as he uttered the name. Nodding, he addressed Mr. Collins. "It is good to know that chivalry is not dead in England. You will remain here with the ladies. Since you are unacquainted with the Lucas family, it might embarrass Miss Lucas to be seen by a strange man."

Setting aside his book, Mr. Bennet exited the room with Mr. Collins on his tail.

Strange man was an excellent description for Mr. William Collins. Darcy appreciated Mr. Bennet's cleverness at delivering an insult under the guise of polite conversation.

Collins opened the front door for them, walked with the two men to the stables, attempted to coerce the pony into action by telling the poor creature that Lady Catherine's exalted nephew required its services immediately, then grabbed the harness for a draft horse from the tack wall.

Mr. Bennet's patience came to an end. "Mr. Collins!" the older man barked. "Miss Lucas is suffering while your clumsiness delays us. Step back, I pray you."

Taking the harness from the fool's hands, he handed it to a waiting groom to replace it on the wall while he gathered what was needed for the pony.

"Lady Catherine says...," Mr. Collins began only to have Mr. Bennet growl.

"Mr. Collins, tell me something," Mr. Bennet left the task of harnessing the pony and cart to the groom. Approaching his cousin, he continued, "If Lady Catherine commanded you to jump into the sea off a tall cliff, would you do it? If she insisted you have the meat served at your table raw and bloody, would you eat it? If she demanded that you shave your head and your eyebrows bald, would you do it?"

The clergyman sputtered and stammered. "You do not understand, cousin. Lady Catherine's exalted..."

"Enough!" Mr. Bennet's hands were fisted, his knuckles white. "Mr. Collins, it may surprise you to learn that none of the intelligent men of my acquaintance consult your patroness before making decisions, yet their properties and their families flourish. We think on our own. We act on our own. We breathe on our own, without any help from Lady Catherine." He shoo-ed him away with the wave of his hand. "Now, off with you. I insist."

"But Mr. Darcy needs..." Mr. Collins began only to have Mr. Bennet interrupt him again.

"Mr. Darcy is one of us who can think, act, and breathe on his own, if I am not mistaken." The older man lifted a brow at him in the same manner his daughter had done at the Lucases.

"I can," Darcy agreed. Moving forward, he took the reins for the cart as Mr. Bennet seated himself in the back. With a gentle brush of the leather, the pony moved toward the pathway. They left Mr. Collins standing in the yard.

"Imbecile," Mr. Bennet muttered.

Darcy agreed.

Once they were out of sight of the manor house, Darcy informed Miss Elizabeth's father of his daughter's injury.

"That is very unlike my girl," Mr. Bennet commented. "She is typically fleet of foot."

"I do believe there was a crow involved," Darcy suggested.

"Ah, *Jeanne de Valois-Saint-Remy*, the scourge of Meryton. Should we ever locate her nesting area I suspect we will find the button she snatched from my favorite shirt when it was hung out to dry along with pilfered ribbons, small children's toys, and page 32 of Coleridge's poems that Lizzy left open while selecting a treat from the orchard."

Darcy chuckled under his breath. Then, he sobered. "You must be wondering how I happened upon Miss Elizabeth. Please allow me..."

"No, no." Mr. Bennet insisted. "I shall wait to hear the story from you both, so I do not have to listen to a telling and retelling. Thus, the account will be without confusion." He paused, "I offer my sincerest appreciation for not naming my daughter in front of my cousin. In the space of a few hours, in fact, almost as soon as he entered Longbourn, he singled Lizzy out as, and I quote, 'the companion of my future life,' end of quote. We would not have been able to rid ourselves of him had he thought his presumed bride-to-be was injured."

Darcy was horrified. "You allow such a man to remain in your house?"

"Mr. Darcy, know thy enemy and know yourself; in a hundred battles, you will never be defeated." Mr. Bennet added, "Keep your friends close; keep your enemies closer."

"Sun Tzu, is my cousin's favorite philosopher and military leader." Darcy admitted. "Richard is an army colonel."

"It is good you have protection, Mr. Darcy. We never know what danger lurks in the dark."

Reflecting on the events of the prior few days, Darcy

easily admitted that what Mr. Bennet said was the complete truth.

Considering what he had learned of the man bouncing along behind him, Darcy added it to what Miss Lucas had shared. He was a strategist, was intelligent, knew when to draw the line with Mr. Collins, was not averse to humor at the expense of a crow, and appeared to be a caring father. Was he more than the sum of all these parts?

A portion of his mind accepted Miss Elizabeth's innocence. However, there were still too many coincidences. The salient fact was that she herself admitted that she had not returned from London until before the assembly. Thus, it could have been her that John Lucas saw. A lady's hair could be taken down and put up fairly quickly. He had watched his mother do the same many times when he was young. A new hairstyle changed a lady's appearance substantially.

Was her father in on her operations? He would have to be, or he would throw everything off course with one command for her to remain at Longbourn when she needed to be elsewhere.

Dash it all! He wished he knew whom he could trust. A sick feeling started churning in his gut, sending the sour taste of bile up his throat. Had he made a mistake in confessing to her the events with the marksman? Had his loose tongue provided her with some sort of information to use against him? He was a dolt!

He knew his reputation, how closely he held things to his chest. Why had he spilled forth everything to her? What was it about her that had inspired his confidence, at least at that moment in time?

The pounding of his heart sped up. The real question was, what would she do with the information she now owned? *Drat!* He should have pretended a romantic interest in her as the reason he was at Oakham Mount. Or, at the very least, he could have insisted that the purpose for his presence was because he wanted to contemplate small beginnings like she did.

Perhaps Mr. Collins was not the only idiot in Meryton.

* * *

THE CART HAD NOT COME to a complete stop before Mr. Bennet jumped from the back to hurry to his daughter's side.

"My Lizzy, what have you done?"

Before he could drop to his knees, she moved her walking boot aside.

The suspicious part of Darcy was relieved. Her injury was real. She had not been acting the victim to throw him off her trail. The gentleman in him forced him to turn his eyes away while Mr. Bennet examined her ankle, despite the lingering need to see for himself if there was swelling.

"Papa, I was engaged in battle with the gnarly root of this big oak. I lunged and parried. The old tree offered a brilliant riposte. I next feinted and counterattacked. Where my battle wound is minimal, I believe my wit has skewered the heart of the wood. Truly, I doubt not that my next encounter with my enemy will find this massive example of arboreal splendor withered to a sapling."

"Hmm," Mr. Bennet chuckled as he tenderly rubbed

his thumb over the injured flesh. "Let us hope this will not keep you from dancing around the bonfire with the others. Guy Fawkes Day only comes once a year."

"Do not worry, Papa. I can always sit with the ladies and 'ooh' and 'ah' over the fireworks display while sipping the apple cider you men share when you think we are not looking."

Mr. Bennet laughed. "Always a pert reply, my Lizzy."

Darcy could not help himself. He peeked. Glancing quickly away, an image of that small slender foot with her short pink toes remained in his mind. How could someone so delicate be evil? It was inconceivable! Nevertheless, Richard had said that both France and England recruited innocent children and females to do their dirtiest of deeds. Miss Elizabeth certainly had the needed intelligence to disseminate information where the intended parties could do ultimate harm against their enemies.

He would need to watch her carefully.

ELIZABETH CAUGHT Mr. Darcy's glance at her bare foot. Heat from complete embarrassment flooded her face and chest. Of all things to have happened, she had not expected his face to be the same color red as hers at being caught.

This was no worldly man. No, if he was used to seeing a lady's uncovered limbs, he would not have blushed. As her father probed around her ankle, she watched the man. He looked anxious or at the least, highly disturbed.

Considering what he had revealed to her, had someone unknown been shooting at her, Elizabeth would have been unsettled as well.

She sucked in a hiss when her father's thumb pressed a tender spot. When he pushed against the ball of her foot and then pulled, there was no pain. In fact, she felt the tendons and muscles in her calf relax. Pulling it slowly towards where he sat on her right, she felt nothing. Nevertheless, once he put pressure to rotate her ankle in the other direction, a sharp pain shot from her ankle up her shin to her knee.

"Let's get you up on your feet, Lizzy. Gratefully, it appears your wound is not fatal. I suspect you will be running wild before the se'nnight is out."

Laughter bubbled forth at her father's comments and the ridiculousness of the situation. She was chased by a mad man and felled by a crow.

As soon as she attempted to stand, Mr. Darcy leapt from his seat on the cart to assist her. With a man on each side holding her elbows, they fairly lifted her from the ground. Hanging onto their forearms, Elizabeth stabilized herself. She discovered that by placing her weight on her heel instead of her toes, she could stand on her own. Gingerly, and with their help, she took a step. Then another.

Glancing between the two men, she said, "If we are to continue the subterfuge that we are helping Charlotte then I will need to walk into the house on my own."

"Will you be able to without further harm?" her father asked.

"I will do what needs done, Papa." Stiffening her spine,

she walked to the back of the cart, turned, and slid herself onto the blanket her father quickly spread. "Thank you, Papa. It would break my heart to ruin my favorite dress on the rough boards."

"Ah, but then Lydia would stop harassing you to borrow the garment, would she not?" Her father quipped as he clambered up to sit next to her.

"If I willingly parted with my gown to my youngest sister, she would have it covered in unnecessary ribbons and lace after begging you for more coins to give to the haberdashery. It would be better should it remain in my care."

"I suppose you are correct." As Mr. Darcy stood at the pony's head, her father teased "Lizzy gave this recalcitrant pony the moniker of Beatrice the first time she read Shakespeare's *Much Ado About Nothing.* The little lady has proven to be true to character. She is likely far from the Four-in-Hand Club with which you are accustomed, Mr. Darcy, however, our little pony will see us home."

To her utter amazement, Mr. Darcy chuckled under his breath. Whatever was he about, having a sense of humor? Who was this man? And why did curiosity about him fill her to the point that he was all she could think about? Frustrating man!

Remembering her manners, Elizabeth thanked him for his help.

He bowed. "Miss Elizabeth, had I not been chasing you; I imagine that you would have avoided the root that tripped you like you had done every other time you have traveled the path. Therefore, it is I who am in your debt.

Please accept my regrets. Your injury was my fault, not yours."

"Chasing!" Her father's gaze went from her to Mr. Darcy and back. "Perhaps the two of you need to tell me what happened, why it happened, and how exactly my Lizzy was injured."

CHAPTER 10

*A*fter a thorough review of the morning, Mr. Bennet directed Darcy to drive down a short pathway that joined the road into Meryton. There would be less jostling of his daughter's ankle on the smoother surface.

Darcy's heartbeat was beginning to return to normal. Once Mr. Bennet heard the events of the morning from each of them, and the confession Darcy had made as to why he had sought out Miss Elizabeth, the master of Longbourn boldly insisted that she take the pins from her hair.

Darcy gulped at the memory. The vision of her removing one pin after another until her lustrous tresses cascaded down her back, far beyond where the marksman's hair had rested, was indelibly inked on his memory.

Egad! He was a bonehead! Believing he would feel that same sense of protectiveness as he had for his mother's and sister's femininity when he happened to see their hair down, he refused to look away. Rocking back on his heels, a practice he had attempted to mitigate since his youth, he almost lost his balance.

His chest tightened just thinking about it. The reality was...Elizabeth Bennet was magnificent, and it was not protectiveness he felt—it was awe.

Mr. Bennet said, "There now, Mr. Darcy, this should put the matter to rest. A woman cannot easily pretend to have hair longer than she does. This should convince you beyond doubt of Lizzy's innocence."

As Darcy had started to nod in full agreement, Miss Elizabeth said, "No, Papa. For you see...," she turned her back to both men. Gathering her hair together in both hands, she twisted the mass this way and that before tucking the pins in tightly. Placing her bonnet back over the knot on the crown of her head, the bottom fringe of her hair hung to the middle of her back—exactly where the marksman's hair ended. "It is easy enough to make my hair any length I desire so your argument is not positive proof at all."

Mr. Bennet growled. Miss Elizabeth's eyes twinkled, and Darcy forgot to breathe.

Fortunately, the pony knew the way to the roadway.

Before they had departed the oak grove next to the orchard path, Mr. Bennet had suggested that they drive to Lucas Lodge to give the impression that it was Charlotte Lucas whom they had aided. Darcy vehemently disagreed.

"I abhor deceit of any sort."

Mr. Bennet replied, "Then you would make a terrible spy."

Miss Elizabeth chuckled. "As would I. In this I do agree with Mr. Darcy. Since Mr. Collins is the only one who knows that a lady was injured, I can hobble into Longbourn where I will be able to avoid him by gratefully remaining in my chamber. Should he inquire about Charlotte, we can explain it as a case of mistaken identity. If he has gossiped to the rest of the household, my sisters will laugh at his error."

Mr. Bennet asked, "Will this satisfy your honor, Mr. Darcy?"

"It will."

"Stop here, Mr. Darcy." Mr. Bennet jumped down from the back of the cart. "I will take the reins."

Darcy handed them over then stepped away from the cart. He was surprised at the regret filling his heart. For a certainty, it was the course of wisdom for them to part company whereupon he could return to Netherfield Park and the Bennets to Longbourn. However, glancing at the young lady's profile, he yearned to stay in her company.

He was a fool! He was mostly convinced she was innocent but there was this niggling, skeptical part of his mind that would not let go of his doubt.

"Papa, Mr. Darcy, it appears to me that the best way to prove my innocence and separate myself entirely from this other female is to find her and be seen with her."

"Lizzy! No!" Mr. Bennet roared.

"No!" Darcy insisted loudly.

She smiled. "I thank you both that your first response was protecting me. Yet, the implications of confusion between the two of us could devastate my reputation and Mr. Darcy's continued good health."

She was correct.

Miss Elizabeth continued, "If this woman has been

tracking you, she could be close to Meryton, if she is not already here. I would not want my neighbors to believe her to be me if we are indeed similar in looks."

"What you are suggesting is sensible, Lizzy." Mr. Bennet glanced at Darcy. "Either you will need to begin spending an inordinate amount of time with my daughter, which could raise speculation as to your intentions, or you could leave the area which would remove the threat from our proximity. My preference would be for you to depart and take the young lady with you. However, I am not your master. Therefore, which appeals to you, sir?"

Darcy considered both options. "A question, if you please, Mr. Bennet. Do you have family other than Mr. Collins who have the same coloring as Miss Elizabeth and are approximately the same age?"

He rubbed his chin before replying, "I seem to recall that Mr. Collins might have a sister or two who are considerably younger than he is. However, I could be wrong. Once his father, a hard man if there ever was one, realized that I was a healthy heir who desired to marry and fill my nest, he attached himself to an older couple with no children, taking their name, and acting their son so he could have their small property once they died. The animosity between us was such that we chose not to keep in touch. At his death, I was informed he had a son who was next in line to benefit from Longbourn's entail. I vaguely recall that there were girls, but again, I am not certain since they were not important to the business at the time."

"Would you ask Mr. Collins about his sisters or any

cousins he is aware of who might resemble Miss Elizabeth?"

"I will, although why one of them would want to kill you is a mystery to me?"

"To me as well, sir." Darcy tipped his head to the older man and bowed to the lady. "I bid you farewell. Until we meet again, I will consider all we have discussed to determine the best course for all of us."

"As will I," Mr. Bennet stated before turning the pony towards home.

Darcy had not reached the first bend in the road before a horseman, easily identified as Major Gerring, approached. He had forgotten all about the man and his promise to keep in contact with him before leaving Netherfield Park.

Blast!

* * *

JANE BENNET SIGHED, her hands at her chest. "Mr. Darcy is your hero."

Elizabeth giggled. "I believe the better part of the rescue was Beatrice pulling the cart so I could safely make my way back home."

"Oh, Lizzy, you still do not hate the man, do you? I mean, how could you continue to despise a gentleman who was tender in his care of you. And he was so diligent. Why, he walked all the way to Longbourn for Papa's help, did he not? His clever ploy of calling you Miss Lucas was brilliant. How could you not admire such a man?"

"Jane, he thinks I tried to kill him!" Elizabeth pulled

herself more upright on the bed. Where she was eager to tell the events to Jane, she should not have. *Drat!* It was not her desire to hear praise being heaped upon the man. Yes, he was kind to Charlotte. Yes, he had shown her kindness as well. Nonetheless, he still believed her to be an attempted murderer who was not handsome enough to tempt him. *Brute!*

Jane whispered as her eyes darted around the room. "You will never guess what I learned."

"What!" Instantly, Elizabeth was curious. Her sister rarely acted sly. "About Mr. Darcy?"

"No, not at all. I learned from Lydia who spoke with Aunt Phillips that Mr. Bingley's first name is Charles." Jane said the last in a revered tone. "Is that not an elegant name? Charles Bingley."

Giggling, Elizabeth teased, "Are you thinking of him alone or are you dreaming of how Mr. and Mrs. Charles and Jane Bingley sound together? It does resonate well; do you not think?"

"Oh, Lizzy," Jane dropped down into the chair next to her bed. "He is everything a gentleman should be. He is fashionable without being a dandy, never is one hair out of place, and he must bathe regularly since he smells divine."

"As should every man," Elizabeth grinned.

Sitting forward, Jane asked, "What do you think Mr. Darcy's first name is?"

"How would I know?" was Elizabeth's sarcastic reply, which was entirely lost on her sweetest sister. "Probably Egbert or something imposing like Pinckney or Abercrombie."

Learning the first name of a man felt intimate. She was not sure she wanted to hear Mr. Darcy's full name.

"At least he is not Mr. Plumbottom," Jane snickered.

"I suspect we shall never know." Elizabeth admitted, not wanting to think of the man any longer. Nevertheless, every inch of her mind was full of Mr. Darcy.

Without his perpetual frown, he was exceedingly handsome. And Jane was right, he was kind. Was the man her hero? How could he be? Until she could somehow convince him that she was exactly who she claimed to be, the chasm between them would remain too vast to overcome.

Why did the idea of them being separated bother her? She was being nonsensical.

Jane hesitated before speaking. Rather than try to guess what she was about, Elizabeth waited.

"Lizzy, our father's cousin had much to say about your hero." Jane grinned before continuing. "Apparently, Mr. Darcy is engaged to marry Miss Anne de Bourgh, who is a diamond above all others. Why, Mr. Collins said there is not a feminine accomplishment that she has not mastered. And her beauty is beyond comparison. Additionally, she is heir to the finest estate in Kent, Rosings Park. Therefore, I would hope that your heart is not touched by the gentleman, Lizzy, for he is already attached."

Every syllable dropped like heavy rocks into the pit of her stomach. Why that was, she would need to ponder later. Surely, her heart was not affected by him, was it? No! It simply could not be. She was only now beginning not to hate the man.

* * *

MAJOR GERRING's morning was productive. He had interviewed several families under the guise of procuring enlistments for the Regulars. It was an easy task to have the residents of Meryton speak of their neighbors. The Bennets, in particular Miss Jane and Miss Elizabeth, were generally spoken of highly. He then sought out the foremost member of Meryton society, Sir William Lucas, introducing himself as an officer of the crown in search of recruits for Britain's army. It had taken little probing to discover that Sir William's achievement of having once been invited to St. James, was the highlight of the man's life. A few well-placed questions indicating interest had spurred Sir William to invite the major to his home.

"Where her father easily tells everything that he knows to anyone who will listen, his daughter, picks and chooses which details about her neighbors are to be shared." The major mused, "She seems a discreet woman."

"She is intelligent, I will give you that," Darcy admitted. "What did you learn?"

The major cleared his throat, "The neighborhood considers the Bennet family to be a mixture of polished and rough. Mr. Bennet is reclusive, his wife has a whimsical mind, the middle daughter is rather proud of herself, the two youngest are flighty flirts, and the eldest is an angel. Miss Lucas and others consider Miss Elizabeth Bennet's intellect to be superior to her own."

"Did you learn anything that might lead to them having connections to France?"

The major hesitated before replying. "One of Miss

Lucas' younger brothers volunteered that his eldest sister writes notes to the newspaper that no one is supposed to know about. Miss Lucas' reaction was telling. Her face turned white as a bedsheet. She stammered and stumbled when she hushed the lad. I teased the boy about it being love notes to a beau, whereupon the boy said that the letters had strange-sounding girl's names."

"This is not good," Darcy observed. "I found Miss Lucas to be uncommonly forthright."

"Since then, I have discovered the same about the lady. When I am not needed for you, Mr. Darcy, I shall stick as close to her as possible."

"A good plan, I believe." Darcy pondered the information. "My exposure to the others of the Bennet family was at Lucas Lodge where I find your descriptions to be accurate."

Major Gerring added, "Sir, if Miss Elizabeth is truly our target, it is my belief that Miss Lucas would be complicit."

Darcy nodded in full agreement. "There is nothing on earth more dangerous to a man as a smart female, whether she is a spy or not."

CHAPTER 11

o sooner had Darcy decided that he needed to distance himself from the Bennets for his own personal safety than he found himself requesting Major Gerring's company to ride to Longbourn. Bingley offered to accompany them. Hurst, as usual, remained behind.

Darcy needed more information, and his best sources were Mr. Bennet, Miss Elizabeth, and—heaven forbid—Mr. Collins.

The uproar they heard at their arrival quieted into a semblance of decorum once they stepped into the drawing room. Oddly enough, the matron of the household completely ignored him and Bingley. Her eyes landed on the uniform of Major Gerring and there they remained. Mrs. Bennet was voluminous in her welcome.

"An officer!" Their hostess almost swooned. "Welcome to Longbourn. I will call for tea."

While the niceties were performed, Darcy glanced around the room in hopes of finding either Mr. Bennet or his second daughter. Neither were present. His plan of discovering more clues about the Bennet family died a quick death when his aunt's parson approached.

"Mr. Darcy, I am delighted you returned," Mr. Collins lowered his chin, his eyes closing, a smirk that could only be described as intensely smug on his face. He continued, "I am to be the bearer of bad news, for you see, it was not Miss Lucas who needed your assistance, it was my...," he leaned closer to whisper, "intended", before raising his voice so the others could hear. "It was Miss Elizabeth Bennet who was gravely injured, I am sorry to say. You will be pleased to know that upon her father returning her home, I censured her in the manner Lady Catherine de Bourgh would have done had she been here. Elizabeth's inelegant display as she limped into Longbourn was simply not to be tolerated in a young lady."

Indignation at the oaf casually using Miss Elizabeth's first name in addition to referring to her as his future bride raised Darcy's ire and his pulse. It was exceedingly bad form to claim a relationship that simply did not exist except in the mind of the claimant. He had no clue how to respond to the buffoon. This was not a man of sense.

Inhaling deeply, Darcy slowly let out his breath to calm himself. "Mr. Collins, do you not recall that it was I who came to Longbourn for Mr. Bennet's assistance and who accompanied him to assist the lady? Thus, you spreading this tale exposes my error in calling Miss Elizabeth by her close friend's surname. Was it your intention to embarrass me, the nephew of your esteemed patroness, Lady Catherine de Bourgh?"

"Never!" Mr. Collins sputtered, his face ashen. "I would never embarrass you..."

"Yet, you did, Mr. Collins. Therefore, I suggest we speak of this no more."

"Yes, sir. I will be quiet." Bowing, Mr. Collins returned to the sofa, leaving Darcy with the impression that he had just whipped a pup.

"Well met, Mr. Darcy." Mr. Bennet stepped into the room with Elizabeth on his arm. She had changed from her peach gown to one of ivory cream. Gone was the mud and grass stains on her arms. She was lovely, yet not quite as vibrant as she had looked at the orchard. Her efforts to move gracefully on an injured ankle showed in the paleness of her face

Mrs. Bennet began fussing, "Lizzy, you must be seated next to Mr. Collins. Mr. Bingley, there is a place by Jane where I am certain you will be comfortable. Major Gerring, I do believe that my youngest would be a delightful companion." She glared at Darcy. "You may sit anywhere there is an extra chair, Mr. Darcy."

Mrs. Bennet, whose reputation for seeking any unattached male for any of her daughters, had snubbed him, Fitzwilliam Darcy of Pemberley and Darcy House in London. The shock temporarily robbed him of speech.

Mr. Bennet came to his rescue. "Come, sir. I believe we have a discussion to finish." Directing him to a sofa directly across from where Mr. Collins was seated next to Miss Elizabeth, he asked the parson, "Cousin, you have not mentioned how long you have had the patronage of Lady Catherine. Were you recently appointed to the position?"

Grabbing the lapels of his coat, the clergyman's chin rose high into the air. "I was offered the post six months past. There were many candidates vying for the privilege. I was blessed to have been chosen by someone as illustrious as Lady Catherine de Bourgh."

"I see," Mr. Bennet crossed his legs as he tapped his chin with his knuckle. "Is her estate far from where you were raised?"

"We are in the same shire." Mr. Collins leaned forward. "Lady Catherine believes that a man should not reach above his status or leave the vicinity where he grew up since it adds stability to a community if everything and everyone remains the same."

"Hmm, how feudal," Mr. Bennet mused. "Your patroness stays in Kent then?"

"She does, although she would be welcomed into the highest circles should she travel to London, I am sure."

"Yes, yes," Mr. Bennet said, giving the impression that the matter was of little importance. "How is your family? How do they get on with you away from home?"

"I have no family to speak of," was the parson's immediate reply.

"Hmm, I seem to recall that you have younger sisters, am I not correct?"

Mr. Collins pulled at his collar, his face the hue of a ripe tomato. "I do not speak of them, sir, and that is the end of that!"

Mr. Bennet glanced at Elizabeth, who immediately took up the conversation. Had they planned this before they entered the room? If so, Darcy was impressed.

Miss Elizabeth looked directly at the man, her expression one of kindness, "Mr. Collins, having younger sisters can be both a blessing and a source of annoyance. As an older brother you cannot know the frustration of having favorite ribbons or gowns being borrowed and not returned in a timely manner."

"I do not." His tone was stern, his words clipped.

Miss Elizabeth added, "I understand how your newly elevated position would leave you uncomfortable speaking of your sisters, however, having relatives on the Bennet side of the family is a rare treat for me as we are few. Could you please tell me the age of your sisters and whether either have the same brown hair and dark eyes as both you and me?"

Had she turned those mesmerizing eyes upon Darcy, he would have given her the complete sum of his fortune had she asked. Mr. Collins was no less immune.

The parson cleared his throat before replying, "Claire reached her majority not one month ago and Sarah was but fifteen. They both have the Bennet coloring. Claire is remarkably similar to you in appearance, Miss Elizabeth. Enough so that I almost mistook you for Claire the first time I saw you."

"Oh, how exciting," Elizabeth clapped her hands together and rested them under her chin. "Mr. Collins, you cannot know how happy you have made me on this day. To know that I have cousins is a gift. Are they much like me in character?"

Mr. Collins squirmed on the sofa, his fingers nervously tapping on his knee. "I do sincerely hope that my sisters and you are dissimilar. Claire is very forward. She does not know her proper place. Lady Catherine kindly brought her into Rosings Park where she was introduced to Miss de Bourgh. I deeply regret to tell you that Claire was dissatisfied, if you can believe it, with the elegance displayed before her eyes. Miss de Bourgh kindly gifted my sister with garments she was no longer using. Claire gratefully accepted them, as she should have done. Then, she immediately left for London. I have not heard from her since. Sarah...remained at home."

The implications of his words stunned Darcy. Miss Elizabeth's cousin Claire Collins was bold and close enough in appearance that her own brother mistook them. Was she the lady who wanted him dead? He had never met her. What could possibly be her motive?

Miss Elizabeth, who was still smiling at the oaf, asked, "If you do not mind one more question, I would like to know if Miss Claire enjoys the finer ladies' sports of hunting, riding, and marksmanship?"

"She does not!" Mr. Collins was emphatic. "We have not been able to keep riding horses nor afford the fees to join a hunting club."

Disappointment almost crushed Darcy. He had rested his hopes on Miss Collins being his mystery murderer.

Mr. Collins continued, "However, as a man who sought the church for my employment, my conscience would not allow me to kill the Lord's creations. I have carried my ideology to my new situation. My cook does not procure meat for my table on Sundays when it is only myself in residence at Hunsford Parsonage. Nevertheless, Claire insisted that she learn to handle a weapon so we would have venison for our table when I was at home, which she did well to provide. I was opposed, of course, but gave in one winter when produce was slim."

Mr. Bennet noted, "Your conscience allows you to eat the game, does it not? You did not hold back from the roast beef and potatoes my wife provided when we dined last evening if I recall clearly. There was little left on the platter once you served yourself."

"Yes, well..." Mr. Collins paled. "A man needs to eat."

"As does a woman, Mr. Collins." Miss Elizabeth's smile made everything right with the world so that Mr. Collins relaxed against the back of the sofa.

"As do I," proclaimed Bingley from the corner. Miss Bennet smiled, agreeing with his opinion.

Mr. Bennet stood, offering his hand to his daughter. "Mr. Darcy, I would ask that you accompany me to my study where I can show you the book I was telling you about. Lizzy, you will need to return to your room where you can rest your ankle."

Mr. Collins continued speaking to the air as the three left the parlor. Bingley and Miss Bennet put their heads back together and the others ignored the clergyman as they sought their own entertainment. Major Gerring appeared miserable being seated between the two youngest Bennets. Darcy figured the man could fend for himself.

"WELL, THAT WAS INTERESTING," Mr. Bennet stated once they were settled into his study.

"I thought so as well, Papa." Elizabeth considered what

Mr. Collins said and what he did not say. "He failed to speak of his younger sister at all. This leads me to wonder if something is very wrong with her."

"Possibly she found it to be better for her own health and safety to keep from being noticed by her father, and then her brother," Mr. Darcy suggested.

Elizabeth considered his suggestion carefully. If she was residing in the same house as Mr. Collins, she certainly would do anything within reason, and perhaps anything outside of reason, to avoid him like the plague. He was a foolish man and entirely disgusting for wanting to marry a woman whom he would confuse with his sister. *Yuck!*

"Papa, what do you know of the parents of Mr. Collins? Perhaps understanding how he and his sisters were raised could give us insight into their inclinations and motives."

Her father nodded as he considered the question. "My grandfather, who was a younger son, never intended on becoming the master of Longbourn. His chosen career was the law, an occupation he savored. Upon the early death of his elder brother, he quickly realized how differently the ladies looked at his prospects. Before he became the master, the daughter of one of his legal clients caught his eye. The lady and her father rudely rebuffed the advances of a mere fledgling barrister. After inheriting Longbourn, they approached him with an offer he gratefully accepted only to discover that this lady, and I use the term loosely, was already with child. My grandfather packed her up and returned her to her father's house. She died giving birth as did the babe. If my memory serves me correctly, it was a girl child. This treachery resulted in the entail on Longbourn where only the heir's male will inherit the property."

Elizabeth knew none of this history. "Papa, he must have married and had at least two sons or you would not have cousins."

"You are correct, Lizzy. My grandfather became even more cautious with his decisions. He was careful with his income, with his associations, and with the choosing of his next bride. My grandmother was a wonderful woman in many ways. She was kind and caring to me, to the staff, and to the tenants. She was also as frugal as my grandfather. Nevertheless, in the way they trained their two sons, they were intemperate. Showering attention on the heir to the exclusion of their younger son created a bitterness between the two brothers. This acerbity widened the void between my father and Bertram for the rest of their lives. I met my uncle at my grandfather's funeral. I saw Bertram again when they buried my grandmother. I did not see him until after my own father passed. Bertram, accompanied by his young son, came to Longbourn with every intention of remaining. I was fresh out of university, had just lost the most powerful influence in my young life, and had no idea what to do with them. I found out about Collins' sisters when Bertram died. I never knew what sort of woman Bertram married. I assumed when the father and son came to Longbourn alone that she was deceased. With the advent of two younger sisters, I must have been wrong."

"Papa, I am sorry." Elizabeth's heart ached for what her father must have felt.

Mr. Darcy said, "I, too, had recently returned from university when my own father died. Pemberley has over ten thousand acres of prime farmland. The main house is larger than Chatsworth, the gardens were designed by none other than Capability Brown, and the stables housed prime horseflesh bred from imported Arabian stock. The complete contents of my father's investment portfolio were unknown to me until I met with his man of business after the reading of the will. I was overwhelmed, to say the least."

Mr. Bennet nodded. "And then the long-lost relatives come out of the woodwork to snatch and grab anything they can get their greedy hands upon, am I correct? As well, strangers began throwing their daughters and unwed sisters my way in hopes of them taking advantage of an inexperienced youth. I did not know whom to trust."

Mr. Darcy agreed. "It was the same for me. My biggest concern when my carriage departed Cambridge was the grand tour I was planning to the Orient. I arrived home to find my father extremely ill. We had two days together before he passed. Since my father's death, I have not stepped one foot out of England. Instead, I have spent the last five years avoiding the marriage mart and any business and personal entanglements that are risky. The Darcy family has few relatives on my father's side. In that, I clearly knew who belonged at Pemberley and who did not." He rubbed his hand over his mouth.

"Then your upcoming marriage to Miss de Bourgh will bring you relief, I suppose," Elizabeth said, even though the words tasted bitter on her tongue.

"I am not, nor will I ever be betrothed to my cousin,"

Mr. Darcy did not hesitate to reply. "I suppose you have heard of my supposed attachment from Mr. Collins, who is as incorrect as is my aunt, who continues to promote the match despite my firm refusal."

"What a kettle of fish," her father muttered. "The person at the root of this rumor and the one where he believes he is attached to Lizzy is the same man. How odd."

"He is odd, Papa." Glancing at the man seated in the chair next to hers, she asked, "Do you have brothers and sisters?"

"Only one. I was left the guardianship of my sister, Georgiana. She recently turned sixteen."

"Poor Miss Darcy," Elizabeth uttered. "Her life must have changed as much as yours. Is she with your mother then?"

"My dear mother died shortly after my sister was born. Georgiana is currently in London with my mother's brother and his wife, Hugh and Helen Fitzwilliam, Lord and Lady Matlock."

"Is she well?" Elizabeth could not stop herself from asking. Mr. and Miss Darcy were alone, which rendered their situation as pitiable. She would far rather have family surrounding her than all the gold in their accounts.

Mr. Darcy sighed. "As well as she can be, I suppose. A recent disappointment unsettled her to the point that I worried she would not recover. However, with the assistance from my aunt along with a cheerful association with a fairly new acquaintance she is recovering."

"I am sorry to hear that her heart was damaged but pleased to hear it is mending," Elizabeth admitted. "Fifteen seems to be one of the most challenging years for females, as Papa can confirm." She smiled, as did the men.

Elizabeth's heart ached for the young lad whose life had gone from joy at welcoming a baby sister to utter despair at the loss of his mother. She observed Mr. Darcy closely. His hands were gripping the wooden arms of the chair, his shoulders were unyielding, and his chin was firm. His dark blue eyes, the color of rich sapphires, were deeply troubled.

He was wealthy and arrogant. But he was also an orphan who was left with the care of an estate ten times the size of Longbourn. He worried about Miss Darcy; Elizabeth could see it in his face. And someone was trying to kill him—someone who looked remarkably like her.

Clarity hit her directly between the eyes. Mr. Darcy was not the brute she had accused him of being. For the first time in her twenty years, her propensity to quickly form opinions as to the character of a person had failed her. Through her humiliation, a tiny seed of interest in this Mr. Darcy began to grow. Should she pluck it out or allow it to flourish? If only she knew.

CHAPTER 12

*E*ven if Elizabeth Bennet was not the marksman, she was dangerous. Sorting through the stack of letters forwarded to him from Darcy House, he kept getting distracted by the image he held in his mind of her letting down her hair. It felt intimate and very private.

Upon their return from Longbourn, Bingley recommended they retreat to the billiard room. Major Gerring followed them. However, Darcy had business to care for and a lot to ponder before he was free to relax.

Pulling a note Georgiana had written from the pile, he broke the seal, determined to give his full attention to her words. When Aunt Helen first reported on the acquaintance they had made with his sister's new friend, Miss Hobbs, the young lady was described as lively and delightful. Despite being a few years older than Georgiana, Miss Hobbs apparently was personable, ladylike, and well-dressed despite her gowns being several seasons out of...

Darcy gulped. Mr. Collins had described his eldest sister as being forward, wearing garments that Anne de

Bourgh had cast off. Aunt Helen said Miss Hobbs approached them as a close friend of Anne's with enough details from Rosings Park and Lady Catherine to confirm the relationship. Mr. Collins' sister would have known those small details from her short time there.

Could it be? No! Surely, Lady Matlock had screened any stranger who, without an invitation or introduction, approached Georgiana. Although his aunt knew nothing of Ramsgate and the treachery of Wickham, she would scrupulously guard his sister from strangers, would she not? And Georgiana herself, certainly she would be cautious after almost falling into a trap set by a scheming companion and an old acquaintance from Pemberley's past? Of course, she would be! Or would she?

Lady Matlock was part of a vast social web where her attention was often sought by others when she was about town. Had she not been paying attention when Georgiana met the young lady? And his sister? She was desperate for a trusted friendship like he had with Bingley.

Unfolding the parchment, he almost ripped the paper in his haste. Searching every word, he looked for clues.

Dear brother,

I hope this finds you doing well and enjoying the company of Mr. Bingley and his family. I surmise that the majority of your time is spent helping Mr. Bingley manage his new estate. Pray help the poor man with his correspondence. I have seen you struggle to read his script with all the ink splotches and crossed out words. Nevertheless, how exciting it must be for him to go from being a perpetual guest to offering hospitality to his friends.

Fitzwilliam, I am pleased to report that il maestro Amato told me yesterday morning that my Italian is improving. According to him, should we travel to Italy, I will be able to order bread, meat, and wine for our meal. However, when I repeated the lesson for requesting lodging, he informed me that we would be sleeping in the straw above the stalls in a stable instead of a comfortable bed at an inn. When I later met Miss Hobbs in the bookstore, we chuckled as ladies should at my error. I do not believe Miss Hobbs has had the advantage of masters since she expresses no interest in anything other than reading. Rarely a day passes that we do not meet at Hatchards. Aunt Helen approves of my sudden appetite for literature. Should Miss Hobbs ever see the main library at Pemberley, I fear she would never depart the room.

Aunt Helen begged me to ask for your speedy return to town. Lord and Lady Barrington have scheduled their annual ball which is Thursday next. According to our aunt, this is the one social event you would not want to miss.

Now, brother, I can see you in my mind's eye rolling your eyes at the request. Nonetheless, aunt insists it is high time that you find a wife. "Pemberley needs an heir," she says at least two or three times each day. I believe that she has several candidates in mind, as does Lady Barrington.

Miss Hobbs has left London for an indeterminate length of time to visit family to the north. I shall miss Claire's company. Yet, I do miss you much more.

Darcy's heart almost stopped beating. *Blast!* Claire? Georgiana's close friend's name was Claire?

Dropping the pages to the desktop, Darcy pulled a clean sheet of parchment from the drawer. Grabbing the quill so roughly that it snapped in two, he deliberately slowed his breathing until he calmed. Random puzzle pieces began falling into place.

None of his staff reported being asked about his schedule. None of the groomsmen in the stables had any inquiries as well. The only other person with knowledge of his comings and goings was Georgiana, who Darcy had not even considered asking.

He was a fool! Mr. Collins admitted that his sister was bold. And she could shoot. Someone as inherently timid as Georgiana would flourish in the presence of a lady who willingly took the lead. Darcy admitted, if only to himself, that he felt the same in Miss Elizabeth's presence. Miss Claire was given cast-offs from Anne, whose mother insisted that her daughter wear the latest fashions made from the best fabrics. Had a dark green traveling coat with a black bonnet been included in the pile of clothing Claire Collins, or maybe Hobbs, had received? Georgiana would know if it was something her friend wore. He would not upset his sister by asking.

The pertinent fact was that Miss Claire Hobbs was traveling north. He was north of London.

Carefully removing another quill from the desk, he quickly wrote a note to Mr. Bennet. *"Does Mr. Collins know Miss Claire Hobbs?"*

Within minutes, the note was on its way to Long-bourn. As he waited, Darcy took out another sheet of paper, drew a line down the middle, and placed the names of the two ladies at the top of each column. Under each name he listed his suspicions.

Miss Elizabeth Bennet:

- *Her appearance matched the lady who aimed and fired at me twice.*
- ~~She is impertinent.~~ (He crossed that out.)

Yes, she was impertinent but that did not make her a murderer. She...she... Sitting back in the chair, he considered each interchange they had since his arrival in Meryton. Not once had she acted aggressively towards him. Instead, he had witnessed a kindness so fundamental to her character that it was at the root of her teasing as well as her concerns. She would never willingly harm any living thing, not even a greedy crow.

Then, there was Miss Claire Hobbs. He knew nothing about her other than she might be the younger sister of Mr. Collins and she possibly was trying to kill him.

He needed to tell Major Gerring what he might have learned.

* * *

ELIZABETH'S FATHER moved her favorite chair closer to the fire. Placing the footstool where she could elevate her ankle, Elizabeth pretended to read. Her body was cozy and relaxed. Her brain spun with images of Mr. Darcy—standing by the fireplace, seated across from her, kneeling at her side when she was on the ground, atop his gigantic horse. He was an impressive man.

She blushed at the thought. Should her father notice the rosy hue of her cheeks, she would blame it on the heat of the fire.

Jane had taken their younger sisters to visit the Lucas family followed by a short stroll into Meryton. Mr.

Collins offered to accompany them but at the last minute, chose to write to Lady Catherine instead.

Mrs. Hill, Longbourn's housekeeper, interrupted with a brisk knock on the outer door.

"You have a message from Mr. Darcy. His rider is waiting at the entrance."

"What is this?" Her father asked as he accepted the folded parchment. Breaking the seal, he scanned the words. Speaking to the housekeeper, he said, "Let Mr. Collins know he is needed."

As soon as Mrs. Hill retreated, Elizabeth's brow arched, her head tilting to the side.

In answer to her unspoken request, her Papa offered, "I believe Mr. Darcy might be close to identifying the person who shot at him as someone other than you, Lizzy girl."

Before she could reply, Mr. Collins burst into the room. Sliding to a stop in front of the desk, in one breath he blurted, "Are you well? Is it a pain in your chest? Your head? Do you need help to lie down? Should I call the apothecary? Do you have any final instructions for me to carry out after your passing?"

Of all the ridiculous things to say! Stunned at his assumption, Elizabeth slid her feet to the floor, pressing herself back in the chair. She did not want to miss her father's reply.

"Mr. Collins, I fear you will not be inheriting Longbourn today." The anger that flashed across her father's face melted into a grimace as he lowered himself into his chair. He moaned rather loudly, "Perhaps it should be me who sits close to the warmth of the fire with my favorite

blanket draped across my lap as I wait out my final days."
He held up the parchment. "Mr. Darcy requires information from you."

"Mr. Darcy! Why did you not say so?" Mr. Collins
eagerly reached for the note. As soon as he read the
words, his pallor turned a chalky shade of beige. "Why
would he want to know this?"

"Is Hobbs your mother's name?"

"My mother's maiden name was Carlson—Mrs.
Mildred Abigail Carlson Collins."

Elizabeth's hopes plunged. Without a positive identifi-
cation that Mr. Collins' sister was the guilty party, this left
herself as the primary suspect.

"Thank you, Mr. Collins," Her father relaxed back in
his chair. "I will reply to Mr. Darcy that you do not know
Miss Claire Hobbs."

"I did not say I did not know her," Mr. Collins said
after a somewhat lengthy pause. "You asked if my mother
was Hobbs. I spoke the truth when I answered. However,
after my dear mother died, my father remarried a terma-
gant named Harriet Hobbs. It was she who birthed Claire
and Sarah."

Elizabeth was stunned to have her growing suspicions
confirmed. Her own cousin, Miss Claire Hobbs Collins,
attempted to kill Mr. Darcy.

Warring emotions surged through her—guilt that a
distant family member was responsible for his distress
and concern for the man's continued health. Poor Mr.
Darcy!

As her Papa began scratching across the parchment
with his quill, Mr. Collins asked, "Why would Mr. Darcy

be interested in Claire? Does he know her? Has she caused some sort of difficulty that affects his good name? If she has, then I will hunt her down and see that she gets what is coming to her."

He was breathing rapidly through his nostrils. The knuckles of his fists were white, his face was red, his brow and upper lip dotted with sweat. His spine was stiff with his head tipped back. The evidence of the man's increasing ire was frightening.

Elizabeth made herself as small and imperceptible as possible in the leather chair. She was eternally grateful she was not Claire Hobbs Collins.

"Cousin, pray settle yourself," her father admonished several times before Mr. Collins was able to gain control. "I happen to have it on good authority that the nephew of your patroness was impressed with the kindness that his aunt showed to Miss Collins. Sharing the contents of her daughter's closet was extraordinary. It is my firm belief that Mr. Darcy intends to warn his sister not to be embarrassed if she were to identify Miss de Bourgh's garments but not the lady wearing them should they meet in London. That is all."

Elizabeth admired her father's quick thinking.

"Oh, well yes, I do suppose that ladies pay far more attention to clothing than gentlemen usually do." Mr. Collins glanced everywhere but at the master of Longbourn. His eyes settled upon her.

"Miss Elizabeth! I would not have believed it possible that you have infringed upon a gentlemen's discussion. Why did you not identify your presence or depart as soon as we began discussing a topic of interest to Mr. Darcy?

You are guilty of eavesdropping. Lady Catherine would chastise you severely if she were here."

Shaking her head, she glanced at her father to see if he would answer only to see a smirk behind his whiskers. Elizabeth was on her own.

"Sir, my injury prevented my speedy retreat, this is my home, I am here at my father's invitation, and Lady Catherine is not here."

"Miss Elizabeth!" he stammered. "I sincerely doubt that an esteemed man like Mr. Darcy would want you to know his business. Forget everything you have heard."

His insistence irritated her.

Pushing herself up from her chair, Elizabeth sternly reprimanded him, "When Mr. Darcy or Lady Catherine gives you permission to speak for them, then I shall listen."

As he sputtered and fumed, she glanced at her father. "Papa, I shall be in my room should you need me."

Straightening her shoulders and lifting her chin, she exited the room with as much dignity as an injured ankle allowed. *Of all the fools alive on the planet they happened to have one at Longbourn!*

By the time she ascended the staircase, she had determined an indissoluble fact—Mr. Darcy could occasionally act as a gentleman. Mr. Collins could not.

NOT A QUARTER HOUR LATER, Charlotte Lucas arrived. The climb up the stairs must have been dreadful. Entering Elizabeth's bed chamber, her friend sat next to her on the bed, stole the pillow out from underneath Elizabeth's ankle and stuffed it under her knee.

"Major Gerring is asking a lot of questions." Charlotte rearranged the pillow to her liking. "As soon as he finished gaining as much information as was available from my verbose brothers and sisters about *your* family, he began to gather information about mine."

"Questions? What sort of questions?" Elizabeth asked.

"The sort that makes a body wonder if there is a decided lack of loyalty to the crown in the neighborhood." She mumbled, "As if my father would be anything but devoted to anyone attached to St. James!"

Elizabeth said nothing at first. Major Gerring might not trust Charlotte, but Elizabeth did. Despite this, the information Mr. Darcy shared with her and her father was private. If it got out, it could make it more of a challenge to find Claire Collins and discover why she was shooting at him.

Into the silence Charlotte asked, "What are you not telling me, Lizzy?"

But this was Charlotte. Finally, she told her friend everything from the insult at the assembly until the discovery that Claire Collins matched the description of the female who shot twice at the gentleman from Derbyshire.

"Can you imagine that Mr. Darcy thought I was a spy?" Elizabeth asked.

Charlotte immediately replied, "I well and truly can imagine it because I believe Major Gerring believes me to be your partner in crime."

They both snickered.

Leaning over to bump her shoulder into Charlotte's, Elizabeth boldly suggested. "Then let us make it our mission to see what the men are about. I will keep my eye on Mr. Darcy if you would do the same with Major Gerring."

Charlotte's head slowly dipped up and down. "Oh, yes, Lizzy. It will not be a hardship to learn as much as I can about the major. As he spies on me, I will spy on him."

They shook hands like a gentleman's agreement. "It is agreed."

CHAPTER 13

$\mathcal{M}$ ajor Gerring appeared at the same time as the rider from Longbourn. Before they could remove themselves to the privacy of the library, Miss Bingley insisted the two men join the others for tea. For the long minutes required to partake of the small feast and chat about the weather, the note from Mr. Bennet burned in Darcy's pocket. If Darcy's suspicions were true, Claire Collins was headed his way, if she was not already in Meryton.

It chilled him to the bone that his own tender-hearted sister had been in the company of a potential murderer.

At one point, he was unable to hide his desperation. His knee started bouncing. Wanting the social niceties to come to a quick end, he, Darcy of Pemberley, did the unthinkable. Risking the ire of his valet, he waited until Miss Bingley was refilling Mr. Hurst's plate to put his plan into action. Making sure that the only eyes upon him were the major's, he tipped his cup until liquid spilled on his thigh.

"Good heavens! I have gone and spilled my tea," Darcy admitted with absolutely no shame. "I beg your pardon while I return upstairs to change."

"Mr. Darcy!" Miss Bingley was horrified. Whether it was because he was clumsy or he would be leaving the room, Darcy had not a clue.

Before he left, Darcy addressed the officer. "Major Gerring, I have a letter from Colonel Fitzwilliam you need to read."

It was not exactly a lie since he had received a report from his cousin that morning. Richard's ship sailed immediately after the letter was posted. Whether the major found any of the information interesting, Darcy could not know.

His subterfuge worked. Within seconds, both men were heading to his sitting room whereupon Darcy ripped open the seal from Mr. Bennet's note.

He was correct. Claire Hobbs was Claire Collins. She must have sought out Georgiana for the specific purpose of gaining knowledge of his schedule. Her betrayal would devastate a girl who already suffered from having misjudged Wickham. For that damage alone, he would see that justice was wrought against Miss Claire Hobbs Collins.

"This is consistent with what I have found with my interviews. Miss Elizabeth is generally regarded as law-abiding." Major Gerring asked. "This makes 'why' the most salient question. Why is the sister of your aunt's parson targeting you? Does she only want to scare you, or does she want you dead?"

Rubbing his hand over his chin, Darcy replied, "I wish I knew."

"We need a plan," the major suggested. "Until we have one, I recommend you remain with the Bingleys inside Netherfield. In the meantime, I will search the area for Miss Collins."

It was not Darcy's preference, but it would satisfy his hosts to be in their company, therefore he agreed. Glancing out the window in the direction of Longbourn, disappointment at not being in a certain lady's presence begged him to rebel. At that moment, he finally admitted to himself that both ladies were a danger—one to his life and the other to his heart.

FRUSTRATION BOILED under every inch of Elizabeth's skin. Each time she made the effort to join the family downstairs, Mr. Collins viewed her presence as an invitation to instruct her in the delicacies common to ladies of elevated status with Miss Anne de Bourgh and her mother's conduct as his guide.

Elizabeth's sore flesh had improved dramatically, proving that she had merely rolled her ankle slightly instead of permanently damaging the joint. She was able to walk about her bed chamber without pain. Nevertheless, it was a convenient excuse that kept her from being in the company of one Mr. Collins.

During the few days she remained in her chambers, she exchanged notes with Charlotte. Her neighbor's wit was infectious. The first time she had aided her friend to get her article to *The Times*, Elizabeth had impatiently waited for her father to finish his thorough perusal of the newspaper before snatching it away to search for the words Charlotte had penned. The column was deep in the inside pages on the lower corner. The article was entitled, *Bucolic Life in the Far North for Young Ladies.* It was a witty piece intended to entertain the jaded residents of well-populated cities such as London, Manchester, or Liverpool. Since it first appeared, readers have clamored to hear more of the rural lives of the five Hopper sisters, Heloise, Trinette, Irene, Solange, and Catrinel. As the demand from readers increased, the position of Charlotte's column moved closer toward the front of the newspaper and the amount of money placed directly into Charlotte's account grew.

Elizabeth praised her for her brilliance despite the Bennet family providing fodder for Charlotte's pen. The name of each character was the exact opposite of their counterparts. Serene Jane was Heloise, whose name was French for a famous warrior. Each time Charlotte wrote of Heloise fighting for justice or standing up for herself, Elizabeth wanted to giggle. Not one word was like Jane's character.

Elizabeth's counterpart of Trinette, translated as a very innocent child, was usually deep into mischief with every tale. Pious Mary's character name, Irene, was Greek for peace. Mary never seemed to understand social signals so blurted out fiery counsel at the most ridiculous times. Solange, a well-grounded religious woman should have been Mary, but Charlotte dubbed flighty Kitty with the name. Lydia, the loudest and brashest of all the Bennet girls was written as Catrinel, one who is chaste and pure. Elizabeth could only hope it were true as the youngest Bennet spent more time in society.

Folding the latest article from Charlotte carefully, she wrapped it in another layer of parchment to send out with the next post.

Finally, Elizabeth decided it was time to set Mr. Collins straight. She was not interested in becoming an imitation of his patroness or Lady Catherine's daughter. What she was interested in, or rather, *who* she was interested in failed to appear at Longbourn.

Frustration and disappointment warred inside her. If she asked her father whether he had heard from Mr. Darcy, the teasing Elizabeth would receive would be unbearable. As well, she did not want to give her father the impression that she had an interest in the gentleman since she was not at all interested.

Oh, what a lie! The man consumed her thoughts and...well, she simply refused to think upon him anymore.

On the other hand, Mr. Bingley promptly arrived almost every day, except Sunday, reporting that Mr. Darcy kept busy with the business of running his properties and corresponding with Major Gerring and his sister, Miss Darcy. Occasionally, the major would make a brief stop at Longbourn before proceeding to Lucas Lodge. According to daily notes from Charlotte, he was an intelligent man with an engaging wit that matched her own. Elizabeth hoped he would not leave a brokenhearted best friend behind when he had to go back to his regiment.

Returning her attention to the man sharing the sofa, she boldly examined him from head to toe as he gave attention to her mother's chatter. Mr. Collins was not bad looking. His features were even, and he was well formed. He was gainfully employed. His prospects for the future were good. Had he possessed a brain between his two ears, he would be considered quite the matrimonial catch.

This was a powerful observation to Elizabeth. His actions and attitude had rendered him unattractive in her eyes. It was a not very subtle reminder that first impressions were not always accurate.

Men! Were they all this much trouble?

Dropping her gaze to her fingers twisting around each other, she considered how to tell the parson seated next to her that she had no interest in a future with him should he ask. Before she could say anything, Mr. Collins caught her attention.

Speaking softly so no others could hear, he said, "Miss Elizabeth, this morning I received word from Lady Catherine that I am required to return at the end of the fortnight. It occurred to me after reading her letter that I have not been forthright with you about my intentions. I, as was proper, let it be known to your father and mother that one of the reasons I came to Longbourn was to choose a wife, yet I have not spoken to you of my hopes."

"Mr. Collins," she interrupted, desperately wanting him to go no further.

"Pray allow me the opportunity to speak, my lady, for I prayed for the courage to tell you what is in my heart."

No! No! No! Her stomach suddenly felt like she had eaten the large rock next to the spring at Oakham Mount. The palms of her hands began to perspire. She needed to be kind in her rejection, no matter how nonsensical his words were. He might be an oaf, but she would not be mean.

"Miss Elizabeth, I will confess that my expectations were high before my arrival to Longbourn. Nevertheless, you have exceeded them all. I have witnessed with my own eyes your patience with your younger sisters as you attempt to guide them, the respect you show your mother when she says something silly, and the love you have for your eldest sister and your father." He paused, inhaling deeply. "There was very little affection in my family after the loss of my mother. We were made to work for our keep, despite my father's ability to afford help. My father felt the loss of Longbourn deeply. From my infancy he instilled in me a desire for status. Being in close association with Lady Catherine de Bourgh served to increase my ambitions. However, after watching your family and the way you and your sisters respond to your father's oversight, I realize now that I need to readjust my thinking. It is I who desires to please a lady worthy of being pleased. Therefore, I beg your forgiveness for believing I knew better than you the path to true happiness. Instead of insisting on my way, I ask for your guiding hand to lead us to a future filled with the affection I sorely miss."

What was happening? Elizabeth gulped. *Who was this man and what had he done with Mr. Collins?*

Speaking her thoughts aloud, she said, "In all honesty, I do not know what to say, sir. You have quite taken me by surprise." Glancing at him, she noted genuine concern on his furrowed brow. "Whatever the future holds for each of us, I will recall this moment with pleasure. I thank you, Mr. Collins, for sharing with me the contents of your heart. As for my own feelings, I will confess for your ears alone that confusion reigns supreme. For most of my years, constancy was the order of the day. I could always count on Papa and Mama to evoke a smile, Jane to bring calmness to our daily chaos, and my younger sisters to enliven the day. Except for traveling with my aunt and uncle, little changed in my routine. Yet, for the past ten days since the assembly in Meryton, our lives seem to have been turned upside down."

He nodded. "I agree. Arriving here to discover Mr. Darcy in residence only three miles from Longbourn certainly changed my plans."

His admission confused Elizabeth. "Truly? In what way?"

"In what way, you ask?" Mr. Collins clasped his lapels, his chin lifting in arrogance. "Why, I wait upon him daily in hopes of being of assistance to him. He is the master of a large estate. One day I will also be the master of my own property. His rank secures my humble obeisance in the manner equal to that of my patroness, Lady Catherine de Bourgh. Rather than focusing solely on obtaining joy for my own lifetime, I need to guide him to seek his own happiness with the daughter of my patroness, Lady Catherine de Bourgh. Miss de Bourgh is...well, although there have been some recent challenges, she is a diamond who would grace any man's arm and home."

Elizabeth's mouth gaped open. Where had the gentle man with the lovely words gone? Where she had relaxed with his revelation of his desires, his quick change in attitude rendered her exceedingly uncomfortable.

Leaping to her feet, she took a small step away from him as he too stood.

"Pardon me, Mr. Collins. I need to share a thought with Papa before my sisters take their walk to Meryton."

He bowed. "Certainly, Miss Elizabeth. Until we are betrothed, your father has the first claim upon your time."

She had no intention of remaining behind to argue the point. They were not courting. He had not asked, and she had agreed to nothing with this man. Nor would she ever!

DARCY LOATHED BEING IDLE. Firing off one letter after another, he requested information from his housekeeper about any strangers Georgiana might have brought to Darcy House. He wrote his aunt Helen to determine why his sister was keeping company with...*Blast!* The simple truth was that Georgiana had met Claire *before* she went to Matlock House. That meant that it was under his oversight that she had cultivated a friendship with a stranger.

He wanted to whip himself bloody. What sort of a guardian was he that all this went on under his very nose?

Pulling another sheet of parchment from his writing desk, he penned the next letter to the butler at Rosings Park, a man who delighted in small rebellions against his mistress. Darcy needed to know how long it was since Miss Claire Collins was in Anne's company and when she left for London.

Rubbing his eyes, he wished they could all go back in time to before these events began. But then, he would not have come to Hertfordshire, to Netherfield Park, and to Elizabeth.

* * *

ELIZABETH'S younger sisters burst into the room bringing with them disorder and noise. They had been in Meryton searching out the perfect ribbons to wear that evening for the Guy Fawkes bonfire. Gratefully, Mr. Collins had gone upstairs to write to his patroness—again.

"Lizzy, we saw a lady who could be your twin," Kitty blurted. "She had on a lovely dark green traveling coat with a bonnet I covet. Why, the ostrich feather must have been at least eighteen inches tall."

"You exaggerate, Kitty." Mary, who firmly believed she was always right, added, "It was about ten inches tall. It was not a full foot in length."

"The officers have arrived!" Lydia announced over the top of her sister's voices. "Why, they look fine in their uniforms, finer than Major Gerring. Some of the men are exceedingly handsome. I simply cannot wait to dance with them all." She pranced around the room, humming an unknown melody.

"Captain Carter, with his bright red hair and blue eyes, was dreamy." Kitty's hands were clasped together under her chin. "Mr. Chamberlayne is too short, and Mr. Denny needs to avoid the dessert table. His coat does not fit properly for an officer."

Lydia piped in, "It was Mr. Darcy, Mr. Fitzwilliam Darcy, who outshone them all. What a handsome gentleman with his stately form and charming countenance. His hair! Kitty, did you see the length of his hair? If he had not tied it back, I believe it would be longer than mine! Once he has a uniform, he will be the man every female will want to partner at our next dance. I will tell you right now, he is mine!"

"Mr. Darcy?" Elizabeth asked. She had never heard the surname until the arrival of Mr. Bingley's guest.

"Yes, Mr. Darcy, Mr. Fitzwilliam Darcy." Lydia continued to dance around the room. "He is mine! He is mine! He is mine!" She stopped. "I do not believe he is related to snooty Mr. Darcy at Netherfield Park. Their coloring is fairly similar as is their height. However, *my* Mr. Darcy smiles where the other frowns. Besides, Mr. Bingley's friend's name is probably Archibald or Wilbur, nothing as elegant as Fitzwilliam."

"Officers!" Their mother fanned herself with her handkerchief. "Girls, we will have a wedding at Longbourn chapel before spring or I am not the mistress of Longbourn."

The two youngest giggled. Elizabeth's emotions were still too raw from Mr. Collins' declaration to appreciate her outburst. In the midst of the revelry, she hurried to her father's study.

"Papa, we must let Mr. Darcy know that Miss Collins has arrived."

Her father responded immediately by ordering his cart readied. "Gather your things, Lizzy. You will accompany me."

After almost a se'nnight of not seeing the man, Elizabeth was more than willing to agree. She had no claim to him, nor was she certain she even wanted Mr. Darcy. But the need to be in his presence was stronger than her internal voice of reason.

As the cart bounced over the roadway, Elizabeth told her father about the new Mr. Darcy's arrival in Meryton.

"How can that be?" Her father looked perplexed. "Mr. Fitzwilliam Darcy is at Netherfield Park. For a certainty there cannot be two of them with the same unusual first name."

What! His name was Fitzwilliam? The oddness of these events churned inside of her making chills run up and down her spine. Something unsettling was happening in Meryton, something she feared would impact the residents of Longbourn in a way they could not begin to imagine.

Her father slapped the reins on the back of the pony. Danger lurked around every corner, and it all centered around the man they were journeying to see.

CHAPTER 14

From the expressions on their faces, this was not a social call. Both Mr. Bennet and his daughter were visibly distressed.

Darcy and Major Gerring had excused themselves from their hosts, welcomed the Bennets into Bingley's unused study, then locked the door behind them.

Mr. Bennet got directly to the point. "Claire Hobbs and Claire Collins are one and the same. She has been spotted in Meryton by my younger daughters who all believe that her resemblance to Lizzy is remarkable."

Although he expected Mr. Bennet's comment, Darcy felt each word like a blow to his chest. The realist in him accepted that the conclusions he had reached were sound. Nevertheless, the small fragment of the dreamer inside of him that had hoped this was not truly happening to him died a rapid death at the confirmation.

Mr. Bennet was not yet done. "Additionally, my youngest became acquainted with a Mr. Fitzwilliam Darcy who she described as being similar in coloring and height with a far more pleasant countenance than the one you are currently wearing. According to them, the man's long hair is divine.'"

He was stunned. The pool of anger boiling inside of him threatened to explode from his skull. The only person of his acquaintance who matched this description, including intense pride in his hair, and who had pretended to be him in the past was none other than George Wickham, the same vile man who attempted to elope with Georgiana. *The scoundrel!* This was too much!

Before he could state his conclusion, Major Gerring asked, "Who would have the temerity to pretend to be you, Mr. Darcy?"

Darcy growled in frustration. "George Wickham was the son of my father's steward and my constant companion from my youth on. Where he once was my friend, I have severed all contact with him. He would rather trade upon his looks and charm to keep his pockets jingling than to do a thimble full of hard work." He stood to pace the floor. Speaking aloud his turbulent thoughts, "During university, Wickham assumed my identity to satisfy debtors or to obtain credit. Everywhere he went he left a trail of angry shop owners behind. It caused no end of difficulty for me until I visited each business he frequented to end Wickham's theft. Once my father died, I was no longer responsible for his godson. I refused to provide the man any advantage. He cost Pemberley and the Darcy family enough."

Unclenching his fists, he continued, "For five years I have not heard of a single occasion where Wickham resumed using my identity. Not one merchant has approached me or my man of business to collect overdue funds. Until today, I have not known him to use my name with young ladies. His propensity is the more ignorant of the world that they are, the better and easier for him to ease his way into their chambers. However, the simple truth is that he would do or say anything to get what he wants, of this I have no doubt. He is bold enough to claim to be the Prince Regent should he think a callow young lady would believe him."

His gaze settled on Miss Elizabeth. "I beg your pardon for addressing a delicate subject in front of a lady."

Elizabeth's startled, her head jerking towards him. "That is it! To a lady, delicacy comes in different forms than I suspect it would to a man." She sat forward in her chair. "Gentlemen, what I am about to suggest may appear incredulous, but please bear with me as I attempt to put my thoughts in order." She closed her eyes for a moment. Breathing deeply, she had the full attention of the room, especially Darcy's, once her lids lifted, and she began to speak. "What if Mr. Wickham, pretending to be you, harmed or took advantage of Miss Claire Collins, leaving her in a delicate condition?" She shook her head. "No, it cannot have been her since he approached Kitty and Lydia rather than Jane, who generally attracts the attention of men before anyone else. Your comment, Mr. Darcy, that he prefers to toy with those who are not yet out would be more consistent with approaching the younger sister. What if he fooled Miss Sarah Collins into believing that he was you, that he could supply her with a future beyond her imagination if she would bow to his desires? If he left her in the same condition as some men do, the shame upon the family would be irreparable."

Mr. Bennet rubbed his chin. "Collins did speak of his youngest sister in the past tense, if I recall correctly."

Darcy's mind followed the path the Bennets were traveling. "If Miss Claire Collins only heard my name as the one who compromised and threw away her sister, she would be justifiably angry at the man whom her brother, Lady Catherine, and Anne praised—me."

Elizabeth continued, "As well, it would explain why a lady the same age as me would wear her hair down like a schoolgirl. She is attempting to appear young enough to tempt the man she believes to be you. It would also explain why she would not fear being recognized by you. She has nothing to lose. The damage to the family name is complete."

If their suppositions were correct, all the details were coming together into one picture. Miss Elizabeth was likely correct. Additionally, Darcy was an eyewitness to Wickham being in Kent, specifically at Ramsgate, in July. Mr. Collins had said that his family resided close to there.

"*Confound it all!*" he exclaimed, immediately catching the notice of the others in the room. Dropping into his chair, he said, "What I am about to tell you is not to pass beyond these doors or an innocent will be irreparably harmed." As the major, Mr. Bennet, and Elizabeth nodded, Darcy cleared his throat. "My sister, who was fifteen at the time, was established with a companion in Ramsgate for the summer. At first, I received a letter from her almost daily. They were filled with the delights of a seaside town with quaint shops and an active presence of a few of her friends from school. In mid-July, her letters became few. Fearing she had become despondent for some reason, possibly that her friends had departed Ramsgate, I hastened to Kent only to find that George Wickham, with the help of Georgiana's traitorous companion, had convinced my sister to elope. My arrival the day prior to their departure for Gretna Green brought their plans to a halt. Wickham chose to take his bitter ire at the loss of my sister's dowry out on Georgiana. His words crushed her. Seeing my anger, both he and Mrs. Younge fled. I did not know where they went, nor did I care." Dropping his head into his hands, he continued, "These events place a frustrated George Wickham in the location of the Collins property. He would justify taking out those frustrations on a different young girl to make him feel empowered again. As always, he would toss her aside, completely uncaring if she was carrying the burden of his child or not."

"And this man met my daughters," Mr. Bennet muttered. "Because of her travels, Lizzy knows something of the world, but Jane, Mary, Kitty, and Lydia do not. They have never been confronted with evil, until today." He stood. "You do what you must, Mr. Darcy. I shall return to Longbourn to protect those who are my own. I had not planned to attend the bonfire, but now nothing will keep me away. Not a word about your sister will come from my mouth, nor will Lizzy say anything. Reputations are a fragile treasure that once gone can never be fully restored."

Darcy stood, his mind automatically jumping ahead to what he needed to do to clear up this mess.

"Sir," Miss Elizabeth stepped closer. "My sympathies for your sister are sincere. Her heart will feel the blow when she learns that her new friend is treacherous. However, knowing that there are others who are trustworthy will see her through." She reached up to touch his arm, then dropped her hand before there was contact. "Trials can easily be turned into training with a gentle reminder that discernment, which she will learn from this, is a valued commodity for a lady. Rather unfortunately, the bitter pain of being ill-used again will help her gain maturity far quicker than what she could learn from school or from her peers."

He nodded, unable to formulate a word. His heart was touched, as if she had taken a crumpled cloth and smoothed out the wrinkles.

"I thank you." His appreciation was sincere. Before him stood an intelligent woman with an empathetic heart, one who suffered the pain of others. She was lovely in character and form, lively and joyous, yet serious and temperate when she needed to be. Elizabeth Bennet was...

He gulped. Through all the multitude of developments demanding his attention: the need to protect himself and his sister, the need to learn Miss Collins' motive from her own mouth, and the decision to bring a menace like Wickham to justice, Darcy felt the danger of Miss Elizabeth Bennet. If he was not careful, she would steal his heart without him knowing it was gone.

* * *

LONGBOURN'S RESPONSE was sadly as Elizabeth expected. Jane shook her head in denial that anyone, especially a man in the militia, could be that evil. Mary sermonized. Mr. Collins inserted his opinion that Lady Catherine never would tolerate officers in her home. Kitty and Lydia squealed in delight at an honest to goodness rake being in their midst.

"No officers at Longbourn?" The matron of the house wailed. "How can you be so cruel, Mr. Bennet? Tonight is the bonfire, the night for our girls to sing and dance in hopes of making a match before tomorrow. Your own daughters will starve to death in the freezing cold when you die, leaving us impoverished and without aid if they do not wed one of the officers."

Elizabeth knew the futility of attempting to reason with her mother so she could correctly guide her daughters as a mother should. Glancing at her father, his frustration was clearly written on his face.

"Pray, calm yourself and be seated, the lot of you," her father insisted. So rarely did he stir himself to act like the head of their household, everyone, including Mr. Collins, obeyed.

"Mr. Collins, I believe that *now* would be as good a time as any to write to your patroness." Her father winked at her before continuing. "I imagine her wanting to know that the militia in all their splendor have arrived in Hertfordshire. Likely, she will need to detail exactly how you should act during this invasion to best reflect upon her good name."

Mr. Collins shot to his feet. "Such wisdom! Such

condescension of my Lady Patroness' Cousin, I will pen my letter immediately." Bowing, he left the room.

"There, we are now alone." Her father brushed his hands together like he was removing the evidence of snatching a biscuit from Cook's tin.

"Lydia, tell me what it is that you and Kitty find attractive about knowing that a rogue is in our community?"

In unison, her sisters sighed. "Mr. Darcy is so handsome and charming."

Kitty added, "Lydia insists that he will be hers, but I am just as pretty as she is, plus I am older so I should have him first." Her bottom lip jutted out, rendering her silly and unattractive.

"Have him? For what purpose?" Papa asked with an air of innocent ignorance.

"Why, as my husband, of course," Lydia insisted, sticking her tongue out at Kitty.

"I see," Papa tapped his finger to his chin. "Lydia, did you know that your monthly allowance is almost as much as a militia officer makes? Yet, you cannot buy all that you desire from the funds I give you."

"What do you mean?" she asked. "Mama says that the best husbands are officers. Surely, they could keep a wife in ribbons and new gowns. I will be the most popular wife at all the balls we will attend. I will dance every dance."

"Is that true, my dear?" Papa looked directly at his wife, his eyes piercing. "You who cannot manage to keep within our own budget of two thousand a year, could you dress five daughters in new gowns plus keep a house on a mere twenty-five?"

"Certainly not!"

"Yet you would condemn our daughters to this life of drudgery. An officer's wages in the militia are to cover his expenses and nothing more. There would be no money to pay for the needs of a wife. The wants of a wife and any children who resulted from the marriage would be ignored."

The changing expressions on the faces of her mother and sisters was revealing. Gone was the eager anticipation. Instead, Elizabeth could see the moment her mother realized the full extent of what Papa was saying.

"Mr. Bennet, Longbourn does not have the funds to support the wife of an officer. We would not be able to come to their aid, would we?"

"We could not."

"But, Papa," Lydia wailed, not wanting to give up on her dreams. "With my allowance, I could pay my own way."

He snorted. "My dear girl, the day you say 'I do' in front of a clergyman and sign your name to the register, your allowance ends. My responsibility is done."

As he had done with Mr. Collins, he brushed his hands together before resting them on the arm of his chair.

The facts were cold and hard. Both Kitty and Lydia were having a difficult time accepting this new reality.

Attempting to help them to better understand, Elizabeth said, "The idea of being singled out by a man of the world is exciting, is it not?"

"Oh, yes, Lizzy. It is." Lydia and Kitty both lit up like lanterns with a new wick.

"What happens once the excitement of being chosen is over?" she asked, then continued before they could formulate a reply. "I cannot believe that having a husband with a roving eye would make a good marriage mate."

"No, Lizzy, that is where you are wrong." Kitty boldly claimed. "To be the wife of a man whom all the other ladies want is the height of prestige. Why, it would keep me happy for a lifetime for me to know that from all of them, he chose me."

"That is not sound," inserted their mother. "Rakes continue to choose others after they marry. You will only be exalted by the ignorant, Kitty. Those with any wisdom at all will render you an object of pity as you wallow in your loneliness in some hovel while he polishes his buttons and his boots to spend his evenings with some other female who is attracted to a rogue. No, in this, your father is correct."

"But, Mama," they whined.

"I shall hear no more from either of you."

Frances Bennet put her foot down on her two youngest for the first time in Elizabeth's memory. Hopefully, it was not too little, too late.

Later, finding herself blessedly alone in her chambers, Elizabeth pondered over all she had observed that day. Her parents were managing their youngest, which was a shock to her. Mr. Collins had remained in his rooms for almost an hour, departing only to see his thick letter left in the silver tray at the entrance hall for the post. He had not reached the top of the stairs before returning to the drawing room to announce that the better course would be for him to depart immediately for his home to be by Lady Catherine's side to receive personal instruction about the militia. Within an hour, the pony cart carried him, his thick letter, and his luggage to Meryton to catch the post coach for Kent. If he had not been too late, the parson was already on his way.

Jane remained downstairs should her mother or sisters need her calmness. Mary recited passages from *Fordyce's Sermons for Young Women* to unreceptive ears. With all that was said and done, Elizabeth hoped it was a new beginning for the family, one where cohesion ruled the day instead of chaos.

Then, there was Mr. Darcy. Whatever was she to do about him?

She sighed, playing with the curtain fabric that framed the window seat.

In truth, there was nothing she could do. Ladies had no power to change the course of their own lives. There was nothing they could do to affect the lives of others. Or could they?

If Mr. Darcy approached Miss Collins by himself, his honor would place him in danger for Elizabeth could never see him harming a female. Ever!

Wait! How and why was she certain of this about a man whom she had known for less than a fortnight? What exactly did she know about his character?

For starters, his first name was Fitzwilliam. She giggled. It was an imposing name, much like the man.

Secondly, ... She caught movement out of the corner of her eye. Pushing aside the curtain to get a better view, she sucked in a breath. It was Mr. Darcy approaching from the orchard. Behind him, his beast of a horse was being held by Major Gerring.

What were they...?

Mr. Darcy waved, then pointed down to the room below hers.

Her father's book room.

Waving back, she jumped from the seat to grab her boots, her bonnet, and her spencer. Using the back stairs, she approached her father's sanctuary on stockinged feet.

"Papa, Mr. Darcy needs to see us." Pointing out his window, her Papa hastened to gather his jacket to join her.

CHAPTER 15

"*C*harles, what is this you say? Murder? Who would want Mr. Darcy dead? What has he done?"

Bingley ran his hand through his hair. He never should have repeated what Darcy told him about the reason he had left London. Now, he would never hear the end of it.

"Darcy has done nothing," Bingley insisted, despite not knowing all the details.

Caroline tapped the tip of her finger on her chin. "Hmm, at least as far as you know he has done nothing wrong. I wonder...how might we use this to coerce Mr. Darcy into fulfilling all our dreams by...*Good God!*"

"Caroline, there is no reason to be vulgar," Louisa chirped from where she was seated next to her snoring husband.

Waving away her older sister's words, Caroline dropped into the chair next to Bingley. "Charles, you did say that Colonel Fitzwilliam had sailed off to a battle somewhere, did you not?"

He nodded.

"If whoever this person is were to kill Mr. Darcy, then Georgiana would be alone. To protect her from grasping relatives, you could marry her which would make you the master of the grandest estate in England."

Bingley's first inclination was to reject the thought. However, if someone did do Darcy in, it would be the act of a friend to protect Miss Darcy.

The master of Pemberley. That would finally get Caroline off his back. As well, he would be able to repay the moneylenders who were hounding him. How he wished he had never picked up dice in the first place. The winning streak he started with soon turned into a series of losses. Bingley had thought he could win his money back with a few more games. He had been wrong.

"Major, in a little while we will have our suspicions confirmed or we will be back where we started with nothing in our pockets except unanswered questions."

"Do you believe that to be true, sir?" the major asked.

"Indeed, I do not." Darcy admitted. "My confidence in the identity and guilt of Miss Claire Collins is as high as can be. We only need to confront her with our accusations whereupon she will have no reason to claim innocence."

His horse snorted, pawing the leaves under its hooves as if it sensed the crackle of anticipation in the air. He knew that as soon as he mounted, the horse would be ready to run.

Darcy was as restless as the animal. The desire to see justice served as well as to escape the clutches of a female who was aiming to kill the wrong man, disturbed his peace and his routine. He was the one who was used to being in control of his life, not some emotionally charged stranger.

"YOUR PLAN IS NOT SOUND," Darcy replied in shock at what he was hearing. "You should be at Longbourn preparing for the bonfire tonight, not confronting a dangerous female carrying a gun."

Elizabeth's fists rested on each hip, the point of her chin jutted out, her nostrils flared. "And yours is?"

Ripping his hat from his head, Darcy ran his fingers through his hair until his nails scratched his scalp. She was the stubbornest, most recalcitrant, female who...who had ever crossed paths with him.

"Sir, this lady is my cousin. She is in a public inn belonging to a family I have known since my birth. She has no reason to feel threatened by me." Elizabeth scoffed. "You, on the other hand, have a target on your chest as big as Derbyshire. You most likely represent everything that is wrong with her life. You are the one she is after, not me."

"I am attempting to protect you, Miss Elizabeth." Each word was forced through his clenched teeth. "Were you to remain at Longbourn, the three of us men will scour Meryton until we find her knowing you are safe at home."

Elizabeth gritted her teeth. "Do tell, Mr. Darcy, what

will you do once you do find her? It would create a multitude of questions should you, a single man possessed of a
fortune, seek out the company of a young lady who is
undoubtedly traveling alone—with a pistol—aimed at
you. How will you convince her to reveal her motives?
Will you demand she tell you?" Miss Elizabeth
harrumphed. "I cannot see you having any success at all."

He huffed, pacing back and forth in front of her. "I do
not like this." She was most likely correct in her observation. His intention was to charge into the village cloaked
with the full authority of Darcy of Pemberley to insist
Miss Collins reveal everything about her plan. Rubbing
his jaw, he looked to Mr. Bennet for assistance in
reasoning with his child. The older man leaned against
the trunk of a tree with his arms crossed. The slight lift of
his shoulders into what appeared to be a shrug convinced
Darcy that he would receive no help from that quarter.
Major Gerring had his back to them, pretending he could
not hear every word.

Miss Elizabeth unclenched her fists. Gazing into the
distance she sighed, then she clarified, "My goal is not to
interfere, nor is it some mission to prove to you
gentlemen how brave I am. I am not seeking to thrust
myself upon your business for gossip to later share with
the ladies of our community."

"I did not suggest that you would." Darcy growled.

"Mr. Darcy, I offer you my word that I will quickly
retreat to safety should the situation become volatile." Her
small hands stretched towards him; palms turned to the
sky. "Sir, I will offer you this—if your purpose is to
confront Miss Collins with your pistols blazing, then I

J. DAWN KING

will gladly remain at Longbourn. However, if it is information that you want before you enact whatever justice is on your mind, you will need my help."

He barely kept from stomping his foot. "I am not a violent man, nor have I ever been. Never would I harm a female be she a queen or a rag-picker." He was astounded that she assumed he would hurt anyone. *Blast it all!* Was not the fact that Wickham still lived enough evidence that he was not a vicious man?

"I cannot...," she began when her father interrupted.

"The air is beginning to chill. If you two remain in a stalemate much longer I believe winter will arrive and my breath will freeze. Mrs. Bennet would give each of you a piece of her mind should I come to harm before she settles the future of all five of our daughters so she can live in comfort the rest of her days. I would hate to be standing here waiting for you both to agree when I welcome my first grandchild from one of my other daughters who will have had time to find a husband, be courted by him, and marry. Therefore, I offer this suggestion," he dropped his arms and approached. "I see wisdom in the paths each of you have chosen. I also see the danger. If I have not lost my perceptive powers, knowing the reason behind Miss Collins actions is primary, am I right?"

He waited until Darcy finally nodded before continuing. "I shall accompany Lizzy inside the inn. We will seek an interview with my young cousin. The two of you will remain hidden in an adjoining room or outside. Once my daughter and I learn why Miss Collins has traveled to Hertfordshire, we will remove ourselves promptly."

Although Darcy did not like it, he was forced to agree that this probably was the best course.

* * *

ELIZABETH and her father were greeted by the innkeeper.

"Say Bennet, I did not know until today that Miss Lizzy has a twin. Had I not seen all your babes grow from birth 'til now, I would've mistaken her for one of yours."

"She is here then?" Her father inquired.

The innkeeper pointed down the hall. "Second door on the left. Quiet one, that."

Mr. Darcy and the major retraced their steps out the front door. They would approach the hallway from the back of the inn, staying out of sight of Miss Collins. Her father clasped Elizabeth's hand in his. "All will be well, Lizzy, if we keep an eye out for danger. Do not be afraid to run."

She nodded, her heart pounding. They approached the entrance to the hall. From where they were standing, they could see that the second door was closed.

The four of them were in position when Charlotte walked into the inn.

"Thank you, dear friend, for coming." Elizabeth could see the effort Charlotte made to walk without limping. Her face paled. Her breathing was labored.

"It was easy for me to get away. Everyone is so busy that no one noticed." Charlotte added, "Father has the bonfire lit already and John is setting up the fireworks show. As many as he brought to Lucas Lodge, the display

161

should last all night." Shifting her weight to her uninjured leg, she said, "Let us proceed."

Charlotte's calm and reason could tame Elizabeth when she was emotionally charged. If Claire Collins was like her in more than looks, Charlotte's skills would be needed.

"Major Gerring and Mr. Darcy are already in the room next to where Miss Collins is enjoying tea. Papa will join us." Elizabeth whispered, although the common room was sparsely populated with only two men at the counter sipping ale. It would be hours before another post coach arrived with more passengers. The one containing Mr. Collins must have departed for Kent on time.

Nodding, Charlotte followed closely behind her toward the door.

At her father's knock, a lady called for them to enter.

"The pot has run dry," the lady observed without turning to face them. Instead, she flicked the curtain back from the window, peering outside.

"I shall see it filled, Miss Hobbs," Papa answered. He had asked the innkeeper upon their entry about their guest. Claire Collins was using her mother's name as she had done in London.

"I thank you." She flicked her fingers to hurry him on his task. When the door did not close behind him, the lady finally turned to face them.

The expression on her face surely mirrored Elizabeth's own. Mouth agape and eyes wide, Elizabeth stared at the person who looked as much like her as she did. When her sisters told her they had seen her twin, she had assumed there would be a family resemblance. This level of similarity was unbelievable.

"Who are you?" Miss Collins demanded, her hand flying to her chest. "Do I know you?"

"At the moment you do not," Elizabeth answered, unsettled by the similarity. "Nonetheless, I do hope we can repair the lapse with a bit of conversation."

Papa bowed as Elizabeth curtseyed. Charlotte merely tipped her head.

"Miss Hobbs, my name is Thomas Bennet. I am the master of Longbourn."

Elizabeth observed the young lady closely as her father mentioned the name of their estate. Miss Collins almost leapt from her skin.

"Longbourn," she snarled.

"Yes." He bowed again. "I am delighted to meet you as will my family be happy to know you are here."

"You are?" The lady was hesitant in her inquiry.

"Indeed." He gestured to the chairs before glancing at Charlotte. "Our neighbor, Miss Lucas, was told by her brother that my daughter has a twin staying at the inn. Charlotte was anxious to be introduced to you. Elizabeth and I hurried to meet you, dear girl."

"Dear girl?" She looked upon the master of Longbourn with doubt. Then she glanced toward the ladies. "Elizabeth. You are my cousin, then?"

"I am," she answered.

Eyes sweeping the room as the ladies moved to the chairs, Elizabeth noted that there was no maid. Miss Collins was alone. Additionally, not only was the teapot empty, but the plate that held bread and meat had not a crumb left behind. The lady was short on funds since a full meal had not been ordered.

Offering a hesitant smile, Elizabeth suggested, "Papa, mightn't you obtain refreshments while the three of us ladies become better acquainted?"

He hesitated, then agreed. Once he left the room, Elizabeth took the lead in the conversation.

"Rather than delicately speaking of the roads or the weather, let us establish a beginning for us." Elizabeth suggested.

Miss Collins was on the edge of her seat, as if she was prepared to run or launch herself across the small table at Elizabeth.

Lifting her chin, Elizabeth boldly pressed her point. "You should know that I care not what our ancestors squabbled over in the past. Family is very important to me. Therefore, pray allow me to tell you that four out of five of my sisters look like golden angels. As the only Bennet girl with dark hair and eyes, I can safely say that the color looks far better on you than it does on me."

Miss Collins' first reaction was surprise. Then she snorted inelegantly. "I will say exactly the same of you, Miss Bennet."

"Pray, call me Elizabeth or Lizzy as do those who are close to me." She smiled at her cousin. "What shall we call you?"

After a slight hesitation, she replied, "Claire. I am Claire Hobbs Collins."

This confirmation of her identity was key. The lady's purpose was not to assume a different persona or to hide who she was. This would make matters less complicated.

Charlotte, as Elizabeth fully expected, attempted to put Miss Collins fully at ease.

"Lizzy was raised as a gentleman's daughter; however, I was not. My father owned a business in Meryton and was content to do so for most of my youth. Elizabeth is not one to judge a person based on their background, Miss Collins. Neither am I." The calm on Charlotte's face inspired trust. "I mean no criticism at all when I suggest that you appear to be traveling alone. Are you in distress, Miss Collins? Is there some way that we may be of assistance?" Charlotte tipped her head to the side and smiled. "Once you are settled and comfortable, you will understand that you are wanted here."

The lady gulped, her fingers gripping together so tightly that her knuckles were white. "I can't...I cannot understand." She looked at Elizabeth. "You are..."

"The dreaded Bennets of Longbourn? Thieves of one of the largest estates in Hertfordshire?" Elizabeth commiserated. "Is that close to what you probably have heard your whole life?"

With a smirk, Miss Collins admitted the truth of the statement.

"Claire, I meant what I said about the feud. Nevertheless, while it is not of importance to me, your viewpoint must be quite different. Had your grandfather, then your father inherited my home, your circumstances in life would have been different, as would mine."

Miss Collins' gaze dropped to the floor as she chewed on her thumbnail. Glancing up at Elizabeth, she said in hushed tones, "If only things were different."

"How?" Elizabeth boldly asked, all humor gone. "Please

share with me how your life would have been different, Claire."

"You would never understand in a million years." Miss Collins shook her head, her tone laced with bitterness. "My life is so far removed from Longbourn as the earth is from the moon."

Charlotte piped in, "But it is not different from mine." Sitting back in her chair, Charlotte never took her eyes away from Elizabeth's cousin. "The eldest son in our house is six years younger than I am. Yet, because he is a male, any wisdom I have gained from my education or additional years is ignored. Because I am female, I am ignored. Even when I see how a decision my father and brother make will result in harm for themselves or the family, I am ignored. In the ridiculous future they have planned for my younger sister Maria, who is but fifteen, I am ignored." Charlotte leaned closer to Miss Collins. "Tell me, is your situation not the same as mine?"

"It is strikingly similar." Miss Collins closed her eyes, her lips pressed tightly together. Once she regained control, she began to speak. "There was no room in my Father's thoughts for anything other than the unfairness of him not inheriting Longbourn. I grew to hate the mention of that place." She spat out the name like it was revolting medicine. "He gave no consideration to the future of me or my sister since he was constantly burrowed in the past. My only brother, who is the eldest, is a stupid fool. Like our father, he sets his mind on a course and will not bend, even if it is proven beyond measure how unreasonable his decision is. He cares for his happiness and his alone. Thus, it was left to me to look after myself and Sarah. Not knowing much of the world, I did the best that I could. However, my best was not nearly good enough."

Miss Collins did nothing to contain her angry tears. Instead, she continued, "I thought I was free when my father died only to discover how much my brother coveted the authority of being the lone male." Her gaze focused on Elizabeth. "I hope you never know how little a female is valued by a selfish man who insists on a standard of perfection for his sisters that is both unreasonable and impossible."

"I am sorry." Elizabeth meant each word.

"I suppose you are." Swiping the moisture from her cheeks, Miss Collins said, "I have a mission. Once that is complete, I will finally have peace." She shook her head. "I will do anything, become anything or anyone, to see it done."

"Can we help?" Charlotte asked.

To Elizabeth's frustration, her cousin immediately replied, "You cannot."

Claire stood, "I thank you ladies for seeking me out. For me, it is good to know I have family of whom I can be proud." Her smile was slight. "I must attend to my business for I do not intend to remain long in Meryton. Before you ask, I have no interest in seeing Longbourn. If I never hear that name again in my lifetime, I will be satisfied."

"Your brother was at Longbourn until he left for Kent earlier today," Elizabeth stated, curious how Miss Collins would react. It was like pouring gunpowder on a blazing fire.

Her cousin's face paled, then turned beet red. Elizabeth would not have been surprised had her hair stood on end.

"I have no brother," she spat out each syllable. Stepping back from them, her frantic movements signaling an end to their conversation.

Charlotte attempted to put out the fire by calmly asking, "May we help you?"

Claire Hobbs Collins stopped pacing, turned, and faced them with such a look of agony in her eyes that Elizabeth stepped back.

"If you truly want to assist me, then you will leave me alone," Miss Collins snapped, turning her back on them.

They were not wanted. Nevertheless, she could not leave the room without some form of confirmation of the lady's plans.

Into the silence Elizabeth asked, "Are you looking for someone?"

Miss Collins spun back around; the appearance of haughty belligerence was the same as what Lydia Bennet frequently wore when she was told, 'No!' There would be no reasoning with her cousin.

With slow deliberation, Miss Collins replied, "I am looking for someone I was told had arrived recently. Perhaps you have met him. He is tall, reputedly wealthy and handsome, and universally charming. Yet, underneath his fine clothing beats a heart as evil as a viper. His name is Mr. Fitzwilliam Darcy. Until now, I have taunted him so he knew the fear I lived with during the past few months. Now, I am ready for this to end. When I find him, I will kill him."

CHAPTER 16

As soon as Mr. Bennet left the ladies to order a meal for his cousin, he joined Darcy and the major in the adjoining room. Through the thin walls of the inn, Darcy and the other two men heard almost everything.

"She does not look like a blood-thirsty killer," Mr. Bennet observed when he first arrived.

After a long stretch of eavesdropping, Major Gerring noted, "No, she does not. She sounds like someone with nothing to lose."

Darcy was torn. His inclination to burst into the room demanding an explanation for why she hunted him like a deer would not have worked. Miss Elizabeth was correct. Her asking Miss Lucas to accompany her was the course of wisdom.

"What do you do now?" Mr. Bennet asked. "I cannot take the lady to Longbourn since I will not expose my family to her wrath."

"I would not suggest that you offer her hospitality,

family or not." Darcy knew what could happen to a household to have a snake let loose. The victims would be numerous. "She is dangerous."

"I do not believe she would harm anyone physically since we are not her target. If she is like her brother who attempted to berate Lizzy..."

"What!" Darcy was instantly livid. "How dare he speak to Miss Elizabeth in anything other than deference! What has he done?"

"Hush!" Major Gerring hissed. "The tone of their conversation has changed."

Darcy set aside his ire at the parson to listen. Should there be a need, the three men could bust through the door with little effort.

When Miss Elizabeth asked, "Are you looking for someone?" Darcy held his breath. Just as Miss Collins began her reply, raucous giggling was heard from the taproom, followed by the bellows of men bent on teasing flirtation.

"Blast and damnation!" Mr. Bennet's reaction to the disruption was unexpected. With an angry growl, he threw open the door at the same time that Miss Elizabeth threw open hers. The three ladies followed a stomping Mr. Bennet down the hallway. "Kitty and Lydia, what in God's good name are you doing away from Longbourn?" he roared.

Darcy's stomach churned. Miss Lucas might have been able to overlook the childish behavior of the two Bennet misfits, but their silliness had placed them in the middle of a perilous situation. The female who most wanted him dead had followed Elizabeth out of the room and was standing between Darcy and the Bennets. Fortunately, her back was to him and the major where they remained in the hallway.

"Papa, Lizzy, Charlotte, what are you doing here?" The one called Kitty asked. "We thought you were still at Longbourn."

"Obviously." Mr. Bennet pressed into the circle of officers surrounding his youngest, grabbed both girls by their arms and pulled. "You will come with me now."

"But, Papa," Lydia whined. "You said such mean things about this Mr. Darcy that I simply could not believe it to be true. Of the other Mr. Darcy, the sour one, I would have no difficulty in believing your charges." She purred, petting the arm of one of the officer's whose back was facing them. "This Mr. Darcy is such a charming gentleman."

The chaos that took place at the mention of his name almost shook the room.

From behind Mr. Bennet, Darcy saw Miss Elizabeth and Miss Lucas startle. Miss Collins stepped back then reached into the pocket of her coat, pulled out a small pistol which she had hidden in her skirt. The major moved directly behind her. Darcy would have given anything to have seen the expression on her face. The officers promptly began to defend one of their own.

"Lizzy, Charlotte, take these children home," Mr. Bennet barked. He looked around, saw Mr. Bingley and Mr. Hurst at one of the tables and commanded, "Gentlemen, would you escort these silly girls to Longbourn."

Bingley jumped up from the table, eager to please. "Certainly, sir. It will be our pleasure."

"But Papa," the younger girls pleaded to no effect. Miss Elizabeth and Charlotte grabbed their arms just as firmly as Mr. Bennet had done and pulled them toward where Bingley and Hurst were now standing. That left only Miss Collins and Mr. Bennet standing between Darcy and the officers.

Finally, the one who called himself Mr. Darcy turned to face the angry father, flicking his chin to the side so his hair splayed out behind him—a practiced move.

"Mr. Darcy, save me," Miss Lydia Bennet pleaded.

Wickham's eyes darted to the girl before he spoke. "You are mistaken, Miss Lydia. I did not say my name was Darcy."

Egad! The slime coming off Wickham would have made a slug proud. The man was entirely bereft of morals.

"Yes, you did," claimed the youngest Bennet, her bottom lip sticking out in an unattractive pout. "You told me yourself that you are Fitzwilliam Darcy of Pemberley. I heard you. Kitty heard you, too."

"He is *not* Mr. Fitzwilliam Darcy of Pemberley since the man himself is currently staying at Netherfield Park." Mr. Bennet stated in no uncertain terms.

"No, Papa. I believe our Mr. Darcy and Mr. Bingley's friend are cousins or something," Miss Kitty reasoned.

"Mr. Darcy is in Hertfordshire?" Wickham paled and sputtered. "Then, you truly must have misheard me, Miss Lydia, for I recall telling you my name was Fitzwickham of Pemberley. My father was Mr. Darcy's steward."

Darcy wanted to laugh when Wickham's eyes drifted from Miss Lydia to survey the room. When he saw Darcy within hearing distance, his countenance went from the confidence of knowing how to soothe an outraged parent to fear of being held accountable for his actions.

Slapping his forehead, he chortled, beads of sweat popping up on his upper lip. "How could I be so foolish? I said that wrong. My name is and has always been Mr. George Wickham, son of Mr. Samuel Wickham, Pemberley's former steward."

Miss Collins spun around to see who was behind her. Immediately, she pointed her weapon at him. "You! I want you dead!"

Darcy raised his hands into the air.

Miss Elizabeth deliberately rushed at her cousin, bumping her shooting arm hard enough that the lady lost her balance. As both of them flailed to remain upright, Elizabeth clasped her arms around Miss Collins' waist, capturing her firing arm in her grip. The major pulled the pistol from her fingers.

"You have the wrong Mr. Darcy, Claire, and I can prove it." Elizabeth's voice easily carried above the furor.

Regaining her footing, Miss Collins looked directly at Darcy.

"Not me, Miss Collins. It is him you are after." Tilting his head towards Wickham, his heart pounding. "I can explain."

Lydia Bennet guffawed, "Isn't this a hoot! We have two ladies who look like twins and two men claiming to be the same gent. What fun! Isn't it fun, Kitty?"

Miss Elizabeth spun towards her sisters. "Shut up, Lydia. You know nothing."

With the murderous look of confusion on Miss Collins' face, fear on the now cowering Wickham, righteous indignation on Mr. Bennet and Miss Elizabeth, and pain flickering across Miss Lucas' countenance from standing too long, Darcy was outraged.

Claire Collins' eyes moved back and forth between Wickham and Darcy.

Darcy stated, "In the past five years, I have spent a total of three hours at Ramsgate with the sole purpose of retrieving my young sister and returning her home. I have receipts in my possession for purchases made by George Wickham when he pretended to be me in the past for the purpose of gaining credit for a lifestyle he cannot afford. As well, he spent the summer in that part of Kent. Of this I also can offer proof."

The lady nodded, then focused solely on Wickham. Darcy felt inclined to step back. He would not be surprised if lightning bolts shot from her dark eyes.

Major Gerring stepped closer to her. Whispering something in her ear, the lady nodded without taking her eyes off Wickham.

"There now," Wickham sighed in relief when she looked away from him. "This slight misunderstanding can be cleared up in no time." Signaling the innkeeper, he ordered a round for the room.

Mr. Bennet growled again before retrieving Kitty and Lydia from Bingley, herding his complaining youngest girls toward the door.

"No, Papa," Lydia wailed. "We simply must see that Mr. Darcy/Fitzwickham/Wickham is safe." She dug in her heels and splayed her arms to keep from going through the door.

Miss Elizabeth urged her cousin, "Be cautious, Miss Collins, I beg you."

Miss Collins stepped away from Miss Elizabeth and rushed past Mr. Darcy to the room she had occupied, slamming the door behind her.

Facing the man who had cost him an abundance, Darcy wondered how someone with so much potential could have become such a wastrel. A quick list of Wickham's crimes against the Darcy family popped into his mind. Perhaps Miss Collins had the right idea. Wickham needed to be stopped.

"This is the last time you will take advantage of my name, Wickham." Darcy kept his voice calm, although he was raging inside. "You will find that I am done making excuses for you. The pain and misery you leave behind you is over. I will see that you finally pay for your crimes."

"Are you threatening me?" Wickham boldly sneered. "You never have done anything before. Why should I believe you now?" He had the temerity to laugh in Darcy's face.

"Consider yourself warned." Darcy knew how to act. In a leather pouch in his bed chamber was a stack of debts Wickham left behind from university. Darcy's man of business had paid them all, collecting proof of the rogue's profligacy. It was time to call in those debts. Wickham would be in Marshalsea, a greedy man's worst nightmare, before the morrow.

* * *

"Papa, I cannot think that it was wise to leave Claire alone." Worry flooded Elizabeth.

"You are afraid for her, then?" her father asked.

Before they stepped out of the inn, he offered to help Charlotte to climb up to the seat of her pony cart. Like Kitty and Lydia, Charlotte had no intention of leaving. Eventually, Mr. Bingley and Mr. Hurst helped two whiny girls into their carriage after her father forcefully dragged them to the conveyance. Bingley joined the driver in the front and Hurst stood in the back where a footman usually rode. Kitty and Lydia could be heard complaining until the carriage turned the corner. Elizabeth, her father, and Charlotte let themselves back inside.

Mr. Darcy and the major walked down the hall, stopping before Claire's door.

Elizabeth, watching the men, said, "I cannot help but be worried. She has set a course to destroy Mr. Darcy only to discover that she has been after the wrong man. I cannot begin to imagine the fear and confusion she is feeling."

"I suppose you are correct," her papa mused. "However, I will not sacrifice the health and safety of any of my daughters for another, not even a vulnerable, misguided cousin. Unfortunately, the first time she fired upon Mr. Darcy, she set her course. The penalty should she ever go to trial is severe. If Mr. Darcy has a mind to see her charged with attempted murder, there would be nothing that anyone could do to save her." He snorted. "Speaking of Mr. Darcy, that fool of a man tossed a coin to the innkeeper to care for her every comfort as soon as she left the room. She will have a maid to see to her needs, plus the best food and drink the inn has to offer."

Was that not like the man? Her heart swelled at the thought. Elizabeth was confident that Mr. Darcy would never bring harm to Claire Collins. Not only had he told Elizabeth that he would never hurt a female, but the man had also shown in his treatment of her and now with her cousin that his words were true. He was a man of honor. He spoke the truth as he saw it and acted accordingly.

Her brain froze on that thought.

Yet, despite her thinking of Claire, it was not the lady's safety and health that was concerning her. It was Mr. Darcy's. Surely, being in the same room with the lady who had fired bullets at him in addition to the miscreant who had tried to ruin his beloved sister was enough to cause a man to act wildly. Should something happen to him...well, Elizabeth, well...she...she cared for him.

Admitting that to herself was *hard.* He was a man who stirred deep emotions within her, whether it was loathing or love. Love? *By all that was good and holy!* Love? Where had that idea come from? Was she in love with Mr. Darcy? What a horrifyingly terrible thought.

"Charles," Caroline drew out his name, alerting him that she wanted him to do something that would benefit her personally. From where she stood, the light from the moon shining through the window shone at her back, giving her the appearance of being an avenging angel. At times, she scared Bingley. "I have an idea," she intimated.

"I will not attempt to get Darcy to marry you, Caroline. He has said he will not, and I will not try to force him." Charles knew exactly where every advantage he and his family had received during the past five years originated—with Fitzwilliam Darcy. He would do nothing to endanger his association.

"You have been a wonderful friend to Mr. Darcy." Caroline brushed her fingers over the back of the chair directly opposite from him, her head tipped to the side. "I wonder if you would be a wonderful brother to me."

"What do you want, Caroline? I will not take you back to London if that is what you are after," Bingley insisted.

"No, not at all." She came around and took a seat. "I was merely thinking about this situation in which Mr. Darcy finds himself. You reported that a lady arrived in Meryton with the goal of killing him." She quivered dramatically. "Additionally, this Mr. Wickham, who you say is a rake, was practically threatened by Mr. Darcy. Am I correct so far?"

Bingley, wondering where she was going with her line of inquiry, admitted, "You are."

Caroline continued, "He has become quite friendly with the Bennets. What do you suppose will happen if he keeps going to Longbourn? Why, I believe one of those vile girls, probably Eliza, will sink their claws into him and he will never escape. What will become of us then? I cannot imagine Eliza Bennet would allow us access to Pemberley even if you were to wed her sister. Why, the only way to guarantee the freedom to stay would be to marry dear Georgiana."

"Georgiana!" Bingley shook his head. "This is the

second time you have mentioned the possibility of me marrying her. She is a lovely girl, but marry her? She is but sixteen, I believe."

"Do think, brother. If something were to happen to the lady at the inn or Mr. Wickham, all fingers would point to Mr. Darcy as being guilty. If he were tried by a judge, he would likely never return to Pemberley again. Who would the new master be? Why, the husband of Georgiana Darcy. With Colonel Fitzwilliam away and Mr. Darcy possibly going to the gallows or being transported, the dear girl would be at the mercy of fortune hunters. It would be a kindness to Darcy should you marry her, Charles."

It made sense. Jane Bennet was a lovely lady, but she would bring little to a marriage. Georgiana Darcy would be one of the wealthiest females in England if she inherited the Darcy fortune. She would need a man to guide her, and he could then afford the life he longed to have, the life his father wanted for him.

"Caroline, to think of Darcy being harmed and Miss Darcy being alone is untenable. However, having my debts paid, being free of those ruffians who keep hounding me for more money, and the interest they charge me...well. I was winning. I only needed one good toss of the dice." He flinched, his hand twitching like it was still holding the gaming pieces. "I have relived that round of play a million times, even in my sleep," Bingley closed his eyes and laid his head back on his chair. "I was trying to keep up with Darcy, having his tailor make my clothes, joining the clubs he attended, and even purchasing a town coach like his. I tell you, it is impossible!"

"Shame on Mr. Darcy for the hardship he has created for you, dear brother." Caroline was full of sympathy. "He needs to suffer some of the consequences for holding such high expectations of you." She changed her course. "Think of the future. Think of the welcome we will receive in the best houses of London once you are the master of Pemberley. No debts, no worries."

It was easy to imagine himself climbing the front steps of Pemberley with an air of confidence. The housekeeper would welcome him. The butler would see to his every need. People from the highest levels of society would beg for his company. He would be sought after more than a new debutante with a fortune.

Mr. Charles and Mrs. Georgiana Bingley. It had a nice ring to it.

"However," Caroline's voice burst rudely into his dreams. "We will never have Pemberley if Mr. Darcy is found to be innocent. Why, he might walk away from this awful evening as a free man whereupon he would marry Eliza Bennet. We would forever be shifted off to the side, always begging for entrance to Pemberley and never being received there again."

Bingley knew he was not the smartest man in the world but even he could see that his sister was correct. "What can we do about it?"

Gilbert Hurst interrupted the conversation. "The only way would be to make certain that Darcy was charged."

"With what?" Bingley asked, not completely following what was being said.

"With murder," Hurst bluntly replied.

"But nobody has died." Bingley did not like the turn the conversation had taken.

"Yet." Hurst stood from the sofa where he had been napping to join them. His wife remained behind, playing with her bracelets. "Through you, Bingley, we have had a taste of the life we want, the life we deserve. If we choose to take the next step of guaranteeing Darcy is permanently removed from society, we can have it all."

Bingley hesitated. "Someone would have to kill either the lady, Wickham, or Darcy. I could never hurt anyone."

Caroline scoffed. "Firing a gun in the dark would be no different than shooting those adorable little quail that fill the coveys. You have no trouble with that, Charles. If you want Pemberley, this is the only way."

He gulped. He did want Pemberley, but framing Darcy for murder? Or killing him? He could not do it.

"Charles," she purred like a satisfied, fat cat. "As I said, you would be doing Mr. Darcy a tremendous favor if you got rid of those two who threatened him at the inn."

He sat up. "I suppose I would, wouldn't I?"

"There is no real inconvenience to anyone to have the girl and Mr. Wickham gone, am I not correct?"

"You are." Bingley agreed. "But to have Darcy accused of murder? He will not like that."

"Oh, Charles, it is nothing with which Mr. Darcy cannot easily cope. Why, I am sure he has been accused of worse over the years. Do not worry, I know what I am about."

"You had better be sure, Caroline, or we would be the

ones in trouble." Bingley asserted, concerned at the way his sister's mind worked.

Hurst rubbed his belly. "Don't you worry about a thing, Brother. We will each have a weapon. I will be the only one who needs to fire."

"The shots will be heard, Hurst." Bingley reasoned.

"It is Guy Fawkes tonight. You said Lucas promised a grand fireworks show, am I right?"

"As long as I do not have to kill anyone," Bingley murmured to himself. "Darcy cannot know anything."

"You deserve this, Charles," Caroline pronounced.

After a long pause, he said, "I do, do I not?" By his agreement, he firmly set his course.

"For Pemberley!" Caroline hissed loudly.

"For Pemberley!" the three others responded.

Before many minutes passed, a plan was developed, how to get Miss Collins and Mr. Wickham away from the inn, what to do with the bodies, and how to guarantee that Darcy would be the guilty party.

"The town will be empty as will all the houses since everyone will be at the Guy Fawkes bonfire," Hurst offered. "No one will see us," he promised.

CHAPTER 17

*I*nhaling slowly to calm himself, Darcy tapped on the door. Before Miss Collins could bid them to enter, he was joined by Mr. Bennet, his daughter, and her friend. Instead of allowing Elizabeth to walk through the door first, Darcy stepped inside, followed by the others.

Miss Collins was at the window, her back to them. She said, "I have been foolish, but I am not a fool." Her cheeks were tear stained. Her fingers were twisted together. Her breathing was shallow. Her eyes sparked determination. "I am aware of the consequences of my actions. Should you allow me to walk away from this room I will hunt that man down and kill him for what he has done."

"What has he done?" Darcy asked, softening his tone. She looked like a threatened doe ready to bolt away from suspected danger.

Swiping the tears from her cheeks, she glanced at Elizabeth and Miss Lucas. "You both treated me with kindness, something of which I know little. To tell my sordid tale is to repay your goodness with the sort of badness that ladies should never hear. Yet, ignorance of that evil is what cost me the life of my sister. You both have sisters of your own to protect so prepare yourselves."

Darcy glanced to where the two ladies were standing together. Recalling Miss Lucas' injury, he asked if they would make themselves comfortable. At Miss Collins' nod, the major helped Miss Lucas to a chair. Elizabeth stood between her father and himself, exactly where Darcy wanted her to be.

"By July of this year, my brother was established at Hunsford with Lady Catherine. The small property he inherited was run into the ground by his lazy insistence that as master, he was required only to oversee matters rather than do any work. Sarah and I toiled from morning to dusk but nothing we did was good enough or provided enough. The ground is rocky, and the trees were stunted from the wind. The vegetables from our small garden and a few pear trees in the field put a meager amount of food on the table. With my brother using the rent from the two parcels the tenants worked to purchase books he never read, there was nothing to use to pay for help."

Pausing to study her audience, she continued. "When the tourists came to Ramsgate at the beginning of summer, I began working in one of the shops that sold delicacies to the visitors. Sarah, who was painfully timid, remained home alone. I worked through mid-August until I came home to my sister casting up her accounts. Afraid that she had caught something horrible, I asked the apothecary to stop by. He confirmed that Sarah had allowed..." She covered her eyes with her hands, bent at her middle, and groaned.

"He told her that his name was Mr. Darcy. Mr. Fitzwilliam Darcy, the nephew of Lady Catherine de Bourgh. He promised Sarah that he would marry her and take her to the most beautiful place in England, Pemberley. She, in her innocence, believed he was sincere." Miss Collins scoffed. "When the apothecary contacted my brother, the good Christian that he is, threw us from the only home we had ever known. The few coins I had saved from my employment allowed me to rent a cheap room where the two of us stayed until it was over for Sarah." Running her hands down the sides of her skirt, she closed her eyes, breathing slowly in and out. Standing taller, she looked directly at him. "I vowed over her unmarked grave to find Mr. Darcy and make him pay. I wanted him to know fear, the same emotion that ruled me the minute Sarah took her final breath. I wanted him to worry when death would come to him unexpectedly. And I wanted him to know that there was an accountability to his actions and that it was time he paid."

The silence when she finished was thick enough to cut with a blade. Stepping away from his side, Elizabeth approached her cousin, wrapped her arms around Miss Collins and said loud enough for all to hear, "I would have done the same."

Mr. Bennet gasped. Miss Lucas nodded. The major shook his head.

Darcy's knees began to shake. Of all this, he was most

at fault. Had he put a stop to Wickham's machinations when they were at university or had he revealed the true character of George Wickham to his father, possibly the rogue could have been made to learn the humble truth of his position and worth. Instead, by allowing him to feel entitled and freely prey on others, Darcy was culpable. He, who knew what sort of person Wickham was, did nothing to stop his loathsome course.

He tasted bile at the back of his throat.

Elizabeth began speaking. He could hardly discern the words over the sound of his own blood coursing through his veins.

"Claire, pray listen. Let us discuss your future, where you go from here."

"Future?" She tried to step back from her cousin. "I have no future."

Elizabeth refused to let her go. "I will not pretend that your situation is not dire. However, you have the ear of three highly intelligent men, two of whom have daughters and a sister who are dependent upon their care. They understand the vulnerability of a lady with no one to protect her. Allow us to discuss what might be done, I pray you."

Miss Collins' eyes slowly moved to each individual in the room. "Very well."

In his heart Darcy knew that this was his opportunity to redeem himself.

"Miss Collins, until this moment, the only crime you have committed was against me. Other than a hole in my hat and my carriage, I have suffered only in wondering why you intended me harm. Should I not press the charge of attempted murder, then the law will know nothing." Darcy pondered before adding, "However, you cannot remain on English soil. I would not have been the only person who saw you the day you fired upon me in London. Should you wish a fresh start, I will see that you have safe travel to Plymouth where passage can be obtained to either Canada or the Americas with enough funds for you to settle into the future of your choice, if this is agreeable." He raised his hand before she could reply. "But know this, Miss Collins, I will guarantee that George Wickham finally pays for his misdeeds. As I said in the public room, I am done with him."

Elizabeth released her cousin and turned toward him. Her magnificent eyes were filled with warmth and joy. He vowed to himself right then to do everything within his power to earn her good opinion. He had not set forward this path to freedom for Miss Collins alone. Rather, it was for himself and for Elizabeth that they would not have either Miss Collins or Wickham's actions come between them. He needed to sweep the garbage from his own front porch, and it began with Wickham.

Gratefully, Miss Collins accepted the offer. With tears and the promise to see her on the morrow, the Bennets and Miss Lucas left for their homes. He walked outside the inn with the major.

* * *

DARCY TURNED TOWARD MAJOR GERRING. "Come. We have an interview with Colonel Forster before he leaves for

Lucas Lodge." Darcy ordered as if he were Colonel Richard Fitzwilliam himself.

If Wickham had already enlisted, there was an authority he answered to above the law. Interestingly, joining the army during the war with France had become competitive. Since the Regulars and Volunteers competed for men, the signing bonuses for actual military service had gone up. Therefore, there was an incentive for someone as greedy as Wickham to become an officer. With the militia it was different. Each shire had a quota of men that were required to enlist. Landowners were exempt. Men like Wickham were expected to serve.

Upon enlisting in the militia, he would not be expected to be a skilled marksman, horseman, or trained in fencing. He did have to provide his own weapon. Darcy could not help but wonder whose gun Wickham had borrowed since he often sold everything he possessed for another round of gambling at the tables. Because Wickham had received a gentleman's education paid for by the Darcy family's purse, he would enter as a junior officer.

Colonel Forster welcomed them to his quarters. It was a small house with an even smaller parlor.

"How might I be of service, gentlemen?"

Darcy took the lead in conversion. "I am Fitzwilliam Darcy of Pemberley in Derbyshire, and this is Major Robert Gerring who serves under my cousin, Colonel Richard Fitzwilliam. We are here to share information with you about a man in your regiment who is unscrupulous and is a danger to the local citizens."

"How odd," the colonel began, "For there is a different

gentleman with the same name who has spoken to me several times about the possibility of enlisting under my command. It appears he is delaying obligating himself in hopes that he will receive a signing bonus, which he will not."

Darcy was not surprised. "I was born Fitzwilliam Darcy, son of George Darcy, Esq. and Lady Anne Darcy. I am the master of Pemberley. The man attempting to steal my identity is none other than George Wickham. He is a bold rake who would not hesitate to use your name, Colonel, if he thought it would bring him an easier life. Of this information, Wickham publicly admitted a short time ago at the inn in front of several of your officers."

The colonel shook his head in disgust and said, "That may be. Unfortunately, since he has not yet enlisted, I have no authority over him."

Darcy was relieved. It was one less barrier to seeing justice done. "Then, I thank you for your time, Colonel Forster. I will take matters into my own hands to see that the neighborhood is protected and make certain that Wickham is taken out of commission."

"Very well."

And that was the end to that! If only the rest of his tasks would be that easy.

On the ride back to Netherfield Park, Darcy asked the major what he had whispered to Miss Collins to stop her from shooting him or Wickham.

The major grinned, "I merely said, 'there is no justice in killing the wrong man.' She got my point and dropped her hand."

Darcy nodded, appreciative that the major was on his side.

"Mr. Darcy, I suspect that you will not be attending the bonfire for I imagine you have letters to write to settle Mr. Wickham's future, as well as speaking to the constable." Darcy acknowledged the truth of the comment. "Now that Miss Collins is aware you are not the man whom she seeks, the danger to you has passed. I ought to check to make certain that Miss Lucas returned home safely."

Darcy was not surprised. The major was spending a considerable amount of time at Lucas Lodge. The lady was Miss Elizabeth's closest friend. Darcy would make sure that nothing or no one would harm either female.

"Is it Miss Charlotte Lucas who has gained your interest?" he cautiously inquired, knowing he had no right to the major's business.

"I appreciate the company of an intelligent female who enjoys a calm exchange of ideas. That is all." The major added, "Additionally, I might gain needed information at the bonfire so I will attend."

Darcy noted how quickly the major replied, or rather, defended his interest.

"Very well."

The major reached into the breast pocket of his coat. "By the way, the colonel sent this to me to give to you before he left England. He knows that I find the study of ballistics educational. This is the bullet that was dug out of the back wall of your carriage. It barely penetrated the wood. It is from a woman's pistol." Handing the smashed metal ball to

Darcy, he continued, "If you would, please notice the shape after impact. Because Miss Collins' extended arm would be approximately the same height as the bottom of your carriage window, the bullet would have projected from the barrel of the pistol to the squabs at between ten to fifteen degrees less than level. As you likely know, unless it is a smoothbore, the barrel of a rifle or pistol has grooves, which puts a spiral spin on the bullet for accuracy and greater trajectory. The marks on the undamaged rounded end are singular to the pattern that would be inside the barrel of her pistol. These two factors, the angle at which the shot entered the carriage and the rifling inside the barrel can identify the weapon and the exact location where the marksman was standing when the gun discharged."

Richard was a proponent of ballistics during crime investigations. As an officer who had seen several battles on the continent, knowledge of the laws of motion and trajectory provided him information he could use during the campaigns. Many times, Richard had spoken at length about the very things the major mentioned. Darcy wished he had paid more attention. It was why his cousin had asked him to recall exactly where the spectators were located in relation to his carriage when the shot was fired, which confirmed that Claire Collins had indeed shot at him.

"I thank you, Major Gerring." Darcy rolled the small piece of iron in his palm before handing it back. That something so meager could rob a man of his life, humbled him. Of course, he had always known it intellectually, but to have solid evidence that his own life was on the brink was another matter entirely. "Do you still have Miss Collins' pistol?"

"I do not," the major admitted. "She is no longer a threat to you, and she will need it for her protection. I placed it on the table before we left the room."

"Very good." He deeply regretted that ladies were not guaranteed safety by the men around them. It made him more determined to protect Georgiana and Elizabeth.

CHAPTER 18

"I have never seen Papa so angry," Jane paused. Running the brush to the ends of Elizabeth's hair then back up to the crown of her sister's head, she continued, "Once we return from the bonfire, Kitty and Lydia will reach their majority before they are free to leave Longbourn again."

Shaking her head, Elizabeth regretted the conduct of her sisters and the loss of Jane's ministrations.

"Jane, for the first time Papa saw how their poor conduct reflected on our household. Their flirting with the officers was innocent fun to them. They had no idea of the danger they were in."

"I suspect you are correct." Jane set the brush aside, giving her full attention to her sister as she wove a ribbon through Elizabeth's curls. "Lizzy, tell me about our cousin. What was she like?"

"My first impression, after the shock at thinking I was looking in a mirror, was that she was alone and afraid. I saw a vulnerability in her that had me concerned for her future. Lydia's blurting out that my twin was in Meryton where mama could hear will not protect Claire from gossip, I am afraid." Elizabeth anticipated no good when Lydia opened her mouth. She was correct.

Mama's cheeks puffed up and turned the color of a tomato until Elizabeth feared her face would explode. After a moment of trying to bring herself under control, the matron of Longbourn said, "Is this not like one of Mr. Bennet's cousins! Come to survey our house just like her brother did. Well, I hope she is not planning on chasing Mr. Bingley or Major Gerring while she is here since she cannot be anything next to my Jane or Lydia."

It had taken Jane almost thirty minutes to calm their most volatile parent.

Jane asked, "Did she truly look like you?"

The question was easily answered. "Enough that I doubt that after a brief glance, even Papa could tell us apart if we were to exchange clothing."

"Will she be well?"

In truth, Elizabeth wondered the same. Claire was vulnerable in being alone. "Jane, I know my first concern should be our cousin. What Claire learned tonight would have turned her life upside down. That she had committed violent acts against an innocent gentleman while the real guilty party continued to prey on other young girls, had to have upset everything she would have believed to be just reason to pursue her course. But Jane, I also worry what this could do to my reputation should she take it upon herself to act further against Mr. Wickham here in Meryton."

"I wish the situation was different, Lizzy," Jane

soothed. "Perhaps Miss Collins will put this all behind her and press forward with a brighter future."

Poor Jane, always seeing rainbows amidst the darkest storm clouds.

Jane left to gather her gloves and warmest scarf. The evening was chilled. The whole town would be at the bonfire, pressing close to the fire. She wondered if the Bingley party would be there...if, Mr. Darcy would be there. Three hours later she had her answer. None of them were in attendance.

* * *

"YOU AND HURST are to be praised for the thankless task of returning the two youngest Bennets to Longbourn." Darcy admitted.

"My friend, it was our pleasure." Charles Bingley greeted Darcy's return with his ever-present grin. "I mean no criticism when I say that I believe I saw you more in town than I have since you have been under my roof. I had no idea when I extended the invitation that you would seek the company of my neighbors more than mine."

Sheepishly, Darcy began an apology only to be interrupted. Bingley slapped him on the shoulder.

"Do not concern yourself, Darcy. I understand what has distracted you, the threat to your life and all, however, I am glad to see that you are busy. You are a fearsome thing when you have nothing to do." Bingley chuckled, then directed them to his study where they would have privacy.

Once they were settled, Darcy said, "Thank you, Bingley. I believe the threat to me is over. Now I have the unenviable task of informing my sister, which will break her heart, I am afraid."

"Is Miss Darcy well?" Bingley set his drink down on the table with such force that liquid sloshed onto the table. "Surely, she is unharmed."

What a good friend he had in Bingley!

"Georgiana is in perfect health and spirits; I am pleased to report." Once Bingley relaxed back in his chair, Darcy added, "I thank you, Charles. You cannot imagine how sincerely I appreciate your concern. She will have fortune-hunters enough pursuing her when she comes out in society. Knowing I have someone I can trust to help Richard and I protect her is crucial."

The flush covering Bingley's face was evidence of the man's modest opinion of himself.

"I will do what I can, Darcy. In many ways I can see how I have failed both Caroline and Louisa. They both suffer by thinking too highly of themselves. Yet, someone like Miss Darcy who has a true claim to excellence, has never put herself forward, at least not in my presence. She is a wonderful girl, Darcy. You have every reason to be proud of her."

"I thank you."

Darcy chose not to comment about either of Bingley's sisters for he had absolutely nothing positive to say other than if persistence was rewarded, they would be two of the wealthiest females in the Kingdom.

"Do let me tell you of what transpired after you left the inn." In the retelling of the events, he left out the details, only explaining that Miss Collins had confused him with Wickham, who would be paying for his crimes.

"She no longer wants you dead?" Bingley looked puzzled. "Well, that is wonderful, Darcy, thank heavens for that!"

Darcy could not help but agree.

"Perhaps you would join us this evening for cards or charades. Caroline and Louisa have no interest in the Guy Fawkes bonfire held in a farmer's field. In truth, I plan on an early night tonight. In the meantime, being surrounded by something familiar might take your mind off your troubles, albeit temporarily."

Darcy's inclination was to grumble. However, Bingley's subtle reminder that he was their guest was valid. Choosing to accept a man's hospitality obligated him to join in at least occasionally. Apparently, tonight would be one of those nights.

BINGLEY ALREADY KNEW what had happened at the inn since Hurst had bailed off the back of the carriage at the first turn into Longbourn's driveway. Returning as quickly as he was able, he hid himself in the room next to where Darcy and the Bennets met with Miss Collins. Thus, he overheard the whole of the conversation.

They needed Darcy relaxed and asleep while the rest of the house celebrated Guy Fawkes at Lucas Lodge. When Darcy went upstairs to his chambers early in the evening, their quickly constructed plans were set in motion.

* * *

THE NEXT MORNING, Darcy woke early to a heavy mist coating the Hertfordshire countryside, which was perfect for a quick ride alone over the fields. Nothing cleared his head like a good gallop down the lane into Meryton. His sleep had been disturbed by the sound of the fireworks that easily covered the distance between Lucas Lodge and Netherfield Park. Young Lucas was correct. The fireworks display must have been impressive.

Passing through the market town, he rode until the peace and quiet of the autumn season settled upon his shoulders. His only stop was to help a recalcitrant calf stuck in the mud join its mother. It was likely frightened by the explosions.

His mind drifted to the woman from Longbourn. Elizabeth, for she was no longer Miss Elizabeth to him, had saved his life by pushing her cousin off balance then capturing her shooting arm. How could he ever repay her for her courage in thwarting his foe? He spent the rest of the ride wondering what he could possibly do to reward the lady who was taking up more and more space in his heart.

Returning to Netherfield Park, he was greeted by the arrival of Mr. Bennet and Elizabeth shortly after he changed out of his riding clothes. As was their habit, none of the Bingley's were yet awake. Leaving his muddy boots and trousers for his valet to clean, he met them in the front drawing room.

"Mr. Darcy, we are hoping to accompany you to the inn. Both Lizzy and I are desirous of seeing Claire one last time before she heads to Plymouth." Mr. Bennet held his hat in his hand.

Elizabeth smiled at him, increasing Darcy's gratitude for the day.

They had not yet taken their seats when hurried footsteps approached the entrance.

John Lucas ran into the room, deathly pale and out of breath, Bingley's butler right behind him. "Mr. Bennet, I...I think I am going to be sick." Looking to the side of the fireplace, the young man hurried to the ash bucket and cast up his accounts.

Darcy and the others could do nothing other than wait for him to finish to learn the cause of his distress.

Once the young man set aside the bucket and dropped down to sit on the hearth, he looked toward where Elizabeth stood beside Mr. Bennet, only to turn green once more as he swayed in place.

"How is it possible? Lizzy? Is it you?" John Lucas stammered. "I saw you as clear as day with a bullet in your chest lying next to the other Mr. Darcy." His voice raised until he was shouting. "I saw you! As God is my witness, I saw you." Tears streamed down his cheeks. "Lizzy?"

Good God! Darcy's knees weakened. His hands started to shake. Despite Elizabeth standing in front of him where he could see with his own eyes that she was well, the idea of her being harmed shook him. Protective instincts surged through Darcy until he wanted to clasp his hands around Wickham's neck and squeeze, for it had to have been him lying next to the lady. Blinking, he sought a cool head. If young Lucas was correct, a double murder was committed in Meryton, one of them a lady who regretted trying to kill him, the other an unscrupulous man who wanted everything Darcy owned.

His stomach roiled until he thought he would need the bucket as well. Inhaling deeply, he counted until he could feel the pounding in his chest calm.

* * *

No! Elizabeth shouted to herself. *Not Claire!* Her poor cousin. And Mr. Wickham? Dead? Poor John Lucas. The young man was completely undone.

Elizabeth approached her friend's younger brother, her hands shaking, her voice trembling. "It was not me, Johnny. It was not me. The lady you saw was likely my cousin, Miss Claire Collins. I am here, Johnny. I am unharmed and alive." Kneeling in front of him, she asked, "Did not Charlotte tell you about our conversation at the inn?"

"No, she did not. I was busy with the fireworks, then helped Mr. Caudle with his livestock until early this morning." He dropped his head into his hands. "I am sorry, Lizzy. I thought..."

Major Gerring demanded, "What do you mean that you saw her lying next to Mr. Darcy?"

John Lucas covered his eyes with both hands. "Mr. Darcy, the one with the militia and the long hair, had a pistol in his hand pointed at his temple. Blood splattered the wall and the floor behind him. It was everywhere."

"Suicide?' Mr. Darcy mumbled, his palm covering his mouth as if to stop the words from being said.

"Where were they?" The major insisted. "Where did you see them?"

John's whole body was shaking. Three times he began to speak, only to stop and start over.

Mr. Darcy approached him with a small glass full of spirits. After a few sips, John was able to reply. "They were in the stable behind the blacksmith." Dropping his hands, he wiped his cheeks. "Last night, one of our horses went crazy from the noise. It kicked out the railing in the corral, then ran into the barn. Father decided to sell the horse, which was the same one that dumped Charlotte to the ground. I had taken him to the smithy early this morning for new shoes hoping to at least get father's money back. After discussing terms, I led the horse back to the stable so Haniger could put his own halter on the beast. The door to the first stall was unlatched. I assumed the smithy would want the horse in there while he retrieved the halter from the tack room, so I opened the door wider. It was then that I saw them." Young Lucas shuddered. "It was...it was the worst thing I have ever seen in my lifetime."

The major asked, "Was there anyone else about? Did you see anyone other than the blacksmith, and the victims?"

"The only other person I saw was this Mr. Darcy, who is standing right here, riding his horse through town," was Lucas' quick reply. "He did not see me walking up the lane from Lucas Lodge to the smithy."

"Close your eyes," the major ordered. "Now, tell us exactly what you did see."

After a long pause, Lucas began his description. "Mr.

Darcy's coat was of fine wool, although the hem was frayed. His gloves were white. His hat had rolled across the floor into a pile of…" He looked up at Elizabeth and changed his choice of words despite everyone knowing what he was thinking. "…debris." Glancing at her again, he continued, "The lady's hair was draped across her arm and chest where…well, where the bullet… Her bonnet was askew and her traveling coat was…*Oh my word!* Lizzy, it was the same lady I told you about that I saw in London, the one who looked like you so much that even I had a hard time telling you apart. The coat was dark green and black. It was her!"

Elizabeth took his hand. "Johnny, after you saw what happened, how did you know to come to Netherfield Park?" she asked.

"I didn't. I went to Longbourn first. Hill told me your father was here."

"Come, Lizzy." Mr. Bennet held out his arm. "Longbourn must be in an uproar. We need to return immediately. Once you are settled, I will ride to Haniger's to reassure those who have seen the crime scene that it is my cousin and not my daughter in the stall."

Major Gerring assisted Lucas to stand as Darcy did for Elizabeth. "Mr. Lucas, as unpalatable as it may sound, I believe we need to return to the scene of the crime. Murders of passion are usually easily explained but I do need to file a report. It will be necessary to examine the scene before some well-intentioned soul interferes."

* * *

"I WILL JOIN YOU," Darcy offered. His testimony in addition to the major's would be needed to identify the lady and Wickham.

Elizabeth lifted her eyes to his. They stood close enough that he could see a gold ring around her dark iris. She was so beautiful. She completely robbed him of the ability to breathe.

"I am grateful you are unharmed," he whispered for her ears alone. He spoke the truth. Before him was a lady unlike any other. She was remarkable. "I am grateful your father will look after your safety." He leaned a fraction closer. "I am grateful you were not the one trying to kill me."

She smiled, a reflection of the fire's flames dancing in her eyes. "I am grateful, too."

Mr. Bennet cleared his throat. Loudly. "Lizzy?" He glanced at Darcy. "Pray come to Longbourn once your investigation is over, gentlemen."

It was a request for which Darcy was more than willing to comply. He would need her peace. He felt like there was much they needed to say to each other.

"Miss Elizabeth, I..., I am deeply sorry about your cousin. This was a crime that never should have been committed," he paused, trying to contain his thoughts. "Without you, I would not have been able to identify Miss Collins, nor would I have obtained the information necessary to protect myself. Had you not distracted her, I would have lost my life."

"It did not need to come to this." she whispered for him alone, her eyes filling with tears. "I simply cannot believe that she is gone."

He yearned to pull her into his arms and hold her until the tears went away. He had no right to comfort her. Instead, he said, "Pray know this, if something should have happened to me, my sister would have been alone to face a harsh, grasping, population of men who would not care about her tender heart. When I think upon the consequences of someone seeking to harm me, it reaches far beyond my person. I do not yet have the words I need to thank you. In essence, I needed you and you saved me, Elizabeth. I will never forget what you have done."

The softness of her eyes, the fullness of her lips, and her intake of breath stirred him until all he saw was her.

"Lizzy!" Mr. Bennet's patience was done.

Slowly she smiled, her lovely eyes glistening. "My pleasure, Mr. Darcy."

Turning, she moved to her father's side. Blinking rapidly, she said, "Johnny, please tell Charlotte that I will come to Lucas Lodge later. Good day, gentlemen."

With the dignity of a queen, Elizabeth left the room.

The major slapped him on the shoulder. "Come, Mr. Darcy. We have work to do."

He should be joyous that Claire Collins was no longer a threat. Neither was Wickham, someone who would do his family harm. Instead, his heart was brimming with an emotion he failed to recognize. Could it possibly be...love?

CHAPTER 19

$\mathcal{B}$y the time Darcy and Major Gerring arrived at the blacksmiths, a small crowd of men had gathered. Colonel Forster and several from the militia were closest to the stall. Sir William Lucas was as far away from the bodies as humanly possible whilst still being part of the fray.

"Who is the magistrate? The constable?" Darcy inquired. Within seconds, it was determined that Sir William held the position of magistrate while the blacksmith, Mr. Haniger, was the constable. Yet, it was Darcy who took charge.

The scene was gruesome. The bodies were so close that they touched at the knee. Miss Collins had fallen with one hand extended towards Wickham. The other was resting under her head like she was trying to soften the hard wooden surface to be more comfortable for resting. Examining her face closer than he had done the evening before, Darcy could see that there were points of similarity with Elizabeth, yet they were not identical.

Elizabeth's cheeks were slightly fuller and her chin more determined. Where the resemblance was striking were their eyes. Fortunately for those gathered, including himself, Miss Collins had died with her eyes closed.

Wickham had not been as fortuitous. His eyes were open enough for Darcy to see a blank stare. He could not help but wonder what the man was thinking before he pulled the trigger. In fact, he had a hard time imagining Wickham doing such a thing. He was lazy and greedy, but a cold-blooded killer who shot a lady before he killed himself? It was unfathomable. Until twelve hours before, the two victims were strangers. Miss Collins expressed her eagerness to start her new life. Wickham would not care a fig for any of her complaints. This...this travesty made no sense at all.

Movement behind where Wickham lay caught Darcy's attention. Major Gerring was presently digging into the wooden slats in the midst of the blood and detritus. Pulling something from the wall, the major quickly wrapped it in his handkerchief and tucked it in his pocket. Not one person from the crowd said anything, which was odd.

Looking around, Darcy understood why.

Three of the officers were heatedly complaining to Colonel Forster, fingers pointing to where Wickham lay.

Sighing in resignation, Darcy approached them knowing his purse would be lighter when all was said and done. His father had adored George Wickham's playful, zest for life. Out of respect for his father, Darcy would see George given a proper burial next to Wickham's parents at Pemberley and that his final debts were paid.

While the men were outlining their extensive list of grievances against Wickham, Mr. Bennet arrived on horseback. Following not far behind were Bingley and Mr. Hurst.

"Darcy, we hurried as quickly as we were able when I heard there was trouble in the village. My staff informed me that young Mr. Lucas was upset and that you were somehow involved." Bingley jumped from his horse.

Mr. Haniger, the smithy, approached. Wiping his hands on his leather apron, he looked like he was far more brawn than brain. However, the first words from his mouth dispelled that notion. Major Gerring appeared at his side.

"Now, I've been wondering. Reports from last night at the inn are that the miss that gone and got herself killed, had a powerful hatred for one Mr. Darcy." His brow lifted at Darcy. "Word has it that you, good sir, had a powerful hatred for the man who appears to have shot the lady before shooting himself. Now, why do you think he did such a thing?" Before he could reply, he continued. "Myself, I've known many worthless scoundrels. Once they rid themselves of what was antagonizing them, they usually skip town, never again to be seen in the area. As well, it was the lady's pistol he had in his hand. How do you think that happened? Had they planned together to rid humanity of their presence? Me, I can't imagine the two of them would or could agree upon anything since the reports indicate they were strangers until yesterday."

"I concur," Darcy stated, listening closely to every word.

"Now, you, Mr. Darcy, you appeared to those at the

inn last night to have knowledge of both of the victims. What have you to say for yourself?"

What! He was being accused? Of What! Murder? What a dreadful turn of events!

Before he could put his words together, the constable/smithy continued, "Now, I am not accusing you of anything, mind you." Mr. Haniger planted his fists on his broad hips. "I'm just saying that you, of all the people at the inn last night, were the only one who seemed to know both Miss Hobbs and Mr. Wickham. That's all."

Darcy was not reassured. "You are correct. I have known Wickham from my youth on. His pretense of being me is not new. As I warned Colonel Forster after the major and I left the inn, the man was an opportunist who always looked for the easy way out of a bad situation, usually of his own creation." The smithy nodded. "As you said, men of his sort typically run from the area, rather than face the consequences of his actions. George Wickham was disinclined to work, preferring to use his charms and his skills at the tables to provide for himself. His desires were always larger than his purse could maintain."

"Hmm...I see," the smithy scratched his chin. "Then it makes me wonder what would have made him change his character so much that he acted violently rather than flee. Do you have any idea?"

This was no casual question. Darcy could not miss the fact that although Mr. Haniger's stance was relaxed, his eyes pierced Darcy like a lance holding him in place.

Darcy offered, "I last saw Wickham mid-July. He was the same as he had always been, indolent and selfish. His countenance and comments last evening were nothing out of the ordinary."

"Hmm...I see," the smithy rubbed the back of his neck. "And the lady? I was told that she met with Miss Lucas and Miss Elizabeth before she drew a pistol on you. They are fine ladies. Was Miss Hobbs equally as fine?"

It was at that point that Mr. Bennet and Sir William joined them.

"Nigel," Mr. Bennet addressed the blacksmith. "You are doing a fine job with the investigation; I can say with all honesty. Did you happen to hear gunfire?"

"I was at the bonfire with everyone else. I doubt anyone could have told the difference between the black powder of a pistol and the gunpowder in the fireworks." The giant man shrugged.

Mr. Bennet continued, "Mightn't I suggest that we return to the scene of the crime to continue this discussion in private? With you mentioning our daughters by name, I beg you to consider the possible ramifications of having them, even in a small amount, attached to what has happened here."

"I beg your pardon, Bennet." The constable spun on his heels, directing those gathered to return to their homes or their businesses.

While the major and Mr. Haniger stepped into the stall, Mr. Bennet and Mr. Darcy remained where the door was ajar. The sight was no less revolting for having already seen it.

"Nigel, Miss Hobbs, as you know her, happens to have been my cousin. Her full name is Claire Hobbs Collins. Her brother arrived ten days ago with a report that his sister was given clothing and good counsel by his patroness, Lady Catherine de Bourgh of Rosings Park in Kent. Shortly after, if my understanding of the timing of the events is correct, the lady traveled to London and attempted to kill Mr. Darcy."

The blacksmith's head turned from Miss Collins to him. Instinctively, Darcy held up both hands. "I did not attempt to kill her in return, if that is what you are thinking."

After a lengthy pause, Mr. Haniger asked for more details. To clear himself of any possible charges, Darcy shared what he knew of both times the lady had fired her pistol at him. In the retelling, Darcy realized just how little he knew about Miss Collins. What he had gathered from Georgiana's letter and what he was told by the Bennets and the lady herself would have fit in a thimble.

Good heavens! He dreaded the prospect of explaining to his sister not only the treachery of her friend, but her death and the death of a man who attempted to charm her by remembering precious memories from when she was young. At that moment, Darcy hated being himself.

Recalling himself to the conversation at hand, he continued, "Until this morning, the four times I saw Miss Collins was at a traveling inn in Bromley, the streets of London outside the office of my man of business, yesterday at the inn in Meryton, and this morning in this stall. The one time I actually spoke to her was yesterday in front of several witnesses to confirm I was *not* the Fitzwilliam Darcy who had wronged her. Since Wickham also was in the room, it was easy enough to point out who pretended to be me."

The constable shook his head. "Well, this is a sad thing to be sure. I am sorry to say it because she was a relative of yours, Bennet, but wasted lives is what we have here. The young tend to act before they think. I am sure that whatever ruin she believed this Mr. Wickham committed against her was probably not bad enough to die for."

Darcy disagreed, although he said nothing. Since his adulthood he heard reports from older brothers and fathers of ruined females of how a damaged reputation altered the lives of the whole family. Miss Claire Collins felt the loss of her sister deeply.

When the major approached, the smashed metal bullet in his hand, Darcy asked if he also carried the one from his carriage fired from Miss Collins' gun.

The major cleared his throat. "Mr. Darcy, gentlemen, the bullet used to kill Wickham was not fired from the lady's pistol."

"What are you saying, Major?" Nigel Haniger reached out and took the bullet pried from the wall. When the major added the one that he had taken from his coat pocket, a blind eye could see they were not the same size.

"If you notice the bore pattern on both pieces of metal, they are vastly different."

"Where did you get this?" the constable held out the one in his right hand that the major had just handed him.

"From Mr. Darcy's carriage where the lady's shot smashed through the glass before embedding itself in the back panel."

Darcy spoke up. "Wait a moment. There was no blood behind Miss Collins. If the bullet exited her back, then she was not inside the stable when she was killed."

Mr. Haniger said, "Come on. We had best be more thorough in our investigation."

The only thing behind where Claire Collins lay was dirt, pieces of straw, and the wooden slats that served as a barrier to the next stall.

The major retrieved the pistol from Wickham's grasp. Feeling the inside of the barrel, he noted, "My question to you men is, since this pistol was not the weapon that killed Wickham, where is the firearm that did?"

Darcy noted, "Additionally, there is no residue on Mr. Wickham's pristine gloves to indicate he fired a shot. Notably, both have mud on their shoes despite the floor of the stall being covered in straw."

Darcy's mind spun until he felt queasy. There was no evidence of suicide. Both were murdered.

Mr. Haniger voiced his concerns aloud. "Are you saying that someone murdered them both elsewhere, then deposited them in my stables to look like it was a suicide?"

"That is exactly what I believe we are saying," the major's claim and stance were solid.

As hard as it was for him to say it aloud, Darcy explained, "From her own mouth, Miss Collins loathed Wickham for taking advantage of someone she loved until she wished him dead, even by her own hands. Nonetheless, he was the one left holding the weapon so she could not have killed him, then herself. Additionally, if I understand what my cousin, Colonel Richard Fitzwilliam, has told me, the energy or force of a projectile from a gun this size would have dissipated within a few inches. I cannot imagine the bullet being able to go all the way through her. No, it would take a much higher caliber of weapon to have caused this much damage to each of them."

"Perhaps Mr. Wickham killed himself because he felt like he would be charged for her death," Mr. Bennet suggested.

Darcy added, "I do not believe so, Mr. Bennet. Men like Mr. Wickham would care nothing about the scorn of the residents in Hertfordshire. He would have moved on with no guilt for any damage he left behind."

Major Gerring pointed back at the bodies. "As I understand it, as far as Mr. Wickham is concerned, his reputation was one of avoiding consequences at all costs. He would have much experience at being confronted with his sins, I suspect, so her making accusations would have been like water off a duck's back. He would have walked away from her without giving her another thought."

Darcy agreed. His insides roiled. His father's heart would have been broken had he known the lengths Wickham had gone with his debauchery. That Darcy had at one time considered George Wickham one of his closest friends made him sick to his stomach.

The constable interrupted his thoughts. "We are left with a third party who, for reasons of his own, wanted them both dead. I ask you gentlemen, who in Meryton had anything to lose at the hands of these two miscreants? And who had the most to gain by their passing?" The blacksmith scratched his chin. "Now, I suppose Mr. Wickham had many enemies. Perhaps one came in search of him and found him talking to Miss Collins. The killing of one would mean getting rid of the other who witnessed the crime. Mightn't you know anyone who would target the man?"

He was sick. The victims Wickham had abused the most was the Darcy family. First, he took advantage of Darcy's father. Then, he stole Darcy's name and cost him untold amounts of money to hide his depravity from the elder Darcy. Finally, there was Georgiana. For a certainty, Darcy was murderous when she sobbed all the way from Ramsgate to London and for weeks beyond. But to point a weapon at someone and end their life? Never!

Darcy glanced around to find all three sets of eyes looking directly at him. He knew he was innocent. He would never have hurt either Miss Collins or Wickham. Nevertheless, all three of these men were new acquaintances. They did not know him. *Dash it all!* How could he prove that he did not commit cold-blooded murder?

Colonel Forster stepped forward, cleared his throat, and declared, "Only yesterday, Mr. Darcy, in front of myself and Major Gerring, said, 'I will take matters into my own hands to see that the neighborhood is protected and make certain that Wickham is taken out of commission.'"

Blast! Could matters get any worse for him?

Despite not having anything to do with the horrid scene in front of him, beads of sweat gathered at his temple and in his palms. This was not looking good for him.

Stepping closer, the constable asked, "Mr. Darcy, where were you last night and early this morning?"

CHAPTER 20

*E*lizabeth paced her chambers. This was dreadful. Mr. Darcy had not been directly accused of murdering Claire Collins and Mr. Wickham, but he was told he could not leave Netherfield Park. If the real murderer was not found quickly, the least that would happen was that the Darcy name would be destroyed, ruining the future of both Mr. Darcy and his sister. The worst was that a judge would make an example of him, which could cost him his freedom or his life.

Heart pounding, the need to act almost shook Elizabeth. Someone wanted both Claire and Mr. Wickham out of the picture. Who could it be? Surely, it was not Mr. Collins. The man was gone by the time of the confrontation at the inn. He hated guns but he loved the admiration of Lady Catherine, who would never favor him should he act in a manner that would endanger her nephew. No, although he was the obvious choice, it could not have been Mr. Collins.

Were the murders committed to purposely frame Mr.

Darcy as the guilty party? Who in the community would have done such a thing, and why would they have done it? No doubt, many of the ladies were piqued by his initial insult at the assembly but who would murder someone for having their vanity hurt? If anyone should want to shoot Mr. Darcy, it should be her since it was she to whom he had directed the harsh words.

She snorted. She might not have been tolerable enough that night, but he had let her know without words that he no longer felt the same. No, he called her *Elizabeth* and told her he needed her. These tender words were not the mark of a man bent on murder, but a man on the verge of..."

Her hand went to her mouth. Did he return the tenderness she was beginning to feel in her heart?

Dropping to her bed, she lay back with her arm over her brow. She sighed. There was no benefit for either of them to go down that path. Under these changed circumstances, he desperately needed someone to help him. Who of his friends would provide that help? Mr. Bingley was too amiable. He was like Jane in believing that cruelty and hatred existed on some unknown planet, not in their sphere. Mr. Darcy's cousin, the colonel, might have the power to assist but he was not in Hertfordshire.

In truth, what Mr. Darcy had done the day prior in offering Claire a choice of where she wanted to live and the means to make a life for herself was heroic. She sighed again. Mr. Darcy was...she smiled. He was nothing like she had thought him that first night at the assembly. How things had changed!

Nevertheless, if proof was not found of the guilty party, Mr. Darcy was in trouble.

Elizabeth pondered each piece of the mystery that her father had revealed after his return from the blacksmith's stables. In a flash, she donned her walking boots then rushed to her father's study.

"Papa, you mentioned that the victims had muddy shoes. Do you recall if it was the brown where someone might have dumped the water after washing the laundry or was it the rich loam from the fields?"

"The debris on their shoes was dark—almost black," he stated. "Let us head to Oakham Mount, dear girl. I believe you may be onto something."

In silence, they approached the orchard. After a few moments they could hear the caw of *Jeanne de Valois-Saint-Remy* flying toward them.

"She will be disappointed today since I have brought her nothing she can steal." Elizabeth was in no mood to be pestered by the bird.

Her father began to reply when they noticed the crow circling a spot not far from where Elizabeth had fallen when chased by Mr. Darcy. Squawking and flapping, Jeannie dove into the grass. Elizabeth turned away in case the bird had a mouse or a snake in her claws. She hated snakes.

"What in the world?" her father whispered to himself. To the bird herself, he yelled, "What did you find, Jeannie?"

Looking up, Elizabeth shaded her eyes with her hand. The bird's talons were opened ready to gather a treasure in their clutches. Hurrying to the spot where the crow was about to land, they discovered the sod disturbed with assorted sizes of footprints in the mud, blood everywhere.

"Oh, Lord!" Thomas Bennet clamped his hand over his mouth.

There in the grass was a crumpled ostrich feather amidst broken blades of grass next to a brass button, dotted red. Not far from them were clearly marked hoof prints and the tracks of a cart.

For the first time in her life, Elizabeth nearly swooned.

* * *

ABOVE ANYTHING ELSE, Darcy wished Richard was still on British soil. In spite of Major Gerring's skills and the confidence of owning his own innocence, he needed help. Graciously, Bingley offered his assistance.

"I thank you, Bingley. At this point, I truly do not know what needs to be done. No formal charges have been made against me. Until the guilty party can be found, I am to be a prisoner in your home." Darcy could not sit. Standing to pace in front of the fireplace in Bingley's study, he would not have been surprised to see lightning shoot from the tips of his fingers. Having his life turned upside down energized him to do something...anything to fix this mess.

He was livid at Wickham for his reprehensible conduct against the Darcy family. Nevertheless, he had not wanted him dead. There was a place in his heart that had long hoped Wickham would learn his lessons, come to his senses, and change for the good. Now, the opportunity for redemption was gone; stripped from George with one fatal shot.

Blast! This news would add to Georgiana's burden when she heard of his death. Even though Wickham had treated her cruelly, she, too, had expressed the desire to have him repent of his sins, if only to have reflected well upon their father's memory. Added to the report of how Claire Collins abused her friendship, it did not bode well for the tiny steps Lady Matlock had made instilling confidence in his sister. Georgie would be devastated.

In truth, so was he.

"I hope you know that you are welcome under any circumstance," Bingley gratefully interrupted his somberness. "Thus, I will strive to make your stay as pleasant as possible. Perhaps we could have Caroline invite Miss Bennet and Miss Elizabeth to tea."

Although he would appreciate seeing Elizabeth, Darcy was aware that, under the circumstances, pleasant was far from what he was feeling. Someone had murdered two individuals in the neighborhood. Wickham was closely connected to the Darcy family. Miss Collins was related to the Bennets. The discussion at the stables was that the only person with an apparent attachment to them both was Darcy. He would be crushed if something happened to Elizabeth because of him. It would be best if she remained at Longbourn.

Before he could reply that it might be best if the ladies remained at Longbourn for their protection, Mr. Bennet accompanied by Major Gerring and Mr. Haniger arrived at Netherfield.

Bingley offered refreshments. They all refused.

219

Mr. Bennet came directly to the point.

"Once Lizzy asked me about the color of mud on Mr. Wickham's boots, we were able to retrace the path of the murderer. Apparently, Miss Collins was killed close to the big oak tree where Lizzy injured her ankle. As soon as I returned my daughter safely home, Nigel, the major, and myself returned to the scene of the crime with Mr. Wickham's and Miss Collins' shoes. There we were easily able to match the prints to the ones in the mud."

"Were there any other prints?" Darcy asked. "I would willingly offer one of my boots as evidence of my innocence if there were."

Mr. Bennet cleared his throat, looked to the major and the blacksmith, then replied, "Yes, Mr. Darcy. There is a third set of prints that were clearly marked."

When nothing more was said, but covert glances were still taking place between the visitors, Darcy offered, "Allow me to have my valet bring the same boots I wore to the inn yesterday, on my ride this morning, and when we were at the stables."

The men nodded.

As they waited, Bingley repeated over and over, "It cannot have been you, Darcy. I just know it."

Finally, Darcy reassured his friend and himself. "No, it cannot have been me. Under no circumstances did I wish Wickham dead. Had the events of last night or this morning not happened, he would be on his way to Marshalsea as we speak."

"I knew you could not have killed him, Darcy. You are too honorable to do something so terrible."

"Thank you, Bingley. Your support means everything to me."

His valet entered the room with a pair of boots in his hand. The leather was scarred, giving evidence of regular use. "Sir, you brought three pairs of boots from Darcy House, a new pair I believe you have only worn once since our arrival in Hertfordshire, these, and the ones you are currently wearing."

"Thank you, Parker. If you would help me out of these boots, I will exchange them for the ones in your hand, so the others know they are, indeed, my boots." In only a moment, that set of boots rested beside the other pair already in his valet's possession.

"As you can see, they both are the same height since they have the same heel. The toes are rounded, which is my preference. I dress for comfort not fashion. The wear pattern on the bottom should be the same."

Mr. Haniger selected one set from the grouping. "Come on, let us take care of this business so we can get on with finding the killer." Throwing the door open, he walked out of the room carrying Darcy's boots.

Stuffing his feet into the ones he had been wearing, the rest of them followed.

Bingley's grooms quickly saddled two horses as he and Darcy gathered their outer garments. Within minutes, the five of them rode toward Longbourn's orchard.

Had it only been the day prior that he had ridden through the trees with Major Gerring to speak to Mr. Bennet and argue with Elizabeth? It seemed like a lifetime ago.

From a distance, the serenity of the location was

deceptive. Movement from above captured his attention. The crow was circling, cawing her mournful cry. He felt each plaintive note in his soul.

They were almost to the corner of the pathway where Elizabeth fell when Mr. Bennet reined his horse to a halt. Knowing what he was about, the man dismounted and waited until he was joined by Bingley, the major, the smithy, and Darcy. Forming a circle around where Mr. Bennet pointed, Darcy studied the print. As Mr. Bennet had said, it was clearly molded in the dark mud. After a slight pause, Mr. Bennet lowered the boot.

Oh no! Bile rose in his throat. He blinked to clear his vision. *Surely, it could not be!* Swallowing, Darcy shook his head. *How was that even possible?*

He looked at each man standing alongside him. Disappointment covered Mr. Bennet's countenance, the smithy was angry, Major Gerring shook his head, and Bingley was in denial.

Darcy himself was stunned. The boot—his boot—was a perfect fit.

CHAPTER 21

"r. Darcy, you are hereby placed under arrest for the murders of Miss Claire Collins, also known as Claire Hobbs, and Mr. George Wickham," Mr. Haniger glared at him. "I know men like you, ones who have it all and want more. What have you to say for yourself?"

"I am innocent of these charges." His voice rang out clearly amongst the trees. He was grateful it did not crack like a fifteen-year-old adolescent. "I cannot yet explain how this has happened, but I did not kill anyone."

There was no give to the blacksmith. "Be that as it may, you will be kept under guard until you can be transported to St. Albans for the assizes in a fortnight. I suggest you call in every marker you have ever held against your friends in authority, or you will hang."

Bingley offered to keep Darcy at Netherfield Park for the duration of his stay in Hertfordshire. "You may send over as many men from the militia as you need to make certain that my friend goes nowhere. They will have full access to any of the buildings, I promise."

Eternally grateful that he would not have to spend the next two weeks in Meryton's makeshift jail, Darcy refused to complain when the reins were taken from him after he mounted. Led by Major Gerring, he returned to Netherfield Park with his spine erect, his face looking forward. He had murdered no one. He needed to prove his innocence, find the guilty party, and see they were brought to justice. But how?

"LIZZY, I regret to tell you that all of the evidence gathered so far points to Mr. Darcy killing both victims."

"No! It is impossible." Elizabeth was stunned. And terrified for the man. The Mr. Darcy she knew arranged for Claire's future. As far as Mr. Wickham was concerned, Marshalsea was his intended destination. Mr. Darcy simply would not have taken matters into his own hands, robbing someone of their life because they were a threat or a nuisance. No, she had once thought poorly of him due to his deficient manners but that was not reason enough to believe he would choose to kill anyone. Several times he had shown himself to be honorable. "Papa, he is a man of his word."

Her father agreed. "The clues look rather damning right now, I must admit."

Her mind scrambling for ideas, Elizabeth recalled her

comparison of Mr. Darcy and Mr. Collins. "Papa, did you not notice how Mr. Collins and Mr. Darcy are the same height and size? Why, I suspect they could have exchanged garments without any tailoring at all. They differed only in the fabrics they wore, as well as the design of their clothing."

He snorted. "Are you telling me, your own father, that you peered so closely at a man's body that you could discern what would fit him and what would not? Lizzy! I expected this of Kitty and Lydia, but not you."

Embarrassed to her toes, Elizabeth refused to allow shame to keep her from doing what was right. With each detail, her conviction that Mr. Darcy was innocent flourished.

"Papa, pray think," she begged. "Mr. Collins had a motive for the deaths of both Mr. Wickham and his sister. Mr. Wickham soiled Sarah Collins. Her brother would feel justified in making him pay for his sin. With Claire's rejection of Lady Catherine's counsel and her pursuit of Mr. Darcy, firing upon him twice, your cousin would be even more inclined to his patroness's brand of justice."

Her father held up his hand. "Stop, Lizzy. Mr. Collins left on the post coach for Kent hours before the confrontation between Mr. Wickham and Miss Collins. He was not here."

"Are you saying that he could not get off the stage, hire a horse to ride back to Meryton, where he hunted down his sister and Mr. Wickham? Surely, he was strong enough to carry his sister to the stable. Mr. Wickham was apparently killed there. The shots would not have been discernable from the fireworks. It would take little effort to plant the weapon and leave." Pressing her point when she realized she had her father's full attention, she said, "I would like to know exactly when Mr. Collins arrived in Kent, Papa. I would like to know if his boots fit in the print the same as Mr. Darcy's."

Her father nodded. "Your points are valid, Lizzy. I will go and speak with Nigel."

Standing, he added, "Daughter, I want you to consider carefully what it means that you defend Mr. Darcy so thoroughly. Have you lost your heart to him already?"

She hesitated before replying as honestly as was possible. "I do not know."

TWO OFFICERS from the militia paced back and forth below Darcy's window. Two more were outside his chamber door in the hall. Two were perched at the servant's entrance below the stairs that led up to his rooms. One remained in the room with him, standing at attention each time Parker came in to care for his needs.

Bingley's sisters kept sending him notes asking if he wanted more tea, a book from the library, or a deck of cards to entertain himself. Several times during those first few hours, Caroline Bingley came to his defense.

"Charles, you must make these men understand that Mr. Darcy of Pemberley could not have killed anyone."

One of the officers responded, "Do you have evidence that would prove his innocence, ma'am?"

She sputtered. "Why would I need evidence? Mr.

Darcy is the grandson of an earl and nephew to the current Earl of Matlock."

"Yes, and..." the officer began, only to be interrupted.

"The Darcy legacy stretches back hundreds of years. They are known and respected throughout the land."

"Yes, and..." Darcy had to give the officer credit for patience and for trying to get a word in.

Miss Bingley ended her defense with, "Why, I have half a mind to write to Lady Matlock immediately. With the power she wields in society, she will have you ejected from the militia before morning."

"Ejected? Most likely she will hold a ball in our honor for performing our duty for the safety of the neighborhood," the officer snickered, as did his fellow officers who appreciated his form of sarcasm.

"You know nothing!" Miss Bingley huffed and puffed, but the man simply would not be moved. Finally, she gave in only to return not an hour later with nothing new to add.

Darcy sighed. It was going to be a long two weeks until he left for St. Albans.

Bingley himself marched up and down the hallway of the guest wing, stopping at his door to inquire as to his health each time he went by. Of Gilbert Hurst or his wife, Darcy heard nothing, which surprised him not at all.

Major Gerring arrived approximately two hours into Darcy's confinement.

"Sir, Miss Elizabeth convinced Mr. Bennet to ask the constable to send a pair of your boots to Kent for Mr. Collins to try on. She suggested that with the two of you gentlemen being about the same size, it could have been his footprint instead of yours. Miss Elizabeth also reminded Mr. Haniger that Mr. Collins would have been motivated to get rid of both Mr. Wickham and his sister." He looked directly at Darcy before adding, "Mr. Bennet will be traveling with me to Kent to Mr. Collins' residence at Hunsford parsonage. There we hope to receive a confession of Mr. Collin's guilt. We will leave on the morrow."

Pride in Elizabeth's intelligence swelled his chest. That she came so readily to his defense with a motive that was plausible increased her value in his eyes. She was remarkable!

"Please know that I appreciate your efforts on my behalf, Major."

Once Darcy was alone, he pondered the series of events that led to his arrest. If the boots did not fit Mr. Collins, then who else would have killed the two victims? Back and forth his mind went to those he had met in Hertfordshire and those in other parts of the country who might have wished Wickham dead. The list was long and distinguished.

Then, there was Elizabeth. That dear lady chose to believe him innocent enough to attempt to determine who had committed this heinous crime. If he knew her at all, he knew she would be resolute until the true murderer was found. Darcy was grateful to have her on his side. Bingley, too. If only Richard was still in England. However, he was not without help.

He sat at the small writing desk in his chambers. Recalling every event and encounter since he departed Rosings Park in Kent until that morning, he began making lists, attempting to see a pattern or someone he knew acting out of character. As page after page was filled, his mind settled, and his heart calmed. Elizabeth was not the only one looking for a motive for murder.

Next, he penned a letter to the Chief Magistrate of the Bow Street Runners with a detailed explanation of his case. Afterwards, he wrote to his uncle, Lord Matlock, who held more power than any other in the House of Lords. Finally, he began a letter to his sister only to realize that he could not. No, he would not tell her of his current distress. It would be too much for her fragile heart to bear.

* * *

WAITING WAS the worst part of the investigation as far as Elizabeth was concerned. With her father gone, there was nothing for her to do except avoid the gossipers who were arriving almost by the minute to whisper amongst themselves about the possible reasons why a lady would have been killed by a handsome officer, who then killed himself. Each teller seemed to revel in the inside knowledge they appeared to possess, embellishing details until the story contained very little facts and an abundance of speculation. And then there was the slander of Mr. Darcy's name. None of these women knew him. Yet they reviled him as a murderer and a scoundrel. Elizabeth defended him until she was blue in the face, but they would not listen. She could no longer give heed to their lies.

Removing herself to her father's office, she seated

herself behind the desk. As if they had a mind of their own, her eyes darted to where her father had written Mr. Darcy's name. Sliding the paper closer, she read her father's notes.

Mr. Darcy:

Claire:

·	*She shot at him twice before Meryton – thought he was someone else*

Wickham:

·	*Harmed Miss Darcy*

·	*A blight on the Darcy family name*

·	*Financial costs to the Darcy family*

o	*His education – books, tuition, lodging, clothing, food, etc...*

o	*His gambling*

o	*~~Several~~ Many ruined women*

o	*Foundlings*

o	*Presumed to assume Mr. Darcy's identity*

Mr. Collins:

Claire:

·	Disowned *Claire Collins*

·	*Rebelled against Lady Catherine*

·	*Took justice into her own hands*

·	*Provided for family where he did not*

·	*Would not have shown her brother deference – at least not willingly*

Wickham:

·	*Ruined youngest sister*

·	*Fathered a child*

·	*Abandoned Sarah*

·	*Destroyed family name*

Longbourn:
- *Wanted a bride   Elizabeth*
- *Wanted me to hurry and die*

Lady Catherine de Bourgh:

- *I suspect that if she told him to get rid of Claire and Wickham, he would do it without batting an eye, such is her power over him*

- *Opinionated*

- *Senseless to her true position in life (has someone ever informed her that she is NOT the queen of England?)*

Conclusion: Mr. Darcy and Mr. Collins have motives, yet the stronger position of guilt, at least on paper, goes to Mr. Collins.

Elizabeth lowered the parchment to the exact place where it had been found. Her father was more thorough than she was. She had not considered Mr. Collins' quest for his rights to inherit Longbourn.

Turning the parchment over, she added her own notes. Rather than choosing to rewrite the facts as her father had outlined, she focused upon the emotions. She wrote:

Claire:

Distraught at the discovery of her sister's plight. If something like this happened to one of my younger sisters, I would be murderous toward the man who caused this outrage. Not only was the future of Miss Sarah Collins destroyed, so was Claire's future. She would never be able to improve her situation with an unmarried sister who was with child. With the death of Sarah and the babe, the desire to end the life of the man responsible would intensify. As well, she had no one who would attempt to call the man to account on her behalf. Her only source of protection had abandoned them to serve at Lady

Catherine's feet. She would feel alone, discarded, responsible, frightened, determined, and fearless since any attempt at justice would result in the end of her own life. Would she have killed Mr. Wickham in cold blood? Absolutely!

Mr. Wickham:

His motives would always come back to self-preservation, I suspect. He cared for his own pleasure. He felt entitled to have a lifestyle of ease and elegance where he could be the Lady Catherine of his current residence. His efforts were for finding the best advantage—for himself alone. Was he lazy? I suspect he was. Was he indolent? I suspect not since he exerted himself if he thought there would be gain. Was he capable of murder? I suspect he would think it was too much trouble when moving on would have been an easier option. Did he fear the consequences of his actions? Absolutely not!

Mr. Collins:

He is a greedy man who also feels entitled. His servitude toward Lady Catherine is not out of true love and devotion. No, he has found a position wherein, with little effort on his part, his needs and wants are cared for. He does not need to extend himself to make decisions since she willingly does that for him. Due to this, he is even more loathsome than Mr. Wickham since that man makes his own choices and acts on them. For a man to be unwilling to go to the effort of thinking something through until the right path is revealed shows a selfishness that is entirely offensive. Could he have murdered his sister and Mr. Wickham? Absolutely! In doing so, he would believe himself to be justified in ridding society of two deficient individuals, as if he had done a service to humanity—and Lady Catherine. What a disgusting man!

Side note:

· *Who else wanted not just Claire Collins dead but Mr. Wickham dead?*

· *Who In our area knew them both enough to be aware of the sort of people they were?*

· *Have there been any newcomers to Meryton staying at the inn?*

· *Who spoke with Claire Collins?*

· *Who interacted with Mr. Wickham?*

· *Besides Mr. Collins, who departed Meryton after the murders?*

· *Who would benefit from the deaths of the two who died?*

Elizabeth reread her list several times before a thought occurred to her that robbed her of breath. Sitting back in the chair, she considered this new angle to the investigation. Her heart pounded and her eyes teared. Swallowing, she looked again at what she had written, her eyes blurry. *Heaven Forbid!* What if it was not Mr. Collins who had killed his sister and Mr. Wickham?

Blinking her lids rapidly until her vision cleared, she mustered up her courage to reread the final line:

· *Who would benefit from Mr. Darcy's death or permanent removal from society?*

Before she could contemplate the consequences, she sanded the paper, folded it, wrapped it in a blank sheet of parchment so no eyes, except Mr. Darcy's, would see her handwriting, and sealed it with her father's wax seal.

Once done, she placed it back on her father's desk. Staring at the packet, she weighed the possible consequences should she send it. If it was discovered that she had penned information on the letter, it would ruin her.

Sending a letter to an unmarried man was social suicide to a lady's reputation but this was life and death.

On the other hand, could she live with herself if she withheld the information from Mr. Darcy and he came to harm?

Putting her hands over her face, she meditated on one question; what if it was her who was unfairly accused? She would be desperate for someone to help.

Elizabeth closed her eyes and slowly inhaled.

Why was she certain Mr. Darcy was innocent? Why was she considering putting her future on the line for someone she barely knew? Were her emotions blinding her to his true character? She had already been entirely wrong about him once. Elizabeth could not place her finger on the exact reason she knew Mr. Darcy was not a murderer...or could she?

The gentleman had not only said that disguise was his abhorrence, but he proved it when he refused to deceive Mr. Collins that it was Charlotte and not her that they had aided on the orchard path. Although it was a seemingly small thing, this revelation of the true nature of his character was massive. At the cost to his own reputation, he had provided his coat for Elizabeth to sit upon under the tree, insisting that her comfort was paramount. Mostly, it was his honest recitation of Miss Darcy's plight that was most revealing of his true character. He shared information with her and her father as equals.

With that said, Elizabeth knew beyond a shadow of a doubt that Mr. Darcy would not have sought justice with his own hands. Had he been so inclined, Mr. Wickham would have been dead before he left Ramsgate. No, the man was honorable, considerate, and most of all, innocent.

Tapping the tip of her finger on the parchment, she reviewed her options. Again, it went back to the question; what if it was her?

Grabbing the letter, she gave it to Hill to have delivered right away to Netherfield Park. For justice to be served, to prove Mr. Darcy's innocence, she would risk everything. Later, she would meditate on why she was willing to pay that price for a man she had known for less than a fortnight. For now, he needed to know that he had others who cared what happened to him. And she did care, very much.

CHAPTER 22

"From Longbourn, sir." Parker held out the silver tray containing the letter.

Mr. Bennet must have penned the missive prior to his departure for Kent.

Ripping open the seal, Darcy was stunned to see not only Mr. Bennet's list but the man's daughter's as well. *Elizabeth!* He cared nothing about propriety that demanded no written messages be shared between couples who were not yet betrothed. His life was at risk. Darcy scanned both sides of the paper before seating himself by the window where he read each word several times. Mr. Bennet's findings were remarkably like his own. Elizabeth's page was a revelation.

Her final question chilled him. Who wanted him dead or out of the way? The answer was simple. Anyone who wanted Pemberley, which left the field wide open. Had Wickham not been dead, his name would have been at the top of the list. Yet, to contrive the death of two individuals who happened by circumstance to be in Meryton at the same time would have been the work of a brilliant mind. That alone reduced the number of those who could use the deaths to do him harm.

His stomach churned. A vision of Georgiana left alone and defenseless tormented him. He needed help with his investigation so he could be proven innocent. Richard was gone. The major and Mr. Bennet were not available. Bingley was, well, Charles would have no idea how to begin an investigation. He would wait impatiently for someone else, specifically his youngest sister, to take the lead then follow.

Elizabeth was his best resource. Rereading the list of facts outlined by the Bennets, he came to the same suspicion as Elizabeth. Likely, it was Mr. Collins who murdered his sister and George Wickham.

Shuddering at having been in the same company as the man, he prayed that the evidence against Mr. Collins would be collected swiftly and thoroughly. Darcy would not rest until he was free to walk from his chambers with his head held high.

"DID YOU HEAR?" Kitty Bennet bounced on the sofa after her return from Meryton, so anxious was she to be the bearer of news. When even Jane leaned forward to glean new details of the killings, Elizabeth knew that nothing could be done to restrain the females in her family from spreading gossip. "Abigail Goulding told Maria Lucas who told Cordelia Long, who I happened to see at the haberdashers, that Mr. Wickham was shot through the heart." She sighed; her hands pressed to her chest. "Isn't it romantic?"

Elizabeth was stunned. "Why ever would you think a murder would be romantic, Kitty? And are you certain of the facts? Mr. Wickham's wound was at his temple, not below."

"Hah!" Lydia chirped. "Little do you know, Lizzy. For I spoke with Denny and Captain Carter, and they saw the body before it went to the undertaker. They said," she paused for dramatic flair. Clearing her throat, thoroughly enjoying being the center of attention, Lydia drew out each word like she was a revered sage, "The bullet wound at his chest was hidden by the folds of his coat. Since there was no blood at his back, there was no reason to suspect another bullet was fired. He was shot twice. Likely he was already dead before he was in the stall since Denny said there would have been more of a disturbance to the scene if he was killed there." She lifted her chin in satisfaction at having bested her older sisters.

Elizabeth felt like someone hit her hard in the stomach with a walking stick. This was horrible if it was true. Before she could recover, her mother gave her opinion of the report.

"What does it matter if it is one bullet or two? Dead is dead, I say," The matron pulled her handkerchief from her sleeve and sniffed.

Behind their mother's back, Lydia stuck out her tongue at Kitty, who immediately began whining. "It was supposed to be my turn to tell the news, not Lydia's. Why does Lydia get all the turns?"

Bewildered, Elizabeth shook her head and glanced at Jane. For the first time that she could recall, her eldest sister rolled her eyes at the fiasco in the drawing room. Standing, she excused herself from the room. She needed to send this latest information to Mr. Darcy.

Thinking quickly, Elizabeth moved her ankle to the left. The twinge she felt was minimal. Willing to pass it off as a small deceit, she said, "Jane, after I write a quick note, would you be willing to drive the cart into Meryton? I fear the walk would be too much for my ankle."

Remembering not to run up the stairs to her chamber, she hurried down the hall once she was out of sight of the others.

Her note to Mr. Darcy was brief.

Sir,

Rumors are rife. Two bullet holes in the body but only one bullet in the stall. Verifying now. Be cautious as will I.

E

In less than thirty minutes, Beatrice was hitched to the cart, and they were on their way. Before they reached the end of Longbourn's drive, Elizabeth asked Jane to go directly to the blacksmith.

"Mr. Haniger, I suppose you are weary of being disturbed," Elizabeth could see by the force the smithy used to pound the molten metal into place that he was irritated. "I will not keep you from your work."

"Then how may I help you, Miss Elizabeth?" The blacksmith asked, his hammer falling heavily on the anvil. "Is there something wrong with Beatrice or your wheel?"

Stiffening her spine, Elizabeth boldly inquired, "I am needing only one word from you, sir. Were there two bullets fired at Mr. Wickham or only one?"

Mr. Haniger dropped the hammer to his side, his eyes piercing Elizabeth. After a short pause he said, "Two." Turning away from her, he poked a metal rod into his forge, stirring the coals.

They would get no more information from him on this day.

"Walk on, Jane," Elizabeth instructed.

Clearing the market town, she asked Jane to bypass Longbourn's drive. Turning down the path Mr. Darcy had used at her rescue, they arrived at the scene of the crime.

The morning mist had collected inside the footprints. Oak leaves in variegated shades of orange, yellow, and green hues were tossed about, covering the area where possibly not just one person, but two, had died.

Their father often included a gift for her when he placed his order from the bookseller. The mix of subjects he had given her was broad. Elizabeth kept them in a small bookcase next to her bed chamber window. For this morning's purpose, she had selected her least read text, "*A Treatise on Plane and Spherical Trigonometry*" by John Bonnycastle. Elizabeth loathed mathematics.

Pulling out a folded piece of paper from inside, she asked Jane to hold it while she carefully approached the scene where the scuffle had taken place. Gently, she pulled away the leaves.

Climbing back aboard the pony cart, she used the advantage of height and the hardness of the back of the book to sketch the location of every indentation or disturbance to the grass, as well as the trees surrounding the area. To satisfy her own curiosity, once she finished her task, she stepped down from the cart and again approached where the majority of prints were located. Carefully, she placed her booted foot where Miss Collins must have stood.

Ahh! She and Claire were not identical since the print was slightly longer than her boot.

"Lizzy, whatever are you about?" Jane asked, shivering from the chill.

Glancing around the area one last time, Elizabeth replied, "Autumn has set in. When the rains come, the prints will fill in and be indiscernible later. I do not know if this information will be helpful, but I did not want to regret the lack of record later."

"Would this be helpful?" Jane pointed to the trunk of the southernmost English oak that stood behind the other two. The trunk was fissured with age, the canopy dotted with leaves that had not yet fallen to the ground.

Elizabeth's eyes moved from the bottom of the trunk up to the first of its branches, carefully surveying every inch. Immediately below the crook where the branch shot out, a shard of wood was missing, exposing the lighter-colored flesh underneath.

She could not look away.

Lifting her skirt to protect the hem from the damp, the walk to the tree was over far quicker than Elizabeth wanted. On one hand, the need to help Mr. Darcy was the weightiest reason she was there. On the other hand, the cousin she had only just met, likely lost her life near that very spot. Pain and sorrow flooded her heart.

When, on close inspection, her small finger penetrated the trunk easily, she knew the cause. Inhaling deeply, she placed the toes of her boots as close to the trunk as possible. Stretching to her full height, she placed her finger back in the hole. It was right where her heart was pounding so fiercely that Elizabeth was afraid it would leap right out of her chest.

"Do you have a knife?" she looked back at Jane.

"One moment, Lizzy." Jane dug through the box kept under the seat. "There is a knife, though I cannot determine how sharp it is."

Grateful to be away from the tree, Elizabeth retrieved the blade from her sister. Despite her efforts to calm herself, her heartbeat had moved up into her throat.

Expecting to have to burrow into the wood for several inches, she was stunned when the bullet popped right out into her hand. Her instinct was to drop the offensive item. Bracing herself, she studied it instead. The metal was flattened with only a small, rounded bump on one side. Removing her handkerchief from her sleeve, she wrapped the piece in the cloth and placed it in her pocket.

Walking back to the footprints, she noticed something she had not seen before, cart tracks. Standing behind where Jane was seated, Elizabeth stretched her arms out until each hand would have rested on a wheel of their cart. Returning to where the other tracks were, she kept from moving her arms to see if it was a perfect match. It was. Next, she stepped toe-to-toe inside the tracks before moving back behind where Beatrice had pulled their cart.

Again, the measurements were exact. *What did that mean?* Were all carts built to the same specifications? If they were, did it mean they came from the same manufacturer? Did someone who was known to the Bennets borrow the transport from Longbourn?

She slapped her forehead with her hand. Mr. Collins was the last person to use the pony cart. She needed to tell Mr. Darcy.

When she showed the smashed bullet to Jane, there was a small streak of something on the white linen surface of the cloth she had wrapped it in. Most likely it had not come from the bark of the tree. The sour taste of bile shot up the back of Elizabeth's throat. Jane began crying.

Clamping her hand around the metal, Elizabeth shoved it into her pocket. Swallowing repeatedly, Elizabeth insisted that they return to Longbourn. She had another letter to write.

* * *

THE KNOCK on his door startled Darcy. He was sitting by the window, his mind holding a sorrowful picture of what his sister's life would be if his innocence could not be proven. His own life as well. He would never be able to marry, to feel the joy at the birth of his first child, and the delight of growing close as a family. He would not be able to see the colts and lambs born in the spring later producing young ones of their own or the orchards newly planted bearing fruit.

He wanted to sob.

Clearing his throat and his mind of these maudlin images, he commanded whomever it was who had disturbed him to enter. Parker came in bearing the same silver tray. This time, a thick packet wrapped in parchment and string rested on the surface with, again, nothing to identify the sender on the outside.

"Sir, this came from Longbourn."

By Jove, he was grateful she was on his side!

"That will be all," Darcy said as his fingers worked the knot from the string. Once his valet had stepped away to confer with the officer sitting at the inside of his door, Darcy poured over the information inside.

Glancing at the map, he set it on his lap until he read what Elizabeth had to say.

Mr. Darcy,

I do hope you are seated, sir, since the news I bear, which is already being whispered in every drawing room and parlor in the area, is dire.

Mr. Wickham was shot in the heart and the temple. Yes, two of the officers reported that they saw both wounds. Mr. Haniger also confirmed that there were two bullet wounds rather than the one. Therefore, my conjecture is that both victims were killed elsewhere, brought to the blacksmith's stables after they were dead, planted there to look like a murder/suicide with Mr. Wickham being shot again for effect. Who would do such a thing, I ask? It would, out of practical necessity, be someone who was strong enough to lift the bodies into a cart by himself or who had comrades to assist in the transporting and repositioning of the corpses. If this was the case, I suspect there would have been a pact of loyalty since unscrupulous strangers performing an illegal task could be bribed to point the finger of guilt at any party other than themselves. Do you know anyone in this position, sir?

I have also enclosed a crude drawing of the orchard where the oak trees are. The compass points in the upper right corner are as accurate as I know, Mr. Darcy. Jane located the damaged area on the bark of the southernmost tree where the enclosed bullet was retrieved. With no little amount of trepidation, I will tell you that I stood against that tree to confirm the range and height would have matched the location of Claire's fatal wound had she been standing with her back to the tree. From the location of the second set of boot prints, which I assume belonged to Mr. Wickham, he was positioned immediately in front of her, facing her, since the toes of their footwear pointed to each other less than two feet apart.

Sir, I am anxious for my Papa and Major Gerring to return with the evidence needed to resolve the issue and have the guilty party arrested for this heinous crime. In the meantime, I will pray for your safety. If it was not Mr. Collins, then you are in danger.

In case you wondered, Hill can be trusted implicitly.

I beg you take care,

EB

Darcy was gutted. The murders were not a spontaneous reaction to an emotionally charged setting. This was cold-blooded killing with an intent to deceive. If he was not careful, he could be the next victim.

Grabbing paper and quill, Darcy did something he had never before done, he wrote to an unmarried female completely unrelated to him.

EB,

If Mr. Collins is not the murderer, then all of us are in

danger. I would request, no, I would beg you to remain inside Longbourn along with the rest of your family at least until Mr. Bennet returns from Kent. Once your father and Major Gerring are here and it is confirmed that the murderer has been apprehended, it may be safe. Please do not take any more risks on my behalf.

I thank you for the information you have shared. In return, I shall report my suppositions.

1. Whomever was in the orchard would have left the murder scene covered with mud and blood. Where are these damaged garments and footwear? Where is the pony with the black mud from that location in its hooves?

2. Pray forgive me for mentioning this, but consideration needs to be given to how much heavier a dead body would be to carry than one who could place their arms around the carrier's neck, therefore better distributing the weight evenly. Mr. Collins did not impress me as one who developed strength and dexterity from hard work. From his own mouth, he admitted that he did not keep a horse so his thigh muscles would likely not give him the power he needed to lift and shift a body weighing as much as his own. I apologize, EB. You now have a mental image you never wanted; I imagine.

3. Something I did not see in your drawing were the hoof prints from the horses that your father, the major, Bingley, John Lucas, and myself were riding. This leads me to believe that the thicker clumps of grass might have hidden the existence of a second person's prints. With that in mind, it bears asking, who would have assisted Mr. Collins with this crime?

I despise being idle. The need to participate fully in this investigation is overwhelming. Yet, I am forced to wait on your father's return. Nevertheless, please know that the second I am able, I will do all within my power to bring the guilty party to justice,

Your servant,

FD

Folding and sealing the letter, he tasked Parker with the delivery to Hill at Longbourn.

CHAPTER 23

$\mathcal{B}$y the end of the first day without her father in residence at Longbourn, Elizabeth and Jane had visible proof that Mrs. Francis Bennet was not a good decision maker.

Blatantly rebelling against the direction of her husband, Mama invited two of the officers from the militia to tea. During the conversation, Mr. Denny and Captain Carter competed to share the most vivid details about the recent murders. The ladies, including Elizabeth if the truth were known, leaned forward to not miss a word.

"Why, I heard that the lady and gent from Netherfield Park were more than friends," Captain Carter sneered, "If you know what I mean."

Mama fanned herself with her handkerchief while Lydia begged for more salacious details.

Denny added, "Well, I heard that the lady and Mr. Wickham were sworn enemies of Mr. Darcy, that he had ruined and then tossed the lady aside like refuse. From

Mr. Wickham he stole a valuable living. Mr. Darcy is an evil man who needs to pay for his crime."

How dare they vilify Mr. Darcy!

Elizabeth opened her mouth to defend the gentleman against their vile claims, then snapped it shut. They would not understand why she, of all people, would stand up for him. Likely, they heard the rumors about Mr. Darcy's insult to her at the assembly. More importantly, to openly side with a suspected murderer would not allow her the freedom to investigate. Mouths would close and tongues would wag behind her back.

"Could this be true?" Jane asked, her eyes tearing up at the claim. "Mr. Bingley, who is kindness itself, would never have a close friend capable of doing anyone harm."

Both men blushed at her innocent chastisement.

Elizabeth used their discomfort to further her own purpose. Creating doubt in their minds would be a more effective tool than confrontation. With the way the two officers liked to share information, any uncertainty created had the potential to spread. At least, that was her hope.

"Gentlemen," she began. "It was reported to our family by our beloved father that Mr. Wickham was not an honest man. Although I do not know of these matters," Elizabeth closed her eyes, sighed, and dipped her head in mock humility, something she had observed often when Mr. Collins was at Longbourn. "We were all given to understand that despite his recent arrival to Meryton, Mr. Wickham left behind debts with the merchants and debts of honor with the militia. Is this information not true?"

"Well, ah...," Mr. Denny sputtered. "Indeed, Mr.

Wickham owed me money that I wish he had paid. However, Mr. Darcy made it right."

"He owed me a fair amount too," Captain Carter poked himself in the chest with his thumb. "We aren't the only ones, I hear. Wickham was one who took risks with his money."

Elizabeth lifted her eyes from her lap, her posture as demure as was possible. "It appears as if he liked to risk the funds belonging to others, as well, Captain."

"Yes, well," Captain Carter said. "It does not mean the man deserved to be murdered for a few coins."

"Hmm...I wonder," Elizabeth paused. "If a man showed no integrity to those like you whom he claimed as friends, would he inherently lack integrity in other areas of life...such as with the fairer sex?"

"Oh, yes, Miss Elizabeth," Mr. Denny immediately replied. "Why, I could tell you many a tale about the times that Wickham...well...they would not be stories fit for ladies, I am afraid."

"Pray, do tell," Kitty and Lydia begged. Even their mother seemed eager to hear something nefarious she could later share with the other matrons of the community.

Elizabeth sought to nip the conversation in the bud, "I thank you for your restraint, Mr. Denny. That you show ladies far more dignity than Mr. Wickham had is commendable. I am certain that your mother would be proud."

He blushed, then gulped the rest of his now tepid tea.

"Gentlemen," Elizabeth's tone rang as if it was solid steel. "You do recall that Miss Claire Collins, the lady you implied as having a torrid affair with both Mr. Darcy and Mr. Wickham, is our cousin, do you not?"

She paused briefly, not allowing them time to gather their thoughts. Continuing, she said, "If you recall the scene at the inn, Miss Collins did not know which man was actually Mr. Darcy. Mr. Wickham had used the man's name to perpetuate theft and dissolute behavior. Had they not identified themselves, she would not have known either man. Do you remember?"

"We beg your pardon, ladies." Mr. Denny stood, bowing deeply. "I had forgotten that she was family. And, yes, I do recall the conversations and accusations at the inn. Wickham was mortified to have been discovered as a liar."

"Which makes him a liar and a thief, does it not?" Elizabeth boldly challenged.

"Lizzy!" Jane reprimanded. "To speak ill of someone dead will not serve you well."

Elizabeth pretended embarrassment. And humility. Bowing her head, she stated, "As usual, you are correct, my sister. In my quest to get to the truth of the matter, I expressed opinions when I should not have."

It galled her to promote the sorry viewpoint held by most men that ladies were empty-headed fools. Yet, there was a certain amount of power in her actions. Anything she said or did outside of what was expected from a lady would be excused because she was of the "weaker" sex.

Mr. Denny cleared his throat. "What you say is true, Miss Elizabeth. Mr. Wickham's decisions could make a grown man blush. And you are correct in that Miss Collins appeared to not know either man for it was the name Darcy she was familiar with, not the man himself." He bowed. "I beg your pardon, ladies. Carter and I, well, we need to be more cautious about what we say, I suppose."

"Mr. Denny and Captain Carter, your motive was to warn us that people are not always what they seem." Elizabeth wished her words were the truth since that had not been their motive at all. "For this, we thank you, kind sirs."

Within moments, the two officers excused themselves with their heads held high, likely to share their adjusted opinions in the parlors of as many citizens of Meryton as possible.

Their statements were a bold reminder to her that Mr. Darcy had already been tried and judged in the opinions of the public. Their neighbors had cruelly and unfairly declared his verdict as guilty.

DARCY STUDIED the documents from Elizabeth as if they were a detailed map leading to a gold mine. Each time he reread the pages he came to the same conclusion—Mr. Collins murdered George Wickham and his own sister.

The thought made his heart sick. How could a man end the life of a sibling, especially a girl he would have watched learn to toddle, lose her first tooth, and go through that gangly stage between childhood and becoming a young lady? Darcy could not conceive of committing something so egregious against a cherished family member. It spoke of an unfeeling heart, a damaged soul void of human feeling. The mere idea of hurting Georgiana was repugnant.

A brother's greatest responsibility, especially that of an older brother, was to serve and protect; to foster a life where a little sister would run to you with confidence that you and only you could make her world better again if she was troubled.

For a certainty, he was enough of a man of the world to know of the treachery in some families where fathers, brothers, and uncles mistreated young girls in heinous ways. Those acts were untenable, unthinkable, and unspeakable. Never should such an abhorrent idea come up into a man's heart. Grown men who harmed a female in that way deserved to be...

Inhaling deeply to slow the galloping of his pulse, Darcy unclenched his fists and relaxed his jaw.

That Mr. Collins had been in the same residence as Elizabeth, selecting her as his future mate made Darcy's stomach rebel.

He would stand up at the trial and speak against the evil that was Mr. Collins. He would do it for Miss Claire Collins, Miss Sarah Collins, and Elizabeth. Collins could rot in a penal colony or hang until he was dead, Darcy would not care.

Oh, but how that would infuriate his Aunt Catherine. Although Darcy had no doubt that she would manipulate the information until she believed she knew all along of Mr. Collins' guilt.

With so obvious a criminal who could be swiftly brought to justice, Darcy merely needed to wait until the major and Mr. Bennet returned with Collins arrested and in chains. Then, Darcy would take on the prosecution, seeing it through until justice was served. Only then would he feel truly free.

Unless...unless Collins did not do it.

Was he, Fitzwilliam Darcy, passing judgment like everyone else in Meryton was likely doing without knowing all the facts? In truth, the mental image of Mr. Collins lifting and carrying a limp body hinted at the impossible. Darcy was strong from a lifetime of riding, fencing, boxing, and working at Pemberley when needed. Even for him to lift a man equal to his size would be a challenge. Unless he had hidden occupations, Mr. Collins simply could not have carried out the task. So, who *could* have helped him? Who *would* have helped him?

Darcy paced his chambers, his mind questioning his theories as his heart begged for an easy resolution to the crimes.

When the first day passed since Mr. Bennet and Major Gerring departed Netherfield Park, Darcy refused to worry. It was a four hour journey to London by carriage, then another four to Rosings Park in Kent. At the earliest, they would not return until late on the morrow. Then, the matter could be settled.

After a sleepless night, he penned a note to Bingley.

My friend,

To protect the reputation of your sisters, mightn't they return to town, distancing themselves from the events of the past few days? I would hate for the suspicions against me to afflict their names and their futures.

To be sure, I am sincerely appreciative of how you have generously allowed me to remain in the comfort of your home.

Nonetheless, I also recognize that the burden I have placed upon you is more than a friend should ask. I willingly volunteer to be housed at the jail in Meryton until I am sent to the assizes.

I regret that your first foray into the management of a property would turn out this way. Because of the accusations against me, I do not want you to come to harm.

Darcy

Bingley's reply was that he was confident that the true guilty party would be revealed once Mr. Bennet and Major Gerring returned. The Bingley family would remain where they are.

* * *

ELIZABETH QUIETLY LEFT Longbourn through the kitchen on her way to the stables. The two grooms were quietly going about the task of raking straw into Beatrice's stall.

"Pardon me, Billy," she caught the attention of the older man. "Did Beatrice go out and play in the mud the night of the bonfire?"

The groom chuckled. "Well, she must have because I dug black mud outta her hooves for a whole day."

Elizabeth's heart dropped to her stomach. It was as she suspected, but not exactly what she wanted to hear.

* * *

WHEN THE MOON was visible in the dark of the sky at the end of the second day, Darcy refused to allow himself to be concerned. Mr. Bennet was wily enough to avoid any machinations tried by his cousin. Major

255

Gerring would have no difficulty at all in restraining the criminal.

Earlier, the militia officer who was assigned to remain inside his room chose to relocate to the hallway with his comrades. There they passed the time playing dice, cards, and gossiping like the harpies who flitted from drawing room to drawing room spreading their poison. Darcy heard their voices but not the words. His first instinct was to escape, to investigate on his own. However, that would have added to his guilt had he been caught. Thus, he was stuck in the chamber alone with his thoughts, which were many.

The daily change of guard occasionally brought a tidbit of information he could add to the little he already possessed. According to one of the officers, Mr. Bennet arranged for Miss Collins to be buried in the Longbourn graveyard. Darcy was able to convince the guard to deliver the necessary funds to have a carved stone placed at her grave.

He shook his head. A series of foolish acts by Wickham caused a chain reaction leading to his own demise at the hands of Mr. Collins, as well as the death of others.

By the end of the third day, Darcy's disappointment at not hearing anything from Mr. Bennet, the major, or Longbourn left him restless. Neither had he received a response from his uncle or the Bow Street Chief Magistrate. He had not even received a letter from Georgiana. It was as if he had disappeared off the face of the earth where no contact was allowed. Had he been able to travel with the others, he would have made sure that matters moved forward quickly.

* * *

ELIZABETH WAS SURPRISED to have not received a message from Mr. Darcy after writing to him about her discovery of the dark mud in Beatrice's hooves. That someone was bold enough to enter Longbourn's stables the night of the murder to move the bodies while the staff was at the bonfire was appalling. Additionally, a close inspection of the back of the pony cart yielded nothing. Whatever blankets were used to protect the surfaces had to be hidden somewhere. Where were they? Why did Mr. Darcy not write?

* * *

ON THE FOURTH DAY, Darcy woke to rain pounding against his window. The downpour lasted two days, soaking the ground and dampening his spirits. He had received not one word about the progress of the investigation. His only correspondence was business letters his staff forwarded from Darcy House in London and a daily note from Bingley asking after his health. With the officers not allowing any contact other than his valet and the maids, Darcy had an abundance of time to simmer and stew over the smallest details he knew of the murders.

Dropping into the chair by the window, he reconsidered what he knew of the scene of the crime from the two times he was in that portion of the orchard along with the drawing Elizabeth sent to him. The rain would have erased all the footprints. The wind would have stirred the grass and leaves so that nothing would look the same.

Blast! He pounded his fists on the arm of the chair. If only he could do something. He would gather the evidence that existed, find Mr. Collins, shackle him to the inside of a carriage, deposit him at St. Albans for the assizes, then hurry to Longbourn to offer...to offer...

He swallowed. Was he truly thinking what he was thinking—that he would hurry to Longbourn to offer for Elizabeth? Marriage? To Elizabeth Bennet?

Darcy held his breath waiting for panic to settle in. Only once before had he seriously considered marriage. Miss Millicent Moore was considered a diamond in her debut season. She was as blonde as Jane Bennet with light blue eyes and a fair complexion. The first time he had stood up with her at a ball, she moved so lightly it felt like he was dancing with a feather. She exuded gentle charm, was witty in her speech, and delighted every cell of his body. With the exception of Lady Catherine, his family approved of the lady as the future mistress of Pemberley. The evening prior to his offering a proposal, he instructed Parker to have his best suit brushed and pressed, roses to be delivered ten minutes before his scheduled arrival, and his mother's ring polished.

It was not until he exited his carriage and he saw the line of gentlemen waiting for entrance to Miss Moore's residence that it hit Darcy square in the head. His motive for being there was selfish. It was not love or affection that moved him to propose to her. He wanted her to choose him above all the other candidates. He wanted to bc the winner of her hand over all the others in contention. Darcy stopped in his tracks going no closer to her door. Perspiration beaded his brow at how close he had come to one of the most foolish decisions in his life. His treacherous heart had convinced him that she was a prize to be gained, a bride to be won. Except, he did not love her and as far as he knew, she did not love him either. Besides, his preference was for a brunette with dark eyes, not a blonde.

After that misstep, he vowed to himself and his cousin to only marry for the deepest love. Richard, too, had almost fallen prey to the fear of missing out on someone every other man craved. Both men desired not to settle for less than what their own parents' possessed, true love and deep affection.

Was that what he was feeling for Elizabeth? Was it true love or was his heart pounding out a cadence of deceptive beats? In truth, Darcy was not quite sure.

CHAPTER 24

*E*lizabeth worried about the continued absence of her father. And she fretted over not hearing from Mr. Darcy. By the end of the seventh day since her father and the major departed Hertfordshire, only Charlotte was able to calm her frayed nerves.

After a short conversation, Charlotte handed her latest in her series to Elizabeth. The paper was folded, wrapped, and sealed with the direction for *The Times* on the outside. As they had done many times before, Elizabeth would pass it over to Hill for him to post the next time he took the pony cart to Meryton.

"Have you had news from your father?" Charlotte asked.

Frustrated, Elizabeth admitted, "We have not."

"Hmm. I wonder if he has written directly to Mr. Darcy then." Charlotte mused.

"No, for Mr. Bingley reports that the only mail his guest receives is from his house in London or from Miss Darcy. Papa would send a letter directly to Netherfield

Park should he write to Mr. Darcy." Elizabeth pulled the brim of her bonnet down to keep the heavy mist from her face. Charlotte had driven her family's pony cart which had smaller wheels than the one belonging to the Bennets.

"Mr. Bingley comes to see Jane daily, then?" Charlotte asked. "I suppose your Mama is over the moon with excitement at the possibilities. Has Jane decided that he is the one?"

"Other than two days away to care for business in London, Mr. Bingley has been a constant visitor." Elizabeth said. "I am not privy to Jane's private musings, as you know. However, she anticipates his arrival at Longbourn and welcomes him when he is here."

"And what of him? Has he spoken to Jane about their future?"

Elizabeth appreciated that Charlotte most often came directly to the point. She claimed it was because she was old enough to be considered on the shelf, so she no longer needed to guard her tongue. Elizabeth scoffed at the idea since her friend would be forever young in her mind.

"They often have their heads together. Their conversation is kept between the two of them. Nevertheless, just yesterday, he rejoiced in the smooth running of Netherfield Park under his own hand loudly enough that all in the room were able to hear. He speculated that he might be willing, in the future, of course, to take on a larger estate should one come available. The joy his accomplishment brought him was written on his face. He is a modest man who seems to complement Jane's character very well."

Charlotte nodded. "I am pleased for her if the two of

them agree to wed. I fear Jane would shrivel and fade away should she be attached to a cruel or selfish man. She is not like the two of us, Lizzy. A vicious man would rue the day he tangled with either you or me, would he not?"

Elizabeth chuckled. "Then let us keep away from those sorts of men, I say."

Clicking her tongue, the cart moved forward.

Elizabeth waved until Charlotte made the turn at the end of the driveway.

The ribbons of her bonnet snapped in the stiff breeze. Pulling her jacket closer, she shivered. Autumn was welcoming the upcoming change of season with open arms. Yet, despite the cold, Elizabeth remained outside.

Change had blown into Meryton with the arrival of Mr. Darcy and the Bingleys to Netherfield Park. Once Mr. Collins and then his sister appeared, the gusts increased. Then Mr. Wickham showed up and the dam holding back the four winds broke, leaving the residents stunned with the force of destruction. Their lives would not return to normal until Mr. Collins was brought to justice. Then fear would dissipate as the air currents headed away from their small community. Elizabeth could not wait.

A WEARY MR. BENNET arrived at Netherfield Park along with the major, Sir William and Mr. Haniger. Bingley also was in the room.

It was a relief for Darcy to be outside his chambers for the first time in a se'nnight, especially to receive good news freeing him of suspicion. When none of the men spoke right away, a wisp of apprehension began to grow. As the minutes passed, trepidation blossomed into fear. Darcy had a million questions he wanted to ask to have his curiosity satisfied. However, he remained quiet and waited.

Finally, Mr. Bennet cleared his throat, shook his head, and said, "We arrived at Hunsford Cottage to discover Mr. William Collins splayed in his chair, an empty bottle of spirits at his side, a cup shattered on the floor."

Darcy nodded, unsurprised that the man's guilty conscience had driven him to drink.

Mr. Bennet continued, "A pistol was in one hand, a poorly-written note confessing to the murder of his sister in the other. Nothing was said about Mr. Wickham's death." He glanced at the others. "We assumed his loss of life was circumstantial rather than intended."

No! No! No! Darcy's stomach began to churn.

"He was dead."

What! Darcy felt behind him for a chair, his knees no longer able to support him.

Mr. Bennet was not yet done. "Your aunt, Lady Catherine, upon being informed, declared it impossible. We said nothing to her about Mr. Wickham since he was likely unknown to her." Mr. Bennet shook his head in disgust. "As Mr. Collins' closest heir, I saw to the man's burial, the disposal of his possessions, and the closing of the cottage until another occupant can be chosen by your aunt."

Darcy dropped his head into his palms.

"Before we departed, the major retrieved the pistol,

the bullet lodged in the wall behind Mr. Collins, and one of his boots from his closet."

Darcy's head shot up, his eyes on the speaker.

"They were similar enough to yours that we, the major, the magistrate in Hunsford, and I, believe justice would be served by clearing you of all charges and suspicion, Mr. Darcy."

The relief was incredible.

After a long pause, Bingley slapped him on the back, "Well done, Darcy."

Not wanting to take anything for granted, Darcy glanced at Sir William and Mr. Haniger. Both agreed with the findings. William Collins was guilty of murdering his sister and George Wickham, then himself.

Moments later, Bingley left to inform his family. Sir William returned to Lucas Lodge and Mr. Haniger went back to work at his blacksmith shop.

Major Gerring moved a side table to the center of Bingley's study. Placing three chairs around the small table, he gestured for the two others to be seated. Once they were settled, he put four small wads of paper onto the surface in a straight line. Unwrapping the first, he put the smashed bullet back on the table.

"This was the bullet we retrieved from your carriage."

Unwrapping the second, he said, "I dug this out of the stable behind Wickham's head." It was almost twice the size of the first bullet. "The third was just given me by the blacksmith. It was removed from Wickham's heart before he was buried."

Darcy shuddered.

The third one almost matched the second.

The fourth one was similar. "This was from Mr. Collin's wall."

"One moment, if you please." Darcy hurried back to his chambers to retrieve the bullet that Elizabeth had retrieved from the oak tree she sent in her second letter. Returning to the study, he placed the metal next to the others. "This came from the tree in the orchard." It was approximately the same size as bullets two, three, and four

Mr. Bennet rubbed his eyes.

Darcy said, "Four similar bullets that killed three people. This proves that the same weapon fired bullets two through five if I am correct?"

The major nodded.

"Which proves that Claire Collins murdered no one and that Mr. Collins killed the others and himself?" Darcy asked.

Neither the major nor Mr. Bennet answered right away.

Finally, the major said, "Not necessarily. You see, the curious thing was that there was no smell of alcohol about Mr. Collins. Recall Mr. Wickham's white gloves which were remarkably free of powder stains? It was the same with Mr. Collins. There was no residue on his fingers. Additionally, there was no black powder burn in the barrel or in the flash pan, no scarring from the spark initiated upon repercussion in the gun he held. It is impossible to wipe a weapon completely clean to restore it to condition once it has been fired. Also, it was a much smaller caliber than the one that fired these four bullets."

"You are saying..." Darcy wanted to be sick.

"I am suggesting that Mr. Collins was murdered by the same person who killed Miss Claire Collins and Mr. Wickham."

"Dear God in heaven!" Darcy exclaimed. His stomach plunged to his knees.

Mr. Bennet added, "We know you were not the guilty party since you were kept under watch during your confinement. Upon our arrival here, the staff reported that you did not leave your chambers once during the past se'nnight. Therefore, you are no longer under suspicion."

"But, who...?" Darcy asked, stunned at the information.

Mr. Bennet shook his head. "We do not know."

"Then there is a murderer on the loose in Meryton." He shuddered as a cold chill shot down his spine.

"We believe so," Mr. Bennet admitted.

Major Gerring wrapped the bullets back in the paper from which they came. Each was labeled with the place where they were retrieved. "Sir, you should also know that we spoke with a midwife in Ramsgate who cared for Miss Sarah Collins just prior to her sisters' arrival at Rosings Park. We were told that the young girl started bleeding early in her pregnancy. Neither survived what the midwife called a miscarriage. The girl was buried in a plot in the family cemetery near their home. This confirms that Miss Claire Collins was telling the truth."

Mr. Bennet added, "Yes, well, since there were no heirs to the Collins estate who survived the atrocious events since the loss of young Sarah, I arranged for the property to be placed with an agent who will lease it or sell it. It is modest in size and in rather poor shape. Any funds gener-ated will be donated to a charity benefiting girls in the same situation as Miss Sarah Collins, may God have mercy on her soul." Mr. Bennet wiped his hand over his eyes. "Gentlemen, I have five daughters, one the same age as Sarah. I cannot begin to stress how much these events put the fear of God in me. I need to go home to see my girls."

Once Mr. Bennet had gone, Darcy retrieved the papers Elizabeth had sent from Longbourn. Handing them over to the major, he waited impatiently while the officer studied the information.

"She is an intelligent woman," the major offered when he handed them back to Darcy.

"I agree." Folding the parchment to place inside his waistcoat, he asked, "Tell me what you are thinking, Major Gerring, for I simply cannot believe you have not pondered these events as you traveled."

"In that you are correct, sir." The major hesitated before looking at him directly. "The mystery of why Miss Claire Collins shot at you is solved. It was a clear case of mistaken identity based upon Wickham's lies. As far as her intent, Miss Collins' case is closed." He inhaled, then exhaled slowly. "The easy course would be to believe Mr. Collins perpetrated these crimes. Yet, although he most likely killed his sister and George Wickham, I do not believe he was responsible for his own death. Which makes me wonder...did he actually kill them?"

Darcy was beginning to believe the same. A thought occurred to him, "Just how close did his boot compare to mine?"

The major rubbed his hand over his mouth before replying. "They were about the same length although narrower on the sides. Where they differed was in the heel. His were almost double the height of yours." He paused to let that fact sink in. "Now, Collins was probably a stone heavier than you and, from the wear of the heel and sole, he walked on the outside of his feet. If you compare Miss Elizabeth's drawing with what we know from his boots, they do not match. The print left in the orchard was level with only a slightly deeper impression at the heel."

"Then it would *not* have been Mr. Collins who was there?"

"It would not," the major confirmed.

Blast! "Then who murdered Claire Collins, her brother, and Wickham?"

"As of yet I do not know," the major admitted. "But I am determined to find out."

"As am I," Darcy muttered to himself.

CHAPTER 25

"I told you Collins was too much," Bingley growled. "But you always think you know best, Caroline."

His sister paid him no attention. Instead, she grinned maliciously. "No, Charles, in this you are wrong, as usual." She purred, before showing her metaphorical claws. "Only two men, Mr. Darcy and the parson, were motivated to have both the girl and the rogue dead. With the preacher out of the picture, the person who will eventually be charged and found guilty is Darcy."

"Then why did you have me write a suicide note? Why did you make it so Darcy will go free?"

Caroline scoffed. "Because the only thing better than having Darcy dead is to have him under our power."

"Blackmail? We did not talk about this, Caroline," Bingley ran his hands through his hair, pulling at the ends.

"Hurst agreed," Caroline admitted. "You know, Charles, having our brother-in-law leave for Kent as soon as the bodies were put in the stable was a mark of brilliance, if I do admit so myself. The timing was perfect." She smiled her malicious smile. "I must confess that I had no idea Hurst was a capable man. Returning to the inn after getting rid of those Bennet girls to overhear the parson's sister's confession by hiding in the adjoining room was smart. I had no idea he could be of use to us in a practical way."

Bingley paced the room. "This is not right, Caroline. We never talked about blackmail. I..., *Good God in heaven!* I know what you were about!" Bingley swore a blue streak. "Because Darcy rejected you as mistress of Pemberley, you want him to pay, to suffer humiliation at your hands as you suffered under his."

Her elevated chin and the tilt of her head told him more than words that he was correct.

"You had Collins killed for your vanity, Caroline!" Disgust riddled his voice. Cupping his hand over his mouth, he considered the mess they were in. "You have left us with no choice. We have to make sure Darcy is dead before he works out what you did or we are destroyed."

"You worry far too much," Caroline soothed. "Besides, who are a blacksmith and Sir William to us? They read Mr. Collins' suicide note and believed every word. Mere simpletons, they are. However, as you reported, Mr. Bennet and Major Gerring are much more discerning. The finger of guilt is still pointed at Mr. Darcy for the murder of Miss Collins and that rake, what was his name? Doubt has to be brewing in their gut." Before anyone could reply, she continued, "Never mind them. They are not important. Once Louisa and I journey to London to retrieve dear Georgiana we will have no difficulty getting her into the carriage when we tell her that her brother needs her here because he is in danger. By the time we are north of the city and she realizes we have none of her luggage, it will be too late. Like Sir William, she is a simpleton. She will do as we tell her."

Bingley dropped into his chair. "You had better be right, Caroline."

"I am right, Charles. Stop worrying." Caroline flicked her wrist at him. "Do you recall your part of the plan?"

He huffed. "Hurst and I will follow you to London, then we head north for a quick trip to Gretna Green. I will marry Miss Darcy, making me the new master of Pemberley."

Her tone sharpened. "Do not forget, Brother. You will not become master as long as Mr. Darcy is alive. I suggest we bleed him dry before he dies. He needs to pay for his arrogance."

Bingley ran his fingers through his hair. "No! We are too involved to veer from the course we already set. This had better work."

"Fine!" She pouted. "If you insist, we will do things your way." She tapped her fingers on the back of the chair. "Trust me," Caroline insisted. "Just do one thing for me, Charles. Do not kill him right away. Allow him to suffer knowing his end is near and that he is powerless to prevent it. Only then will he have paid for his crimes against *me.*"

"Yes, Caroline," Bingley sneered. "Whatever you say, Caroline."

Ignoring his sarcasm, she added, "No one will expect the 'accident' that will befall him if everything goes as planned. When he goes missing, Mr. Bennet and Major Gerring will no longer doubt who murdered Claire Collins and Mr. Wickham. Before we leave Hertfordshire, we will plant enough clues to lead the investigation right back to him."

ELIZABETH'S PATIENCE was almost at its end. Her mother and younger sisters captured and held her father's attention as soon as he walked into the door. All they could talk about was nonsense about ribbons, officers, and local gossip. When he asked his wife about the lace on the neckline of her gown, Elizabeth's chin dropped. Instead of ignoring their prattle, he sat as if they spewed the wisdom of the world.

Who was this man and what had happened to her father?

When Lydia insisted that their father rescind the order restricting officers to Longbourn, his reply confirmed more than words that something had happened in Kent that changed him.

"My dear girl," Papa gave his full attention to his youngest. "Do you not yet understand why I do not want them to call?"

"Sure, Papa," Lydia reasoned. "You don't want us to have any fun until we are old like Jane and Lizzy."

Elizabeth barely restrained herself from rolling her eyes. Even Jane was having difficulty.

"No, Lydia. The five of you are my babies. Your

mother and I know the best of each of you. We see your beauty, your kindness, and your charms."

What! Elizabeth was stunned. Never had her father spoken like this to any of them.

He continued after loudly clearing his throat. "We also see those small areas where improvement can be made. Nevertheless, it is my role as your father to make certain that any man who approaches me to ask for your hand is not only a good man, but a responsible man as well, one who will see beyond your loveliness to the fine character you are within. Thus, let it be known to all five of you that I will not hand you over easily. I am not in any hurry to see any of you go. I will not tolerate a man who acts less than a gentleman should. If he flirts with you, he is gone. You will be treated as the ladies you are, or they will answer to me." He poked his chest with his thumb.

Glancing around, Elizabeth noted that she was not the only one shocked at his words. Mary, Kitty, and Lydia shifted in their chairs until their spines were stiff and their chins were tipped to the perfect posture for a lady. Even their mother sat up straight, a small smile on her face.

Jane recovered first. "I thank you, Papa. Your wisdom and protection will see us all happy."

"Thank you, Papa," Elizabeth added, puzzled by the exchange. Impatient for information, she began, "About your journey to Kent..."

"We shall speak of it later, Lizzy." His voice was unexpectedly stern. As he looked away from her to his other daughters, he said, "I would like to enjoy the company of *all* my family, if you do not mind."

The next hour was a lesson in frustration. Desperate to learn of the arrest of Mr. Collins and the freedom of Mr. Darcy, Elizabeth's mind traveled the three miles to Netherfield Park. Had her father and Major Gerring already informed Mr. Darcy of the charges being dropped? Surely, they would have wanted to ease the mind of the innocent even as they sought just punishment for the guilty.

She wondered how Mr. Darcy responded. She knew how she would feel to have that weight taken off her shoulders. The relief would be unimaginable. It would renew a person's zest for living, possibly opening new vistas for the future like...well, maybe the potential for...marriage?

* * *

CAROLINE BINGLEY WAS UNBEARABLE. From the second Darcy stepped into the drawing room, she fawned over him to the point that if he asked her to breathe for him, she would have done it willingly.

Her elder sister, Louisa Hurst, ignored him and everyone else in the room. Gazing off into space, she sighed heavily then muttered, "If only this had never happened. If only we had remained in London."

Her husband, Gilbert Hurst, was laid out on a sofa next to the fire, snoring with every rise and fall of his chest. He was by far the most indolent man of Darcy's acquaintance. In the years he had known Bingley's brother-in-law, the only thing that stirred Hurst from his personal comfort was shooting at birds. The man was a marksman.

Darcy glanced at Hurst's slippers as they hung over the edge of the sofa. They were short and wide. No, despite Hurst's comfort with firearms, he simply could not be budged from the house unless grouse were involved.

Miss Bingley mused, "Yes, Louisa. We can pretend this never happened. Let us leave here for London or winter at Pemberley where no one would deign to accuse Mr. Darcy of so repulsive a crime as murder."

Darcy stared at her, refusing to agree to her bold suggestion. Was she capable of arranging the deaths of three strangers to her? For what purpose, if she were able?

He groaned inside. Would everyone be under suspicion from now until they found the murderer? Darcy hoped not. Bingley's sisters were ambitious, and his brother-in-law was lazy. They were not cold-blooded killers. Bingley would not hurt a fly if it landed on his last bite of supper.

Shaking his head to change the directions of his thoughts, he was frustrated when Miss Bingley said, "Surely, you do not want to remain here where they had the nerve to insist upon your guilt? I cannot imagine what would happen should word get back to London that you were suspected of killing someone you knew. Poor Miss Darcy! She would be crushed, I am certain." She smiled insincerely. "Of course, in your stead, I would offer the girl guidance and comfort to see her through the darkest period of her young life. Why, she would need my consolation, I am sure."

Each word spewing from her mouth increased Darcy's ire.

"Caroline!" Bingley reprimanded. "You have gone too far."

"How can you mean I have gone too far, Charles? These rural sorts have loose lips, telling their betters everything they know within the first few minutes of meeting them. Dear Georgiana would be devastated to be left alone."

"Enough!" Bingley finally put his foot down. "Darcy has been through enough. The matter is settled. He is innocent. There would be no reason to have any gossip come from this household. From us, Miss Darcy will hear nothing, am I clear?"

As emotionally trying as the past weeks were, Darcy was relieved that he was not standing alone.

Refusing the tea that was offered, he stood to leave.

"You cannot be leaving, Mr. Darcy." Miss Bingley was appalled. "You just arrived."

"I beg your pardon," bowing properly, Darcy added, "I need to speak with Mr. Bennet."

"I will join you," Bingley quickly offered.

To the tune of Miss Bingley's inelegant harrumph, the two men left the drawing room.

Although Darcy would not admit it to Bingley, it was not Mr. Bennet he needed to see. It was Elizabeth.

MR. BENNET FINISHED his narration of events upon his arrival in Kent along with his discussion with Major Gerring and Mr. Darcy at Netherfield Park.

Elizabeth was troubled.

"Papa, I fear you will be unhappy with me when I reveal that I shared your list of suspects with Mr. Darcy. On the back were my suppositions as to motive." Elizabeth chewed on the side of her thumbnail.

"Yes, he showed me both papers delivered to him from this house."

"Both? There were a total of four I sent through Hill. I wonder what could have happened to the other two. One addressed the gossip of the militia and the other reported finding mud in Beatrice's hooves."

Her father shrugged nonchalantly. "Perhaps they were in a pile with his other letters." Waving his hand over the papers strewn over the surface of his own desk, he grimaced.

Elizabeth was disappointed. Had Mr. Darcy not taken her discoveries seriously? She could not imagine he would not. His life was on the line.

Her father said, "Yes, well, be that as it may, I spoke with Mr. Phillips before returning home."

Mr. Phillips was her uncle, the husband of Mrs. Bennet's sister. As an attorney, he had studied the entail on Longbourn thoroughly.

"Papa, with the death of the whole Collins family, where does this leave Longbourn?"

Her father nodded. "With Collins dead, the question was, who will own the estate when I am no longer here? The entail was written by my grandfather in a way particular to his situation. I have long known that should Mr. Collins predecease me, Longbourn will remain in the family as long as one of my daughters has a son who would take the name Bennet." He rubbed his jaw. "Thus, it is not a giant leap to suppose that someone might suspect *me* of using the current circumstances to rid myself of Mr. Collins to possibly end the entail, whereupon I could leave the estate to a grandson."

"Papa!" Righteously indignant, Elizabeth stood to pace the small confines of his study. "No one who knows you would ever believe you would resort to violence to save our home."

"Ah, but is that not the point?" A tap on the door came as the words left her father's mouth.

Expecting Jane, Elizabeth spun towards the door. Jane would never be able to tolerate the subject being discussed. However, it was not her sister. She was surprised and, at the same time, joyous to see Mr. Darcy.

"Good, I am pleased you have arrived," her father insisted, gesturing to the seat next to Elizabeth.

Once the three were seated, Mr. Darcy began, getting to the crux of the matter, "Miss Elizabeth raised a question in one of the letters she sent that begs to be answered: Who wants me dead or away from society? I have not been able to stop thinking about this since I read her words."

Glancing sideways, Elizabeth caught his eyes upon her rather than her father. The corner of her lips rose higher the longer he gazed at her. Heat rose from her neck to settle in her cheeks. Mr. Darcy's face was rather flushed too. She closed her eyes momentarily, breaking the connection between them.

He did not look like he had suffered too much from his confinement. He looked...windblown from the ride between properties, rumpled from having been in the saddle, and....particularly handsome.

Her bones might have melted as her breath caught in her throat. Her father's next words broke the spell. She was mortified that either man might have noticed her acting like a... female.

"Mr. Darcy, murder is nefarious business. Greed or shame can move a man to commit acts of atrocity against his fellow man if gain is to be had. Lizzy and I were discussing how myself and Longbourn will potentially benefit by having Mr. Collins gone."

"Does his death break the entail then?" Darcy asked.

"As far as I know," her father admitted. "My wife's brother, Mr. Phillips, does all of my legal work. He reviewed the original documents when I told him of Collins' arrival three weeks ago. Unless he is mistaken, which I sincerely doubt he is, Longbourn now has the potential to remain with my family."

Mr. Darcy nodded.

Into the silence that followed, Elizabeth said, "Papa was speculating that someone might believe he might have killed Mr. Collins."

"What! Why would anyone think you capable of murder?"

Her father sat back in his chair. "It is the same as with anyone else who has not been cautious with his income. Anyone in the business community of Meryton could tell you that I have allowed my wife the freedom to spend as she pleases. Perhaps I sought to assure my family a home upon my eventual death? Once a rumor or a conjecture is expressed within someone else's hearing, it is rife for retelling until what eventually comes back around bears little resemblance to the truth."

"Mr. Bennet, we need to aggressively search for the person who killed Miss Collins and Wickham. Once we locate him or her, we would likely have the murderer of Mr. Collins." Mr. Darcy sat forward in his chair. "I have studied the list provided by Miss Elizabeth diligently." He glanced at her and smiled, before continuing, "The one clue that is most telling is the boot print. Unless a woman was of extraordinary size, which would be noticeable, the perpetrator was a man with the same size feet as mine."

"It was not you," Elizabeth stated, causing both men to focus solely on her. "I have proof," she added.

"What do you mean, Lizzy?"

"Papa, the heel print of the boot was embedded into the mud slightly lower than the sole. When Mr. Darcy stands still for any length of time, he rocks back on his heel. Had it been him at the orchard, the print would have been embedded much deeper into the mud."

Oh, good heavens! Had she truly said that aloud? Without touching her cheeks, she knew from the heat radiating from them that she was as red as a beet. This was the second time she had admitted to her Papa that she had studied Mr. Darcy's form. *What must her father think? And what of Mr. Darcy?* If only the floor of the study would open and she could fall to the cellar below.

She peeked at Mr. Darcy only to discover that his mouth was wide open, as were his eyes.

"She is correct. My father attempted to break me of the same habit as did my tutors. In fact, if you look..." he crossed his left boot over his right knee, pointing to the back of the heel. "I always wear my heels down right here."

Her father rubbed his hands over his face, groaning into his palms. "If only it had not rained. Although I trust your memory, Lizzy, I am sorry to say that the drawings you made did not indicate the depth of the heel print. We have no proof now."

"Papa, Mr. Darcy, pray consider this since I feel this is the most pertinent detail," she swallowed. "We know who did *not* murder Miss Collins, Mr. Collins, and Mr. Wickham. What we need to determine is who did? Who stands to gain from the death, not of one of them, or even two of them, but all three of them?"

After a lengthy silence, Mr. Darcy exclaimed. "*Blast it all!*"

CHAPTER 26

"It comes back to me, does it not?" Darcy looked at them both before continuing. "Although you are willing to accept that a charge of guilt could be pointed at you for the death of Mr. Collins, you benefited not at all from Miss Collins and Wickham's passing. Thus, any reasonable person would erase any thought of accusing you from their minds. Having Collins arrested for the murder of the others would have served your purpose as easily as his death. You are acquitted, sir."

"I thank you," Mr. Bennet tipped his head in acceptance of Darcy's opinion. "Now tell us, why do you calculate that it comes back to you?"

Tapping his finger on his mouth, Darcy sorted the list of facts into order before replying. "Firstly, by removing Miss Collins, I removed a threat to my life. Self-defense would have been my motive. Secondly, having George Wickham dead meant that an era of deceit and harm against the Darcy name would be gone. Finally, by arranging for the apparent suicide of Mr. Collins, I deliberately pointed the finger of guilt at him and away from me for the first two deaths. This, I could have arranged via messages to some of Wickham's most unsavory contacts who I have had the unpleasant task of coming to know during the course of my dealings with George." He paused, again sorting his thoughts. "To an amateur these few facts would tie up the case with a pretty ribbon whereupon I would be presented to the courts as an evil, though not very brilliant, criminal. Far be it for me to claim I am more intelligent than the average mind since it would take very little to realize how unreasonable these claims are."

Sitting straighter, he added, "All it would have taken to remove Claire Collins as a threat was to point her in Wickham's direction. The lady was not without intelligence. In fact, that she possessed more mental acuity than her brother was evident. As far as Wickham was concerned, having him removed to Marshalsea, which was my intent, would have rendered him ineffectual against me or anyone else. Mr. Collins was not a threat to me or to my family."

Elizabeth spoke up, "Please recall when John Lucas came to Netherfield Park to report the initial crime to Papa. Major Gerring mentioned that murders of passion are often easily explained. Mightn't someone suggest that the emotions of the moment have been the motive for you committing these atrocities?"

Darcy's gaze shot towards her. "Are you suggesting that you believe me capable of committing these heinous crimes?"

"Not at all, Mr. Darcy, I am merely speculating on

what might have been churning in the mind of the real murderer." Elizabeth was quick to reply. "Someone killed those three, someone who, as we speak, is frustrated that you have been released from confinement and cleared of all charges. Or...," she paused, glancing between the two men. "Or we have someone who took advantage of the public confrontation at the inn with Claire and Mr. Wickham to quickly formulate a plan whereupon the finger pointed at you. He cared not if his decisions were shoddy since it was prison or death that he wanted for you. Or, perhaps his desire was to hold this over you as blackmail. Someone who believes they have proof they could resurrect when they feel it is the most advantageous to them. Have you considered this as a possibility?"

What a brilliant woman! He was grateful she believed in him. So grateful that he...no, now was not the time to think along those terms.

"Blackmail is an interesting theory. Although I considered it during my confinement, anyone who knows me well would comprehend that I would rather own my guilt, if I was indeed guilty, than rob my estate to satisfy someone's greed." He added, "My greatest wealth is Pemberley. In past history, men have proven willing to lie, steal, or kill to obtain my estate or at least a portion of my wealth."

"Like Mr. Wickham, I suppose," Elizabeth suggested.

He nodded. "Yes, like Wickham."

"Mr. Darcy, let us take Lizzy's idea and see where it might lead." Mr. Bennet suggested. "Why would someone want you out of the way? If it was to obtain your estate, then it could only be by marriage to Miss Darcy. The man would need to be unwed. It would also need to be someone who was not financially solvent enough to purchase an estate similar enough to yours to be satisfied. They would have been in the vicinity on the night of the murders, possibly at the inn to have learned enough to have used it to entrap you."

Elizabeth added, "He would know how to use a weapon, how to stage the scene to look like both murder and suicide, and had help to move the bodies into position. How well do you know Major Gerring, sir?"

"My cousin trusts him implicitly."

Her left brow arched. Darcy knew that look. He needed to justify his opinion.

"Richard is my closest friend. At two years older than me, he was my constant companion when our families would gather at Pemberley or his family estate in Matlock. Although he is a second son, he never has had a desire to possess an estate as deeply rooted as Pemberley. His heart yearns for a simpler life, a quieter, more peaceful existence. To saddle him with a large property and all the responsibility it contains would be a burden, rather than a blessing. In addition, he takes his responsibility as Georgiana's guardian as seriously as do I. When I say that I trust him implicitly, I have absolutely no doubt about his character. Therefore, I have no doubt about his recommendation of Major Gerring."

"Thank you, sir. I do appreciate your candor." Elizabeth chewed on her thumbnail. Dropping her hand, she said, "We must not overlook anyone despite any attachment to them. Nor can we forget motive. Papa, perhaps you might make a list of those who stood to gain from the deaths of Mr. Collins, Claire, and Mr. Wickham. In another column, we can think of everyone who knew of the orchard, who was at the inn, and who wants what Mr. Darcy owns."

Gathering pen and paper, they spent a long while considering and rejecting suspects from Bingley to the blacksmith, from the militia to Kitty and Lydia Bennet. Every time a name was listed, it was immediately crossed out as being ridiculously impossible.

Darcy's frustration grew exponentially each time the tip of the quill was dipped in the inkwell. Deep inside, he felt as if there was only one piece of the puzzle or one link holding them back from revealing the name of the murderer. Yet, as hard as he thought of every piece of the clues available, nothing was coming to mind.

Finally, Mr. Bennet placed the quill on its holder and rubbed his eyes. "We are forgetting something important, or rather someone obvious, I feel it in my bones."

"I feel the same," Darcy admitted.

Elizabeth said, "Then let us consider the most outlandish suspects possible. I will begin with Miss Georgiana Darcy."

Immediately Darcy's ire shot through the roof. *How dare...*

"Pray do not become upset, sir. I do not believe it possible that your young sister would harm you. As you have described her, she is far too timid to lift a feather to hurt anyone, much like Jane. However, in considering her, we might inadvertently stumble on the true suspect."

Hesitantly, he replied, "Carry on."

She squared her shoulders, inhaled deeply, then began. "Miss Darcy was angry at Claire's deception. The desire of every young girl is a kindred spirit, a friend who can be trusted with their most intimate thoughts. To discover this friend's treachery could make a volatile girl on the brink of maturity murderous. Add to this the damage Mr. Wickham did to her heart with his own deception, why, you can see why your sister would want him permanently out of her life. Perhaps with Mr. Collins, your poor sister was in Lady Catherine's company where my father's cousin prattled on enough that Miss Darcy wished him silenced forever. There are your motives which are completely independent of...wait, no, I am wrong. Perhaps in the back of her mind your sister craves the same sort of control that your aunt, Lady Catherine, apparently has of her estate. With you incarcerated or transported, *she* would be mistress of Pemberley. Let us say for the sake of fiction that Miss Georgiana Darcy wants it all."

"Never!" Darcy understood Elizabeth's purpose but would have nothing more said against his sister.

"I agree with you wholeheartedly, Mr. Darcy." She sat back in her chair. "I have no more to add. Therefore, it is your turn, Papa."

Exaggerating the clearing of his throat like an orator would do to make themselves heard over the masses, her father said, "After finding my cousin at the parsonage, I was thrust into your aunt's company several times over the next two days. Major Gerring and I quickly learned that Lady Catherine de Bourgh has both the will and the capability of commanding enough troops to perform any task she insists be done, would you agree?"

"Assuredly," Darcy agreed since Mr. Bennet was looking directly at him.

"Although the time I spent with her was short, I will confess that her influence remained with both Major Gerring and me when we traveled to Ramsgate then back to Hunsford Parsonage. She impressed me as the sort who prefers to have her way."

"And her say," Darcy muttered.

"Yes, well. The little I know of her makes me readily agree with you." Mr. Bennet grinned, then continued. "Lady Catherine, angry that Claire Collins rejected the friendship of her daughter as well as any suggested improvements made by the great lady herself, wished Miss Collins away from her estate. Once she discovered that Claire intended to end your life, the lady chose to step in and take control of matters. In doing so, she learned of Mr. Wickham's crimes. Within her power and command are several loyal servants who would easily blend into our farming community. They would have the brawn needed to move the bodies and place them to look like murder/suicide. Once the two victims were out of the picture, Lady Catherine's focus was on her parson who had returned to Kent without a bride, which was a direct failure to obey one of her orders. With the two sisters of her clergyman being of low moral character in her exalted opinion, she needed to dispose of Mr. Collins since the law says she cannot rescind an appointment without consent of the archbishop. By wiping them all out of existence, Lady Catherine receives justice for the crimes committed against her family members, allows her to appoint a man more qualified for the living she holds, and removes all obstacles against your name which will allow you to finally marry her daughter, gaining a permanent entry to Pemberley." He stood and bowed; his performance done.

"I will not marry Anne." Darcy insisted even as his mind considered the facts. Lady Catherine was everything and more than Mr. Bennet described. Her belief in her own infallibility was well-known. As the self-proclaimed expert on any topic, she would have the reason and the means to see it done. She coveted Pemberley. She resented marrying Louis de Bourgh for providing her a smaller estate than the one her younger sister obtained at her marriage to George Darcy. It is why she continued to insist on a marriage between Anne and himself.

The pieces of the puzzle were beginning to come together, but his aunt? A murderer?

Before he could consider the matter further, a commotion was heard outside the room.

"Where is he?" an imperious female voice demanded. "Where is my nephew?"

Blast! As if his own thoughts and their conversation had conjured her from Kent, his aunt, Lady Catherine de Bourgh had arrived.

CHAPTER 27

$\mathcal{L}$ady Catherine swept into Longbourn like a cyclone bent on destruction. Commandeering the drawing room, the matron, followed by a young lady who appeared to melt into the background, stood in front of the fireplace waiting for the room to hush.

Bingley, who had arrived earlier, stood in front of Jane to protect her. Kitty, Lydia, and Mary huddled next to their eldest sister.

Never in Elizabeth's lifetime had she met a woman whose very presence evoked blatant superiority. Nevertheless, Elizabeth and every other resident knew who ruled their home. It was *not* Lady Catherine de Bourgh.

"Welcome to Longbourn," her mother's delight was evident in her smile. "You are...?"

"Aunt Catherine!" Mr. Darcy roared. "What are you doing in Hertfordshire?"

Elizabeth's mother ignored him. "Oh, you are a relative of Mr. Darcy? Well, I should have known you anywhere then. You both have the same furrowed brow and way of elevating your chin just so." Mama demon-strated by tipping her jaw exactly like theirs, giving them a perfect view up her left nostril. "I can see you are used to the finer things in life, so I will have a room prepared for you, milady. I will also order tea." Without taking a breath, the matron of Longbourn continued, "Is this your young companion with you? She has lovely hair and the lace on the end of her sleeves is divine." As she moved to ring the bell for their housekeeper, she waved towards the sofas, "Do sit down. Your journey from London must have been long and uncomfortable. Our fire is warm and the cushions on the furniture are soft. You will be well-settled here."

Lady Catherine pounded her cane on the carpet. "I do not know who you are, nor do I care. I do not want tea. My daughter and I will not remain here. We do not need a fire, nor do we need your sofa. What we need is to speak to my nephew in privacy. Can you do this, Madam, or is this too much to ask."

From years of observing her mother's expressions, Elizabeth knew she was thrilled with the arrival of a person of elevated rank to Longbourn. It would give Mama bragging rights to the neighborhood during the cold winter months to come. By the time spring arrived, every inch of Lady Catherine's hairstyle, outer garment, accoutrement, and feathered bonnet would have been described repeatedly. Whatever verbal exchange that took place between the two women would have rendered them the closest of friends. That was, until Lady Catherine played the master in Mrs. Francine Bennet's home.

Her mama stopped in her tracks, then slowly turned to

face Lady Catherine. With a slight lift of her chin, Mama walked past her to the younger woman. Curtseying, she said, "Then you must be Miss de Bourgh. I am delighted to make your acquaintance. Is there anything I may offer for your comfort? Are you weary from the journey? Do you need a moment to gather yourself before I introduce you to the ladies of the house?"

"Mrs. Bennet!" Lady Catherine bellowed.

Mama ignored her. Leading the younger woman close to the fire, she said, "Pray do be seated. I will arrange for refreshments right away. Or do you need to lay down? A room can be readied right away where you can have both privacy and silence. No one," she glanced in Lady Catherine's direction, "will bother you there."

"Anne, come," Lady Catherine ordered.

To her consternation, the young lady sat by the fire where Mama grabbed a lap robe from the back of the sofa to drape across Miss de Bourgh's lap. "There, there. You shall be comfortable here."

Approaching the three of them, Mama told Mr. Darcy, "Sir, I am sure it would make your cousin more comfortable if you and Lizzy sat in the chairs next to her. I imagine she would enjoy some pleasant conversation."

With a bow and a smirk, Mr. Darcy offered his arm. Elizabeth did not hesitate to accept it.

In all of this, Lady Catherine de Bourgh's mouth gaped open. Once Elizabeth was comfortable, her right side immediately warmed by the fire and the rest of her heated by the warmth of his eyes, Mr. Darcy went to his aunt's side.

"Aunt, pray come and be seated next to Anne. You will

be away from the fire but will be across from me for easy conversation." He held out his arm.

Elizabeth thought him the bravest man she knew. Almost as brave as her mama. She grinned.

"Pardon me," Miss de Bourgh said, her chin lifting to the same angle as her mothers, "Why are you smiling? Have I done something you find to be humorous?"

"Not at all," Elizabeth admitted, soothing the young lady's temper. "I was contemplating how much I think I know someone until I am proven wrong. How foolish it is of me to put stock in my own opinions."

"I see," Miss de Bourgh said, only to follow it with, "Actually, I do not see. I do not understand. Are you speaking of my mother? I did not think you had ever met."

"In truth, it was your cousin, Mr. Darcy, of whom I was speaking." Elizabeth refused to elaborate since the pair were drawing close. "I am Elizabeth Bennet, Miss de Bourgh. It is a pleasure to have you in our home."

Glancing at the scowl on her mother's face, Miss de Bourgh said quickly, "I shall not marry Fitzwilliam, no matter how much it is mama's desire. I have my own plans for my future."

"I cannot imagine why you are telling me, Miss de Bourgh, but I thank you for doing so," Elizabeth admitted. Inside, she was relieved at hearing the news.

"What are you whispering about, Anne. You know I cannot hear you when you speak softly." Lady Catherine slowly seated herself, her scowl growing when she looked at Elizabeth. "I suppose you are one of *that woman's* daughters. Which one are you?"

"Elizabeth, Lady Catherine. I am the second born."

"Ah, you were the upstart who refused to accept Collins." Lady Catherine sneered. "That man was a fool who had no idea how to follow the simplest command, God rest his soul. He did not even know how to die properly. Leaving a bloody mess in *my* cottage was highly inappropriate. If he were here right now, I would give him a piece of my mind. Suicide! It is intolerable, I tell you. A blight on the name of de Bourgh for which I will never forgive him."

"Mama!" Miss de Bourgh scolded her mother—to no effect.

Lady Catherine brushed off the reprimand like lint on a table. "Well, never mind him. He is gone now, leaving me with the task of finding someone skilled to replace him." She muttered under her breath, "Ungrateful oaf!"

As the lady castigated her former clergyman, Papa gathered the rest of the Bennet daughters and removed them from the room. Bingley followed closely behind Jane. Mama had yet to return from speaking to Cook. Closing the drawing room door, he asked, "Lady Catherine, I never expected to see you again once I left Rosings Park. Let us dispense with the niceties and get to the reason you traveled from Kent to my estate. Why are you here?"

The lady's hand shook where it rested at the top of her cane. Miss de Bourgh's chin quivered, her hands tightly fisted together.

Tilting her head to give her most aristocratic pose, Lady Catherine replied, "I am looking for Mr. George Wickham, a charming man who is a longtime friend of the Darcy family. I do not suppose you know him for the circles he moves in are much higher than yours, Mr. Bennet."

Mr. Darcy's mouth dropped open as did Elizabeth's. It was the last thing they expected Lady Catherine to say.

Mr. Darcy blurted out, "Why?"

Catching sight of Miss de Bourgh's cheeks, Elizabeth worried. The young lady's pallor was almost white.

"Why I am looking for him is not your concern, Darcy. Tell me where I can find him. I have business with him entirely unrelated to you."

Mr. Darcy's eyes pierced his aunt. "Tell me what you want with him, and I will direct you to Wickham's exact location."

"I will not be denied, Fitzwilliam Darcy. Have you forgotten who I am?"

Mr. Darcy replied, "I know exactly who you are, Aunt Catherine. This has no effect on me. Tell me about your business with George Wickham and I will tell you where he is."

Elizabeth's eyes volleyed back and forth between the two adversaries. This was not a pleasant conversation between two close family members.

Until this moment, Elizabeth was suspicious of Lady Catherine's motive for her arrival in Hertfordshire. Her father's descriptions as well as Mr. Collins' adulation had placed an image in Elizabeth's mind of an arrogant woman who commanded "off with their heads" to anyone who refused to kneel to her authority. Was she, indeed, the one who arranged for the murders? She gave no impression that the loss of life bothered her. A woman with ice flowing through her veins was as accurate a description as Elizabeth could picture until she looked closer.

A thin bead of moisture dotted Lady Catherine's upper lip. Her face was almost as pale as her daughters. The fingers holding her cane were wrapped so tightly around the handle that the knuckles facing Elizabeth were stark white.

After a moment of consideration, Lady Catherine harrumphed, "Very well. When I find George Wickham, I will haul his charming self to the closest chapel to marry Anne. Once the register is signed, I will kill him."

"Aunt!" Mr. Darcy sat back in his chair.

Elizabeth clapped her hand to her mouth. Her father dropped into the closest chair.

Mr. Darcy looked at his cousin, then at his aunt. "Are you saying that Anne..."

Lady Catherine snorted. "I am saying nothing, mind you." Tapping her cane on the floor, she said, "Well, are you going to tell me where I can find the rake?"

Mr. Darcy ran his hands through his hair. "You truly do not know, do you?"

"Know what!" Lady Catherine insisted, recovering her strength of mind. "Where is he?"

"Blast!" Mr. Darcy exclaimed.

"Do not curse in front of Anne," his aunt sneered, her haughty attitude firmly in place.

Before answering, Mr. Darcy turned his attention to his cousin. "Are you well?"

Miss de Bourgh raised her brow, the corner of her mouth tilting up at a memory no one else shared. "Well enough, I suppose."

Shaking his head, Papa spoke, "Lady Catherine, Miss de Bourgh, it is believed by the constable and the local magistrate that George Wickham and Miss Claire Collins were both murdered by her brother, Mr. Collins."

"No!" Miss de Bourgh's hand went to her throat.

"How can that be? When you were at Hunsford, you spoke only of the death of Collins' sister. Not one mention was made of Wickham's demise." Lady Catherine's shock was visible in every pore of her body. "Mr. Collins murdered George Wickham? It cannot be!" she glanced at her daughter. "What are we to do now?"

"Lady Catherine, you asked where he could be found." Her Papa directed his attention to both ladies. "His body was transported to Pemberley to be placed next to his parents. Your nephew and many others can confirm the truth of this account."

The lady's chin fell almost to her chest before she suddenly snapped her jaw closed. "You will marry Anne tomorrow, Darcy. She needs a husband, and you need a wife."

"I will not," Mr. Darcy insisted to Elizabeth's intense relief.

"Yes, you will," Miss de Bourgh demanded. "I need a husband and you will do as well as any other."

Elizabeth was stunned. What happened to the declaration only a few minutes before from the same young lady's mouth that she would never marry her cousin? She wanted to laugh although nothing happening was humorous. With the horrible farce playing itself out in front of her, any suspicions that Lady Catherine or Miss de

Bourgh had arranged Mr. Wickham's death vanished into thin air.

Mr. Darcy stood. "Aunt, Cousin, you can have no further business in Hertfordshire. I will escort you to the inn where you may stay the night before returning to Kent to decide what you will do for Anne. As for me, this is not my concern."

"You will do as I say, Fitzwilliam Darcy." Lady Catherine rapped her cane on the floor several times to no avail.

"No, Aunt Catherine. I will not marry Anne. I do not love her. She does not love me. She carries another man's child, not the heir to Pemberley. No," he held up his hand to stop her from speaking. "Nothing you say has the power to induce me to change my mind." Glancing at Elizabeth, he said, "I have someone else entirely in mind."

Clapping her hand over her mouth, Elizabeth's eyes shot wide open. Had he just said what she thought she heard him say? *Good heavens!* Did he mean it or was he trying to rid himself of his relatives once and for all?

"Her?"

Lady Catherine pointed her cane directly at Elizabeth's chest. She was grateful it was not a pistol loaded with powder and a shot. The look the lady gave her was deadly.

Stiffening her spine to not hide herself behind Mr. Darcy, seeking his protection from his aunt's wrath, Elizabeth stared back at her, refusing to blink.

Mr. Darcy glanced at her before addressing his aunt "Whom I choose to wed is none of your concern."

Her heart was racing with Lady Catherine's perceived

threat but this...she feared her chest might burst. Then reality set in. What was a mere glance after all? Had Mama been in the room, it would have been enough for her to assume that wedding bells were soon to chime. Yet, a look could have meant anything other than a commitment to offer for her.

You are being nonsensical, Elizabeth Rose Bennet! Stop this foolishness now!

Papa shook his head then settled his eyes upon Lady Catherine. "Enough! Perhaps your aunt and cousin should be directed to the inn or may be they would be offered hospitality at Netherfield Park. Mr. Bingley seems a good sort who would open his house at the last minute for strangers. He is still at Longbourn unless he snuck out when Jane was not looking."

"Very well," Mr. Darcy ignored her Papa and his relatives, finally speaking directly to Elizabeth as the others in the room watched. "Do I have your permission to call on you in the morning?"

He looked calm everywhere, except his eyes. Through the turmoil, Elizabeth thought she saw hope.

"You may," she offered.

Lady Catherine barked, "Collins was a fool. His sister was a fool. George Wickham was a fool. You, Fitzwilliam Darcy, are a fool." Without looking at her daughter, she said, "Come. Perhaps we can get that upstart Bingley to marry you. Being from trade, it would be a considerable step up to be attached to the de Bourghs."

"Bingley? You would attach me to *him*?" Miss de Bourgh asked right before she placed the back of her hand on her brow and fainted.

CHAPTER 28

*C*harles Bingley slumped into the leather chair next to the fire in his study. The hour was late. Netherfield Park was quiet—finally.

"I shall not offer for your cousin." Sipping his brandy, Bingley boldly looked Darcy in the eye. "Rosings Park is not enough of an inducement to propose to her, I am afraid. Besides, in comparison to Miss de Bourgh, Jane Bennet is an angel, is she not?" Bingley sighed. "No, I said that wrong. In comparison to any female, Jane is an angel."

Darcy could read every expression on the younger man's face. It had gone from a sour look to Bingley's eyes glazing over as he stared into the distance at nothing.

Darcy knew the feeling. In spite of all the current challenges, in particular a murderer on the loose, he preferred to spend his leisure time dreaming of Elizabeth. For in that moment standing alongside her while confronting his aunt, he knew that she was the only one for him. For a certainty, he had not been smooth in stating his intent.

Bingley sat up in his chair. "I have been thinking of taking a wife. I will need a mistress of my home."

Darcy truly looked at Bingley to discover he was serious. "You need a wife to take care of you. You have a button missing on your infernal green waistcoat." Darcy smirked. "Tell me, do you wear the same one daily, or do you have a dozen that you rotate?"

Bingley patted his chest where the button was gone, grinning from ear to ear. "I will have you know that your very own sister told me that the green in my garment brings out the blue in my eyes."

"Georgiana? She commented on your eyes?" Darcy was stunned. His sister was naturally timid. It spoke well of Bingley that she was able to relax enough to share a personal observation.

If anything, Bingley's grin grew in width. "Yes, she did. Caroline admired the blue you often wear, wanting me to purchase the same fabric from your tailor. Even though Caroline can be a fearsome thing, your delightful sister, who has an artist's eye for color, noticed that the dark green of the chair I was sitting on at the time complimented my coloring. I immediately went to your tailor, who agreed with Miss Darcy, and ordered six vests made to your design."

Darcy did not know what to say. Learning these small details about his sister recalled to his mind the conversation Elizabeth had with them the first time he saw her at Oakham Mount. She discussed with Bingley the importance of small beginnings. The little details he had learned about Elizabeth over the course of the past several weeks had grown into a complete picture of possible future felicity. Unless he was mistaken, she felt the same.

"You need a wife to care for you, Darcy." Bingley snorted. "Not that it is likely to happen now that Miss de Bourgh is...well, I am sorry to say that matters will not go well for her. Nevertheless, with her out of the running as the future Mistress of Pemberley, you are unlikely to find a female on the planet who can meet the high standards of Fitzwilliam Darcy. Oh, they will want the position, but I cannot see you wanting them."

Darcy pondered Bingley's comment. He knew why Bingley said it—he knew how others viewed him. He expected much out of others, but even more so out of himself. Even Richard teased him about having a solitary life since no one could possibly measure up to Darcy's requirements for a wife.

"You might be surprised, my friend." Darcy smiled behind the brandy snifter he lifted to his lips.

Bingley's eyes shot open, his mouth the shape of an oval. "What is this? Has the great Fitzwilliam Darcy finally met his match?"

"I might have," he admitted, joyously watching Bingley's reaction.

"Do I know her?" Bingley slapped the arms of his chair, then leaned forward.

"You do."

"Who?" Bingley boldly asked.

Not willing to play games or tease about a topic so important that it would be life-changing to him, he replied, "Should you marry Jane Bennet, there is a chance we could be brothers."

Bingley's brows almost jumped to his hairline. "Miss Elizabeth? Are you going to offer for her?"

"There is no entail on Pemberley. Once I wed, the property would pass to her should something happen to me. I trust her to care for myself, Georgiana, and Pemberley."

"Well," Bingley relaxed back into the leather. "Well...I did not know you...well, you know, considered Miss Elizabeth with enough affection to offer a courtship, but...well," he swallowed, breathing in and out several times. "I am happy for you and for her. She is a lovely lady with an angel for a sister. There is nothing I would like more than for us to be brothers in fact, Darcy. Yes, I am, indeed, happy for you and for Miss Elizabeth." Bingley stood and offered his hand.

Pleased at Bingley's response, Darcy accepted his best wishes. With Richard out of the country, perhaps Bingley would stand up for him. Of course, he needed to ask Elizabeth first. He would ask—tomorrow.

* * *

THE EARLY MORNING sun struggled to fight its way through the chill of the morning. Low clouds dampened the air. The grass was heavy with dew. Pulling her shawl tighter around her shoulders, Elizabeth smiled at Jeannie's antics until she realized the crow was taunting a small field mouse scurrying between the trees. Choosing to help the furry rodent, Elizabeth stomped her walking boot on one of the apples that had fallen to the ground. Almost immediately, the crow changed direction to scavenge the fruit pieces. All the Bennets knew Jeannie had a sweet tooth...or a sweet beak.

Leaving the bird behind, Elizabeth chose the path cutting through the trees to avoid the area by the old oak grove where Claire lost her life. The senselessness of the ending led Elizabeth's mind back to where it possibly all began. When Mr. Wickham flirted with Sarah Collins, had she been flattered at the attentions of a handsome, indulgent man? For a certainty she was. Having lived under the oppressive oversight of a negligent father then an uncaring brother, the promises of a rogue must have seemed like the only opportunity for future happiness.

Elizabeth understood why Claire would have taken justice into her own hands. The law would never listen to a young lady of less than noble birth, even if she possessed a written note from Mr. Wickham confessing to his crimes. The truth of the matter was that Claire would have been patted on the head like an errant pup, then sent home to do as best as she could under her circumstances.

Stepping over a mud puddle, Elizabeth longed to strike out at someone over the inequity of a man reporting a crime and a woman doing the same. The first stirred a constable to action. The second was viewed as nothing more than an annoyance, no matter the seriousness of the complaint.

What would she have done in Claire's situation? Would she have been able to see her way forward, to carve out for herself a means of living to sustain her life? Having been raised in a noisy household, Elizabeth simply could not imagine what it must have felt like for Claire to be so alone.

Contemplating the choices open to a female with little education other than what she obtained from books, Elizabeth stopped in her tracks. *She* was a female with little education other than the books she read. Like Claire, who Mr. Collins reported had no opportunity for training in those areas of the arts common to young ladies of higher birth, Elizabeth had never been taught by a master.

Stunned, Elizabeth made the final turn down the path leading to the spring. Seating herself on the rock next to where the water trickled forth, she considered the prospects of each of her sisters, including herself. Not one, not even Jane, possessed the minimum required to qualify as an accomplished lady. None painted well, was beyond rudimentary in their drawing, was fluent in a language other than English, played an instrument, or sang with any great level of skill.

Burying her face in her palms, she groaned. How had she come to think so highly of herself? She, who had already been proven wrong about her judgment of Mr. Darcy's character, and who had misjudged her own parents as lacking when they both proved capable of protecting their daughters when under threat. How could she have mistaken their true identities? Even worse, how could she have mistaken her own?

Who was Elizabeth Rose Bennet other than a pretender believing she was knowledgeable when she was not? Shaking her head, she wanted to laugh at her own foolishness.

Humility tasted bitter on her tongue.

Throwing her head back, she closed her eyes, refusing to be diverted by any distractions the vista offered.

Savoring the smell of the damp Hertfordshire air, Elizabeth pictured in her mind when Mr. Darcy poured from his heart the account of his sister with Mr. Wickham. His devotion to Miss Darcy was a living, breathing part of him. She loved that about him.

Her eyes popped open. *She loved that about him?*

She did.

Dropping her forehead back in her palms, her mind filled with the man. She loved his constancy, his caution. She loved the way he dealt responsibly with others and spoke with her like she was an equal. She loved the way his hair curled above his collar and how his eyes warmed when they settled upon her.

She loved Fitzwilliam Darcy and wanted more than anything for him to offer her a courtship with the goal of making her his wife.

Was that what he was planning during his visit later today?

Goodness! She hoped so.

Grinning from ear to ear, she pressed her hands to her chest. She might have discovered that she was less than she had thought of herself, however, she knew how to learn. And she would learn. She would do everything within her power to make him proud to have her bear his name.

The squawking of the crow interrupted her meditations.

Laughing up at the bird, she said aloud, "*Jeanne de Valois-Saint-Remy*, you thief of a bird, you cannot steal my heart for I have already given it to someone else."

Flapping its wings, the crow dove to a spot close to

where Elizabeth sat. Taking off her straw bonnet and placing it close to her so the bird would not pick at the ribbons, she removed a piece of bread from her pocket. Elizabeth was grateful to have snatched it from the basket in the kitchen. Tearing off a corner, she tossed it to the crow. "Today promises to be a grand day, Jeannie, one I will remember for the rest of my life."

The crow devoured the offering, immediately begging for more.

"My greedy companion, you may have one more piece." Elizabeth lobbed the bread to a spot to the right of where Jeannie had landed.

Before the crow clasped the bread in its beak, it squawked loudly, flapped its wings then flew to the other side of the mound.

Elizabeth's heart raced. The idea that Mr. Darcy had sought her out to speak to her in private, thrilled her. Was that why she was eager to arrive early to Oakham Mount? Perhaps her heart led her exactly where it wanted to be. She grinned. She loved Mr. Darcy. If he cared for her in return, this would be the happiest day of her life.

Dusting the crumbs from her hands, she stood to walk around the outcropping, her heart in her eyes and a smile of welcome on her face.

Except, it was not Mr. Darcy seated on a horse, a pistol pointed at her chest.

"You!" she screamed.

CHAPTER 29

*D*arcy tugged on the bottom of his waistcoat, examining himself closely in the mirror. He had never proposed marriage before. For Elizabeth he wanted to look his finest.

"Sir, since I was able to clean all of the mud from the seams of your newest boots, would you like those or were you planning to wear either of the ones you prefer for your daily use?" Parker held the shafts of two pairs of the footwear in each hand.

Darcy shook his head, his heartbeat suddenly racing. "Pardon me? Of what are you speaking, Parker? I have not worn the newer pair since the night of the assembly."

It was not like his valet to become confused over an item of clothing. Parker was fastidious, matching the attitude of his master.

Oh no! The boot prints! Someone had borrowed and used his boots? Who would have done such a thing? No, who *could* have done such a thing?

"When was this?" Darcy asked.

"The night of the fireworks, sir." Parker stated. "They were still damp in the morning when the gentlemen wanted to look at your other boots so I did not bring them down."

Darcy shook his head. This was in every way horrible. Someone with access to Netherfield Park had entered his chambers for the sole purpose of assigning guilt away from themselves, pointing the finger directly at Darcy.

Was it Bingley? Certainly not. What of Hurst? Everything he knew about the man was that he was unwilling to extend himself for anything or anyone other than himself. Likely, it was not him.

Darcy considered the militia officers who stood guard outside his chambers. Had one of them committed murder for the purpose of pinning it on him? After leaving money with Colonel Forster for Wickham's debts, Darcy could not imagine any reason one of the officers would have wanted to do him harm. He shook off his suspicions. Besides, they only had access to his rooms *after* the crime was committed.

The only staff at Netherfield Park who entered his room were the maids. Always, Parker remained where he could observe them going about their business.

That left Major Gerring. The idea that the man had even crossed his mind made Darcy feel like a traitor to his cousin. Richard's trust in Major Gerring was complete. Should not Darcy's be also? Yet, the officer was allowed the freedom to come and go at Netherfield. Had the major taken advantage of Bingley's welcome by stealing boots to commit an atrocious crime? No, he would not. He had no motive.

Darcy hated that he was reviewing his friends as if they were already guilty.

Gratefully, Parker distracted him. "Sir, I apologize. It was my mistake." The valet bowed, his eyes to the floor.

"No, Parker," Darcy approached his long-time valet. Pieces of the puzzle were beginning to fall into place. "I believe there was no mistake. The prints of my boots were found at the scene of the murders of Mr. Wickham and Miss Collins. I knew I had not worn them. Mr. Bennet and his daughter are convinced that it was not me wearing them. Yet, someone must have borrowed them, committed a heinous act, and then attempted to return them."

"Sir!" Parker's face paled. "Your boots were where they were supposed to be in your closet when I lay down for the night. The next morning, they were on a mat in the kitchen. At the time, I had assumed you had retrieved them, mistaking them for another pair in the darkness of the room, then left them for me to clean—which I did."

"Gather my great coat and order my horse, Parker. I need to speak to Mr. Bennet right away." Stuffing his feet into his well-worn boots, Darcy wrote a quick note to Major Gerring to meet him at Longbourn. If there was a slight chance the officer was guilty, Darcy was determined to find out. Rushing downstairs to see that his note was delivered immediately, Miss Bingley attempted to draw him into the breakfast room. She was alone at the table.

"I thank you, Miss Bingley. However, I am needed at Longbourn immediately." Shoving his arms into his coat, he grabbed his hat and gloves from Parker. "When Bingley wakes, pray tell him where I am. I would ask that he arrive at Longbourn as soon as possible. Do not leave the house. It is not safe."

"My brother left Netherfield early this morning along with Hurst. They plan to raid the coveys. We shall have quail for supper." She smirked. "Mr. Darcy," she whined. "Your aunt and cousin are expected down soon. You will want to send them on their way, I am sure."

Wanting rid of her, Darcy said, "They are fully capable of leaving without me to wave them off. I shall return as soon as I am able. Good day."

Before she could reply, he was out the door.

* * *

ALMOST AS SOON AS Darcy entered Mr. Bennet's study, the major arrived at Longbourn. Darcy could not help himself. He studied Major Gerring's face, his posture, and his hands, even his feet, looking for signs of guilt. Either Darcy was blind, or the major was very skilled at hiding any cues that would indicate he was involved with the crimes.

"You requested my appearance, Mr. Darcy?" the major said. "Was there something you discovered that we needed to discuss?"

"I have." Darcy blinked to regain his focus, observing him even closer. Did he appear eager? Nervous? Concerned? Fearful?

Looking the major directly in the eye, the major did the same to him. Being cautious with his wording, Darcy said, "My boots were borrowed by the murderer then returned with mud on them after the deed was done."

"What!" Mr. Bennet exclaimed.

The major's mouth gaped open. If he was the guilty party, his acting ability would have rewarded him on the Drury stage.

The major leaned back in the chair, his face toward the ceiling, his eyes closed. He slapped his hand on his knee. "I have been a fool."

Darcy sat up in his chair. "Pardon me?"

The major straightened his posture, then explained, "Mr. Darcy, your protection was not my first reason for coming to Meryton, although it was impressed upon me by Colonel Fitzwilliam that he would have my head if something were to happen to you."

"Go on."

"As your cousin, Colonel Fitzwilliam, might have told you, the person leading the ring of spies was a female with the skill and intelligence to easily avoid detection. One of our operatives happened upon a series of articles printed in *The Times* that appeared to contain details matching the identities of various agents of the British government. The source of those articles was traced to Lucas Lodge. While the war office suspects the major players are in London and on the continent, they felt the need to check the link in Hertfordshire."

"Charlotte," Mr. Bennet muttered.

"Yes, her characters of Heloise, Trinette, Irene, Solange, and Catrinel matched the now familiar introduc-tion of Napoleon's general, Karl Schulmeister, the chief of intelligence. '*Voici un homme, tout intelligent et sans cœur. Here is a man, all brains, and no heart.'"*

"II, T, I, S, U," Mr. Bennet murmured. "*Homme, tout, intelligent, sans, cœur.* I would not have thought it of Charlotte. Likely, it was something my daughter helped her choose to tweak the noses of the more informed readers of the newspaper."

The major cleared his throat and pulled at his collar. "Yes, Mr. Bennet. Miss Lucas, with the help of Miss Elizabeth, has led the British government on a merry chase only to learn that she is exactly who she is, the eldest daughter of modest circumstances with a brilliant mind brimming with humor and wit."

"I fail to be surprised," Darcy said.

"Yes, well, Miss Lucas was reluctant to share the role Miss Elizabeth plays in getting her writing to the newspaper. Nevertheless, once the secret was out, she revealed that Miss Elizabeth edits and embellishes the articles, with the approval of Miss Lucas, of course, before seeing them delivered to London, either in person or via your butler, Hill."

Mr. Bennet chuckled. "Charlotte and my Lizzy are both far more than they appear to be. It is the lot of a genteel female to seek their fun where they can. Charlotte shares a small percentage of her income from her writing with my daughter, which Lizzy sneaks back into Charlotte's account whenever she is in London. Neither of the girls are aware that I know what they are about, but Hill told me right away in case I did not approve. Miss Lucas will never become rich from having these little tales published, but it gives both Charlotte and Lizzy a sense of accomplishment and independence, of which I heartily approve."

"Be that as it may," the major's cheeks reddened. "I allowed myself to be distracted from my secondary purpose. That your life is still endangered, and I have done little to mitigate your exposure to others is a confession I will hate to make when Colonel Fitzwilliam returns." He paused, then said, "You have my full attention, Mr. Darcy."

Was the man in earnest? Darcy was not yet certain.

Darcy suggested, "Perhaps we should utilize the brilliant minds of the ladies to lay out every bit of information we have concerning the victims and the details we know. With all of us working together, we can bring the perpetrator to justice and get on with our lives."

"Well said, Mr. Darcy." Mr. Bennet stood to summon his butler. "Hill, have Lizzy come downstairs."

"I shall retrieve Miss Lucas," the major offered.

Within minutes of Major Gerring leaving for Lucas Lodge, Hill returned downstairs. "I am sorry to say that Miss Lizzy is not in her chambers. I have searched upstairs and downstairs. She is missing."

"What do you mean Elizabeth is missing?" Darcy was dumbfounded. "Did anyone see her leave?"

Mr. Bennet replied, his voice shaking, "Until this moment, I did not know she was gone."

Hill replied, "Sir, apparently, Miss Lizzy left Longbourn not sixty minutes past. Cook said she greeted the kitchen staff with a smile before pilfering a slice of bread."

During the entirety of the butler's comment, Darcy's heart fluctuated between fear that something devastating happened and embarrassment at the possibility that he was worried over nothing. Except, this was not "nothing". There was a murderer about, likely one known to all of them.

Mr. Bennet's lips pinched tightly together. He groaned, "Stupid me! I told my girls last night that we would not be allowing anyone inside Longbourn whom we might not trust. I said nothing about stopping them from going out."

Darcy did not like it. Elizabeth knew he was coming. She had agreed to see him. Was her leaving Longbourn an indication that she was undesirous of his suit? Was that why she left and had not yet returned? Did she not want him?

The weight of that thought almost crushed him.

He was desperate to see Elizabeth, to see her lovely eyes light with mirth at his fussing over her. To see whether she welcomed his suit or not.

"We must find her," Darcy stood to leave.

From behind him, Mr. Bennet addressed Hill, "Let no one in or out until we return safely with Lizzy. When the major and Charlotte arrive, direct them to join the search."

Without waiting for a response, the two men hurried out of Longbourn toward the stables.

CHAPTER 30

*P*ulling at the ropes binding her wrists, Elizabeth shivered from the cold. It was years since she and Charlotte explored the chalk caves at the far corner on the border between Longbourn and Nether-field Park. Where the cool dampness had appealed to her during the heat of the summer months, it was an unwelcome location deep into the autumnal season.

Hertfordshire's long-abandoned chalk mines and caves were notorious for collapsing. The material was soft, which made it easy for a wall to weaken and fall. The recent rains where water would drip into the crevices and cracks rendered the caves unstable. Both her father and Sir William had forbidden their children to play near the caverns. Once Charlotte and Elizabeth were old enough to realize they were not invincible, the two never played inside them again.

Rubbing the back of her neck on the sharp rocks at her back, the cloth that was tied behind her head moved about an inch below where it was secured. Disregarding the pull to her hair, she pressed her head back, pushed against the hard rock again, then stretched her neck as far as she was able. It worked. Once the cloth was loosened, she was able to move her mouth and chin until the gag in her mouth came free.

"Help me!" She screamed at the top of her lungs. The only reply was the distant squawking of the carrion crow. "Help me!" she shouted, hoping against hope that someone other than Jeannie could hear. She was desperate to return to Longbourn to learn what Mr. Darcy had to say and to tell him who was behind all the evil deeds against the Collins', Mr. Wickham, and the Darcy's.

Elizabeth hoped her father and Mr. Darcy would miss her soon. As soon as she realized the threat, she was grateful she had removed her bonnet, leaving it on the rock at Oakham Mount. Surely, someone would see it. The crumbs of bread she crumbled in her fingers as she walked in front of the horse would leave a trail as long as Jeannie did not eat them.

She needed to be rescued so she could warn Mr. Darcy and others.

She sighed, wondering how she had ever thought him to be arrogant. She needed a hero. She wanted it to be Mr. Darcy.

* * *

WITHOUT A WORD, Mr. Bennet and Darcy mounted and rode like the wind to Oakham Mount. Darcy, whose horse had taken the lead, saw the bonnet when he was still twenty feet from the rock. *Elizabeth! Where are you?* His eyes sweeping the ground, he saw no sign of her. Panic flooded him from his head to his toes. Swallowing, he held up his hand, reining his horse to a stop.

"Let us walk from here," he directed. "If there are any footprints that would indicate the direction she headed, we cannot take the chance of ruining any clues she might have left."

Mr. Bennet nodded, his eyes stormy. "If something has happened to her, I will never forgive myself."

Darcy felt the same. He lifted her woven straw bonnet, holding it to his chest. Seeing the misery on the face of her father, he handed the headwear over to him.

"We will find her," Darcy insisted. He would not rest until she was safely returned home. Neither would Mr. Bennet.

The heels of her walking boots were visible in the muddy sections. Darcy cursed the presence of so many rocks as they got closer to the spring. In the grass to the left of the rock, he discovered a piece of bread wedged between two blades of grass. A clue!

"Look!" About three feet away they found another piece. Four feet from that they saw another one.

Once Mr. Bennet's eyes saw where Darcy pointed, he said, "That's my girl."

Darcy yearned to correct him. *No, that is my girl.* However, he would save those words for her ears alone once they found her.

Studying the ground at his feet looking for more crumbs, the soft snuffle of a horse and the squeak of a new saddle filtered into Darcy's ears. Looking up to see who approached, he was surprised to see Bingley and Hurst.

"Darcy, Mr. Bennet, are you searching for something? Did you lose a coin in the grass?" Bingley asked, a wide smile on his face. When he looked at Elizabeth's father, he sobered. "Oh, did Miss Elizabeth leave her bonnet behind?"

"You saw her?" Mr. Bennet demanded. "Where?"

Bingley glanced at Mr. Hurst before replying. "We certainly did. Hurst told her that we spotted two young deer that must have gotten separated from their mother by Netherfield's ponds. One of them appeared to be injured. Morris was examining it when we left. Miss Elizabeth told us she wanted to help, then immediately took off running." Bingley pointed in the direction she traveled. "I suppose she did not remember removing her bonnet, such was her concern for the poor little animal."

"That sounds like my Lizzy." Mr. Bennet heaved a sigh of relief. "If you do not mind, I shall see her safely home. Mr. Darcy, will you be joining me?" He remounted his horse.

Something unidentifiable held Darcy back. Bingley had never lied to him before and he had no reason to do so now. However, that glance between him and his brother-in-law unsettled Darcy. That and the fact that the three pieces of crusty bread lead away from Netherfield Park and behind Oakham Mount, not towards it.

"No, I believe I will ride along with Bingley, if I am welcome."

"Suit yourself." Mr. Bennet mounted then raced across the field towards the large house in the distance. There were three ponds in front of Netherfield, two small and one large. All three were lined with trees and brush that had yet to be removed. He would have a difficult time finding her—if she was there.

Looking up at the two men, Darcy asked, "How long ago did you see Miss Elizabeth?"

"Not more than ten minutes ago, perhaps twenty," Hurst answered. "She said she wanted to visit the caves one more time before the hard rains of winter set in. I suppose she changed her mind."

This made no sense to Darcy. There had already been enough rain to make the going rough for a lady on foot. Then, there was the bread.

Bingley added, "Hey, it will not take much time, why not go see what caught her interest. Morris showed us where they are. It is not far from here."

Without saying anything, Darcy retrieved his horse. From his height, he could see two more pieces of what appeared to be breadcrumbs directly south of the others. Riding closer, not drawing attention to the clues, Darcy followed behind the two men, his gut beginning to ache.

Something was not right.

They rode for a long while through the tall grass edging the fence between the two properties. Had Elizabeth come this way, there were no more pieces of bread nor any other clues to be found. Still, he said nothing as they rode. Neither did the other men. Again, that was odd. Bingley was normally as chatty as a schoolgirl with tales to tell her friends.

What was happening?

Approaching a rocky escarpment barely taller than

Darcy and his horse, Darcy heard Elizabeth's cry. Swinging his leg over, he jumped from his mount, running through the grass and rocks to a gaping hole in the side of the cliff.

"Elizabeth, I am here." He looked back to Bingley, the question he intended to ask dying on his tongue. Both men had pistols raised pointed directly at him.

What? His friend's treachery hit him like an uppercut by Gentleman Jim. In an instant, anger trumped puzzlement until he determined he would see Bingley and Hurst pay at the first opportunity.

"If you do not go inside peacefully, I will shoot her in front of your eyes before I kill you," Hurst declared without wavering.

"Why?" he could not stop himself from asking. "Why would you do this?"

"Hands in the air!" Hurst barked as he slid from his horse. Bingley followed; his weapon still aimed at Darcy.

Hurst instructed Bingley, "You aim at his heart. I've got him between the eyes if he makes one false move." To Darcy he said, "Go!"

From the depths of the cave, he heard Elizabeth cry out, "Mr. Bingley is the murderer along with Mr. Hurst. Please, Mr. Darcy, use caution. They are dangerous. They mean to do you harm."

The warning was too late. As soon as he turned his back to them to enter the mouth of the cave, one of them used the butt of their gun to hit him between the back of his ear and his jaw, dropping him to his knees, then the ground. Before his face smashed into the rocky floor, he heard her scream. Then his world went black.

* * *

HOLDING HER BREATH, Elizabeth heard the thud. The excitement of knowing Mr. Darcy was close mixed with fear at what happened to him. Had he tripped trying to make his way to her? No. With the striking of a flint on the rock and the lighting of a torch, Elizabeth knew. Mr. Bingley and Mr. Hurst had found Mr. Darcy.

She was livid when the two men dragged him inside, roughly dropping him on the ground in front of her. His hands were bound behind his back and his feet were together like they had done her. She hissed, "You will not get away with this."

"You think not?" Hurst guffawed. "That's a pretty bold prediction from someone in your predicament, I am thinking. Oh, do not be concerned with us, Miss Elizabeth. As soon as Caroline and Louisa bring Miss Darcy from London and she becomes Mrs. Bingley, we will be just fine."

"You wretch!" Elizabeth growled. Looking directly at Mr. Bingley, she said, "Your perfidy will break my sister's heart!"

Bingley shrugged.

Mr. Darcy groaned, his muscles twitching.

"How did you get Claire and Mr. Wickham to come to the orchard?" Elizabeth boldly asked.

Hurst sneered. "A note to her that Mr. Darcy arranged for her to have her say with Mr. Wickham had her scampering to the orchard. Wickham's note promised him a tryst with your youngest sister, Miss Elizabeth. He was as eager as the lady."

"You disgust me!" Elizabeth spat the words. "Why? Why have you done this? What has Mr. Darcy and the others done to you?"

Mr. Bingley replied. "Caroline said that Darcy has everything my father raised me to have. Once he let Caroline know he would not marry her, the only other way to get what my sister says I deserve is for me to marry his sister, which I will do as soon as we get to Gretna Green."

"Ha!" Mr. Hurst snorted. "Tell her the truth. She won't be able to tell anyone else."

"I will," Mr. Bingley pulled at the bottom of his vest. "The cost of leasing Netherfield Park was excessive, as were the items Caroline and Louisa purchased to bring it up to snuff. Additionally, I owe nefarious men a large sum of money, they are after me to pay for my gaming losses. To be honest, at this point, Caroline said it was a choice between my life and Darcy's. With him out of the picture, I gain Pemberley and Georgiana Darcy's dowry of thirty thousand, which will settle all of my debts. Miss Collins, her brother, and Mr. Wickham's deaths were a means to an end. Caroline said they had to die."

"This way we could get Darcy permanently out of the way," Mr. Hurst added, kicking Mr. Darcy's legs.

"Yes, well, that is rather unfortunate," Bingley said, increasing Elizabeth's disgust. "By the way, something to think about while you wait for a rescue that will, unfortunately, be too late is that Darcy told me he intended to marry you. Imagine, you could have been the mistress of Pemberley."

Mr. Hurst taunted, "Now, I am sorry to say that you will be sleeping together forever in your chalky grave.

These walls are fragile, Miss Elizabeth. Once we block the entrance, you will never be able to dig yourself out without burying yourselves. In essence, if you try a bid for freedom, you will kill yourself. So nighty night."

Elizabeth's mouth dropped open at the gall of the men. "How could you! How dare you share private information from a man who only ever treated you as a friend. You are no gentleman, Mr. Bingley! And you, Mr. Hurst, you are the Devil himself."

Elizabeth's rage shook her. Never in her lifetime had she imagined she would want to do another person harm like she did at that moment.

"Now, now," Mr. Bingley's tone was extremely condescending. "Hurst is right. You cannot be joined in life, but you will be in death. How romantic all the ladies will think it when the news flits from parlor to parlor." To Mr. Hurst he said, a grin on his face, "I never thought my dreams would come true in a small town in Hertfordshire. Caroline was correct. How wrong I was."

"Let us go," Mr. Hurst slapped his brother-in-law on the shoulder, almost knocking the torch from his hands. "We have nothing left to do here. Louisa and Caroline should have the house almost closed by now. We need to collapse the opening so they cannot get out."

Mr. Bingley spun on his heels. Without looking back, they left the cave, leaving Elizabeth and Mr. Darcy in total darkness.

Before the light was completely gone, Elizabeth looked around the cave. It was approximately eight feet across and less than six feet high. Near the entrance leading to the shaft, which led to the outside, was a pile of blankets, straw, and clothing covered with mud and... Oh, no! Blood.

She heard them working at the entrance, the sharp sounds of stones and rocks landing upon each other. She closed her eyes against the dust wafting into their part of the cave. She tasted the chalk on her lips. After a time, the sounds became muffled. Then, she heard no more.

* * *

MR. BENNET CALLED his daughter's name over and over. Each time, he stopped his horse and waited for a reply. After encircling all three ponds, he approached the main house at Netherfield Park, deep concern for the safety of his daughter hurting his chest.

Two carriages, one a town coach, readied for travel were in front of the portico. As he handed his horse to a groom, Lady Catherine de Bourgh and her daughter exited Netherfield.

"I take no leave of you nor of your insipid brothers, Miss Bingley." Lady Catherine said over her shoulder. Ignoring him completely, the Lady and her daughter entered the smaller carriage and left.

Stopping a footman as he came through the door with a traveling case in each hand, Mr. Bennet asked, "Are Miss Bingley and Mrs. Hurst going somewhere?"

The footman shrugged. "London, I hear, though I doubt from all that they are packing up that they plan on coming back."

"Have you seen my daughter, Miss Elizabeth?"

As the footman shook his head, Mr. Bennet asked, "Is Mr. Morris inside?"

"No, sir." The cases must have been heavy since the footman put them on the ground. "He left for St. Albans early this morning to look at some cattle Mr. Bingley wanted to add to the herd."

Then, why had Mr. Bingley and Mr. Hurst told him that the steward was tending an injured animal.

"Pardon me," Mr. Bennet stepped inside Netherfield, to hear Miss Bingley barking orders to the waiting staff.

"We are expecting to return tomorrow. Take good care of Mr. Darcy while we are away. See that he has everything he needs." To Mr. Darcy's valet, she said, "Do tell him that we will be pleased to see his sister while we are in town."

"Very well, Miss," the valet bowed and departed.

This left Bennet alone with Miss Bingley.

"Have you seen my daughter, Elizabeth?" he asked.

"Eliza? Why would she be here? I have issued her no invitation," Miss Bingley sneered.

"You have not seen her then?"

"I cannot imagine why you would believe I would, Mr. Bennet. Now, I am rather busy with my preparations, you understand."

"Your brothers are not attending you?" he could not keep himself from asking.

"They are not, Mr. Bennet. Good day."

Mr. Bennet knew when he was dismissed. *What a miserable female!*

His heart raced. Something was very wrong at Netherfield Park. He only hoped it did not affect Elizabeth.

There was nothing for it but to retrace the path he took, hoping to see his daughter. Had she fallen? Was she laying in the field unconscious? Hurrying back to his horse, he mounted quickly and raced back over the field, scanning as far as he could see in either direction. Arriving back at Oakham Mount, he still saw no sign of her. Nor was there any indication where Mr. Darcy, Mr. Bingley, or Mr. Hurst might be.

Choosing the lower part of the field, he rode slowly back toward Netherfield Park, yelling his daughter's name often. Still nothing. Back and forth he went until he saw the coach leaving the residence. *Good riddance, Miss Bingley!*

With each turn he made from one end of the field to the other, the pressure in his chest increased. Worry turned to fear. Something was very, very wrong. Where was Elizabeth? Where was Mr. Darcy? Where were Mr. Bingley and Mr. Hurst?

When the major and Charlotte in her pony cart joined him to search, the panic he felt inside at not having located anyone he was looking for almost did him in.

CHAPTER 31

"*M*r. Darcy," Elizabeth said, her voice echoing in the cavern. "Mr. Darcy, wake up please, I need your help."

He groaned. Then he whispered her name, "Elizabeth."

She was desperately relieved that he still lived. "Mr. Darcy, I will not ask you if you hurt since I saw the way they treated you. *Disgusting men!* We need to figure out a way to escape." She wished there was even a trickle of light coming in from the sky. As it was, there was nothing but blackness.

"One moment, please," Darcy whispered. He coughed several times, then tried to clear his throat.

She heard him shifting his body on the loose gravel underneath of him.

"Elizabeth, I have a knife on the inside shaft of my right boot. I am aware it will be difficult, but can you reach it? Unfortunately, I do not know where you are located in relation to me. Did you see where they dropped me?"

"Yes. You are directly in front of where I am seated. I am at your back. Should I move down onto my knees, I am afraid I will hit you."

"Do not worry about injury to me, Elizabeth. Do not injure yourself. We shall think of something else."

"Sir, I will not break. Bruises will heal." Sliding off the rock, she leaned back so she would not fall forward over the top of him. Her knees brushed against his back.

"Mr. Darcy, if you would position your legs so I can have access, moving your left foot forward, I will put my back to you. My fingers will then be able to search." Saying it was one thing. Doing it was quite another. The jagged edges of the rocks bit into her knees. Guessing that she was about at his waist, she lifted herself up onto her knees then fell to her left, spinning so she landed partially on his leg and on the gravel. "Pardon me!" Elizabeth had not intended to end up on him. She was hoping to miss him completely.

"Do not worry yourself."

She shrugged. Her shoulders ached from the position of her arms, yet the first touch of her fingers to the fabric of his trousers set the tips on fire. *Good heavens!* Her reputation would never survive even if she did. Her heart raced. All moisture left her mouth.

He groaned again. The *poor man. His pain must be tremendous.* She needed to hurry.

Sliding across the floor on her bum, her skirt pulled against every attempt at movement. Mr. Darcy attempted to wiggle himself forward making her access easier. It did not.

"Please remain still. I do not want to take a chance of

causing you further injury or having you injure yourself further."

"I was trying to help."

"Yes, well," she would not tell him how the bunched fabric of her skirt was now directly under his right leg. Leaning back, her fingers moved over the few inches of his trousers that they could reach. Ignoring the lightning bolts shooting up her arms and the intense embarrassment at feeling a man's body, she leaned to the right again whereupon she finally touched the smoothness of his leather boot. Lifting her hands as high as possible meant bending forward to ease the pressure on her shoulders. With her palms pressed together, she fisted her right hand to allow the fingers of her left to slip under the surface of the boot.

"You are close," he said. "If you hold your fingers still, I will twist my leg to bring the knife to you so you can retrieve the blade."

With his movement, she felt the hardness of the hilt. "I have it." Pushing against his calf, she wiggled the knife from its holder. Passing it to her dominant hand once it was free of the boot, she considered how best she could cut the ropes binding Mr. Darcy's hands.

Before anything came to mind, he spoke, "Elizabeth, I will attempt to sit with my back to you. Do not be concerned about nicking my skin. Like your bruises, any injury will heal."

She heard his boots scrape across the surface and a grunt or two. Elizabeth could not imagine the strength it would take to sit up without being able to use his hands. There would be nothing to wedge himself...Oh! He was using her. The weight of him almost knocked her backwards.

"Oof! I apologize," he mumbled as he pushed away from her side. "There, I think I have it."

She waited for her heart to calm before she used the fingers of her left hand to reach out to find Mr. Darcy. Her right hand continued to grip the knife.

Her heart pounded. Perspiration beaded her brow. Hurting him was unavoidable. The fingers of her left hand clasped his. The knot at his wrists was sizable. Gulping, she began.

* * *

HE WAS GOING TO DIE, and it had nothing to do with his current injuries.

Every touch of Elizabeth's fingers sent a current through him that threatened to stop his heart. Pulling his hands apart as far as was possible, he felt the first nick of the knife. Clamping his teeth together he vowed to do his best not to make a sound.

"Mr. Darcy?" Elizabeth paused before continuing, her left hand squeezing his fingers tightly.

"Yes, Elizabeth," he grinned. "Mightn't you consider calling me Fitzwilliam or even Darcy? I believe we have passed the requirements for two polite individuals from our sphere."

She chuckled, the sound a delight to his ears. "Why, I wonder what Lady Catherine would say?"

"Ugh! You think of her now? How could you?" he teased, pleased it was her he was stuck with rather than someone who would weep and wail while doing nothing to help the situation. "Elizabeth," he hissed and flinched when the blade found his skin.

"I am terribly sorry. I wish...," she pulled on the rope, making the knot tighter. "I wish we had some light. However, I do not know how much ventilation this cave has. I believe that Mr. Bingley and Mr. Hurst knocked the rafters from the opening, collapsing the entrance."

"What?" *Blast!* He would personally see those men paid as soon as they could get out of the blasted cave.

"Fitzwilliam, are you familiar with chalk?"

He gloried in hearing his name on her lips. *What had she asked?* Oh, yes, chalk. "I am."

"Then you comprehend the task we have to get out of here, do you not? Without the support of the beams the whole roof could cave in on us. We would never make it out alive. The risk of trying to dig ourselves out of here may be more dangerous to us than waiting for help, do you agree?"

His admiration for her grew by the minute. She was a marvel.

He felt the knot loosen. "I believe you almost have it, my dear."

"Am..." she put pressure on the knife, making her slices more sure. "I..." she bore down even harder on the knot. "Your..." he felt a sawing motion as the blade slid back and forth. "Dear?" she cut through the bindings. "Yes! We have done it, Fitzwilliam."

Pulling his hands in front of him, he rolled his shoulders to stretch his muscles. Pulling off his gloves, he turned in the darkness, his fingers searching for her. He touched her hair, rubbing the silk between her fingers. Resting the side of his face against hers, he whispered, "I love you, Elizabeth. With my whole heart, I am yours."

Drawing her so close that a blade of grass could not have passed between them, he lowered his face to hers, his lips finding her forehead, her cheek, and finally...that soft, welcoming place that held dreams and... *By Jove!* He doubted he could remember his own name.

Tasting her, he lost all sense of...he sighed. She moaned. *Good God in heaven!* He was undone. Running his hands down her arms, he...*Oh, Good Lord!* She was still bound.

"I am a selfish beast." Trailing his fingers down to hers, he lifted his knife from her hand. "Allow me."

Once her arms were free, she wrapped them around his chest, pulling him closer. In the dark, they bumped noses and foreheads. Neither minded. For the longest time they drew comfort from tender words and caresses.

Boldly, Elizabeth kissed his cheek, his jaw, then the tender spot between his high collar and his ear. "I love you too, Fitzwilliam. My heart is yours."

Could he be any happier? Pulling her to his chest, she rested her head on his shoulder while he leaned back against the rock. Brushing his lips over her hair, he felt the roughness of the chalk dust. "Elizabeth, we are in dire straits, I am afraid." Before intertwining his fingers with hers, he used his knife to cut through the bindings on his ankles then did the same for Elizabeth. The blood pounding in his veins rose like fireworks at the realization that either Bingley or Hurst had their hands on Elizabeth's ankles. *He would make them pay for daring to touch her!*

Breathing in and out slowly to calm himself, Darcy said, "Bingley and Hurst told your father and I that you had gone to the ponds in front of Netherfield. I doubt your father noticed the trail of crumbs you left, and fortunately, neither did the crow."

She squeezed his fingers.

"I left my horse at the entrance of the cave."

"Will the animal stay?"

"I doubt it. Without me in his view, he will head to the stables at Netherfield Park." Bingley's treachery hit him anew. "Why? Did Bingley or Hurst say anything to you that would indicate why they plotted this course?"

His heart ached.

Elizabeth lifted their joined hands to her mouth. Brushing her lips over his knuckles, she said, "He wants Pemberley. With the support of his family, they plan to lure Miss Darcy from town whereupon Mr. Bingley will marry her at Gretna Green. All he needs is for you to die to take ownership of your estate." Elizabeth added, "Mr. Bingley told me that the leasing of Netherfield Park drained his funds. By the time his sisters finished refurbishing the property and he paid for the staff, his inheritance must have been almost gone. However, it was his gambling debts and the men pressing him for payment that motivated his course."

"Gambling debts? *The fool!* What does that have to do with me? Marry my sister to pay for his greed? Never!" Darcy almost shouted. "I have warned him repeatedly that he needed to take Miss Bingley in hand. She has long coveted Pemberley where she would rule as queen" Darcy spat the words into the filthy air. "Never!"

Elizabeth interrupted his thoughts. "My dear man, Mr. Bingley had a choice. Easily, he could have decided to imitate you, to be led by you. How different his life would be now had he done so. I do wonder, why did we not figure out ahead of time that it was them who were guilty of the murders?"

Darcy grimaced, "Because I simply did not want it to be them, and I suspect neither did you."

"I believe you are correct. The clues were there. Your boot prints at the orchard?"

"Bingley stole my boots, then had the temerity to return them without cleaning them first."

"The brass button?"

Darcy said, "I incorrectly assumed it was the one missing from Wickham's waistcoat. It must have been from Bingley's ugly green vest, one of which was also missing a button."

"The mud in Beatrice's hooves?"

"What mud?" Darcy asked.

"Do you not recall in the third note I sent you? I told you that the groom had to clean the dark mud from the orchard from her hooves."

"No, I...*Blast!* Bingley took my mail, which explains why I received no letters from Georgiana, my uncle, or the Bow Street Runners. I doubt the letters I wrote to them ever made it out of Netherfield Park," Darcy growled, his anger and frustration boiling over. "I trusted him, Elizabeth. After Wickham's disloyalty, I vowed to only keep as friends those whom I could rely upon implicitly. I thought Bingley was that sort of man. For five years I helped him and shared the bonds of friendship with him despite loathing the family that was attached to him."

She hugged him tighter. He deeply appreciated her empathy. Losing someone's trust hurt.

She asked, "Mr. Collins?"

"Bingley was gone to London for two days. During the week I was confined I never saw or heard from Hurst. It was then that they went to Kent."

"Did you see the so-called suicide note?"

He admitted, "No, I am afraid I did not."

"Papa told me it was covered with ink blotches and crossed out words. He assumed Mr. Collins wrote it after he was inebriated. I had not thought of it until now but Mr. Collins' letter he sent in advance of his visit was neatly formed with letters so small and tightly written that it was next to impossible to read."

"Then Bingley wrote it. Had I seen it I would have known immediately. I would not have recognized Hurst's handwriting. He should have written the note. That was a foolish mistake on their part."

"Fitzwilliam, had Claire and Mr. Wickham not been in Meryton, what would Mr. Bingley have done?"

Darcy sighed. Distractedly playing with her fingers resting on his chest, he mused, "I cannot think that Bingley started down this path on his own. He hid his greed well, so well that I wonder if he was aware of its existence. He has always been an open book, easy to read."

"He impressed me and Jane the same."

"Which means that there was a mastermind pushing,

scheming, and convincing him to act. I cannot see him doing it on his own."

"Miss Bingley?" Elizabeth asked.

He nodded. "When I look back on the sequence of events, I can almost put my finger on the exact moment their plans began. I firmly rejected her dreams of becoming the mistress of Pemberley."

"Miss Bingley does not handle disappointment well, then?"

"Not at all." Darcy shuddered, pulling Elizabeth closer. "One of her most unappealing characteristics is her inherent belief that she belongs in a position of elevated rank. As the daughter of a merchant, she should have remembered her roots."

"Mr. Bingley, with Mr. Hurst's support, also felt entitled, Fitzwilliam. From his own mouth he said that being the master of Pemberley was what his father raised him to be. He is deeply in debt and felt having Pemberley was the only solution to the problem he created."

"That explains it all. He was more like Wickham than I could have dreamed." He was disgusted at the knowledge. "However, the overall plan sounds decidedly like Caroline Bingley," Darcy sneered. He shook his head, closing his eyes. "Bingley might have dreamed of having my estate, but I cannot see him following through on his own no matter how desperate he became. He would act if his sister took the lead and he could follow her orders." He harrumphed. "I knew she was ambitious. I knew she was willing to do whatever it took to gain my regard. What I did not know was the extent of her desires."

Elizabeth kissed his chin. "Speaking of desire, Mr.

Darcy...will you share with me how you possibly managed to avoid her and fall in love with *me*?"

He grinned, grateful for the change of subject. "It is inconceivable for me to admit this, but even when I feared you were attempting to kill me, I was attracted to you."

She pulled her head back and exclaimed in disbelief. "You? Attracted to me, then? How is that possible?"

Gently pressing her cheek back to his shoulder, he kissed her brow. "You have a way about you, Elizabeth. I had a list of requirements for the mistress of my house. You waltzed into my vision with your pert attitude, your lovely eyes, and your kind soul, and I knew right then that I was in danger. When you set aside propriety for the sake of doing the right thing, I realized my heart belonged to you more than it did to me. When I found out you were missing, I...I realized that there was nothing I would not do to see you safe. If the murderer offered me a trade, Pemberley for your life, I would have given it all to him with no regret."

"Oh, Fitzwilliam."

He felt her sigh on his lips. Her passion melted his brain and sapped his muscles of strength.

Mid-kiss, she pulled back, pushing against his chest. "My father. He will be looking for me. When he realizes you are gone, he will look for you as well. Let us ponder the clues they will use to find us."

Even though he wanted to continue kissing her, he saw the wisdom of her idea. "Very well. You begin."

Elizabeth tapped her fingers against his chest for quite a while before she spoke. Finally, she said, "Your horse. Papa will either see it galloping back to the stables at

Netherfield or will think to check there when he does not readily find you. He will next contact Charlotte and Major Gerring for help. Both Charlotte and my father know this area. It will be no time at all before they see the disturbed entrance of the cave with debris scattered outside. Mr. Bingley stated the truth when he said it would be dangerous to attempt a rescue but my Papa will figure it out. We shall be rescued in no time."

He hoped so. Then he would go after Bingley.

CHAPTER 32

*T*homas Bennet reined his horse close to Charlotte's cart. "Mr. Bingley sent me on a wild goose chase to Netherfield's ponds. The ladies of the house have departed for London after Lady Catherine and her daughter left for Kent. The only thing I have found of Lizzy is her bonnet."

Charlotte asked, "She left her bonnet behind? That is not like Lizzy. Where is Mr. Darcy?"

"He is with Mr. Bingley and Mr. Hurst." Bennet replied. "They are looking for Elizabeth."

"Have you not seen them ride by?" Charlotte inquired.

"I have not. However, the three of them could have crossed the fields and arrived at the stables while I was inside the house."

"This is rather suspicious, is it not? Why did they not join you in your search at the pond? What sort of game is Mr. Bingley playing that he would want you separated from the search party? Why can I not let go of the idea that there is a far bigger drama going on than Lizzy wandering off and getting lost? We know her capabilities and her knowledge of..."

From a distance two riders were crossing the field racing toward Netherfield Park. Charlotte flicked the reins of the cart turning the pony towards the fence line between the estates. She never looked back.

Waiting until the others were out of ear shot, she said, "Lizzy is not at the pond, nor was she on the main road to the north or Major Gerring and I would have seen her before we arrived. Returning to Longbourn would be a waste of time in my opinion. That leaves south."

"The caves," Mr. Bennet muttered, having already reached the same conclusion. "Lizzy would never go there alone."

The major said, "If they are chalk caves, I have confidence that neither would Mr. Darcy."

Bennet could not wait for the cart to navigate the rougher terrain. Kicking his horse, he charged ahead.

"WOULD you describe what you can remember about the inside of the cave?" Darcy asked. Had their life not been endangered, he would have rejoiced at being allowed the opportunity to hold her in his arms. She fit against his side perfectly.

"Certainly. We walked seven of my steps on a downward slope until we turned into this room. The back of the wall in this chamber was ten very small steps because the debris on the floor a challenge to cross with the torches burning behind me. On the left side of the doorway to the shaft is a pile of soiled clothing, blankets, and straw used by the murderers when they carted Claire and Mr. Wickham's bodies to Mr. Haniger's stable, I suspect."

He was disgusted. That Bingley had used the clothes to commit a terrible crime. That Elizabeth was forced to remain in the same room with the evidence of their evil was deplorable.

She said, "Dearest, I just thought of something. The shaft did not end at the entrance to this chamber. It continued into the earth. There was not enough light to see how far back it went, I am sorry to say."

"I wonder...Shhh! Did you...?" Darcy stopped speaking. The plaintive cry of a crow was heard as if from a distance. "Did you hear that?"

"I did." Elizabeth's head lifted. "I heard it before but did not consider how that was even possible? The rock is thick, and the grassy roof over the top of the cave would keep sound from penetrating, would it not?"

"It would, unless..." Darcy paused. "Unless there is a hole."

Helping Elizabeth to stand, he shuffled his feet forward. "Extend your free arm, sweeping it to the front and the side. If we walk carefully, we might be able to see if there is a way out at the opposite end of the shaft." He clasped her hand tighter. "Elizabeth, it is entirely possible that we will end up in a situation far worse than we are now. Are you willing to take that chance?"

Without a pause, she answered, "Like the account of Ruth in the Bible, I will go where you go."

"Then let us hope we have the same outcome Ruth

had." He slowly took another step. From a distance they could still hear the crow.

"Fitzwilliam, I propose we stop for a kiss every four steps. That way, whatever the outcome, we have no regrets."

What a brilliant woman! He smiled. "To clarify the rules, is that every four steps with both feet or every four steps with a single foot."

"Whichever gets me more kisses, my darling man."

Of that he was in full agreement. Taking two more steps he leaned in for his kiss. They made slow progress across the room.

* * *

BENNET ARRIVED at the cave long before the others. It looked like an explosion had gone off. Grey dust and debris scattered over the grass. Old timbers had tumbled over themselves, their ends buried under the rubble at the entrance of the cave. Hoof prints leading away from the area signaled that more than one rider had recently been there. The chalk floated on the breeze, filling his eyes and mouth with grit.

Jeannie circled the escarpment not far above the surface, frantically flapping her wings and squawking. Every third circle, she would swoop down to the back of the mound then rise up again and repeat her actions.

He started pulling away the largest stones and boards. When the chalk from further back in the shaft began filling in whatever gaps he made, he stopped.

"Lizzy!" he yelled over and over until Charlotte and Major Gerring arrived.

Sliding off his horse, the major began rummaging under the seat of the cart after helping Charlotte to the ground. Mr. Bennet joined him.

"We need something that will stabilize the roof before we do any digging," Mr. Bennet told the major as he fought to keep the panic from his voice.

"What in the world is that bird doing," Charlotte stood with her hand shading her eyes. "If it is what I think it is, I believe we are looking at the wrong end of the cave."

Tossing aside the rope and hammer he had picked up from the box, the three of them hurried around the escarpment, the major assisting Charlotte. Not thirty feet from where they left the pony cart, a rocky point approximately five feet from the ground signaled the back of the cave. Jutting out from one of the crevices was a massive pile of sticks.

With the adrenaline from his youth giving Bennet the ability he needed, he used the jagged edges to make his way from the ground to the nest. Reaching inside, he held up a shiny brass button to show the others. "As I suspected, Jeannie is a thief."

Major Gerring's brow furrowed. "Sir, Mr. Wickham's waistcoat was missing only one button, which was retrieved from the orchard. Do you have a vest with that style of fastenings?"

Bennet turned the button over in his hand. His heart fell to the pit of his stomach. "No, but I have seen this often enough. Most of the days that Mr. Bingley came to

Longbourn he wore a green striped vest with brass buttons."

"Mr. Bingley?" Charlotte's hand shot to her chest. "Then, if I could venture a guess, Mr. Bingley and Mr. Hurst were at the orchard the night Miss Collins and Mr. Wickham were killed. Likely, there was a struggle either before they were killed, or the button could have come off while lifting and carrying them."

Mr. Bennet growled.

Charlotte continued, "If Lizzy and Mr. Darcy are inside this cave, it is also likely that Mr. Bingley and Mr. Hurst have either harmed them in some way or bound them making their escape impossible."

Major Gerring added, "By chance are either of you familiar with this particular cave?"

Both Bennet and Charlotte shook their heads.

"Then we do not know where they are in relation to us. They could be in a cavern deep underground or right below the surface."

Rubbing his hand over his mouth, Mr. Bennet yelled, "Lizzy! Mr. Darcy! Elizabeth!" He waited for a reply. When it finally came, it was faint, but it was there.

"They are here!"

AFTER TEN STEPS and many kisses, Elizabeth reached her hand out in front of her. They should be at the doorway to the cavern where they were confined. When the only thing she felt was dusty air, they carefully took two more steps. Darcy's arms were longer than hers. He would touch any surface first.

"Fitzwilliam, I would guess that the width of the shaft was approximately four feet. We should have left the room and entered the shaft."

The step he took pulled her hand forward. He stopped. "Something is in front of us, either the wall of the cavern or the wall of the shaft.

She could hear the excitement in his voice. Elizabeth desperately wished she could see the eagerness on his handsome face.

Taking a step to match his, then another, Elizabeth still felt nothing except air.

"Let me run my hand towards you to see where we might be." He took the hand he was holding and put it in his coat pocket. "Do hang on tightly, my dear. I need both hands to search. It would devastate me to not have contact with you now."

When his palm left hers, she clasped the fabric, fisting it in her hand. Like him, she had no desire to let go.

She felt him lean to his left, then his right. When he bent down, his coat pulled against her hand. She kept a tight hold of the fabric.

"What? Blast it all!" he exclaimed.

She heard the disgust and felt the movement of his body as it shuddered.

"I touched the bloody blankets."

"Ewww!" Elizabeth's stomach began to roil. Swallowing down the bile, she stepped to the right, pulling him with her. He willingly followed. "Then the opening should be in front of us."

Taking another step to the right, they moved forward. After four more steps, they both felt the hard surface of the wall. They were in the shaft. It felt like a victory.

She willingly stepped into Darcy's arms at his gentle tug. They had taken too many steps for a single kiss. Reaching the shaft of the cave needed to be celebrated.

Through the haze of passion, she heard the crow. Then she heard her father.

CHAPTER 33

The crow continued circling above. Occasionally, it would caw and squawk before diving down to the ground close to its nest. At the last second, it pulled itself up and shot back into the sky.

"Papa! We are here. Mr. Darcy and I are in the shaft." His Elizabeth yelled although her voice could barely be heard.

"Elizabeth Rose. You have scared me to death!" Mr. Bennet's hand shot to his chest; his heart almost unable to cope with the relief of the moment. Climbing to the top of the escarpment, he stopped. Years of rainy winters and springs would have weakened the ceiling above the shaft.

"Lizzy, where are you in the shaft?"

Darcy answered. "In truth, we do not know. We can see nothing, only feel the surface beneath our palms. At which end of the shaft are you?"

"I am opposite the entrance that has collapsed."

"Good. Then we will come toward you. Can you see any way to access the tunnel from where you stand?"

"Not yet." Bennet surveyed every inch of the area in front of him with his eyes. He did not dare put his weight on the roof. Looking back, he saw where the major had laid out all the tools from the box in the cart. "Major, see if you or Charlotte can find a strong enough stick that I might puncture a small hole in the roof without collapsing the whole of it."

To Darcy and Lizzy he said, "Do not come any closer. I will try to tap a small hole in the roof. If I am able, it means the whole structure is weak. If I am not, then we can attempt to dig an opening for you."

Darcy replied, "Sir, there is already a hole somewhere or we could not hear you. Mightn't you try to find the opening?"

Darcy was correct. Without thinking, Mr. Bennet stepped back, catching his heel on the corner of the crow's nest. Flailing his arms to keep from falling, his boot kicked at the sticks and branches, dislodging the aerie from its resting place. Underneath the pile of rubble, he saw a small hole.

"We see light," Elizabeth shouted, her voice much clearer now.

So *that* was what the bird was about. Where they did not know the location of the opening, Jeannie did.

"Major, bring me what you have," Bennet ordered. "We need to get them out of there."

Hefting all the available digging tools, as well as the rope over his shoulders, Major Gerring soon joined him. While the major chipped away at the hole, Mr. Bennet gathered the sticks together into a bundle, making a torch from the nest. He knew that solid chalk was not flamma-

349

ble. However, the dust particles could ignite. Before the cave-in it was not a problem. Now that the inside was filled with the powdery debris dancing in the air, they would need to be cautious. It was hoped that they would not need additional light once the hole was large enough.

It took little time for an opening broad enough for Darcy's shoulders to get through was formed. Tying a loop in the rope, Mr. Bennet let it down into the hole. The other end of the rope was hitched to the cart after Charlotte steered it to where she was facing away from where they stood. They were ready. They only needed to wait for Darcy and Lizzy to get themselves into position.

"THIS IS IT, Elizabeth. We will soon be rescued, and you will be in your father's arms." Darcy wanted her safety more than his next breath. Nevertheless, the time they shared together gave him unimaginable joy.

"As much as I long to be in the fresh air, I do believe that his arms are not the arms I want to hold me, Fitzwilliam." She tugged his hand to halt his progress. "A moment, please."

He gladly stopped. They were pressed up against the chalky wall, moving sideways at a snail's pace, joined by their entwined fingers. It was more than four steps since their last kiss. Darcy could not let that lapse go. Turning back to her, he gathered her into his arms. His coat, his face, and his hair were undoubtedly coated with white dust as was she. Yet, her lips were as soft and smooth as silk.

He whispered against her mouth, "Marry me? Be my wife, the mother of our future children, and the mistress of Pemberley, please? Marry me?"

She smiled, kissing the lips that still touched hers. Leaning back, she said, "My heart, I can see how it will be." In a tone reminiscent of Lady Catherine she teased, "However, did this happen? Fitzwilliam Darcy of Pemberley has the highest requirements for a wife. Why, she must have a thorough knowledge of music, singing, drawing, dancing, and the modern languages, as the minimum of accomplishments; and besides all this, she must possess a certain something in her air and manner of walking, the tone of her voice, her address and expressions, or the word will be but half deserved." She giggled. "Then I come in with my hair all blowsy and my hem six inches deep in mud and you say, 'I want her for Mrs. Darcy and no other.' My dearest man, I suspect that shock will travel like waves throughout England on the day we wed. Mothers and their unwed daughters will mourn and cry, while their father's sigh with regret at the loss of such a man."

He threw his head back and laughed, while holding her tightly. *What an amazing woman!*

THE RESCUE WAS a series of attempts and failures. Elizabeth stood next to her father while Darcy was raised from the depths. His hair, face, and clothing were covered in grey dust, giving her a glimpse of how he would age over the years. He was still the handsomest man of her acquaintance.

The cuts, scrapes, and bruises on his face looked painful, yet he had not said a word of complaint. Lightly running her fingers over his cheek, she sighed, barely keeping back the tears, "Oh, Fitzwilliam, how you have suffered."

"I will heal." He picked her up and spun her around once they had their feet firmly planted on the ground next to the cart. Darcy kissed Elizabeth until she fairly melted into his arms. Never did she wish to be anywhere else than where she was at that moment.

"Ah-hem!" Mr. Bennet cleared his throat. "You have until our arrival at Longbourn to settle your future and decide the details of your wedding or my wife will be as frazzled as she has ever been. I say this for my peace, not yours." He smirked before jumping into the back of the cart.

"Does he have to come with the marriage?" Darcy asked, a twinkle in his eye as he wiped the dust from his face.

Elizabeth burst out in laughter. "I love you, Fitzwilliam Darcy."

The carrion crow flew above them halfway down the fence line before turning back toward the cave.

Her father chuckled, then said to no one in particular, "I shall need to take from Longbourn's budget enough to repair and maintain Jeannie's nest for the rest of my days or hers."

Darcy immediately offered, "All of my resources are at your disposal, sir. *Jeanne de Valois-Saint-Remy* and her progeny will be forever welcome at Pemberley should she choose to fly north."

Elizabeth grinned at both men. Despite the difficulty of the day and the agonizing turmoil to come, the sun warmed the November air and her heart nearly burst with love for the men seated on either side of her. Her father for his diligence in rescuing them, and Darcy for being the best man in England for her.

INSTEAD OF LONGBOURN, they headed to Netherfield Park. The staff was closing up the house with word from their master that he did not expect to return. Mr. Darcy's valet, groom, and driver were waiting in the front drawing room for his arrival.

"Sir!" Parker stood at attention when Darcy hurried through the door. He had one thing on his mind and that was the need to get to London before the Bingleys to protect his sister.

"Have my horse saddled. The major and I will ride to town immediately. Follow in my carriage."

Kissing Elizabeth, he hurried to where his horse was being readied at the stable. Parker followed. After shaking out his coat and brushing the dust off his hair, Darcy was ready to ride. He cared not that his face was bloodied or that his hair was a mess. Within minutes, he and the major were racing toward the junction of the Old North Road, turning south toward town.

The major yelled at him as he pulled alongside Darcy. "Sir, they probably are close to two hours ahead of us. If

Mr. Bingley and Mr. Hurst were confident that you and Miss Elizabeth would not be found, they may not rush their journey. There would be no need."

"Fools!" Darcy muttered, his determination to protect his sister, see justice done, and return to Elizabeth growing until it consumed him. "They should know that I would be hard to kill, especially when Elizabeth is involved. They will pay, Major Gerring, you mark my words."

THEY CAUGHT up to Bingley's town coach not five miles from London. Bingley was in more of a hurry than the two men expected. Rather than taking justice into their own hands, Darcy chose to follow at a distance to see where the Bingley family headed. Had they directed the coach to Matlock House where Georgiana was staying, Darcy would have not hesitated to make his presence known. However, the coach went to Bingley's townhouse, which was less than a quarter mile from Darcy's residence. After Mrs. Hurst and Miss Bingley exited the carriage, it was driven to the alley at the back of their house to be stabled. Bingley and Hurst left their mounts on the street for the grooms to take away. It appeared to be a merry party that entered the front door of their residence.

Bitterness at Bingley's betrayal burned in Darcy's gut. "Major, I suggest we go to Darcy House to plan our next step. I will send a note to my uncle to not allow Georgiana out of his sight and to keep her safely protected in his home."

"Yes, sir."

"I wish Richard were here," Darcy mused aloud.

"As do I, sir. Your cousin enjoys nothing more than to seek out evil, determine the perfect justice, and see it through to the end. Your enemies would not stand a chance."

Arriving at Darcy House, he apologized to his butler and housekeeper for not letting them know of his arrival.

"Your cousin is in your study, sir."

Darcy barely contained his groan. Richard's older brother only sought him out when he was short of cash and needed to cover either his gambling debts or one of his kept women was insisting on higher support for her extravagant style of living.

"Fine. I will have a message for Lord Matlock as soon as the Viscount departs." Darcy said to his butler. "No, the Viscount can wait." Grabbing parchment and ink from the nearest desk, he quickly scribbled a note for his uncle. Georgiana was his highest priority. "This is to be delivered to Lord Matlock himself, immediately." To himself he said, "Let's just get this over with and be done."

The moment he walked through the door he saw a man's boots crossed one over the other on the polished surface of the window frame immediately behind Darcy's private desk. Bolts of anger shot through him. Of all the nerve! The Viscount, his back to the door, held one of the expensive imported cigars Darcy kept for distinguished visitors, which did *not* describe his cousin.

"Get your filthy feet off of my desk and get out of

here!" Darcy commanded in no uncertain terms. "Come back only when you have learned your manners."

The chair spun around after the man's boots hit the floor. "Is that how you greet your favorite cousin?"

"Richard!" Darcy was gobsmacked. "How did you...? I thought you were on your way to Spain?"

Laying the cigar in the tray, Colonel Richard Fitzwilliam approached. "You look like you have ridden through hell, Darce. You do not look much better, Major." He gestured toward the chairs surrounding the fireplace, which was blazing hot. "I have a tale to tell."

Darcy glanced at Major Gerring. "You are not alone, Richard. We, too, have a story you will not believe."

CHAPTER 34

*J*ane listened to their tale in silence. A tear gathered at the corner of her eye but through sheer force of will, her sister blinked it away.

Both Charlotte and Elizabeth attempted to temper the sorrowful account of the Bingley family's treachery. However, the facts were too horrid. The blinders were ripped from Jane's eyes to where she could no longer see good in everything, especially their former neighbor.

Elizabeth felt terrible at having caused her dearest sister pain. Her own heart ached for the destruction the Bingleys had left behind. At the same time, she rejoiced in her own personal future as Mrs. Darcy.

"You may have thought that I loved him, Lizzy, but I did not," Jane admitted.

Elizabeth was stunned. "You did not?"

Shaking her head slowly, Jane admitted, "Although I believed Mr. Bingley to be all a gentleman should be, I worried about the power his sisters held over him. Until I could settle in my own mind that life with them in control was endurable, I refused to give him my heart."

"Well done, Jane." Elizabeth and Charlotte blurted in unison.

Comprehending that sharing their excitement would not be to her sister's detriment, Elizabeth said, "Dear Jane, I do have news."

"You do?" Jane dabbed at the corner of her eyes with the square of linen she was handed.

Elizabeth looked directly into her sister's tear-stained eyes. "I have gone and done the unthinkable, Jane dear."

"You have?" Jane glanced toward Charlotte. "Do you know?"

Charlotte nodded.

Without a pause, Jane blurted, her face turning scarlet. "Oh no, Lizzy. Please say you did not sneak a peek at Cook's petticoat to see if it was pink lace with ruffles."

All three burst into laughter until they each needed a handkerchief of their own. Elizabeth wrapped her arms around her middle as she fell backwards on the bed. Their mirth was a relief.

"That was funny, Jane," Charlotte snorted.

Moving her arms above her head, Elizabeth's fingers toyed with one of the strings tying the quilt. "I have fallen deeply and hopelessly in love with a man I admire so much that my knees melt just thinking of him."

Jane's mouth gaped open. "Who?"

Elizabeth sat up, a sly smile on her face. "Guess."

Before Jane could reply, Charlotte said, "I, too, have fallen deeply and irrevocably in love with a man I admire so much that my heart beats in tune with his."

"What?" Elizabeth was stunned. "You are in love with the major? When did that happen?"

Jane leaned closer to where the two others sat on the bed. Elizabeth bumped Charlotte's shoulder. "Was it when you were 'helping' him interview our neighbors to find enlistments for the Regulars? Was it when you were plotting to uncover the murderer and see to Mr. Darcy's innocence? Does he know you write for *The Times?*"

"The *Times?*" Jane asked.

"Yes, Lizzy." Charlotte smoothed her skirts, her chin buried in her chest. When she looked up, she radiated happiness. "Major Gerring is a clever man. He earned my appreciation by the manner in which he approached our neighbors. He was kind but firm. He earned my confidence when he repeatedly set aside his personal comfort to seek the truth about what happened to Miss Collins and Mr. Wickham. He earned my trust with his devotion to duty and his loyalty to his assignment."

"How did he earn your love, Charlotte," Jane asked.

"When he told me that my tales of the Hopper sisters were the reason that he read *The Times.*" Charlotte smiled. "Before you ask, yes Jane, I write *Bucolic Life in the Far North for Young Ladies.* Because of the names I chose for the Hoppers, his superiors thought I might be a notorious spy for the French government. Once my name was cleared, I assumed he would be done with me. Yet, he continued to seek me out. Now, I cannot imagine a life without him."

Elizabeth asked, "Has he given you any indication of his feelings?"

Charlotte blushed. "I am pleased to say that he will

speak to my father out of courtesy to me once the Bingley's have been apprehended and this business is over. With my income and what he has saved, he will resign his position. We will settle nearby so I can continue my writing undisturbed." She sighed. "He kissed my hand."

"Ah!" Jane sighed too.

"Charlotte, I am positively delighted for you both." Despite her friend believing she was made for the shelf with the other spinsters, Elizabeth knew Charlotte secretly hoped for a home of her own with a love meant for the ages.

"Lizzy, who has claimed your heart?" Jane asked. "Is it..." She put her hand over her mouth. "Mr. Plumbottom with his hearing problem and lack of teeth or the tall gentleman from Derbyshire?"

Elizabeth knew that if she happened to look into the mirror, she would see stars twinkling in her eyes. "Mr. Darcy loves me, Jane. He said the words to me twice. More than that, he has shown me by his deeds that he cherishes me."

Squaring her shoulders, her sister said, "On this date, I, Jane Marie Bennet, make this vow to not give my heart away easily. I will take the time to look past the exterior a gentleman presents to me to determine his true character. Only then will I share my heart." She giggled. "How was that?"

"Well done, Jane!" Both ladies praised her.

Elizabeth sobered. "I will miss the amazing camaraderie we have together. Derbyshire is very far away."

"As will I," admitted Charlotte.

"Well, I will not," Jane boldly declared. "For I will take

turns traveling between your houses until I meet the man of my dreams. Then, you will see me as content as you are."

It was a worthy goal they could all support.

"CHARLES," Caroline glanced at herself in the hallway mirror. "Do quit pacing. You are quite wearing me out."

"I am afraid something will go wrong," Bingley admitted. "I know it is ridiculous, but I cannot help but wish Darcy was here to make sure we did not miss anything important."

His sister spun to face him. "A note has been delivered so that dear Georgiana is expecting us. You have contacted the agent about giving up this property since we will live at Darcy House whenever we return to London. We are packed and ready to depart for Scotland and settle at Pemberley. What else can there be?"

He ran his hand through his hair then had to look in the mirror to repair the damage. "I do not know, Caroline. I am just anticipating being done with all of this." He turned his chin to the side. "Do you think Georgiana will still find that this green brings out the blue in my eyes?"

"Charles!" Caroline growled.

* * *

LORD MATLOCK WAS quick to support Darcy's plan. As soon as the note was delivered from the Bingleys for Georgiana to expect their arrival, he contacted Darcy.

Then, he joined Darcy, Richard, and the Major in the drawing room at Matlock House. Stationed outside the door and down the hallway were select members of Richard's regiment dressed in the Matlock livery. In the adjoining room were an investigator, a constable, and the local magistrate.

"Where exactly is Georgiana?" Darcy asked.

"She remains upstairs with Helen in her private sitting room. Helen knows not to come down until all is in the clear," his uncle replied. "They are looking at the newest fashion plates, which will keep them occupied for hours, I expect."

Glancing at Richard who nodded, Darcy was confident that everything was in place.

He wanted this done and over with so his life could return to normal. No, with Elizabeth at his side, his normal would change to something far better, he had no doubt.

"What is this?" Richard asked. "Frowning Fitzwilliam Darcy is smiling?" he teased. "Could it be that his mind has happily traveled to Meryton to the home of a particular lady?"

Darcy rocked back on his heels, his hands at the lapels of his coat. "Tease all you want, Richard, I do not mind. Once you have met the lady, you will see that I have every reason for my future happiness as I seek ways to see she is happy as well."

Two taps on the door ended their conversation. It was the signal that the Bingley's coach had arrived. Darcy, Richard, and the major moved into place in the adjoining room with the other men. Lord Matlock would be the Bingley family's first contact.

"Welcome to Matlock House," his uncle greeted the arrivals. "Is it only the two of you? I had assumed that Mr. and Mrs. Hurst would be joining you?"

Bingley began to speak when Caroline interrupted him. "Thank you for your kindness. They remain in the coach, Lord Matlock."

"No. No. No. There are not enough warm blankets or hot bricks to keep them comfortable. I shall send a footman to invite them in. Be seated, the both of you. I will only be a moment."

With a gesture, a footman set about his task.

"Will Miss Darcy be joining us soon?" Miss Bingley asked.

"Yes, soon," his uncle distractedly replied. "Ah, there we are. Here come the Hursts." After a short pause, Lord Matlock said, "Welcome to Matlock House, Mr. and Mrs. Hurst. If I recall correctly, this is your first time here, is it not?"

"It is. We are..."

"Yes. Yes. Yes. Do sit down and make yourself comfortable."

From where he stood, Darcy could easily hear the rustle of fabric of the ladies skirts. Once it was quiet. Lord Matlock began.

"I understand that you have been in Hertfordshire. How did you find it?"

Bingley began to reply when, again, his sister spoke over the top of him. "It was dreadful, Lord Matlock. The society was not as we expected. It is with pleasure that we are returned to London."

"Hmm, yes, well. Is Darcy not planning to join you in town?"

"No, I am afraid a small emergency has taken him to Pemberley. We will be traveling there today to offer our support. It is for this reason that we are here, my lord. Mr. Darcy requested his sister's presence. Although we do not want to remove her from your company, her brother needs her."

"Hmm. How odd that Darcy would need a young, impressionable girl in an emergency. Did you say what the emergency was?"

"I did not," was Miss Bingley's immediate reply. Apparently deciding she was too abrupt; she rephrased her response. "I am sorry, Lord Matlock, but Mr. Darcy did not make us privy to his business."

"Perhaps he did not share his private concerns with you, Miss Bingley, but he likely did with your brother as one of Darcy's closest friends."

Bingley started to speak, then needed to stop and clear his throat to gain control of his voice. "No, my lord, he said nothing of what was occurring."

"Hmm," his uncle mused. "Then I wonder if the course of wisdom would be to keep my niece here. Once this 'emergency' is passed, we could travel north as a family, spending the festive season in the country. Yes, a fine idea this is." His uncle stood. "I am sorry you have delayed your journey; however, Georgiana will be remaining here under my care. I shall make certain Darcy knows my reasoning. In the end, he will appreciate my caution, I have no doubt."

"But Lord Matlock." Caroline Bingley insisted, "In this I cannot believe Mr. Darcy would be pleased."

"You dare to speak for him, then?" Hugh Fitzwilliam's tone sharpened.

"You misunderstand," Miss Bingley began when his uncle broke in.

"No, I believe the misunderstanding is yours. Georgiana will remain safely at Matlock House. Now, do you have other business with me?"

"I...I," she gasped. "She *has* to come with us. Mr. Darcy said she would."

Bingley sputtered.

Mr. and Mrs. Hurst were eerily silent.

"If there is nothing else then I shall say 'good day'." From Darcy's position, he could see his uncle stand.

The others stood as well.

Using the angle of the mirror, Darcy could see Bingley's face. It was beet red for a moment then his cheeks drained of all color, turning them as grey as the chalk.

This was Richard's cue.

Strolling in through the doorway, he said, "Bingley, you are looking rather ashen. Are you well?"

Bingley gasped. "Colonel, what are you doing here? I thought you were on the continent somewhere."

"Why, I live here." Richard went to the side table to pour himself a drink. "Are you leaving before tea could be brought? Where are your manners, Father? Or are you in a hurry to depart, Bingley? Why, it does appear that your sister is suffering from the same malady you are, Bingley. She is as white as a ghost."

This was Major Gerring's cue.

He had not taken two steps into the room before saying, "Mr. Bingley. Mr. Hurst. I am grateful you are here since I have some terrible news to share about the property you leased in Meryton. It seems there was a collapse in one of the old chalk caves at the south corner of Netherfield Park. My understanding is that a few people were affected. Because this exceeds the authority of your steward, he, as well as the magistrate, has asked for your speedy return before the bodies can be recovered and identified. I would be pleased to escort you north."

Never before had Darcy seen Bingley panic-stricken. The man could barely talk.

"Where did you…? How did you…? But I cannot…" Bingley stammered. "We are needed at Pemberley to aid Mr. Darcy."

The major responded, "As a landowner himself, Mr. Darcy would know that your responsibility would be to your estate. With one word from you, a fellow officer from my regiment would deliver a note to Pemberley, is that not correct, Colonel Fitzwilliam?"

"Absolutely correct, Major Gerring." Richard drew closer to Bingley. "Sit down, Bingley."

Bingley immediately did as bid. So did the Hursts. Only Caroline Bingley remained standing.

"Take a seat, Miss Bingley." Richard commanded. "I have a story to tell, one I think will be of interest to all of you, and to you in particular, Miss Bingley." Richard moved to stand in front of the fireplace, placing Bingley and his sister on his left, their backs to Darcy, and the Hursts on his right. The major walked to the area directly behind the sofa where Hursts were sitting, then stood at attention. Hugh Fitzwilliam joined his son by the fire.

"Very good. We may begin." Sipping from his drink, he placed the glass on the mantel. "Due to the war with France, England is filled with treachery. Spies are everywhere, I am sorry to say. Good people have had family members turn on one another. Bad people seem to proliferate. For almost a year the British government has known of a clandestine operation originating from one of the better houses here in London. It was known that the head of the spy ring was a female. We were a week into our sailing journey when one of Napoleon's warships lay at anchor waiting for us. The spy ring had provided the course that was charted before we departed the docks. We ran back to Jolly England as quickly as we were able with the damage and injuries we sustained. Imagine my surprise to discover it was one of my mother's closest acquaintances, Lady Barrington, who was the culprit. As I said, spies, traitors, and treachery are everywhere."

Hurst leaned back in his seat, his eyes surveying the room, a decided lack of interest on his face. Bingley and his sister were both looking down at their feet. Only Mrs. Hurst was paying rapt attention.

Richard continued. "Late last evening, a lengthy letter was received at Matlock House addressed to my father. It was penned in a feminine hand. Inside the pages of the parchment the lines of closely written text revealed a plot so diabolical as to be almost ridiculous. Was it the truth? Was it a work of fiction? I could not help but wonder.

During the whole of the night, I consulted with my superiors and the Bow Street Runners about whether this letter was what is called a 'red herring', a ploy to throw us off the scent of the real scoundrel. Or was it a confession unlike anything I had ever read before."

"What did you decide," Mrs. Hurst anxiously asked from where she was sitting on the edge of her seat.

"Well, Mrs. Hurst, I am delighted you asked the perfect question at the perfect time. Does anyone else have anything to add? I would be pleased to hear your impressions or any questions you may have up to now." Before anyone could reply, he gestured to the major. "Because you have shown yourself to be brave, Mrs. Hurst, I would ask Major Gerring to assist you to stand between my father and myself. Major?"

"What are you doing with Louisa?" Caroline asked, her brow furrowed.

"Stay here," Mr. Hurst demanded. "Louisa!" he growled at his wife.

Bingley exclaimed, "Why are you...? Wait! What was in that letter and who wrote it?"

And that was Darcy's cue.

CHAPTER 35

*F*itzwilliam Darcy strolled into the parlor, his eyes on Gilbert Hurst, who was the first to see him.

"What? How? Where did you come from?" Hurst blathered with his demand for information he did not deserve to know.

Both Caroline and Bingley's heads swiveled toward him, dumbfounded shock on their faces.

In his hand, he carried the letter Richard had mentioned. Standing next to his cousin, Darcy cleared his throat and began reading.

To the Right Honorable Hugh Fitzwilliam, the Earl of Matlock

Dear Lord Matlock,

Help! Your nephew Mr. Darcy has been the victim of a nefarious plot to end his life whereupon your niece, Miss Georgiana Darcy will be left vulnerable. With her co-guardian, Colonel Fitzwilliam away from England, she is particularly in dire straits.

I will confess that the plot sounded exciting to me at first. If carried out properly, it would guarantee my future and that of my family. However, what was supposed to be simple turned bloody with the bullets from my husband's gun.

I do not often participate in the family conferences since my husband, brother, and sister deem me to be less intelligent. Nevertheless, I do listen and easily recall what is said.

Caroline Bingley shot from her seat, her finger pointing at her sister. "How dare you, Louisa? You, who pretended to agree to all that was done are a traitor of the worst sort! I despise you! I loathe you! I wish you had never been born."

Darcy gave her his most scathing look. "I do not believe you know the definition of the word traitor, Miss Bingley. Would you be seated so I may finish?"

"No!" Hurst yelled as he jumped to his feet. "It is a lie, all of it. Nothing but a pack of lies and finger-pointing at anyone other than herself."

"Hmm," Darcy pretended to give his comment due consideration. "Really? Sarcasm dripped from his tongue. "I do not think so, Hurst. Now, sit down!"

Bingley's skin went from pasty white to a light mossy green.

"You say nothing, Bingley? I am not surprised. I will continue..." Darcy paused, waiting for the accusations to come. He was not disappointed.

"It was Charles' idea," Miss Bingley announced, now pointing at her brother. "He was the one who realized that Miss Collins hated Mr. Wickham and they both hated *you!*"

Bingley thumbed his chest. "Me? How dare you, Caroline. All of this comes back to you. I only wanted out from under my debts, Pemberley, the respect of my peers once my rank was elevated, and a comfortable wealth to live on for the rest of my days. It was your idea to kill Miss Collins and Mr. Wickham." He turned toward his brother-in-law. "And it was your plan to kill Mr. Collins and make it look like suicide so the guilt would transfer back to Darcy or you would blackmail him for the rest of his life. Power was what you wanted, Caroline, not me."

"How dare you!" both Caroline Bingley and Gilbert Hurst proclaimed at the same time.

"Enough!" Darcy bellowed. Everyone quieted. "How dare you, Bingley. You, whom I once considered a friend. Even if you did not fire the gun, you planned to benefit from the demise of others. You attempted to steal my good name, my property, and my sister. Good heavens, Bingley. You stole my boots!"

"I only borrowed them." Bingley's voice wavered.

Darcy glared at the younger man. "Are you so weak that you hide behind the skirts of your sister? Can you not even now see that your silence when she acted was a decision in itself? That your inactivity was a choice that you made? You were the master of Netherfield Park. You were the man in charge. Blaming her or anyone else for the consequences of your actions demonstrates the inherent weakness of your character. What would happen should you have been successful with your plans? Would you have been a responsible master of Pemberley? No! Would you have been a good husband to Georgiana? I cannot bear, even in my imagination, to think of you having anything at all to do with my sister. How could you?"

Darcy sneered. "You, your sister, and your brother-in-law deserve what is coming to you. I will see it done!"

"But, but,...Louisa," Bingley whined. "She was in on it too."

Lord Matlock, with all the authority given him at birth, stepped into the fray.

"Young man that is enough from you. I have heard no attempt at an apology, no regret for what you have done, nor any evidence of repentance from any of you, except Mrs. Hurst." He gestured toward the room where Darcy and the others were hidden. "It is time to pay the piper, Mr. Bingley, Miss Bingley, and Mr. Hurst." Waving his hand toward the men entering the room, he said, "Constable, they are all yours."

"You cannot do this. Do you not know who we are?" Caroline Bingley screeched. "We are the Bingleys of Netherfield Park." She turned toward Darcy's uncle. "You want an apology? Fine, I apologize. There! Are you satisfied?"

"Where do you get your arrogance?" His uncle mused, shaking his head. To the others he ordered, "Take them away."

As the three were escorted from the room, Mrs. Hurst moved to join them.

Darcy stopped her. "No, Mrs. Hurst. Although there will be consequences, your confession has saved your life. You have options available to you that your family does not."

The lady dropped her head, her shoulders drooping. Finally, she looked Darcy in the eye.

"I do thank you for your mercy, Mr. Darcy, for that is

what it is." She sighed heavily. "With that said, my letter was too little too late. I do not know how you escaped from the cave, nor do I know if Miss Elizabeth lives."

"She does," he reassured her.

"I am pleased, sir." Mrs. Hurst swallowed. "Nonetheless, the right thing to have done would have been to write to Lord Matlock *before* they attempted to kill you. I knew their plan, and I said nothing. I knew my husband shot all three victims, and I did nothing. I knew what they had in mind for Miss Darcy and Pemberley, yet I kept silent until last evening. While I admit that your kindness is appreciated and your empathy is generous, it is simply too much, Mr. Darcy. I have known the principle of community responsibility and culpability from my youth. I know exactly what I deserve."

Without allowing them time to comment, she hurried to follow the others.

Darcy was gutted. He had enjoyed many years of association with Wickham before the man turned on him. The same had happened with Bingley. Likely in the future, as long as greed and ambition drove individuals, it might happen again. Except, now he would have Elizabeth by his side.

He needed her—desperately.

Glancing at his uncle, he said, "I will speak to Georgiana before I address the magistrate.

"We will join you, nephew. You are no longer alone in your struggles."

"Thank you, Uncle." Darcy's next words were from his soul. "With your permission, I will invite Elizabeth, her father, her sister, Jane, and their friend and neighbor,

Charlotte Lucas, to town. They will be necessary to my prosecution."

"They are welcome to stay here," his uncle kindly offered.

"I thank you."

With a weary heart, he revealed to his sister the treachery of Claire Hobbs Collins and the deaths of her and Wickham. Georgiana's tender heart almost burst. Then he told her about Elizabeth, Miss Lucas, Mr. Bennet, and *Jeanne de Valois-Saint-Remy*, the best things from Hertfordshire.

The next day, Darcy welcomed the Bennets and Miss Lucas to London. Unsurprisingly, the major was on hand to welcome Charlotte.

Lord and Lady Matlock were superb hosts. Georgiana was timid. Miss Bennet had a problem with her hem so his aunt escorted her upstairs to have a maid see to the repair. Mr. Bennet was delighted to have a man who shared his interest in politics and economics. Within moments, he and Darcy's uncle had their heads together over tea and then brandy.

It was Elizabeth who brought calm and joy to his heart.

"My dear man, I must confess that you do clean up rather well," she teased.

He smiled; grateful they were seated together on a sofa a short distance away from the others. "I wanted you to stand at my side, but at the same time I was glad you were safely in Hertfordshire, dearest."

Her magnificent eyes focused solely on him; her fingers lightly stroked his cheek before her palm caressed his temple. "I love you, Fitzwilliam. With you my heart is complete."

He closed his eyes, relishing the softness of her touch and her tender expressions. "You are my heart."

* * *

RICHARD NUDGED GEORGIANA, "Say, Poppet, it looks as if your brother is as happy as a clam."

"Are clams happy?" she teased. "Look at them, Richard. They are so in love with each other. That is the sort of happiness that I yearn to have some day."

"When you are thirty-six, your brother and I *might* allow a gentleman or two to come calling. By the time you are forty, we *may* give you permission to wed."

She snorted softly. "You just wait, Richard Fitzwilliam. One day you will meet a lady who will set you on your toes like Fitzwilliam has done. She will chisel the ice from your heart and chip away at the rough edges you wear to keep the ladies away."

"What sort of talk is this?" He pretended to be indignant. "I will have you know that it is bravery that shields my heart and courage that has built up my rough edges. I like it that way. In fact, I doubt there is a female in all of England who would be worth the effort of taking her on. Why, I plan to wait until a worthy woman comes along and sweeps *me* off my feet. Then, and only then, will I even give her the time of day."

He watched his cousin and Elizabeth closely. In his heart, he envied Darcy for what he had. Oh, not

Pemberley or his bank accounts, but that confidence that the woman in front of him was perfect for him.

"Is that right?" Georgiana grinned. "One day, Richard."

"No, Georgie, it will never hap...," Richard was afraid he was going to swallow his tongue. The lady following his mother into the room was a vision. A queen. A temptress. Who was she? He swallowed, jumping to his feet while running his hand over his hair to straighten it and pulling at the bottom of his waistcoat at the same time. *Drat!* He wished he had worn his dress uniform. He knew he should have worn his uniform. Ladies young and old seemed drawn to an officer who finely displayed his rank.

Darcy and Elizabeth rose to introduce Miss Bennet to those congregated. His cousin presented Richard last.

He bowed to her curtsey.

"Miss Bennet."

"Colonel."

Heavens! She even sounded angelic.

Georgiana approached, an evil gleam in her eye. "Miss Bennet, please be seated between my cousin and myself so we may come to know you better since it appears we will soon be sisters."

While Miss Bennet was elegantly being seated, Georgiana poked her tongue out at Richard. *Why, that scamp!* He would see she paid for her mischief, as soon as he gave her a year of his soldier's pay for placing him and the lady close together.

* * *

ELIZABETH LEANED CLOSE TO DARCY. "I think he likes her."

Darcy laughed. "You think?"

She watched the two and how Miss Darcy directed the conversation until the Colonel took charge. "I was mistaken in hoping Mr. Bingley was the perfect man for Jane."

Darcy frowned. "I was mistaken too, Elizabeth." He glanced to where Richard kept pulling at his cravat to loosen the noose tightening around his throat. "I do think we are right about them, however."

"And we are right about us." Elizabeth leaned closer. "There is no mistake in that."

"There is not," Darcy readily agreed.

EPILOGUE

*T*wo months after Claire Collins fired her first shot at Fitzwilliam Darcy, her murderer swung from the gallows. At the hearings, both Bingley and his sister convinced the judge and jury that Gilbert Hurst was the lone gunman who pulled the trigger. Found in his chambers at Netherfield Park was a pistol with the bore matching the four bullets he had fired at his victims. There was no mercy for him.

It was discovered during the proceedings how deeply into his pockets Charles Bingley and his sister had dug. Once their assets were sold, they had little on which to survive during and after the long trip to the Australian penal colonies. Louisa Hurst would be starting over in the wilds of Canada. What she did with her life after leaving England, the Darcys did not want to know.

* * *

ON THE FIRST Wednesday morning of the year 1812, Darcy took Elizabeth for his wife. Putting the final flourish on the register, Elizabeth teased, "From this day on, I have a new name, a new identity."

"Mrs. Darcy," he kissed her thoroughly. "You will forever be my Mrs. Darcy."

She smiled and kissed him again.

BECAUSE LADY CATHERINE was away from Rosings Park caring for her daughter during her confinement, neither Darcy nor the colonel needed to go to Kent that spring. Instead, it was Darcy who stood next to a nervous groom when Jane Bennet walked down the aisle.

Charlotte and the major had wed the fortnight prior. Since they had purchased a small property close to Meryton, they remained for the wedding.

Elizabeth was delighted for her sister. Richard was a good man, and he was gaining a wife who was perfect for him.

AS SOON AS the carriage with the newly wedded Richard and Jane Fitzwilliam departed the wedding breakfast at Longbourn, Mr. Bennet had the groom hitch Beatrice to the cart.

Darcy clasped Elizabeth around the waist and helped her in the back where a blanket covered the load. Before his father-in-law could flick the reins on the pony's back, Darcy jumped in alongside his wife.

"Do you have it?" Bennet asked.

"I do." Darcy grinned.

During the months they were at Pemberley, he and Elizabeth had discussed in detail how wrong they had been about Bingley, about Elizabeth's parents, and about each other. They vowed to be more cautious in their opinions. As the cart moved closer to the caves, Elizabeth pulled the cloth bag from behind her.

"I cannot believe that you and Papa insisted on keeping one of Mr. Bingley's horrid green vests."

Darcy snatched it from her. "Ha! Little do you know, darling wife, that we have planned this moment since shortly after we were rescued from the cave. As Aesop said, 'One good turn deserves another.'"

Elizabeth shook her head at him, her smile lighting the sky. "I simply cannot believe you intend to carry this through."

Draping his arm across her shoulders, he pulled her tightly against him. They rode that way until they reached the entrance to the cavern where Bingley had confined them. After helping Elizabeth to the ground, Darcy pulled the blankets back revealing an assortment of sticks in various sizes.

Jeanne de Valois-Saint-Remy circled above them. Elizabeth pulled out a biscuit from her pocket, breaking it into pieces and tossing them to the ground. When the bird alighted, she commended her for her help. "Jeannie, because you saved my life, you will have a new home worthy of the masters of Longbourn and Pemberley."

Her father climbed the rock to the nest. Darcy carried an armload of the wood next to where her Papa stood. Placing them on the ground, he dropped the bag holding the vest that was cut into small strips along with the brass buttons the crow could use to decorate her home.

"Uh-oh," her father said when he finally peered into the nest. Stepping back, he jumped to the ground. "I believe we should leave these materials here and allow the birds to redecorate their home without our help."

"Birds?" Darcy asked.

Bennet chuckled. "It seems we have been mistaken all this time as to the sex of *Jeanne de Valois-Saint-Remy*, for he is not a she at all. Inside there is a lovely little female hovering over three small eggs."

Elizabeth's laughter at having mistaken the identity of the carrion crow was infectious.

Bennet shook his head at having been wrong. "I will never attempt to guess the sex again."

"Well, that is too bad," Elizabeth said, her beautiful eyes sparkling. Clasping Darcy's hand in hers, she asked, "Would you help me to the back of the cart, my dear man?"

He did it with pleasure. *Could a man be any happier?*

Mr. Bennet climbed up onto the driver's seat then put Beatrice in motion. They had not gone twenty feet before he pulled the pony to a halt. Swiveling around, he said, "What did you mean, Lizzy, that it's too bad..."

She lifted her left brow in time to see her father's chin drop and his eyes widen to the shape of saucers.

"Oh! Oh! Oh!" The poor man stammered, unable to put his thoughts into words.

* * *

DARCY HAD FELT the same when Elizabeth had told him she had missed her courses for the second month in a row.

A tear gathered at the corner of Bennet's eye. His mouth finally snapped closed. "If it is a boy, Phillips has told me that it will break the entail on Longbourn."

Darcy set him straight. "If it is a boy, he will be the heir to Pemberley. The next son can have Longbourn."

Bennet flicked the reins. "Then you both had best get busy." Laughing at his own humor, he set the cart towards Longbourn and never looked back.

When her lashes dropped to her cheeks and her hand came up to cup his jaw, Darcy knew they would take his father-in-law's advice seriously. Of that, there was no mistake.

The End

ABOUT THE AUTHOR

Joy Dawn King fell in love with Jane Austen's writings in 2012 and discovered the world of fan fiction shortly after. Intrigued with the many possibilities, she began developing her own story for Fitzwilliam Darcy and Elizabeth Bennet. Her first book, *A Father's Sins*, was published in 2014.

In 2017, she experimented with shorter Pride & Prejudice variations using the pen name, Christie Capps.

Joy, and her beloved husband of over 40 years, live in Oregon where she often FaceTime's her daughter, author Jennifer Joy, so they can talk about grandkids, writing, and Jane Austen.

The author is currently working on another tale of adventure and romance for Mr. Darcy and his Elizabeth.

IN APPRECIATION:

Thank you very much for investing your time with this story. A gift for any author is to receive an honest review from readers. I hope you will use this opportunity to let others know your opinion.

NEWS FLASH: Beginning in 2022, my newsletter "Reasons for Joy" (found at www.jdawnking.com) will be resumed after a lengthy hiatus. A free complete short story will be attached to each newsletter so be sure to subscribe now. I have between 4-6 newsletters planned per year.

Made in the USA
Coppell, TX
25 March 2022

75563343R10229